Apprehension

Apprehension

INCANDESCENT SERIES

BOOK 2

SYLVIE PARIZEAU

Library and Archives Canada Cataloging-in-Publication Data:

Parizeau, Sylvie

Apprehension: Book 2 of the Incandescent Series / Sylvie Parizeau

ISBN print : 978-0-9953240-6-0

Interior Design and Formatting by:

www.emtippettsbookdesigns.com

To anyone who seizes each moment lived to the fullest, no half-measures, all in or nothing.

One

ZAC

Apprehension

noun

1. anticipation of adversity or misfortune; suspicion or fear of future trouble.

"Oh. Mon. Dieu. *That's it.*"

The girl's blissful cry reverberates throughout the ski chalet over the gurgling sound of the industrial coffee machine I'm milking for all its worth.

I blink.

For a reason I can't explain, that voice elicits a weird flutter in my chest.

With a will of its own, my finger slackens pressure upon the coffee lever. A trickling of smoldering dark brew inches its way up into my fifth cup to go, stopping at the three-quarter mark.

I tip my head to the side.

"Spot on," the voluptuous voice moans to the high ceiling of the café in what I'd call orgasmic enthusiasm. I look right and left, glad no other patrons are witnessing me ... witnessing her. And then I see her. Or rather, her appendages.

A nimble tongue licks a slender index finger, greedily lapping it up in exaggerated wet suction sounds.

My gut tightens.

I stare, torn between *what the fuck*, and *please don't stop.*

I give the girl the onceover. Facing away from me but bending low over the counter, her tight little body's hot all right. Her black turtleneck and soft-shell ski racers showcasing curves I'd like to palm. Interestingly enough, the fact that we're standing in the middle of a ski resort cafeteria, or that, no shit, it's probably colder than absolute zero tonight up in Québec's Laurentian Mountains, barely registers. Right this minute, I don't really care. My fingers twitch and warm up instantly, and so does my dick.

It's been a little while...

Lost in a steamy daydream, I find myself standing at the counter, coffees in hand.

"Will that be all?" the elderly cashier rudely interrupts me mid-fantasy, ringing up my five coffees to go, stowing them onto a disposable cardboard tray.

"I'd like to have some of what she's having," I deadpan as I hand over some money to the sugarplum fairy manning the cash register.

"You totally should. Mireille outdid herself. Here, have a taste." The splendid specimen of a girl turns to me, offering me half her cupcake.

I quirk one eyebrow, and her gaze tracks mine to the icing that's just about swiped clean. She shrugs sheepishly. "Tell me one of your guilty secrets, and we'll be even," the enchanting grey-eyed creature says, looking me straight in the eye. Her expression is guileless, which only adds to the tease in her words. My heartbeats pick up their pace.

"I think I will," I quip, bending low, trapping her gaze into mine. "Have a taste that is." I take a bite out of the offered cupcake still cupped in her hand without breaking our stare. Her impossibly large eyes grow by a fraction, and she stills. Well, that certainly caught her attention. *Good.* I shift, pinned by the clear silver color of her unwavering eyes. And suddenly, I'm the one who's caught.

Her creamy complexion stains rosy under my scrutiny, eyes wide and full of wonder locked on mine.

My pulse jumps in my throat.

That look. Those eyes. A déjà vu sensation washes over me.

We stare. Just stare. The space of an instant or an eternity, not sure which.

Why do I feel like I know you, like we've met before?

I reel back. Where in the bloody everlasting hell is that shit coming from?

I don't do involved. Ever. My usual type has a universal itch in need of scratching, and not much else.

My best friend Liam's new normality is messing with my head. It must be. After a lifetime of wandering, he's finally—and only recently—settled down with his new wife up here in these mountains. His pregnant wife. And all he can talk about is "normal." Maybe this is me being jealous. I have a sudden yearning for his brand of happiness, yet I have this feeling that I've just bitten off more than I can chew here.

The cupcake is delicious, though.

The girl's wondrous eyes flicker past me, and then back to me. "See? Definitely a keeper," she says with aplomb.

Damn, her smile is enough to knock a bloke off his feet.

"Are you sure?" a middle-aged woman asks from behind the counter, her tone of voice floundering.

"Yeah, pretty much," I say dumbfounded. She knocked years of suave right off me, so it seems, and scrambled my brains by the same token.

The girl, who's too lovely by half, studies me in the space of a second, before answering the timidly voiced question, addressed to her in the first place. "Told you so. A keeper."

Wait, *what?*

A keeper? Me? I inwardly scoff. "Worst pick ever, sweetheart," I say under my breath.

Shifting my weight on one leg, I cross my arms, feigning bored disinterest as I finish my taste of her baked concoction. Curiosity burns a hole in my gut, wondering what this bizarre conversation is all about. "What was that?" I angle a brow, challenging her.

The girl's exquisite face tilts in my direction. She raises her brow, challenging me right back. "A taste of something addictive. So worth keeping."

The woman's audible gasp from behind the counter pops our newest staring contest bubble. "Magali, seriously?" Blonde-haired and of the indeterminate age variety, her eyes dart between us, plump fingers fidgeting with her apron, clearly uncertain.

Ma Ga Lee, I murmur to myself, testing the French musicality of her name on my tongue, and liking it. A tad too much.

The girl stretches over the counter. Long locks of her dark-brown hair stick out every which way from underneath a rainbow-colored wool beanie. Adorable comes to mind. One of her hands clasps the other woman's fidgety fingers, giving them a gentle squeeze. "Seriously. This one above all the others."

I still. Six words. Like a vow. Unheard of. *This one above all the others.* What would it be like to be so chosen? My breath catches in my throat. She can't possibly be talking about me?

Magali. Soft lips ... soft words ... the voice of an angel.

"And ... which one would that be?" I ask, a bit reeling from my wayward thoughts.

A small, delighted chuckle escapes Magali's lips, and I'm strangely pleased to be responsible for eliciting it. Mireille gives her a weird look, but Magali looks down before I catch her eyes.

"This one," Mireille informs me, motioning to the blackboard behind her where an elegant penmanship conveys the cafeteria's treat of the day under the heading *Decadent Bliss du Jour.* A damp spot underneath leaves the blank space wide open to interpretation. She points to Magali's half-eaten cupcake. "I just gave you a leftover diet cupcake I baked for Yolande and I; it's not meant as a special treat ... It's so bland, non?" the middle-aged woman says in a hushed tone as though confessing to a great sin.

Bloody hell. My breath swooshes out, and I'm strangely disappointed. Of course, she'd been talking about the dessert. *Get over yourself, why don't you?*

"You did?" Magali's brow scrunches up in disbelief while her pearly whites take a tentative bite of the cake where a bit of frosting remains. "I don't know where you've put the diet in there; it melts in my mouth. The moist center is pure decadence with that frosting, and you know I can eat my weight in sugar. I'm telling you, this is your Avalanche Cupcake to top them all, and you'll have everyone coming back for more, guaranteed. *Definitely* worth keeping," she says.

"Don't you agree?" Her pale silver eyes light up on me as she smiles the most brilliant smile I've ever seen. Two dimples, cute as all hell, dance at the corner of her full lips.

My pulse jumps. Killer dimples. Kissable lips. *Definitely.*

"Definitely," I parrot. You'll have me coming back for more, I inwardly vow. *Where the fuck did that come from?*

Magali cranes her head above my shoulder. "Yolande, don't you agree as well?"

Three pairs of eyes swivel to the white-haired cashier. She grunts what can pass for a yes. Not quite meeting anyone's eyes, she starts fussing with the display baskets of whole-grain muffins and homemade energy bars arrayed temptingly next to the coffee machine, near the cash register.

I lean back against the counter, crossing my ankles, my ski boots at an angle, waiting for the outcome of this nonsensical debate about plain old vanilla cupcakes. In reality, I can't seem to make myself just up and go before I know more about this girl. She's fascinating.

"I'll be back for more," I say before I can stop myself.

Magali's eyes flick to my night ticket affixed to my left sleeve and the tray with five cups resting on the counter beside me. "See, Mireille? Everyone agrees on your newest treat, even visitors just passing through."

Just passing through. My chest constricts painfully upon hearing the words. What's with that? I've said them myself with a shit ton of relief to back them up more than a thousand times before.

Mireille twists her hands on her apron. "I'm not really sure that cake makes the cut for l'ardoise."

Magali leans closer, putting her hand on my sleeve. A fresh citrus scent worms its way into my sharp inhale. "Mireille's been trying to come up with the perfect Avalanche Cupcake ever since a local blog post mentioned that her Bliss du Jour wasn't worth the detour. Very bad form."

I'd like to wax lyrical on the goddamn cake if just to get on her good side, but for the life of me I can't think of any words; my mind's a blank slate. "Indeed." I rub my jaw, unnerved by the heady rush of warmth her nearness sends zipping through my nerve endings, firing me up. *Does she feel it too? This thing between us.*

"You can say it's a matter of pride now to prove that blogger wrong by the end of the season, and Mireille gets my vote on this one." Magali leans away and I mourn the loss of her hand on my sleeve. *Who's this guy?*

Mireille clucks her tongue on a soft head shake. "I'm still not convinced this afternoon's whipped chocolate berry mousse cupcakes topped with lemony frosting, weren't, I don't know, more ... *it*?" She dips a spoon into a stainless steel bowl, handing it over.

Magali's luscious lips part and she hums while her tongue takes a slow swipe of frosting, licking off the spoon.

Fuck, I can't breathe.

"That's funny." Magali's forehead furrows, her tongue getting in another slow lick. I clutch the counter. "I could have sworn I tasted this, plus a mix of maple and vanilla there, at the end, on mine. You know, less tart. Sweeter."

The grandmotherly cashier, Yolande, clears her throat, looking down at the floor. "I sort of ... spread another layer of frosting on Magali's cupcake."

Spread another layer of frosting on Magali's cupcake? The visual, man.

"Yolande," gasps Mireille.

Yolande shrugs both shoulders. "What can I say? It needed a boost."

Jesus. I don't need a boost. I'm sporting a boner from hell that not even the concept of a negative forty-something wind-chill factor awaiting me outside deflates. Never mind micro-fleece thermal layers stretched to the limits of endurance.

For an answer, Magali's eyes dance with something akin to mirth looking me over, and I wonder for a minute there if I voiced my thoughts aloud ... I grab the coffee tray, making sure it provides adequate coverage over strategic areas. The guys are probably freezing to death waiting on their coffees, and I can't stand here much longer without making a complete fool of myself.

"Time's up, Magaliiii. You coming, or what?" one of the ski resort dudes, in full patrol gear, hollers from the cafeteria doors, a few feet away from where I stand rooted in the quasi-deserted room, a huge bonfire keeping everyone on a ski break tonight out of doors.

Magali hands the bowl back over the counter. "Have to go. Cédric will have my head for sure but it was totally worth it. Here's to one of your tastiest collabs." Magali salutes both women with what's left of her cupcake before opening wide and shoveling it down in one swallow. "Keep it up," she says around a full mouth of baked goods.

Yeah, that's the problem.

My brain's stuck in neutral, my testis drawn tight, and my stomach's clenching in knots.

Great times ahead skiing this off.

"It's off the chart with frosting, you really should try it," she says to me in all seriousness, wiping crumbs from the corner of her lips as she spins on one heel.

"Off the chart with—" I choke, my voice barely audible. I'm struck stupid. What the bloody hell? I don't do tongue-tied. Ever.

"Enough. Come on, already," the hulking patrol guy shouts at Magali, grating on my nerves. My eyes narrow.

"I'm coming. I'm coming. I'm coming," Magali chants away.

Christ above, what's left of me to harden stiffens in a nanosecond. My blood pumps wildly, churning in my ears. The dude spares me a burning glance before pushing back out on his poles and skis, presumably on his way to the lifts.

My hands fist at my side. "Your boyfriend doesn't like you having treats?" I call out to her. I may have something against him if he gives her a hard time for enjoying herself. I may have something against him, period.

"Boyfriend?" She shakes her head on a small laugh. "Won't Cédric have a hoot over that one." The rhythmic thumps of her coordinated moves, heel to toes, make walking in these things sound effortlessly easy, which I know for a fact, is far from being so. "Guess I'll never hear the end of it now, will I?" she adds cryptically.

I clump my way over to her in my ski boots, managing to balance the coffees and myself in an effort to keep pace. "Meaning?"

Reaching one of the long tables a bit farther down, she shrugs on a bright-red jacket labeled Mont-Saint-Sauveur Ski Patrol in reflective white letterings, before grabbing her helmet, sporting the resort logo in front, with her name, Magali, tagged on the back of it.

She's a ski patroller too? Nice ... Maybe not a boyfriend, then. Even better.

She shoots me a smile that turns her from gorgeous to flat-out devastating. A direct hit to the solar plexus. "You owe me one."

"What—?"

"Guilty secret," she says over her shoulder.

For the space of a moment, we fall into each other's eyes, a meeting of souls. "Just so you know. What I said earlier on wasn't just about the cupcakes, either." She winks.

I stare, slack-jawed, as she disappears in a blur of red, pushing her way out, past Leo and P.O., who whistle low.

"Won't ask what's been keeping you." P.O. takes the lid off one of the cups I've almost forgotten I'm carrying. His muddy, green-hazel eyes glint with suppressed merriment, giving me the once over.

"He shoots! He scores!" Leo smirks, quoting the saying on the long-sleeved tee I wore this afternoon at Liam's courthouse wedding. He ties back his shoulder-length brown hair before shoving back down his dark beanie. I give him a look, unimpressed. Liam and Éolie are expecting twins, and the shirt's only funny within context.

"I'd say it was just the usual shit," P.O. says, vastly amused, "but the mouth hanging open's a new one. What'd she do? Say no?"

I shoot him a glare. "*She*," I uncharacteristically bark at P.O., "has a name."

Magali. Her name is Magali, I'd like to say, but refrain. I'm not ready to share any details yet. I'm still reeling from the encounter and my unusual reaction to her.

"I'm sure *she* does." P.O. smirks.

"Give over, man." Leo plucks the coffee tray from my unresisting hand.

"It's not like that," I grumble as I follow them out. I blink.

Shit. It's worse than that.

My eyes scan the crowd of skiers, dismissing one red coat after the other, realizing too late that I've let her disappear on me.

"Of course it's not," P.O. says in an offhand manner, watching me.

"So, tell me again why you're *not* looking for a bright-red coat, and a pretty fucking hot patroller wearing it," Leo says, annoyingly smug, and P.O. low fives him.

I grit my teeth, my gut weirdly churning. "She's ... a friendly sort, that's all," I finally manage, irked to no end by Leo's comment as we approach Theo and Yann waiting by the bonfire.

"Who's a friendly sort?" Yann asks, picking one of the cardboard cups. P.O. sips from his, hiding a smirk.

"A girl, apparently," Leo says knowingly.

"Friendly as in 'just friends?' That's a new one." Yann's face scrunches up as though the notion does not even add up, his bright-green eyes blinking behind his wire-framed glasses. "Girls up here are a different species altogether if Zac can't even score one."

Theo scratches his blond scruff, his mouth twisting, fighting a laugh.

"Want a shot at me, stand in line," I mutter, my fingers gripping my own cup.

"About time," Theo says, snatching a cup. "Level out the playing field for the rest of us."

I cut them a look. "Aren't you guys regular comedians tonight."

"I could have made two more runs down the slope, man," Theo comments, struggling to keep a straight face. "Took you that long to wipe out in there."

The three others chuckle under their breath, and I'd normally join in the ribbing, dishing it right back, but for some unfathomable reasons I have no wish to explore right now, they're pissing me off instead. Big time.

"Wipe out, my ass." I guzzle down the lukewarm coffee before squishing the cardboard into a ball, pitching it into the bonfire. It lands dead center of the roaring flames.

Transfixed, I watch my cup crash and burn, a strange sense of apprehension washing over me.

Two

MAGALI

My patrol partner for tonight, Cédric Daviault, better known as CD, gestures for me to hurry up already as I rush out of the resort cafeteria. Just outside, I clip my skis, operating on autopilot. My mind floats on a hazy cloud, dazzled by the beautiful stranger I just shared my cupcake—and a strangely personal connection—with.

Why does it feel like we've met before?

Cédric hollers. I shake myself out of my unusual trance before skiing over to him, earning a knowing smirk I choose to ignore.

"Well, well, well," he says.

I search for something to say, some way to change the subject before he can start on me about the handsome guy who made my heart flutter out of my chest and my body tingle in a delicious way like no cupcake ever has. *Careful, Magali,* I warn myself. It could turn addictive, and that guy's just passing through. Good thing too, with what I blurted on my way out. Funny how strangers you'll never see again can loosen one's tongue into spilling one's innermost thoughts.

"Well?" CD insists.

I ignore him. "Fancy meeting you here, Alain," I playfully call out to the wiry lift operator from the patrollers' express line.

Alain shakes his head at me, stern lips fighting not to quirk up one side.

He's been working the lifts here at the resort for the past century. Or close to, since I've known him forever. Not that at twenty-two I'm ancient, but still. Since I've grown up on these hills, it feels like forever.

"Get up there, Magali." Alain's leathery face creases, and I'm rewarded with one of his rare smiles as he lets CD and I bypass the line.

As patrollers, we're top priority, and for that reason, we get chairs to ourselves as soon as we show up. I used to think it was the coolest thing. A while ago. Tonight, though, stuck with CD? Not so much.

"Sooo?" CD asks, the minute the guardrail's down. I try and give him my most bewildered look, like I have no idea what on earth he's talking about.

"Come on, don't give me that look; it won't work. Who's the stupendously hot guy?"

Stupendously hot is too mild a description. That guy threw me for a loop. "You should have asked him out when you had the chance, CD," I say, digressing, or hoping to.

"He was eating you up. We're definitely not batting on the same team, more's the pity." He punches me on the arm. "Then again, you were eating him right back."

"Was not."

"Was so."

"Wasn't."

"Was."

"Argh. So what? Enough already," I reply in the hopes of ending the pointless argument. Fat lot of good it does. He takes a deep breath. I inwardly cringe. Here goes the resort's official Gazette.

"Magali finally has the *hoooots*, folks," CD yells at the top of his lungs. And he has quite the set, so his voice carries too well over the wind. My ears buzz from enduring CD's whoops from this close. I hear a few whistles from down below, catcalls and lots of cheers. On top of day trippers and one-nighters, on any given day the resort is at full capacity with seasonal pass holders—most of whom have been regulars for decades if not millenniums—not to mention instructors, patrollers, maintenance crew, and so on.

"And for anyone who ever wondered, myself included," Cédric hollers on gleefully. "It's for a *guyyyy*." He's laughing himself silly.

I thump my helmet on the rail, tempted to stay on the chairlift for the rest of the night. Great.

"You're slipping, CD." I huff a breath, exasperated. "I don't think they heard you over at Mont-Gabriel, Olympia, or Le Chanteclerc for that matter." Three of the closest resorts we see from Mont-Saint-Sauveur.

"Hey, every—" he starts again, but I elbow him. Hard. "What? Just complying." He rubs his side, feigning hurt.

"Quit it. It's getting old."

"You're kidding, right? It'll never get old." He wipes tears, clearly entertained. "I've known you since our bunny slopes days. Lest you forget, messy diapers and all. And I've never actually seen you get heated over the male species. So yeah, it's mind-blowing news."

"The diapers or the guy?" I mutter. But then my irritation gives way to the lifetime's worth of friendship he just mentioned and I join him in admiring the stranger. "Okay, fine. He was stupendously hot. I'll even admit to having a crush on him. You can't blame me for it. But that's as far as it goes. Have you heard him talk?"

"Nope. Talking's overrated," he says, earning him another eye roll on top of a bonus snort. CD could outtalk anyone, even rabid auctioneers in a bidding frenzy. "I'm not recovered yet from his dimpled chin, full lips, bronze skin, and dark stubble."

And I totally get what he means. Oh, le sigh.

He bumps my shoulder. "So, what's talking got to do with any of that?"

"His French is rusty but definitely European, and he's British, or the likes. He's not only from out of town; he's from out of the country. He had a bright-yellow night ticket." Meaning he had a passport or an international driver's license to show as identification, and a busload of amenities and special discounts coming his way from the hospitality industry as a foreign tourist in ski country.

"So? Why is that so clearly depressing you?"

I huff a frosty breath, annoyed anew. "Don't you get that he's just this ... total one-nighter?" I say, referring to the night ticket affixed on his sleeve. I knew the moment I saw it that I would have to walk away.

Casual, non merci. I'm not cut out for it; the awkward sex and tiptoeing around after isn't my thing. I can't seem to do anything other than full measure, and I won't settle. I want what my parents have: enduring, all-encompassing, endless love...

Anticipation of CD's endless teasing has forced me to keep my desires for what he would call a "fairy tale romance" to myself. I know how far-fetched it sounds.

But what if the stranger back there was the real thing? My heart thumps hard against my ribs just at the thought.

No. I readily dismiss my reveries. *You're just in love with love, Magali.*

Moot point anyway. On patrols, we seldom come across the same ticket holders more than once, if at all. Too many slopes.

"I totally get it. One night wouldn't be enough. You'd need at least a week to get him out of your system," CD says. "No. Make that two. A set of full lips and a dimpled square jaw, it gets to me every time."

"Thanks for the visual," I mumble, tingling all over at the thought of those full lips doing wondrous things as I imagine them trailing down my body for the next week, or two, or forever...

I slump back on the chair. I finally get a case of the mythical butterflies by the crate full, but I'll never see him again. Awesome.

No. It's for the best, I remind myself. I don't have time for this insta-whatever that was, and all the drama. I have plans.

An involuntary smile spread across my lips. I'm having babies by the dozens. No, hundreds of them. That's the plan.

I've recently been accepted into the graduate pilot program I've been aiming for ever since kangarooing on my chest my first premature newborn five years ago in a skin-to-skin therapy session, working wonders on preemies' developmental growth. The name being derived from kangaroos completing their postnatal development outside the womb. It clicked right there. Babies are my destiny. And now, it's really happening.

In six short weeks, I will most definitely leave the hallowed halls of l'Université de Montréal, and big city life, behind, for an extensive hands-on internship, studying at the regional hospital in Sainte-Agathe. And two years from now, I'll be a fully licensed midwife, here, in Les Hautes Laurentides. *Home.*

Letting my head fall back against the lift's frame, I hum to myself, sending my overflow of gratitude up to the star-studded sky. Or what can be seen of it, underneath the harsh glare of the resort night lights, anyway.

I sigh dreamily as the lift winds upward toward the Carrefour junction at the top of the slopes. "Have I told you lately—?"

"That you're disgustingly happy all the time?" CD interrupts me. "You're already over your nightly quota, just saying."

"Go ahead, blame my parents, like I do," I say, a smile lingering, and he chuckles under his breath.

"Hey, speaking of? I don't think I've seen them once this past week. Everything okay?" he asks, a slight frown crossing over his face.

"Never better," I assure him.

CD is a full-time patroller. The resort, open quasi year round, turns into a pretty cool aqua-park in the summer, and my parents, now semi-retired, are pretty much habitués in the wintertime here. Not to mention well-liked all around. A week without spotting them once on the slopes is a rare occurrence. "They've been helping Liam, and having so much fun—" I earn a blank look.

"Who's Liam?"

"Hello, Liam and Éolie? The young couple I told you about until you were about ready to gag. Ring any bell?" I prompt.

He smirks. "Not really. I gag too many times to count whenever you talk about sappy subjects like your babies and lovey-dovey couples. It's all a blur."

I thwack him with the back of my hand. "Seriously? I raved and raved about them buying Old Léon's place."

"Oh? That's his name, Liam?" He shrugs.

I grin, recalling my chance encounter with Liam and Éolie at Le Vieux Clocher, a Saint-Sauveur Bed & Breakfast a family friend, Hélène, operates.

My parents and I try and meet there for breakfast once a week before I report here for duty, and as usual, I was running late. But no matter how fleeting our meeting was, they both made a lasting impression on me. Such a lovely, gorgeous couple. One day, I will be as in love as they are, I vow.

Still, what a small world. Now they're my parents' new neighbors. Well, neighbors being relative here, as on back country roads, more often than not, being neighbors means a few kilometers apart in between wilderness patches...

"Merde," CD interjects, and the way he says it grabs my attention with urgency. Bending forward, I quickly scan the surrounding areas looking for a fallen skier. Or worse. Two.

"Yard sale," he says, using a term that sends a chill down my spine. My breath quickens. "Only one. No plow through," he's quick to reassure. "To your left, upper corner of La Grande Virée."

My eyes dart up to the slope he just mentioned. Spotting it, I cringe at the sight of the crash, pieces of equipment spread all over.

As I get ready to report, CD cups his hands and yells down as our chair draws nearer, "Need medical assistance?"

The poor guy gingerly stands, giving us the okay signal. Two other skiers collect his poles, goggles, gloves, and skis farther down the slope, herringboning their way back up. He walks down, meeting them halfway.

I blanch at the sight of death cookies. My mind snags. Death cookies. Such an appropriate way to describe the cookie-sized chunks of ice that can form by grooming and snowmaking, given the right conditions. The plague of resorts this far up north, as they take many unaware skiers by surprise, easily sending them out of control at higher speed, and...

Rafael.

I close my eyes, seeing him so clearly. I swallow and breathe in, count to five, breathe out.

My mind knows there's nothing I could have done, but my heart? My heart never got the full memo.

Talking into my mouthpiece, my stomach twists into a series of pretzel knots as I report the incident and location, sending a maintenance crew to see to it immediately.

I look up, past the landing platform. The needle at the very top of the mountain, or the chute as it's commonly called, has been closed ever since that day. At least there's that.

"Don't go there, M. We're senior patrollers now, remember." CD bumps my shoulder with his.

I nod, silently repeating, *I'm no longer fifteen and helpless.* I shake myself off, giving him a tight smile.

"Hey, it reminds me. I forgot to mention something, thanks to your golden-skinned Adonis blindsiding me." CD gives me a sly glance, visibly trying to distract me away from thoughts of Rafael before the past grips me completely. It works. Despite myself, my thoughts stray once more to the magnetic stranger.

The swarm of caterpillars' gnawing at my guts ever since spotting ice cookies neatly transforms. A flurry of butterflies takes flight in my lower belly, sending me high as a kite.

Tendrils of warmth float in my veins as I imagine those sinful copper-brown eyes burning a trail down my skin. My mind captures anew the intensity of his gaze, like a lover's caress brushing over me when we parted ways in the cafeteria, sensual heat washing over me. No one ever looked at me in quite that way. Over and above desire. With fascination. With longing. What would it be like to be taken by him, I wonder.

I squirm, clenching my thighs together.

Zut de flûte, I'm in so much trouble.

"He's not my anything, got that?" I say, infusing my voice with loads of conviction. I dismiss the tingling fest electrifying my entire body, setting my nerve endings on fire, proving me a liar.

CD looks on knowingly.

"Sure, he's not." He shrugs, the picture of innocence. "Whatever makes you sleep better at night."

My heart flutters, afraid he might be right.

"He's not my anything *and* it will make me sleep better at night." I decisively say.

There. That should do it. I'm totally convinced. Back on track. When I crash in bed tonight, I'll sleep. Just sleep. No slow burning lips lovingly worshipping my body. Nope.

He snorts.

"Besides, I just had one of Mireille's cupcakes. What else could I possibly need?" I stoutly vow.

"An entirely different temptation, that's what," CD says without missing a beat as we get ready to disembark from the chairlift.

A magnetic stranger?

I shake my head. I really had to go there, didn't I?

I groan. "Got a cupcake hidden somewhere?" I ask only to realize that I'll never look at a cupcake the same, ever again.

"I know better than to flash any kind of sugar in front of you," he scoffs. "Besides, I have a much better offering," he adds, entirely too self-satisfied. "It so happens I saw Amélie before you came in."

I perk up. My friend Amélie just received her pre-school teacher degree this semester, and from the look of things, she's back from her last student-teacher assignment, volunteering up in Kuujjuaq, Nunavik.

"I haven't talked to her in ages. How's she doing?" I ask, clearing off the landing platform as the lift delivers us to the Carrefour junction linking the expert slopes.

CD waggles his eyebrows. "She's taking a turn in the park as we speak. Why don't you ask her yourself."

Cédric, Amélie, and I were, once upon a time, part of the Junior Freestyle Canadian Ski Team. And thus, lived out our entire teens together in the ski park, a closed-off area specifically designed for tricks, aerial or otherwise, training here, at 'Saint-So,' for the most part. We couldn't wait to turn eighteen to become full-fledged instructors. At least, I couldn't, up until … Rafael.

I sigh heavily. No escaping his ghost tonight, it seems. My emotions are churning, flying high and low.

"Come on. Go for it. You know you want to," CD says, his tone overly persuasive and definitely tempting me away from duty. It's not like him to offer, nor is it like me to accept. Not while I'm on the clock anyway.

"Hang on. Wasn't I about to be late to report?" I ask accusingly. I lose track of time so easily and so often, I no longer question when someone hails me to hurry...

"Nope. We still have half an hour before reporting. I was just saving you from making an ass of yourself." He snickers as my arm backhands him on the chest. "You owe me, by the way," he adds.

"And just how do you figure I owe you? You're always pushing guys at me, one way or the other. And now that I could have maybe, possibly, tentatively been interested in one, you just what, pulled me away?"

"You're welcome." He flashes me a toothy grin, buffing his night-time lens. He straps the goggles back on his helmet, wearing a smug glow of self-congratulation.

I roll my eyes.

"Look, I'm thrilled you were finally fizzed by one, but that guy was scorching. He'd have burned you to cinders and left you to smolder in your own ash. Couldn't let that happen now, could I? Baby steps, M. Baby steps."

"Point conceded," I sigh, envisioning a scorching kiss, getting hot and bothered all over again. "I'm going to find Amélie. You coming?"

"Nah. I'll let you catch up with Amélie. Talk of babies gives me the heebie-jeebies, thank you very much." He visibly shudders and I shake my head.

"Heebie-jeebies, really?" I let out a snort.

"Yep, and you don't wanna see that, it's not pretty. Come and get me when you're done," he says before delivering the coup de grâce. "I'll be the one gorging up on Mireille's brand-new orgasmic cupcakes in the cafeteria."

"You're so funny." I fight the urge to upturn my eyes and lose.

Waving him off, I veer left for the park.

Three

ZAC

I stare at the bonfire crackling outside the ski lodge, goose bumps prickling along my skin. In just under a few seconds, my cardboard cup is nothing more than ash and a memory. I suppress a shudder.

"Nice. That throw was a perfectly curved half-ellipse," Yann, our very own MIT math brainiac, says to no one in particular, his mind probably getting off on some algorithms.

"Let's hit the slopes," I say, striving for an even tone. Snapping my helmet on, I firmly shake myself out of my trance.

"I'd ask where's the goddamn fire," Theo says in a dry tone of voice, "but then again, it's you being you."

The guys share a long-suffering look, emptying their own cups.

I refuse to comment. I'm known as the adrenaline junkie with good reason, after all. It's as valid cover as any to not let on that my mind is preoccupied with a girl tonight. A sensual, dark-haired beauty with flawless skin and entrancing silver eyes.

Magali.

I can't seem to shake her out of my thoughts, and I'm not thrilled about it. I can't remember having such an instant reaction to a girl. Not since I was what, thirteen? "And even then," I mumble under my breath.

At that age, I was more obsessed with earning my private pilot license. By fifteen, if I recall, I had already logged too many hours to count, flying solo in my twin-engine Comanche, chasing the horizon way more my speed than chasing tail. Girls always had a way of finding me, not the other way around.

Even so, something tells me I wouldn't mind chasing after Magali. No two ways about it, her blend of assertive and wholesome is a killer combination. I'm intrigued by her. *Man, is the world coming to an end?*

"Quad or six pack?" I ask instead, referring to the chairlifts either carrying four or six people.

Not waiting on a reply, I tug my boots down on the bindings of my parabolic skis to clip them on. It's the first pair of skis I've owned since leaving Berlinger International Academy five years ago, the Swiss boarding school we all attended, rooming together for more than thirteen years. And these skis beat rentals, hands down. I had just about forgotten how sweet a ride your perfect match could be. The top layer of the ski's structure is cut lengthwise for superior power transfer enhancing control, and the transversal flex release really improves turn initiation, and makes the skis livelier.

Liam and Éolie putting down roots in Les Hautes Laurentides, Québec's ski country, has some unforeseen benefits. Like skiing day or night in one's backyard with over twenty resorts to choose from, and *not* getting involved with a rather intensely hot, ski patroller named, let's say, Magali.

I never-ever do involved, I remind myself. And even if I wanted to, I wouldn't know how to go about it anyway.

The guys are the only family I've ever known for all intents and purposes, my only constant, and that's fine by me.

Fickle is my middle name. *Here today, gone tomorrow,* as Leo's fond of saying. *That's you, man.* But the familiar pep talk, for once, weirdly enough, has the opposite effect, and depresses me instead.

I ignore the hollow pain in my chest and push off on my skis on my way to the lifts. They respond, as one with me ... I stare down. *A perfect match.*

"Six pack, boys. Take it or leave it," I say over my shoulder to the guys, who are having a heated discussion over which double black-diamond slope to try next. "I want to check their half-pipes." A U-shaped channel with smooth walls used for aerial tricks, and the thrill of a few flips, might be just what I need to regain some of my footing here.

Unfortunately, the mere notion of a thrilling physical release to screw my head on straight, brings me right back to no other thoughts than getting laid. But somehow, Magali's tight little body writhing underneath me is the only one I see.

Fuck me sideways.

Pissed by my own shifting moods, I don't wait for any of the guys. I ski my way over to the six-pack line up, but they join me anyway before I hop on the ride.

"Heads up. You haven't got the skis for tricks," Yann is quick to remind me.

"I know," I grouch, hating that he's right. I'll have to find some other way to let out steam, evidently.

"Like that ever stopped you before," P.O. snorts.

I cut him a glare. "You daring me?"

"What are you, sixteen?" Leo asks.

I scowl. "Don't even go there."

"Yeah, that's the point. Don't even go there with parabolic skis on," Theo says, putting on his best lawyerly *don't fuck with me* face.

The guys know me too well.

I close my eyes for a brief instant, willing myself to shake out of this spiraling down mood.

"Chill, counselor. You won the closing argument," I grumble, my usual laid-back persona clearly missing in action. "This chair travels above the ski park. I'll check it out and see if I'm tempted enough to go back, some other time, with the *right* skis." Twin tipped, shorter ones.

I grunt, more annoyed by my own reactions than I am with them, really.

The line ahead of us moves steadily as the chairlift operator, a dour-faced old timer, keeps the circulation fluid. We're next, so we push on our poles until the tip of our skis reaches the marker. The large chair swivels around the anchoring tower. To the creaking sound of gears slowing it down, it lowers at a knee level as it picks us up, gaining speed once we're up in the air, the handlebar secured.

The ski park spreads out underneath us. I watch keenly as we start our ascent. Single rails and half-jumps for snowboarders mainly comprise the last third of it, and a few adepts are gathered around one, shouting encouragements. A girl flies off to make a front-side grab on the nose of her board.

"Sweet," Yann says, leaning closer, probably figuring out speed and angles.

P.O. gives me a sly glance sideways. "We should rent some."

"Not happening again in this lifetime," I say, recalling my epic fail at snowboarding some ten years ago. With both my feet strapped down on one board, it took me less than half a day to hate with a fiery passion not excelling at it quickly almost as much as feeling restrained.

"Why? With you eating snow more times than you'd be up, it's one hell of a guaranteed way to slow you down, man," Leo deadpans.

I cut them a glare, and they all snicker.

Theo low fives Leo. "Good thinking. Let's strap ZeeMan, here, to a board. Give us all a chance to one-up him—finally."

The bond between the six of us may be thicker than blood, but still.

"Try, and prepare to die," I say, uttering one of our old gaming calls to arm.

Tuning out the typical banter bouncing back and forth between my buddies, my mood turns decidedly introspective.

It's been an age since our last ski vacation together. Liam's missing out tonight, but then again, if a honeymoon weekend isn't a good enough reason, nothing is...

My eyes drop to the bright-yellow lift ticket tagged to my left sleeve. Our ski vacation is almost over. We're all leaving Liam's old farmstead in a few days. No. Leo's old farmstead, I remind myself, as this upcoming summer, it will officially be his. After years of agronomy research and studies to earn his Ph.D., he'll finally start his experimental farm there, cross-breeding new strains of soya beans and whatnots to feed the world. His dream come true, literally.

Envy seeps in. I'd like some of my mates' long-term focus and goals, but I don't think I'm cut out for it.

I zone in and out, letting them argue over which black diamond slope we'll take when there's a lurch forward on the bench seat we're still riding, and everything stops. I know from experience, the whole shebang is only ever stopped manually by the lift operator when someone falls on entry, or automatically, when someone fails to lower the guardrail on the upward swing. This can only mean there's an inexperienced skier who missed his mark down there. I exhale.

"Great," I mumble under my breath, already fretting over being stuck up here, immobile for who knows how long.

"Heard there's a charter bus of never-evers tonight," Leo concurs, using the generic term ascribed to first-time skiers in ski lingo.

"They're pretty cocky if they're trying this lift." My eyes upturn. Even so, knowing quite well I'd have been first in line for the double-black diamond slopes myself, bypassing the carpet or the bunny slopes.

"I'll bet Lucie can optimize this lift's operations." P.O., our computer whiz who never goes anywhere without at least a piece of something connecting him to his computer, Lucie, says, whipping out a wafer-thin pint-sized tablet from his jacket's inside pocket.

"I'd rather you didn't hack into their system while we're dangling up here, if you don't mind," Theo warns drily.

Underneath my ass, the chair swings back and forth. We're left balancing to and fro in the frigid wind, giving new meaning to shooting the breeze. The sudden quiet of the mechanical gears' ground to a halt amplifies the swishing sound of skiers and snowboarders on their way down.

"Hey, check her out. One o'clock!" Yann exclaims in an awed tone of voice.

"She's pretty damn good," Leo says.

"She's a patroller by the looks of her jacket," Theo adds.

My head whips up. I inhale a sharp breath at the familiar resort emblem on the helmet and the bright-red of the jacket—and the curves that fill it out.

Magali.

Four

MAGALI

Closing the gate access to the ski park, I spot Amélie right away in her green, flower-printed jacket. She's surrounded by half a dozen teenagers listening with rapt attention as she demonstrates how to do a front flip, levering on one's poles.

I grin. She's a born teacher all right. Made of awesome.

"Hey, you," she cries out upon spying me watching her. She breaks away from the group and they let her pass, chattering amongst themselves as she slides over to where I wait. "Heard you got into the pilot program in Sainte-Agathe?"

"Yep. I'll soon hold in the palm of my hands all of your future pupils, just so you know." I let my grin blossom until my cheeks hurt.

We fall into each other's arms, laughing.

"When did you get back?"

"This afternoon." She throws her arms wide. "I'm back home!"

We both breathe in, relishing the night's frigid moist air, redolent of the evergreens.

Ah, yes. The comforting smell of home. I sigh, happy.

"Are you officially on duty?" Her head tilts to the side.

"I still have thirty minutes." Raising a brow, I motion with my head to the highest ramp, exhilaration filling me. "Meet up?"

Her face brightens, stunning green-hazel eyes shot with blue, sparkling. Her answering grin mirrors mine.

This is exactly what I need, a thirty-minute session of acute focus, culminating with flying off the ramp, to wipe away any thoughts of coppery-eyed, gorgeous strangers, once and for all.

"I'm almost done with my impromptu lesson here; let me finish and I'll join you up in just a few." Amélie glows, and I shake my head at her. Once an instructor always an instructor.

"I'll be the one in red."

She laughs and we fist-bump on it. I turn to her crowd of young admirers. "Best teacher ever. What she says goes."

Flipping through my iPod's playlists, I select *My Freedom*, an indie epic music mix, and soon get lost in one of the choreographies of an old ski ballet routine of mine, or acroski, short for acrobatic ski, as it's now called. Of all freestyle disciplines, it's still my personal favorite, even though ski ballet is no longer considered an official one and hasn't been since I was a little girl.

As one with my skis, music pulsing in my veins, I let myself be pulled in a place where nothing else exists but the precise movements. The timing and sequences requires my utmost concentration to execute the tricks until they seemingly blend one into another, with me feeling like I'm dancing on air.

I stop at the top of the main ramp, warmed up and primed, waiting for Amélie to join me. It's of no matter that we've done these flips hundreds of times. It never gets old. My chest expands with anticipation.

I see myself gaining speed, breaking free from gravity for the space of a few seconds, soaring, flipping, right up to our landing spot as I visualize every single minute details of the double back flip jump unfolding.

A moment later, Amélie comes up beside me.

My heart pounds in my ears.

We're so in tune that by some unspoken signal, we just push off the deck at the exact same time, and fly down the ramp.

We land spot-on, to the sound of whistling and clapping coming from the chairlifts above, but I don't let any of it distract me out of my happy place.

I just ski on, freely carving out a trail in long sweeping curves on my way down; Amélie's counter curves in synch with mine.

I'm in the zone.

Five

ZAC

I bend forward as far the chairlift's handlebar lets me.

It's her.

I'd recognize Magali's shapely physique anywhere now. It's imprinted on my brain. Even so, as if to leave no doubts whatsoever, her labeled bright-red coat and distinctive helmet jump at me.

My heart pounds, pulse racing as a strange, new awareness sharpens my senses. The hairs on my body stand on end, and my skin prickles in some sort of unforeseen anticipation.

Jesus.

My jaw drops open, and I'm quite unable to tear my eyes away from her, utterly mesmerized.

She's beauty in motion as she goes through a series of intricate flips, rolls, leg crossings, jumps, and spins in a choreographed, acrobatic ski routine.

"Hey, Zee? Looks like your patroller," P.O. says, annoyingly know-it-all. And I don't even care, held spellbound by Magali's freestyle ballet performance.

"Looks like," I reply as nonchalantly as I can. "And she's *not* my anything," I firmly say, yet my chest contracts on the last word. I rub the hollow pain away.

"She's not your anything my ass, man." Leo smirks, never taking his eyes off *my* girl. *Mine.* Bloody everlasting hell. Where did that come from? "Admit you're done for."

"Shut the hell up, Leo." My voice is low, a warning.

Theo shoots me an incredulous look.

"Holy shit. They're right," Yann says, his voice just as awed as before, only now, instead of her, he's checking me out. "You're a goner, man."

Oddly enough, I can't even think of a comeback. I look down over the slope again instead.

Magali now stands motionless at the top of the steepest ramp.

Blood pumping wildly, my heartbeats drum in my ears.

Another girl in a green flowered jacket joins her on deck. They both let go at the same time, gaining speed, soaring off the ramp, executing a perfectly synchronized double back flip.

"Holy hell," I breathe out, eyes bugging out.

"No way," Leo says, his eyes glued on the duo.

They both land effortlessly, skiing on to the sound of whistles and clapping that goes unacknowledged as they speed by their admirers.

With a forward jerk, the lift begins moving again, and I twist my head, contorting my torso, until I can no longer see her behind me.

Christ, it's not like I have a logical explanation for this one-of-a-kind magnetic pull, but one thing's for sure. I don't give a flying fuck anymore. I feel it deep in my guts. I've got to meet this girl. Now. Tonight. And if that makes me a goner? So be it.

A rough estimate of the probabilities of this happening, though, with thirty-some slopes opened up at night, and only two hours left of skiing to do so, calls for drastic measures.

I eye the chute up ahead, a plan forming.

Six

ZAC

Hopping down the chair at the Landing Carrefour, I ski my way over to the billboard, studying the layout of the expert slopes this six pack services, when a "No Downhill" pictogram catches my attention. Hmmm. Maybe getting a warning from one of the patrollers will get the ball rolling faster.

My eyes dart up the chute then back at the board. The chute is crossed out as closed. *Why is it closed?*

This chute is certainly not high enough to be serviced by helicopter like in the Alps, but it's not serviced by a lift or a cable either, and my skis are not equipped with backcountry climbing skins, some add-on sleeves permitting a straight-line climb with alpine skis on a narrow, backcountry trail. Guess my ski boots will have to do.

"What are you scowling at?" Theo asks, adjusting one of his boot clips, the three others having taken off already, scattered down three different black diamond slopes. My bet is on a wager of some kind that I wasn't paying any attention to.

"What they call a chute," I answer Theo back, disgruntled.

A chute by definition's usually a steep and narrow gully surrounded by rocks most often. Almost certainly an expert-run only, and whether it's marked or not, it's a no-fall zone, an area where falling will likely lead to serious injury, but this bump's ridiculously ... just that. A bump compared to the Matterhorn.

Man, schussing from up there at downhill speed will take me less than four minutes to reach the bottom of the hill. And I don't even think I'll reach chatter level, the intoxicating, singing ski vibrations caused by travelling at high speed. So not nearly enough time to be spotted by patrollers for a no downhill warning, the fastest way at my disposal right now to relay a message to Magali to meet with me after her shift. My run will be over before it starts. And I'm not about to lose opportunities just by being stuck on chairlifts more often than being available on the slopes.

It's back to plan A. Climbing the chute and staying put until opportunity strikes. I'll have the perfect lookout all around, and I'll be in a ready position to make my move on the first patroller who comes in sight.

"It's closed, man." Theo levels me a look.

"No shit, Sherlock," I say, still weighing the pros and cons. "Your point?" I ask Theo absently.

"I'd like to try snowblades in their backcountry trails, but they're closed at night," he says, referring to the strips of forests kept in between groomed slopes, and the very short skis used on those trails.

"And ... you're telling me this why?" I ask drily, leaning on my poles.

"If I can wait, you can wait," he warns.

"That's where I beg to differ. I can't wait." I snap him a sharp salute. He curses a blue streak under his breath as I unclip and start the climb, shouldering my skis, decision made.

"What the hell can't wait? It's not only closed, it's darker than pitch up there," I hear Theo say from behind me.

"I'll be fine. I got this," I say, determined.

"Christ. You'll have your ass in a sling for this," he says. "Your funeral. I'm too old for this shit."

I watch Theo take off in a spray of snow for a split second before turning back to the task at hand, undeterred. I'm on a mission.

My breath labors, coming out in frosty plumes. My back dampens with a fine sheen of sweat as I haul my ass up the vertical drop by foot.

The needle, or the very top, is a stumped, snow-covered rock with enough leg room to stand up comfortably. The vertical drop is, at the most, a measly fifteen meters. No challenge.

I don my skis again and face forward. My gaze sweeps the surrounding area.

The view from my vantage point is breathtaking with resorts lit up on the horizon, here and there, as far as my eyes can see under the clear night sky. Yeah, these rolling hills do pull at my heart strings, never mind being puny compared to the Alps as Éolie warned us beforehand. I taste the pungent scent of the evergreens in the moistness of the air. All in all, the quilted silence, only broken once in a while by a gust of wind whistling by me, is soothing, calming my racing heart.

My eyes cut between the chairlifts coming up both sides of the mountain, relentless, searching for the color red, dismissing anything else, when a familiar helmet comes into view below me.

Magali.

Man, my heart stutters out of my chest. Of all the patrollers out tonight, she's back within my sights. Taking it as a good sign, head thrown, I whoop loudly.

How hard can it be to chase after a girl? You're wearing skis, man. A slow grin spreads on my lips.

You're mine.

I push off the ledge.

I fly down the narrow gorge, the trail bypassing the Landing Carrefour.

Magali's up ahead ... and then she's not. She can't possibly have switched slopes on me, once engaged. Going on high alert, I press down hard, sliding a bit longer on a patch of ice cookies than what I originally anticipated, before coming to a quick halt, checking the surroundings. My gaze sweeps the length of the slope making sure she's nowhere in sight, fallen, or worse, injured.

Empty. No one.

I push my goggles on top of my helmet, my eyes narrowing. Where did she disappear to?

A bright halogen headlight blinds me as it bursts out of the backcountry trail.

"You?!" Magali cries out, spraying me up with snow as she abruptly brakes in front of me mere centimeters away. Clicking her patrol headlight off, she pulls her goggles down around her neck, blinking.

My breath swooshes out on a relieved chuckle. "Me." I briefly bow my head, my eyes pinning her down.

"I can't believe it," she breathes out, gawking. *Neither can I, truth be told.* "How could I even remotely think for an instant there..." she murmurs to herself, cheeks flushed, shaking her head in a dazed fashion.

"I don't care about the hows," I say, leaning into her. "What time are you getting off your shift, Magali?" I ask, breathing in her minty fresh skin, one of my gloved hands coming up to brush away the drops of melting snow pearling on her cheek, entranced.

"What?" She recoils, and I straighten, my hands lifting in a placating gesture.

"Too fast? Just tell me," I say softly. "Tonight, I'm yours." I stare at her parted lips, opening and closing, shocked into silence. I shut my eyes briefly, my body overtaken by visions of melding one into another, grinding, exulting. A few spots dance in front of my eyes, reminding me that breathing's not optional.

"We'll go at your pace, not mine. Promessa, mi amore," I murmur, shocking the bloody everlasting hell out of me, never mind her, with the long-forgotten Italian. *Promise, my love.* The very last words she whispered in my ear, on that morning, long ago, promising me she would return. Only, she never made it back ... *di Fiori*, I admonish myself. You're slipping into a dangerous territory, here.

A gust of wind picks up, rustling in the trees. The temperature seemingly drops by a few degrees. Or maybe that's her expression, I finally note.

"On what planet do you live?" Magali asks, just about livid.

"Excuse me?"

"Tonight I'm yours? What does that even mean? Does it normally work for you? Snap your fingers, and the world obeys?"

I frown. "Just about," I say honestly, my breath fogging.

For a split second, my gaze dips to her mouth, lingering there for no longer than a heartbeat before flashing back to meet her angry stare.

She inhales sharply. Her nostrils flare, and her eyes shoot daggers. Yep. It's definitely colder by one-eighty degrees. What did I miss between the cafeteria and now?

"Well, newsflash. Your sense of entitlement is useless here. You're nothing but a reckless, spoiled, bored—"

"Careful," I warn, my voice lowering to a rumble. "You know nothing about me. Don't make snap judgements."

"I know enough." She leans into my face, her eyes crinkling into angry slits. "That chute's permanently closed to prevent uber-privileged guys like you—"

"Who the hell are you to call me privileged? Bored? Reckless?" I say, suddenly seeing red. "That chute's a joke. It's got nothing on the ramp you flew out of, so don't even go there," I hiss, breathing down her face, volatile emotions churning.

"I'll go there all right, you entitled prick. Acrobatic ski requires intense focus and dedication. I knew precisely where I'd be landing and in a secured environment. You just flew out of there uncaring of others you'd plow into—"

"The fuck I did. I was in perfect control at all times," I say through clenched teeth, going toe to toe.

"Yeah, right!" she shouts, her voice over brimming with contempt. Her eyes flash silver, and the air crackles with tension.

Jesus Christ, she's really calling me on my shit, and chewing me off. And for what? Skiing down a puny bump, admittedly closed, but still.

My jaw ticks. On a scale of one to angry, I shoot straight past seeing red, and land on blood boiling. Glaring down at her, I growl a warning. "Get off my back. Your slopes are a walk in the park, no challenge."

She visibly stiffens, closing her eyes.

My stare involuntarily drops to her full, parted lips.

And now I have the insane urge to pull her to me, and kiss the fuck out of her. Breathe in her fire and make the passion burn brighter than anger until we're both drowning in lust, until we both shut the hell up.

"A walk in the park, no challenge?" she asks, eyes popping open, outrage bleeding into her tone. "Tell that to nine-year-old Rafael, who got in the way of an adrenaline junkie just like you, out for kicks," she spits, fisting my jacket one minute, releasing me the next with clear disgust. "He never stood a chance."

Hold on.

What?

What the ... what?

Cold seeps deep within my bones as I absorb what she just said. I blink. My anger fizzles out, my mind in a haze.

Her eyes drop, and then flit back up to mine. I hate that she flayed me alive with some truths just now, but god, the raw sorrow behind her haunted look? Almost brings me to my knees.

"Life's a joke to your kind," she says low, her verdict slicing through me, fleshing out my fears.

There's quiet for a moment as we stare at one another, chests heaving.

Is that what it is? The unspoken question hangs heavy in the air, stripping me of my veneer, leaving me exposed, afraid she might be right.

Another patroller comes to a spraying halt beside us, shattering the moment.

He shoots Magali a churlish look that promises dire retribution. "Never take off on your own. You know better than that," he rants at her, and my thoughts splinter.

The stocky guy she called Cédric in the cafeteria earlier on plants his poles in a pissed-off move.

I pull myself in front of her, cutting him a warning look.

He turns to me. Challenge accepted.

I stand my ground. He can take it out on me all he wants, but not on her.

"As for you, *dude*. That stunt you just pulled? Here's a warning—"

"You're blacklisted for all eternity. Don't ever come back," Magali breaks in. And before I can react, she cuts my ticket holder using a Swiss knife, the irony of which is certainly not lost on me.

I just stand there poleaxed as she pockets it, and takes off in a graceful arch of shaved snow.

"Holy shit. Blacklisted...? Man, that's a first." The guy stares after Magali, and it's a toss-up as to who's the most flummoxed by what just went down.

Seven

ZAC

Apprehension
noun
2. acceptance of or receptivity to information without passing judgment on its validity, often without complete comprehension.

I crack my eyes open the next morning and smother a groan into my pillow as last night's debacle comes back to me. And it leaves a foul taste in my mouth. I can count on the fingers of one hand the number of times I wished I had done things differently, knowing the outcome, but this one tops them all. The guys and I grew up in an all-boys' boarding school, and the stupid dares my teenaged self agreed to, like bungee jumping au naturel, were common enough. But I've never regretted any of them. My impulsiveness most often led to an experience or lesson I could at least appreciate in hindsight. Last night, not so much.

The one time I've been tempted enough to play for keeps and went on a chase, got me blacklisted for all eternity in less than an hour ... That's a new low, even for me.

Magali's exquisite face and mischievous grin as she threw her *definitely a keeper*, out there, in the resort cafeteria, replays in my head, taunting me.

My throat constricts.

Goddamn it.

I'm obsessing over a girl I'll never see again. It just goes to show chasing is obviously *not* on my list of skills. Chalk it up to an experiment gone wrong, man, same as trying to snowboard. She's just one girl.

One in a million...

Disgusted with myself, I throw off the blankets and hop out of my single bed. One of ten that came with Leo's old farmstead, spread out in the three upstairs bedrooms. Leo's bed is made, but P.O., still dead to the world on the bed next to mine, snoring, brings back memories of our days at Berlinger's boarding school. Guess he's lucky there's no Sharpie upstairs, or his baby face would be sporting a neat goatee by now. I grin, briefly entertained out of my funk.

I head for the bathroom, but I get three steps before my toes begin to freeze against the cold and creaky hardwood, tempting me to dive right back under the warm comforter. I double back and pull some thick, woolen socks on. Bloody hell, it's a wonder they had so many kids in the 'olden days up here. It's too fucking cold to get it on, to my way of thinking. There's just no way anyone can sleep in the buff in the drafty upstairs and survive the night with all of their favorite parts intact; things do fall off with frostbite, after all. Wearing my thermal underwear like a second skin, I trudge my way downstairs to the only working shower.

The sound of running water greets me but I enter anyway. After years of sharing rooms and bathrooms with these guys, privacy is nonexistent. I check the daily schedule rotation tacked to the bathroom door. Leo's turn to shower, then Yann's turn before mine.

"If you flush the loo I'll kill you, slowly and painfully," Leo says from behind the shower curtain. I let out a snort. Means he's not yet past the lukewarm portion the ancient water heater spews, and into the cold-as-fuck portion of our Scottish Shower Spa à la Swiss precision style we have going on, the upstairs bathroom being out of commission for the rest of the winter season.

I shake my head, remembering the drenching I got our first day here, with me left holding the rusted-out cut-off valve in my hand and icy water shooting all over me from the broken pipe.

Not daring to flush the toilet, I pee in the sink, more leery of the added pressure it'd put on the antediluvian pipes than by Leo's threat.

I find Yann multi-tasking at the kitchen table, engrossed in one of his quantum physics textbooks all the while chewing on soggy cereal stained red from a mysterious liquid that's sure as hell not milk filling his bowl.

"Man, what's with the red goo?" I ask on my way to the fridge.

"We ran out of orange juice," he answers, not bothering to look up. There's milk, but we all hate the stuff, one of those boarding school hangovers. Unfortunately, so does Éolie, as pregnant as she is. But she likes it well enough if mixed with unsweetened dark chocolate in hot cocoa. And if Swiss made, even better. I inwardly grin. Liam bought what was left of the entire stock a few days ago, only too happy to find some after P.O.'s passage, and stashed it somewhere, as god knows when the village store will get to replenish it.

"So you what? Poured blood on your cereal, instead?" I ask Yann, only to watch him turn a little green around the edges.

"Low blow," Yann mutters, pushing his bowl away. Both Yann and P.O. are well known in our inner circle to pass out at the sight of blood. "I'll never look at cranberry juice with cereal the same now."

"Good for you. Pour it in a glass and drink it next time. That mush looks vile." I toss him an apple, and pick one for myself.

Theo pops in, leaning a shoulder on the kitchen doorway. "I'm running an errand down in the village, need anything? Like a few brain cells to compensate for the ones you lost last night?"

"It's too early for your shit, Theo. I need a few shots of caffeine first." I slam a pot of water on the stove top, shoving two spoonfuls of instant coffee into a mug. What this place needs is an espresso machine, preferably along with a barista who knows her way around it.

"Imagine that," Theo says drily from behind me. "Last night was too late for my shit, and now it's too early."

I rub one hand down my face, and swivel round. "Want me to confess I fucked up, counselor? Fine. Done. Happy?"

"Hardly. But that will do for a start," he mutters. "What were you thinking, man? At least they won't sue for trespassing. But Christ, Zee. You're now automatically blacklisted throughout their affiliated resorts as well, and P.O. checked, that's fifteen more."

"Heads up," I say irritably. "If you're trying to make me feel better, it's not working. Leave it alone, it's done and over with." My jaw locks tight as I lean on the counter and cross my arms. Theo spares me a glance and storms out, slamming the front door shut.

"La Réserve up in Saint-Donat isn't part of the Mont-Saint-Sauveur network. Want to give it a shot today?" Yann says from behind his book.

"Yeah, let's do this." I stare off, waiting for the water to boil in the pan. I don't really feel like skiing today, but if I want last night's incident to blow over I need to act normally or the guys will never let me hear the end of it.

Life's a joke to your kind, she said.

And what kind does that make me exactly? That is the question.

Eight

ZAC

I sigh for what seems like the umpteenth time in the past half hour alone.

La Réserve doesn't offer night skiing, so we went during the day for a change. It's after four, and we end up at an après-ski party at Le P'tit Goulot, the ski resort bistro. And here I am, at one of the liveliest bistro bars this side of les Hautes Laurentides if we are to believe P.O.'s internet search, inwardly twiddling my thumbs, reminding myself every few minutes to stop bouncing my knee or checking my watch.

Awesome.

Beside me, Yann is furiously calculating some mathematical equation on a paper napkin. It looks, strangely enough, like a possible trajectory to the moon and back.

I guzzle down half my sparkling water with a twist of lime, hold the ice. Who volunteered me as the designated driver, again? Oh. Yeah. Me. "Who wants a refill?" I ask, needing to move, exasperated with myself.

"I think we're good," Leo says drily, eyeing the extra four bottles of La Diable micro-brewery beer on the small, round table, still full. I check my watch. Can't blame them, I suppose. Five minutes in between rounds is not enough time.

"Yeah, man. We're soaking up the ambiance here, not getting slushed.

What's with you?" P.O. angles a brow at me.

My gaze takes in the vast square room. Divided into four sections, anchored down the middle by an open-face massive fireplace where one-meter-long logs are burning, the place is hopping with groups of friends and couples having a good time. But I'm not feeling it. That's what.

Yeah, especially the couples.

Man, they're everywhere tonight, laughing, cuddling, kissing.

Christ. I push away from the table. "I need a refill."

Theo, unaccountably quiet up to now, slides his bottle of dark brew, untouched, in front of me. "Take mine, I'll drive. I'll go get a sparkly."

I watch him push his way to the bar. My eyes narrow, speculating.

Guess he's no longer in a snit over last night's fuck-up. It usually takes him a bit more time to get over it, though, and I briefly wonder if something else came up. He's been zoning in and out since he came back from the village this morning. I inwardly shrug. No use asking him; he'll tell when he's ready, not before. A Theo thing.

"Is it me or what?" Leo asks around. "Drinking cold beer with negative forty temperatures awaiting us outside isn't as appealing as I thought it would be. I vote to share a bottle of Cabernet or Merlot, instead. Who's in?"

"I'll go order it." I jump on the occasion but Leo beats me to it.

"No need. I can't read the blackboard from here and I want to check their wine selection before picking one."

"You know, Zee," Yann says, looking up from his calculations with a raised brow. "Last night, odds you'd get the girl with the stunt you pulled were three to five hundred sixty-eight." He slides his napkin over to me before leaning back in his chair, taking a sip of his beer.

"For or against," P.O. asks on a snort.

"Against, by all evidence," Theo remarks drily, plopping his ass back down on his seat.

I bunch the napkin up, shooting them all a glare.

"Liam missed out on your epic crash and burn, man. He'll never believe." P.O. smirks. "And to think this one will go down in infamy."

I scowl thinking of Liam hidden away, honey-mooning it. "Sod off. I don't think Liam's missing out. I think he's got it made," I reply before I can stop myself.

Theo shoots me a sidelong glance but remains quiet as he pours his Perrier into a tall glass. Yann wipes his tortoise-shell glasses on the hem of his thermal ski sweater. Pushing them back on his nose, he stares at me with a speculative glint in his bright-green eyes but refrains from any comments.

"Yeah well, want to know what I think?" P.O.'s muddy, green-hazel eyes narrow on me.

"Not particularly, no," I grumble under my breath, all for nothing, knowing he'll say it anyway.

"I think you're right. Liam's got it made." P.O. salutes me with his bottle. "And you missed out."

I flip him off. But to be perfectly honest, I know I'm pissed at myself for obsessing over silver-grey eyes filled with contempt as they looked me over, or for obsessing over silver-grey eyes I'll never see again, period. "Can't miss out on something that isn't there, now can I?" I mutter.

"You don't really want me to answer that, do you?" P.O. asks.

Theo jerks his chin toward me. "Isn't that your phone vibrating?"

"Whose phone?" Yann and P.O dig into their liner pockets, our ski jackets draped over the back of our chairs.

"Mine." I frown at the caller ID, taking the call. "Liam, what's wrong, man?"

All movements freeze at our table, three sets of eyes zeroing on me.

"Éolie fell dead asleep, almost face planting in her lunch earlier," Liam whispers anxiously. I hunch over, plugging a finger in my other ear, listening over the din of the place. "Should I let her sleep or wake her so she can eat something? Hell, man. She's always so full of energy, is this even normal?"

I let out a pent-up breath. "Let her sleep. Her body knows what it needs right now." My shoulders relax back in the chair, the guys following suit. "This early in pregnancy she's adjusting to the flood of progesterone swimming in her blood and it can make a *normal* day seem as taxing as running a marathon. You're on your honeymoon, need I say more?" A knowing grin tugs at my lips. "Guess you wore her out. Just go with the flow, man."

Camping in the meadow up in the woods behind the old farmstead where their future house will stand, the winter yurt's plush accommodations provided by Off the Beaten Track Adventures, a local wilderness outfitter, is something straight out of *Tales of the Arabian Nights*. That kind of setup would keep me occupied for a while too ... with the right someone. *Yeah, you wish, man.*

"It's been hours, Zee, and she hasn't stirred once. What if..." He huffs a breath, leaving it unsaid. But I know he's thinking of Éolie's preternatural senses and their psychic connection and that he worries when she goes into deep slumber, but I have a feeling this one is truly normal. "Are you positive we can have as much sex as we want without endangering the twins?" he hisses, his breath catching on the last.

Liam must have asked me the same question half a dozen times yesterday morning, eager for some alone time with Éolie. Not that I blame him. The walls at the old farmstead are paper thin and not really conducive to a lot of intimacy on a full house. I can practically see Éolie's blushing cheeks from here. I shake my head, amused. Code Red, we call their afternoon naptime when the rest of the guys and I try to make ourselves scarce.

"Again, that would be a yes, unless you tell me something new. Cramps, spotting, headaches, fever?"

"No, none of that, she's ... glowing." His voice cracks, overflowing with something akin to reverence. "I just got worried she's not eating sufficiently, sleeping too much or not enough ... you know, worried. Otherwise, I could watch her sleep in my arms all day, man."

My ribs squeeze tight, a dose of envy constricting my chest. I briefly close my eyes, inhaling deeply, wondering what that kind of devotion feels like.

The guys shoot me another concerned look. Theo quirks a brow at me, his gaze questioning. "All's good with Éolie and the twins, right?"

Yeah, I mouth, nodding a few times. A collective whoosh of breath releases tension and all three rise whatever they've been drinking, and cheer. "Hear, hear." They rap their knuckles on the table and drink deeply.

I hold my hand up to quiet them, pressing my ear to the phone, unsure if the shuffling sounds coming from the other end of the line are a good thing or not. "Any other worries I can address so you'll keep to your newlywed bliss?" I ask Liam.

"I slept that long?" I hear Éolie's soft voice asking in the background, and some more rustling.

"Éolie says hi. And nope, no worries left. All's good with my world now, thanks," Liam says back to me. "As you were."

I chuckle low. "Take care of our girl."

"Will do."

"See you on Monday, man. Have fun, you four."

"Oh, we will." The call drops.

I press end, happy for him, envious still. I slide my phone on the table. "Yep. Liam's got it made, boys." I take a swig of sparkling water, mulling it over.

If Liam, inveterate globetrotter and famous sci-fi author with a decided bend towards scary, crazy imagination, can do normal and sprout roots here, happily ever after, why can't I?

Magali's dimpled smile and soulful eyes flash in my mind. A taste of something addictive, worth keeping, she'd said staring me in the eye, cupcake be damned.

Yann stretches, crossing his hands behind his head. "Can you believe we'll be uncles this upcoming summer?"

"Stranger still, I can't wait for that to happen." P.O. shakes his head a few times before polishing off his beer.

"You two coming back here for your summer break?" I ask Yann and P.O.

With Leo finishing up his doctorate in agronomy at Cambridge this spring, they'll be the only two students left in our group, the both of them enrolled into grad programs at MIT for another year.

"Yep. I love it here. The cultural flair, the wide-open space, it gets to me somehow." Yann leans forward to rest his elbows on the table. "Outside the math labs, I can't hear myself think in Boston, too many distractions. I'll get more work done on my thesis and get to meet our little twins right off the bat, so it's a win win."

"Ditto." P.O. props his arm up on the side of his chair. "Now that I've upgraded the farmstead with high-speed fiber optic, it's on a par with MIT's computer science labs, minus the crowd. Might as well take advantage of it and debug some of my beta program from here in peace and quiet."

P.O.'s computer hacking abilities led him to develop a new firewall concept, which is the subject matter of the thesis he's working on now, alongside licensing the product.

Between these two, no wonder we were dubbed the Goddamned Geek Squad at BIA, or GGS for short. Owning the nickname to the hilt, not that it took us all that long to elevate it to Geek God Status. Good times, indeed. I shake my head at the memory.

"You?" I ask a taciturn Theo, his thumbnail busy peeling his untouched brew's label slick with condensation.

His eyes snap up. "Maybe I'll be able to squeeze in a few days, not sure though." He lifts one shoulder in a small shrug. "Summer's a prime time away at the firm, and I'm low man on the totem pole of corporate law over there. What about you? Will you fly them in?"

I picked them all up in my Piper from Boston this go around, landing at Mont-Tremblant International, a small airport a forty-minute drive north of here.

"I'd like to." In fact, I'd love to. More than I'd like to admit, truth be known. Not sure how I'll manage to snag a summer break though, this one was hard enough to get.

"Cool, farm hands. I'm all for that." Leo sets an opened bottle of Cabernet Sauvignon on the table. "What else did I miss?"

For the next hour or so, we just shoot the breeze, up until my phone wiggles against my empty glass of Perrier, clinking from the vibrations. Fumbling in my haste to pick it up, I almost knock it off the table, hoping nothing's wrong with Éolie for Liam to call back so soon. "Need anything, man?"

"As a matter of fact, we do, Your Royal Highness."

I toss my head back and glare at the traitorous caller ID. No fucking way. "How did you trace my number—? Never mind. I don't want to know." I scowl, annoyed to no end. "I've already given you my answer. Not interested in your revival. Give it a rest."

"I'm afraid your answer is unacceptable, Your Royal Highness. As the chancellor of the board of trustees, I hereby inform you that you have until your twenty-sixth birthday, next November, to do your duty by us, and conform accordingly."

"Duty?" I sneer.

"Yes, duty, Your Royal Highness."

The hell I will, I inwardly fume.

Christ, it's not like the board of five trustees appointed by my late father's estate, and put in charge of "me" while I grew up forgotten at boarding school, set an admirable example of such. I never even met them.

Thinking on the slew of emails they pester me with ever since I turned twenty-five, is not the way to endear them to me either. Hell will freeze over before I follow in my late *father's* footsteps. They sure can wish all they like now. Not happening.

A shudder of revulsion slithers down my spine just at the thought of that so-called privileged life.

"I'm afraid you'll have to keep up with the times, my good man. This is the Twenty-First Century, not the Middle-Ages. For your info, the island of San Alessio's been a part of Italy for the past two hundred years, pretty sure you're all Italians by now. So am I, last I checked my passport."

"Nevertheless, Your Royal Highness. Come November the twenty-second, your San Alessian's full title will once more be made public at a formal grand ball just as it was in your late father's time. Your presence here from thereon will be required, as you know by now."

"In your dreams." I end the call, tossing my phone on the table. The trustees gave me a taste of freedom by leaving me the fuck alone at BIA, and I ran away with it. Guess they'll have to live with it now. I'm not going to pick up and move to said island so I can dance to their tune.

"Fuck, man. They're still coming at you?" Leo's mouth pinches in a tight line. We share an eye roll. He's yearly required to attend a few outdated ceremonials of his own over at his grandfather's estate, a former grand duché now absorbed within Liechtenstein. He has it worse than me. Well, he had up until recently. My jaw clenches just thinking about it.

Despite being officially the son of the late Principe Filippo San Alessio di Fiori, I've lived my life on my own terms. Absent from the title I've inherited. I just didn't know my relative freedom came with an expiry date. Guess someone fucked up and forgot to send the memo up until the day I turned twenty-five.

"They're fucking ridiculous." I scrub one hand down my face. "It's just a bloody courtesy title on a piece of paper now, empty of all meanings, for chrissakes, not a life sentence!"

"Want me to encrypt your email address?" P.O. picks up my phone.

"They'll still be a royal pain in my ass. Won't make any difference." I sigh up to the ceiling.

P.O. types a series of codes on his tablet. "A few well-placed viruses might make you feel better."

"Don't tempt me."

"Don't they know you're the least likely person to heel on command and do nothing but smile and look pretty?" Yann's forehead furrows. "It's been twenty years, why insist you show up now out of the blue?"

"The fuck if I know." I laugh without humor.

"What's the worse they can do if you don't show up? Cut you off the Swiss trust fund?" Leo snorts. "Like you care."

"Don't I wish." I pinch the bridge of my nose.

I don't want the bloody courtesy title, for chrissakes. Nor do I want to be responsible for the bloody money that comes with the old man's estate, especially as I have little to no say in how to dispose of it. Guess all the previous crowned princes stuck together on that one over the centuries, probably afraid someone like me, a misfit by all account, would come along and be tempted to flush it all out on frivolous things, like investing for the common good. Very bad form, that.

Basically put, I cannot unlock the bloody funds for any other reasons than sustaining *the* "lifestyle," and the amount sitting in the Swiss account is indecent for any one human to sit on. It's enough to give me hives.

"They know I don't give two shits about the money considering the conditions it comes with. I have my own. No, I've been summoned, and the way they talk, they wouldn't be above forcibly escorting me back on island if that's what it takes for their big hoopla to happen. They need a reality check. It's not happening."

"Let me look into it and have some fun." Theo's face visibly brightens, eyes glittering.

"Have at it counsellor, knock yourself out." I shove away from the table. "I'm getting another Perrier, any takers?"

I make my way over to the bar. Or try to. The place is getting more jam packed by the minute. Great. Just great.

"Hey, pretty man, dance with us?"

Pretty man? Give me a bloody break. My eyes upturn and I blow a breath, turning toward the high-pitched voice, intending to decline politely.

But then, two brunettes snag my arms, pushing me to the middle of an improvised dance floor in their section, to catcalls and shouts. I spot a long table in the corner filled with a couple dozen giggling girls, each of them egging on the two who are dragging me by the arms, all of them clearly entertained by their friends' antics. A busload of them probably here to wrap up some kind of ski excursion, by the look of things.

Hmmm. I wonder if ... An involuntary snort escapes from deep within my throat. Nope. I quickly change my mind. If I let them loose on the guys, they'll kill me for sure. They hate dancing, much less being put on the spot in the middle of a crowd. And tittering girls? Forget it, man. They'll likely poke their eyes out.

But maybe that's what I need. A dose of something familiar for a moment. Girls en vrac.

I put my game face on, flashing my most charming smile.

Show time.

I twirl both brunettes a few times to some more shouts and squeals, and half a dozen more girls hop on the floor, surrounding me.

My eyes close in a vain attempt to let the beat of the techno music mix pulse in my veins, but it's no use. All I see is Magali's graceful moves as she danced on air, her choreography on skis replaying in my mind.

My body sways to the music by rote, not in the least engaged. There's just no spark. Bored by their predictable moves, their squealing voices, and bland conversation, I just can't get into it.

"It's been a pleasure, ladies," I say at the next lull in music, unashamedly lying.

"The party just started. You're leaving so soon?" the one to my right says, grabbing my arm, and the others pout.

"Afraid so, but hey, enjoy the rest of your girls' night out," I reply with a tight smile, bowing out.

I'll drag my buddies out if I need to, but I want out of here. I can't breathe all of a sudden. I make a beeline for the men's room, buying myself, or more appropriately, them, a few more minutes before I do drag them out.

I reach inside the pocket of my soft shell ski pants, palming the car keys. I twirl them once, catching them. I'm still the designated driver for all intents and purposes, and I fully intend to collect on the prerogatives, here, and call it a day.

Leaning a shoulder on the wall, I count to sixty before I straighten.

Sorry, boys, looks like today's après-ski is just about ready to be over with.

I tilt my face up and meet my reflection, over the bathroom sink. Lonely eyes stare back at me and I realize the reason her words pierced me so deeply last night ... I want Magali to think I'm worth keeping.

Bloody hell.

Nine

ZAC

The rest of the weekend passes in a blur, even discounting my staring off into space more times than I'd like to count. Up until two days ago, I never had any problems with moving on, quite the contrary. Turns out my laidback persona is not as laidback as I thought it was, and being told no triggered some sort of obsessive compulsive disorder I didn't know I had.

Fuck me, but that girl got under my skin somehow and she plagues my thoughts, curse it all.

Liam and Éolie have been back less than half an hour and, except for Theo, we're all gathered in the kitchen, but the conversation flowing around me is like white noise in my head. Leaning back against the counter, I stare at the maple leaf on the Canadian flag adorning the chipped coffee mug P.O. hands me over, the cheap souvenir part of the mismatched collection of stuff that came with the place.

Bright-red maple leaf. Bright-red ski jacket. Bright-red cheeks tainted with fury. Bright-red lips breathing fire promising ... Promising what, man? To chew you up and spit you out? *Been there done that*, I inwardly scoff at myself.

Leo's peeling an orange, offering half to Éolie, and the waft of citrusy smell overtaking the kitchen is enough to send me into sensory overload. The zesty fragrance fires up my nerve endings in a perfect recall of Magali's fresh citrusy scent as she leaned into me.

I let out a soft groan.

Awesome. I'm sporting one hell of a semi brought by the smell of an orange? Christ, am I ever screwed.

As though reading my thoughts, P.O. snorts and Yann cracks a full smile, watching me.

I take a sip of shit-tasting instant coffee, ignoring them both. Don't know how long I zoned out but I try and focus back on what Éolie's saying.

"Non, non, really, guys, I can't thank you enough, c'était féérique, pure magic. The whole setup in the meadow blew me away and I never even suspected a thing. Not once," she says, one hand pressing on her chest, her unusual pale-aqua eyes lit from within. "I'll never forget."

Liam, his shaggy mane of dark-brown hair sticking up every which way from static electricity as he takes off his beanie, shares a pleased look over her head. I grin into my cup. Last Thursday night, the guys and I really hit it off with Liam's closest neighbors, Vie and Grégoire, the eight of us prepping everything up in the meadow to surprise Éolie last Friday. Not an easy feat in itself considering Éolie's preternatural gifts and psychic connection to Liam. But it was well worth the effort of the stealth operation we had going on. We really pulled it off, her face tells it all.

"Zac, I want to thank you especially," Éolie says, coming up and taking my hand in hers. Her smile is soft and caring, and for the first time since my brooding began, I put it aside and offer back genuine happiness of my own. "Being Liam's literal doctor-on-call can't be easy. Merci beaucoup."

"Anytime," I tell her, and I mean it.

Liam's watchful blue eyes soften, witnessing Éolie's animated features as she retreats to the living room with Leo, Yann, and P.O.

Theo's missing in action, having commandeered Liam's Volvo more than a couple of hours ago for some sort of "me" time down in the village that we all suspect is more in the line of a girl recon mission by now. But then again, hard to tell with him. He could just as well be poring over municipal by-laws at La Mairie just for kicks.

I yank out a chair from the table and straddle it backward. I'm staying put until my body cools off a bit or there's no more citrus scent wafting in the air from the undergoing orange fest in the living room, whichever comes first.

Liam claps me on the shoulder on his way to rinse off Éolie's emptied glass of milk he's still holding in his hand. Plugging her nose, she chugged the cow juice down like a trooper earlier on. No thanks to P.O. and Yann, we're all out of dark chocolate to sweeten the deal, poor thing.

"I owe you big time, man," Liam says, a blissful expression washing over his slightly reddened, wind-chaffed face.

My whacked sense of humor perks up. Can't help it. Liam and Éolie's frozen bliss is still written all over their chapped lips. Catching them making out on the front porch in subarctic temperatures for who knows how long before they stepped inside the house accounts for the frozen part.

"What for?" I joke. "Making Leo close the front door on you two going at it like crazed penguins? Or stopping you before frostbite settled in and numbed all your favorite parts for good?"

Liam smirks, upturning the glass into the dish drainer. "Didn't feel all that cold, but thanks for the save now that you mention it." He grabs a tea towel to wipe his hands, his face turning serious. "I owe you for giving me back my Zen on Saturday."

We share a look of understanding. No more words necessary. Liam's never had anything to lose before reconnecting with Éolie, but now ... he worries more easily. "Anytime, man." We fist bump on it.

"What are you two plotting?" Éolie returns, tilting her heard quizzically in my direction, offering Liam her last piece of orange between thumb and index.

I hold my hands up. "Hey, count me out of it; he's the author. He plots for a living."

Liam bends, his eyes trapping Éolie's gaze. "Want to know what I'm plotting right now?" His mouth sucks the juicy fruit right out of her fingers, his lips licking their tips before he straightens. Her eyes widen by a fraction. His arms coming around her waist, he chews, chuckling low.

I get up, making a big show of tucking my chair back in, neatly. "Obviously, this plotting session is more of a doubles thing."

Éolie rises on the tip of her toes and deposits a sweet kiss on Liam's cheek before replying in turn, "It's more of an individual thing. I've five minutes left on my battery before I crash."

"Hey, I can work with that." Liam tugs on her hand but she doesn't budge. She lets out an airy laugh that a yawn stifles. "I'll be sleeping, go have fun with the guys while you can. They're leaving in just two days."

"For the record, you're more fun to watch than they are," Liam grumbles good-naturedly.

"Go nap, doctor's orders." I tug on her light-blonde braid in passing. "We'll keep him out of your hair," I tease.

Liam's eyes upturn.

As soon as Éolie's down for the count, napping, the guys gang up on me, putting Liam up to speed on my epic crash and burn Friday night.

By the time they're halfway done, I've reached my limit and my temper fires.

I can't get Magali out of my mind and I can't withstand their usual ribbing when it comes to that particular subject either. It's like I'm someone else all of a sudden, someone in a perpetual shitty mood to top it off as evidenced by my latest blowout.

I thump my head on the front door I just slammed shut and sigh heavily up to the twilight sky, my breath fogging. It's no wonder Liam can't even recognize me. I don't even recognize me!

My gut churns with envy. I want what he has. Someone to love, someone who grounds me, someone I'd like to speed home to … And that's pretty scary in itself right now since I technically don't even own a home. It's like I've been thrown a curve that left me spinning in the twilight zone.

I straighten from my slump and reach for the LED headlight kept in the inside pocket of my ski jacket. I pat it to make sure the extra batteries are there. It's a precaution everyone living back in the woods takes, and it's easy to understand why. Far away from big city lights, it's blacker than pitch by four thirty in the afternoon. I click it on and clip on some snow shoes. The six other pairs we have haphazardly sticking out from the snow drift surrounding the front porch make for a colorful, exotic display, I absently note. Well, at least for someone fresh out of the jungle … like me.

I set out at a brisk pace up the trail to the meadow farther down in the woods at the back of the farmstead. Supposedly, to lend a hand to Vie and Grégoire left supervising the outfitters folding down the last of Liam's honeymoon surprise to Éolie. But in reality, it's just an excuse I used for storming out like I did. Our help wasn't required this go around, we were told earlier on. And maybe it's just as well, too. I need to cool off before I face the guys again.

I round the last bend in the trail opening up to the meadow and stop in my tracks. The outfitters have all gone and taken the honeymoon supplies with them. Vie is snuggled up to Grégoire by the bivouac, and the both of them contentedly stare at the dying fire.

I have never, in all my life, been as acutely aware of loving couples before. But they're everywhere I look now. *Shit.*

I fumble, trying to backtrack. I learn in an instant that snowshoes aren't exactly designed to back away. My arms flap, and I almost fall on my ass. *So smooth, man. Way to go.*

"Zac!" Vie exclaims upon spotting me. My flailing must have given me away.

"What a nice surprise, come and join us." Grégoire motions with his head and Vie scoots even closer to him, patting a place beside hers on the bench by the fire.

Envying Liam is one thing, but witnessing the ease and affection flowing between this greying, middle-aged couple is, surprisingly, a comforting sight, inspiring me. Like seeing proof forever truly exists somehow.

Still. "I ... don't want to intrude," I mumble, clicking off my light.

"Who said anything about intruding? There's room for you. Come and share the moment, and sit by the fire while there's still one," Vie invites warmly. In the low light from the fire, her soft smile and expressive dark-brown eyes glow with a glint nothing but welcoming.

I walk over and plop my ass down on the bench. I breathe in, my chest expanding, more touched by the invitation than I let on.

"Vie didn't have the heart to put out the fire yet." Grégoire squeezes her shoulder, kissing the top of her head through her hat. "You're welcome to wait it out with us." His stern features soften in welcome.

"Thanks, I think I will," I murmur, arms coming to rest on my thighs. I stare at the small flames licking at what's left of the charred firewood, red ambers glowing in the dark.

We stay quiet for a moment, but I sense Vie's penetrating stare. She pats my knee a few times. "What's troubling you?" she asks, and I detect genuine concern in the motherly tone of her voice.

"Is it that obvious?" I ask.

"To me, yes," she says, her speech unhurried, laced with caring undertones.

"I have two grown sons about your age. It's a mom thing."

Pushing my beanie up my brow, I swallow to wet my throat. "I don't know much about any of those mom things," I finally say, giving her a sidelong glance. And I don't know if it's the coziness of the bivouac up in Liam and Éolie's meadow under a night sky, white with stars upon stars, or if it's simply the warmth and acceptance they both exude, but I can't help but add something I ever hardly talk about. Especially with a couple of friends I've just met and barely know.

"Mine died in a small plane crash when I was four, and I was shipped to boarding school," I confess. By my father's orders, I silently add, only a few hours after my incidental sperm donor, my mom's lover, officially crashed the royal plane, or so the story says. My jaw tightens.

"I'm sorry about your loss," Vie says quietly, eyes softening with a world of compassion. "But you should know that you're never too old for any mother's advice. They'll always lend a sympathetic ear when you need it." She bumps her shoulder against mine with eyes crinkling at the corner. Holding in a smile, she whispers, "Another mom thing."

I shake my head, and my lips curl up one side, charmed.

Grégoire winks at me over Vie's head, before getting up to put two more logs into the fire, releasing sparks spiraling high up in a vertical column. "We have all the time in the world before this fire dies down now. Try us. We're good listeners."

Affable pale-grey eyes lock with mine, and for the space of an instant, I see in them Magali's friendly silvered gaze as she offered to share her cupcake with me ... I look down, breaking eye contact. Guess I better get used to seeing them in every shade of grey eyes I encounter from now on.

We share green tea in thermal cups, and even though I'm nowhere near ready to talk about my yearning for Magali and love to anyone yet, I spill my guts on everything else like I never did before.

"The six of us, well, we never did quite fit the mold at this elite boarding school, but I fear I'm the misfit in our band of misfits. My mates, they all have long-term focus and this unwavering sense of direction. I get bored easily, I suppose. I've this sort of restlessness inside of me that settles in no matter where I go."

As evidenced by my internship with Doctors Without Borders in the back boonies of South America that couldn't even keep me interested for more than a couple of months. Not even when at one point it was all I could think of doing with my life, and I just couldn't wait.

Life's a joke to your kind. One of my hands comes up and rubs my chest absently.

"It sounds pretty exciting, right?" I stare at the flames. "Flying helicopters to remote corners of the world, assisting die-hard bush doctors, but in reality, it's pretty harsh. The long hours, the debilitating heat, the recurring diseases, the local corruption, but most of all, the apathy, the resignation..." Something which I can't shake, surrounded as I am by it everywhere I turn, and it's killing me. "To survive over there, we have to tune out all of our emotions. Otherwise, we're repeatedly made to feel powerless against the tide, or close to useless in the overwhelming number of losses we deal with month after month." I sigh heavily, rubbing one gloved hand over my mouth a couple of times. "I have to keep reminding myself of the one we saved for another week, another month, god knows, and not the other twelve we lost, and ... for what, so that they can survive one more day of drudgery? I don't think I'm cut out for it."

Grégoire crouches in front of the fire to deposit yet another log, and Vie plumps the cushions at my back and settles her fleece blanket over me. I send her a startled look, unused to being fussed over. She shrugs both shoulders.

"A mom thing," she whispers. And I shake my head, moved.

"And what did you envision when you studied to become a doctor?" Grégoire quietly asks, replenishing our cups from his thermos.

Arms folding on my thighs, my brow dips. No one ever asked me point blank in quite that way. *What did I envision indeed?* "Good question," I say, putting the thermal cup down by my feet. I stare for a long moment at the plumes of smoke and sparks swirling up, looking for answers.

"You could say I wanted to save the world in some capacity, at least according to the few psych sessions I was forced to take, something to do with not being able to save my own mother. Or something to that effect." At least according to Berlinger's most esteemed in-house psychologist, Dr. Englehart. I scoff, and Vie's soft eyes commiserate. "But that would be oversimplifying it," I say with a self-deprecating shrug. Even I know that.

I throw a few twigs into the bivouac and watch them catch fire. Grégoire and Vie simply wait.

And the answer comes to me clearly for once, even before I put it out there. "I wanted to feel alive," I murmur, not walk half-dead pretty much every fucking day out there in the jungle. I look up to the starry sky, searching for Polaris, the North Star. The one star the guys and I used to wish upon as kids from the window of our dormitory bedroom. The Normal Kingdom depicted in Liam's bedtime stories, the Tales from the Enchanted Forest of Laure he used to weave for us at night. I feel it pulsing in this meadow, in the surrounding woods. "I wanted to connect directly to life's pulse, help maintain it, make a difference," I say into the night.

"What's stopping you now?" Grégoire cocks his head at me, and we share a look.

What indeed?

And I'm left wondering that very thing.

The fire crackles on...

Ten

ZAC

The three of us sit quietly for some time, watching the last of the flames die out. Eventually, we cover what's left of the glowing embers with snow, bundling up the last of the cushions and blankets to bring them back to the old farmstead, and I hop a ride in Grégoire's dark-blue pickup truck parked by the side of the road.

But as we pull up the drive, the headlights illuminate Liam, sitting down by himself, his back against the woodshed. *What the hell is he doing?* As we draw near, I see that he's shaking. I scramble out of the truck, hauling ass to his side, but, staring off in a glassy-eyed look, he doesn't react to his surroundings.

Jesus. "He's going into shock," I cry out, double-backing to grab some of the blankets from the truck's backseat and Vie takes them from me, wasting no time in enveloping him, briskly rubbing him down. He blinks a few times, surprised to see the three of us hovering above him like we appeared out of nowhere.

I crouch down in front of my pal, asking him what the fuck happened. He looks at me with indigo eyes glazed over, his shaggy mane of brown hair sticking out as though repeatedly tugged on. My mind goes a mile a minute and my voice grows thick with concern. When I stormed out of the house in no mood to listen to the guys' dry wit as they took turn recounting my epic Friday night crash and burn to Liam, Éolie was quietly napping to my knowledge.

"It's the twins ... Éolie just ... got the news ... They're MoMo, Zac," Liam stutters in a shaky voice, his intense blue eyes searching mine for a reaction. For a second, I flounder at the odd term. What the hell does that even mean? It doesn't—

But then my medical training kicks in and I know. Monoamniotic, Monochorionic, referred to as *MoMo* for short in medical lingo. Only about one percent of identical twins are MoMo. From the initial single zygote they all stem from, MoMo twins split into two embryos a few days later than the norm ... which makes Éolie's pregnancy higher than high risk.

I can't help but inhale a sharp breath and I close my eyes for a brief instant.

"Shit," I mutter, and I almost lose it, feeling my face leach of all color.

Christ, not the twins. *Please, not the twins.*

I hear Liam choke and, somehow, I get my shit together. He's counting on me to give it to him like it is, medically, I know ... When I reopen my eyes, I'm resolute to do whatever it takes to see them through this.

"Are they distinctly separate?" I ask with some trepidation, knowing that if they're past that big hurdle their chances will be better than average.

"Éolie saw them both clearly," Liam says, nodding a few times, and some of my tension swooshes out. Éolie's ability to "see" isn't exactly normal, but I've seen enough evidence of her gift's accuracy to trust the information is good.

"We can fight the odds, Liam," I say with conviction. My eyes lock with his and he nods once, trusting me. I mentally go through a checklist of things to watch for.

"I don't know what MoMo means, but are they at risk right now?" Vie gathers the blankets more tightly around my buddy, cuddling him. And it gets to me, big time. I blink back a surprising rush of moisture in my eyes, and I rub my chest.

"No. Not now." Liam shakes his head. The corner of his lips turns down and his eyes grow tortured. "Later on."

Éolie, with all of her preternatural abilities, heals abnormally fast and, for that reason, letting her go to a regular clinic or hospital is just too risky. Of all her gifts, self-healing in a matter of minutes is the hardest to conceal, and this can't be made public—for her safety.

"Éolie will go into bed rest to help the twins along," I tell him, my voice steady, striving for a confident tone. I can see that he's struggling to stay calm, but he listens to my every word. *Stay with me, bud, we can do this,* my eyes convey. "They're developing in only one amniotic sac with only one chorion, so they've grown past the biggest concern for now. They're separate, meaning no organs or limbs are conjoined. We'll be watching for cord entanglement and compression from now on," I say, and Vie covers her mouth with one hand, her eyes filling up as she finally understands the gravity of the situation.

Liam closes his eyes briefly, and I know he's fighting tears. Man, I hate seeing him so distressed.

"Today their chances are better than average. With daily monitoring, there is a lot that can be done to increase the odds in their favor," I confirm. "And you can help by helping Éolie focus." I grip his shoulder, pinning him with a direct look. *I won't let go, man. I'll be there, for them, for you, for Éolie,* I silently vow.

"I'm worried sick." He looks up to me with reddened eyes.

"Liam, listen up," Grégoire interjects, crouching down in front of him. "Real or imagined, worries have the uncanny ability to taint away every minutes of your day. Case in point, it's already taking a huge toll on you." Liam swallows a few times but Grégoire locks eyes with him, grabbing his full attention.

"Well here's my two cents. You have a worry? Ask yourself if there's something immediate, anything, really, that can be done to either eradicate it, or alleviate it, and go do it. If the answer is no, you're worrying needlessly. Define your when, Liam. When to think about it, when to act on it. And meanwhile? Forget about it."

I could just kiss the man as I see some color returning to my buddy's face and a look of determination etching on his face. "The *when* word." Liam nods to himself.

"Believe in yourself. Believe in your strength, Liam. I guarantee you'll be able to overcome whatever's thrown at you," Grégoire adds, still searching Liam's eyes. "You already did, just so you know. You made it here."

You made it here … The words bounce in my head, my gut churning. I wet my lips and swallow, my throat growing tight.

Grégoire's face softens and, seemingly satisfied with what he sees on my buddy's face, he straightens. "So, any immediate worries left to address tonight?" he asks, squeezing Liam's shoulder once, in encouragement.

Liam breathes out. "No, not tonight," he replies in a self-assured voice, already more like himself.

"It'll be all right, Liam. I feel it in my heart," Vie says, hugging him goodbye. "My thoughts will be with you."

She hugs me next and murmurs, "Those babies are so lucky to have you in their lives." She pats me once on the chest above my heart, and gives me a soft, all-knowing smile.

My muscles lock into place, and something shifts in me. "Thanks," I say, feeling lighthearted all of sudden, on the brink of something new, solid. I can't put a name to it yet, but I can almost taste it. And I like it. My pulse picks up.

"Beautiful night tonight, boys; seize it," Grégoire says in a parting shot.

My eyes stay fix on the disappearing lights of the pickup truck as I say to Liam, "They're pretty cool. I like them."

"So do I," he says, jumping up, bunching the blankets together.

I take a deep breath, shoving my hands in my coat pockets.

"I like it here," I add, one of my booted feet shuffling snow around as I gather my scattered thoughts into something cohesive.

"So do I." He leans one shoulder on the mud room's door, waiting. He knows me well. I usually act, not talk it through. So he knows that I'm not finished, that something I'm trying to put into words is coming by the simple fact that I'm talking now ... instead of leaping into action.

Liam stares up at the starry night, and I follow suit. The dark velvet sky is white with stars upon stars. So white with stars, in fact, it's like standing underneath a constellation shower.

We stay quiet for a moment and breathe in the crisp, night air by the lungs full, our breaths fogging in plumes of smoke.

"So I've been thinking..." I trail off, looking down.

"About...?" Liam breaks into the quilted silence.

My gaze darts up, glancing out toward the abandoned barn and fields. *That maybe, just maybe ... I too made it home.* "Life ... Roots to put down ... This long-ago Normal Kingdom we used to dream about..."

When we were all kids, Liam's Tales from the Enchanted Forest of Laure swept us along, transporting us all to a better world, a better place, a better time. I shake my head at the memories, and my lips curl by a fraction. What a grand time we had with those. We were Knights of the Laure on a quest for freedom, looking for Home in what was the mythical Normal Kingdom.

"Best place there is to live," Liam says with conviction.

My gaze sweeps past the fields to the edge of the woods. Yeah, the Forest of Laure, which happens to be right here, has that kind of pull. Little did we know at the time, though, that the Forest of Laure of our youth would turn out to be a real place three-year-old Éolie saw while she stayed psychically connected to Liam all through the five months of his abduction as a child.

"I'm ready for a change of pace I think, something a little more ... normal. I just don't know how exactly." My mind spins, a bit at a loss on how best to proceed forward, for once. I sigh, rubbing the back of my neck. I'm not used to this indecisive Zac.

A gust barrels through the woodshed, howling by us as it shakes up the rafters.

The wind blows up my sleeves and I shiver, zipping my coat higher up.

"Does this have anything to do with that girl?" Liam cocks his head to the side, angling a brow.

My hand stills. *Does it?* My eyes narrow in thought.

"In a way," I reply after a beat, seeing Magali's haunted eyes all over again. "She said something that really got to me, man." I sigh heavily, my mouth turning down. "And I don't want to be that guy. I'm not that guy," I vow into the night.

Now that I've said it out loud it's as though a switch flipped inside, and plans start to hatch in rapid-fire succession in my head, blooming, ripe for the picking.

I want out of the jungle. I want a chance at a forever kind of love. I want roots grounding me. I want to make a difference in those babies' lives, and in so many others, I realize. At the onset of life's pulse, protecting it, welcoming it into the world. This. This is what feels right.

I stay quiet for a while longer. I'm on a new kind of high, savoring the unusual sensation of knowing deep in my guts that I'm where I'm supposed to be for once in my life. And it's up to me to make it happen.

Something in my chest unfurls. A weight I didn't know I carried lightens in me, and I breathe easier. I know what I have to do now.

I'll be back as soon as I can to intern up here, and take my obstetrics' equivalencies examinations. "I'd like to offer my services as your personal doc. To help keep an eye on Éolie and the twins until the pregnancy's over. Maybe see if the local hospital needs some help." I nod a few times to myself, a slow smile creasing my cheeks, feeling good about my decision like never before.

Liam straightens away from the wall, shoving down his beanie. "You know I'd love that, but it's a big move. Feels kind of permanent, too."

He raises a brow in question, but his eyes twinkle like he already knows my mind's made up. I nod once, determined.

We share a look of understanding.

"I have to go back to South America for a few weeks to tie loose ends and then," I take a deep breath, "I jump, both feet, man."

Liam's grin spreads wide across his wind-bitten cheeks. "House mates?" He pulls down his hand.

"House mates." I give him a low five. "We'll make sure the twins make it out just fine." His fist bumps my shoulder and he nods once, his eyes full of strength and determination.

And come next winter, I silently add, *I'll be ready. I'll find you, Magali. Make you see me—the new me.*

I'm not the kind you think I am.

I'm not the kind I thought I was.

I'll be the kind worth keeping.

Just watch me.

Eleven

MAGALI

"Seriously, Maman, I got this," I say into my phone, looking out the window of the furnished apartment I rented three months ago. It's a finished, private basement in a house just a hop and a skip away by foot from Le Centre Hospitalier de Sainte-Agathe, where I'll intern once my theory is over with. I watch the end of March blizzard slinging sleet and snow pellets on the windowpane, partly obscuring a slate-laden sky.

"You're doing academic-related things more than sixteen hours a day, Magali," she says in her worried mom tone of voice. "Are you sure you're taking time to sleep in between this study marathon you're on?"

"Sleep *is* penciled in my agenda," I reassure her, then quip, unable to resist, "In three months from now." Maybe. I'll see. I cross my fingers anyway. I can see my Maman shaking her head at me from here.

"What about eating? Last time I dropped by, I threw away a garbage bag full of moldy food. This is not like you and I worry."

"Yes, I know you worry, but don't. I eat in between study marathons," I tell my mom, straight-faced. *Just don't ask me what, or you'll worry for good*, I silently add, eyeing the greasy stained fast food wrapper balled beside my laptop. My eyes squint at the email notification that just pinged into my inbox.

I know you're in front of that screen. Get a life little Maggot. Shut it now! Renaud, my eldest brother, is so funny. Not. Once in a while he shoots me a message, and it's sort of our thing to see who gets the other's goat first.

Game on.

"Renaud just emailed me, ordering me to get a life. Like he didn't pull ninety hours week before when he was in school," I huff into the phone. Renaud had to make appointments with himself to scratch his nose while he studied international law in Geneva a few years back. I lean over and type back a quick response to him, the phone propped against my shoulder to free my hands.

Right back at you. And Maggot, really? Original, much. Come and visit, you'll see I'm no longer so little!

"Maman, if you talk to him before I do? Please tell him the diplomatic gene he inherited from you suffers hiccups when it comes to me and it's *not* looking good on his résumé," I say, my eyes upturning. My mom chuckles. Renaud now lives in the Netherlands in the city of The Hague, or Den Haag in Dutch, working at the United Nations International Court of Justice at the Peace Palace.

Beg to differ. I'll always have ten years on you, he pings right back. My mom says something about meeting at Hélène's bed and breakfast for our weekly brunch but I'm not really listening, too busy typing a killer reply.

Ha! Just means you'll wrinkle first, like that's an accomplishment, I type and press send, snickering.

"Are you laughing at my suggestion to take time out to eat with us if just to reassure us you're still eating properly?"

"No, sorry, Maman. I wasn't laughing at your brunch suggestion. I was multitasking, having a convo with you and trading cyber quips with Renaud." I straighten, holding my phone up. "I can't make it. I have an online study group pretty much all day. Maybe next weekend; I'll see what I can do."

"All right, I'll take it." She sighs but leaves it that.

I already know I won't be able to make it. I rub the bridge of my nose, fighting a sigh. I no longer have a life. What possessed me to take my degree in one year instead of two, again? Oh yeah, the fact I don't have a life. I let out a snort. I'm trading sarcasms with myself. A new low has been reached.

Undeniably. I changed your smelly diapers. Hey, have to go. I do have a

life. Get one too. Ciao, little sis. x

Drat, he had the last word.

And it leaves me torn between laughing and groaning. It's as though he heard my inner dialogue, here, and replied right on cue. And knowing him, he probably did. Lucas, my other brother older by six years, and I, often wondered growing up if our eldest sibling could read our minds, as Renaud always knew what we were up to. I can't tell how many times he rescued us from our own cluelessness. Like that time Lucas and I built an igloo, or what passed for one as it collapsed just before Renaud dragged us out...

I shake my head ruefully, remembering many other instances better left unsaid. Now Lucas is a wildlife biologist living it to the hilt in Le Parc National de la Gaspésie, near les Monts Chic-Chocs, well out of reach of civilization, and things like internet connections, most of the time.

"You're the only one who can decide what's best for you, so we'll leave it at that. But don't forget to take care of yourself as well while getting there, chouchou."

"I know, I know." My shoulders slump on a sigh. "I am taking good care of me as best as I can right now, Maman, I swear, thanks for understanding. Take care, and kiss Papa for me."

"I will, ma cocotte. Take care."

"Later." I end the call and slide my phone on the smooth glass top of the table, my fingers freezing on contact.

"Bye, ma petite maman à moi," I murmur into the empty room, truly missing them all.

I stare down at my hands poised over the ice-cold keyboard, ready to resume analyzing ultrasounds showcasing different key foetal developmental phases. I'd put fleece gloves on, but then I wouldn't be able to do much as far as typing is concerned. Frozen digits it is. Whoever thought modern furniture would be a good idea up north never lived up north. Chrome and glass are freakishly cold materials, and not just in looks.

My gaze sweeps by the sleek, one-room loft. As tiny as it is, it doesn't take me long. A sleeping nook, if you can call it that. A microscopic living room, which, in reality, is the sleeping nook with a futon doing double duty, transforming into a bed that stretches wall to wall at night. A tinier kitchen, if even possible, divided by the glass table flanked by two hip, lime-green, plastic chairs. Granted, they bring color to the monochrome white theme going on, but they're uncomfortable to sit on for long periods of time.

I sigh, getting up for a water refill. Jumping out of my skin at the sudden banging on the door, I almost drop the mug I use instead of a glass for its handle alone.

"M, open up. No use pretending you're not in. Your Jeep's parked up front," I hear CD's voice yelling through the thick metal door over the wind howling outside, quite the feat. Heart beating in my throat, I take two by two the four stairs leading up to my door and jerk it open.

"You almost gave me a heart attack. What's wrong with you?"

Amélie follows behind Cédric, who barrels in, and I almost tumble down the stairwell. We're all kind of squished on the small landing until I step back and give us all some breathing room.

"Well come in, CD." My eyes upturn as I follow him down the stairs.

"Took you long enough; we were beaten to death by ice pellets out there." He shakes himself off, raining ice droplets everywhere.

"You two should be huddled in your living room, roasting your toes by a blazing fire, eating supper by now, and I should be studying. What are you doing here?" I shake my head in faux-exasperation. Well, mostly faux. I really do need to study.

Amélie is renting a room in CD's house down in Saint-Sauveur while she's applying for a pre-school teaching position in the area, now that she's back from her stay in Nunavik and fully licensed. I would have rented the other bedroom myself, but Saint-Sauveur is even farther away from Sainte-Agathe and the hospital than my parents' place in Val-David. And, well, if I add my epic losing-track-of-time syndrome on top of everything, I would be a wreck driving up and down in a perpetual rush from either place. I'd rather walk, thank you very much.

"Change of plans. We brought the lasagna over, and we're having supper at your place," Amélie says, walking past me to the kitchen, her hands full of a deep-dish plate wrapped in aluminum foil I didn't really notice before now.

"Well, that's really sweet," I say, touched and torn up at the same time. "But I wasn't kidding, Amélie. Hello, March twenty-ninth, last Tuesday of the month, exam week, ring any bell? And I'm almost late as it is to sign up for my next online session, *and* I still haven't gone through all the required material." I groan now, stressing over it. "I don't have time to kick back and enjoy a meal in good company."

CD tugs on my messy bun, but I'm not quick enough to prevent my hair from tumbling down my back. I give him the stink eye, and he holds his hands up. "Hey, you have to eat like the rest of us mere mortals, SuperStudent."

"I wouldn't call alternating between guzzling down liquid meals and binging on fast food, eating," I mumble, twisting my hair back up and out of my way. "Really guys, I'm touched, but I can't. Rain check." I grab both their arms and steer them toward the stairs. Or try to.

CD waves me off. "No go. Try again."

"And by the way, make it good, you're outnumbered," Amélie huffs.

"Seriously. You know how important this is to me." I throw my hands up.

"Yeah, we do. It's the condensed in one-year thing instead of the regular two that we don't get," Amélie says.

They both cross their arms, tapping one foot. It's almost comical how in sync they are.

"What's the rush again?" CD asks pointedly, daring me to argue.

"Didn't we have this discussion before?" I say, growing annoyed. "Didn't I mention the two-year schedule is too slow for me?" I totally rationalize all over again. Yeah, it's not at all like the regular schedule gives me too much time to think about things I have no business thinking about at this point in my life, like golden-skinned guys with rumbling, magnetizing voices, and missed chances. Nope. "I like that I get all of the theory out of the way in six months, and the full clinical afterwards. It's only one intensive year and then I'll get the life I want that much sooner. What's a year compared to that?"

They share a look. My eyes narrow. "I got this." I huff, crossing my arms over my chest.

"M, anyone ever tell you you're a shit liar?" CD snorts, clearly unimpressed by my superb rationale.

"Look, that guy you blacklisted a few months back changed something in you. And we're not sure if it's a good thing or a bad thing. But one thing we know: ever since, you've been running yourself ragged. Care to share why?"

Amélie asks, turning up the heat by a notch, and it's not on the oven.

"I–I..." I splutter. "What do you mean, changed?"

CD and Amélie share another look, and I have a feeling I won't like what they'll say next.

"Okay, we'll play," CD says, leaning on the fridge, crossing his ankle.

"You've always been focused and driven, but you're taking it to the next level," Amélie says, poking her finger at my chest. "In fact, if you'd like a starting point, it's ever since that night, four months ago. You've quit patrolling at Saint-So, you're holing yourself up studying, never coming up for air; it's like you're obsessed or something. And on the rare occasions we do see each other, you zone out more often than not," Amélie rants at me, and I cringe. "Want us to continue?"

They stare me down, and my stomach twists in a pretzel knot. Is it that obvious I'm still obsessing over a guy I'll never see again? It's so out of character. I don't even know what possessed me to blacklist him in the first place. *And for all eternity, really, Magali*, I huff at myself.

I kind of do know, deep down, if I'm being honest. I just can't explain why everything about him, his sharp wit, the light in his eyes, his quick, charming smile, is calling to me like nothing else, but it does. He shook me up like no one ever did, and I totally appalled myself by the same token. I couldn't get over being so overwhelmingly attracted to an adrenaline junkie out for kicks, something I swore on Rafael's grave I'd never do. Blacklisting him was just for show, pure bravado on my part. It's not like there'll be any long-term repercussions for him, as I rescinded the order right after. It never made it into the data bank. And anyway, he's a foreigner who'll most likely never be back in my little corner of the world, as unimpressed as he was with our hills ... *A walk in the park*, he said, *no challenge*. Exasperated by the direction of my thoughts, beyond annoyed with myself, I shrug it off.

"I do *not* zone out," I deny in one stellar comeback.

But of course CD being CD, I'm nowhere near off the hook. It would have been great, but nope. No such luck.

"Yeah, you kind of *do*." CD lets out an inelegant snort. "Obsessed much?"

"Ha! I'm not obsessing over any other things than this." I challenge them, as well as myself, by scrolling down my screen until the picture of the ultrasound metrics of a healthy sixteen-week old foetus I'm studying, appears. My heart expands at the sight and it grounds me back, away from all thoughts of the entrancing stranger better left alone, like babies always do.

"Interesting. Is that why you still have this?" CD picks up the place holder in my textbook in between two fingers, a brow angling. *Merde alors!* No one was supposed to see that.

My eyes grow wide.

Amélie gasps when she sees it, and I groan out loud.

I snatch it back from CD, my eyes shooting daggers at him. "What? It makes for a great page marker, I'll have you know." Even so, noticing the new crease he put in it, I scowl, bringing it up to my chest in a protective gesture before I can stop myself.

"I rest my case." CD shakes his head at me. "That's what I call denial, folks."

I look down at the bright-yellow lift ticket I hold in my hands, having no other choice but to agree. I'm the Queen of Denial, so it seems.

"Oh, M, you had to go and fall at first sight for someone you'll never see again, didn't you?" Amélie winces on my behalf.

My shoulders sag. She knows me well. I don't do half-measures.

"Looks like," I mumble, staring off. I might as well admit the warm, whiskey-brown-eyed foreigner lives in my thoughts, his face etched on my soul, the burn of his stare invading my very blood stream. Like it, or not.

Which begs the question.

What if a reaction this strong only happens once in a lifetime?

I'm so screwed, my inner voice whispers.

Twelve

ZAC

S pewed from a leaden sky, sleet and snow spatters noisily on the windowpane of my upstairs bedroom at the old farmstead. Hard to think it's the end of March.

I button my dress shirt, holding my phone up in the crook of my neck.

"Let me get this straight. San Alessian's court protocol states that the title comes into full effect at age twenty-five. That's their answer for pestering me?" I start pacing the room. "Theo, that's bullshit. You know it, and I know it. There's no San Alessian's throne, nor Royal Court. It's nothing but inflated air on their part. They just want me to be their crowned prince puppet."

I quickly read through the document Theo just sent me. The trustees, after giving Theo the run around for the past two months, finally sent him a copy of an obscure document dating back to the sixteen hundreds with some recent addendum tacked there at the end like an afterthought.

"Just say the word, Zee," Theo says.

I blow a breath through my cheeks. Christ, I've other fish to fry. Man, are they ever a fastidious bunch. "If the only way I can get rid of them is to abdicate, so be it. Start the procedures, as absurd as it is."

"You made my day. On it, man."

"Yeah, go make mine now." I end the call and check my watch, shrugging on my suit jacket before bounding down the stairs. The sound of running water greets me as I step into the living room, adjusting my cufflinks.

I eye the pile of work clothes on the floor by the bathroom door. Liam has been clearing the road to the meadow alongside Grégoire almost daily now. A few times he's brought Éolie evergreens cuttings bow-tied in aromatic bouquets. The only thing he's brought to the rest of us is the stomach-turning scent of eau de lumberjack. The reek in here is enough to make my eyes water, let alone a pregnant woman.

I pop my head in the open doorway of their bedroom on my way out to the job interview I finally got at the Sainte-Agathe Hospital. One I've been waiting for ever since handing over my equivalencies for appraisal by the Health Ministry when I first got back here, a little over a month ago. I think again of how easily I flew back to my apartment in Bogota and signed the papers ending my month-to-month lease. Giving up everything I knew, including the helicopter, a parting gift to the DWB program. The funny thing is that I don't miss any of it. I left the jungles of South America in my twin-engine Piper Comanche carrying one suitcase. Flying is one piece of the old Zac that remains. That will always remain.

I point my index fingers at a radiant Éolie propped in bed, a sea of pillows at her back, baby Mozart music playing in the background as she reads. "You. Me. Doppler. When I get back," I say, referring to the foetal heart rate monitor I use in order to check on the twins.

She looks up and grins. "I'm not going anywhere," she says, "wouldn't miss it for the world." Her hand rubs her round belly in a gentle, circular motion.

My heart expands. Monitoring the twins' heart rates with a top-notch medical Doppler is one of my favorite routines nowadays. Sébastien and Nicolas are almost halfway there, and doing so well.

"Wouldn't miss it either." I wink. "Wish me luck." I saunter out.

"No need, Zee, it's the other way around," she calls after me.

I pop my head back in. "You wish them luck dealing with me?" I ask, only half-jesting.

Her eyes grow wide. "No! I meant they're the lucky ones to get you."

"What she said," Liam says from behind me. "You've got this, man." He claps me on the shoulder, stepping into his bedroom in fresh clothes, thank God.

"I've got this." I nod, psyched into action. "Later."

"Studded winter tires are quite the marvel," I say under my breath. To think I ribbed Liam mercilessly a few months back when he first mentioned he'd bought a Volvo station wagon, a studded one at that...

Thanks to them, my brand-new Jeep Wrangler, in its more rugged Willys Edition version, effortlessly climbs up the icy hillside avenue leading to a cul-de-sac and the Sainte-Agathe Hospital, or as it is called over here, Le Centre Hospitalier de Sainte-Agathe-des-Monts.

My GPS app flashes a weather update in bright red, a warning of a Spring blizzard in effect for this oh-so-fine Tuesday, March 29. No shit, Sherlock. I've been back from the jungle over a month now, and I shouldn't be that surprised that snow and sleet are coming down faster than the wipers can clear, ice pellets freezing on contact, reducing my windshield's visibility by two thirds, but still. It doesn't look anywhere near Spring or any end of March I've known before, that's for sure.

Bending over my steering wheel, I squint and follow the direction panels stamped with a stylized Fleur-de-Lys, the Québec government logo.

Health care is public over here, government operated and dispensed at no cost to all citizens. Well, at no cost, in a manner of speaking, as income taxes are pretty steep. Even so, I kind of like the principle behind it, and if things go my way today, I guess I'll be one of the cogs in the system from this day forward, receiving my orders from the Health Ministry in Québec City. And as always, when put that way, a sliver of unease slithers down my spine. The rebel in me is at a tug of war with my "save the world" complex, unsure if I'll fit comfortably into this centralized, bureaucratic environment, but I refuse to dwell on it. Not when a certain set of high-risk twins need me. Not when I have high hopes of finding everything I ever wished for, once upon a time, in our long-ago Normal Kingdom, here.

I signal a left turn onto the hospital's visitors' parking lot.

Finding a place near the back, I kill the engine and grab my messenger bag. My heart thudding in my chest, I take a deep breath.

This is it.

Zipping my winter coat up, I hurry over to the administration building, sitting higher up on the hill, sidestepping a few slush piles. The bottom hem of my dress pants is soon soaked through, making me more than happy that my winter boots are waterproof, sturdy and ankle length. The wind blows horizontal gusts of snow pellets, and I tug my collar higher up. Still, I find the slight sting of ice crystals on my cheeks invigorating.

Administration is lodged in an older pavilion tucked in the woods at the end of a meandering path. The stone building, an attractive 19th Century manor, used to house the terminally ill afflicted with pulmonary infections. The article I read this morning, right after receiving the call confirming I had an interview today, mentioned the pure air found in these very mountains was believed to be therapeutic to tuberculosis patients back in those days. They may have been on to something there, I note, as my lungs expand with cold moist air that really tastes of the evergreens. I breathe it in, relishing the sensation of well-being. Breathing deeply never felt this good in the jungle.

I open the ornate wood door, and amble over to the reception island covering a huge square area in the middle of a room with hallways leading down three different corridors, a small waiting room opening up to my left.

"Bonjour, may I help you?" a pleasantly plump, thirty-something woman manning the U-shaped desk asks me in French, eyeing me. I shoot her my most charming grin.

"J'ai un entrevue avec Docteur Garneau à treize heures," I answer, confirming that I have an interview with the head honcho, Doctor Garneau, at one o'clock. "Je suis Zac di Fiori."

She blinks a few times, her dark eyebrows disappearing under her bottled-blonde fringe. "You're Docteur di Fiori?" she asks, her expression skeptical, and I confirm. She blinks some more, looking between me and her screen, her show of incredulity a bit startling.

"Am I at the right place?" I ask, my brows dipping.

"Oui, oui, we just weren't expecting..." Her face flushes bright red, stopping mid-sentence. She straightens in her chair, and points to a coat rack. "I'll notify Docteur Garneau right away; it won't be long." She motions to the waiting room.

I shrug my coat off and straighten the sleeves of my pewter-grey suit jacket, hating the pinch of the fitted cut of my light-grey dress shirt. Well, here's one thing I'll miss about the jungle, wearing cargos and tees to work. At least I'm not choking on a tie, here. I didn't have one to wear.

Noticing what looks like framed period photographs on the neutral, cream-colored walls of the waiting room, I walk over, studying them. They were all taken more than a century ago, I read on the plaques, on the once beautiful landscaped grounds that used to surround this pavilion, on what is now the actual hospital building. My chest constricts, and I rub it a couple of times, fighting a shiver. I turn away, in no mood for the sepia tones underlining even more the melancholy I see reflected in the eyes of so many young patients who are long dead by now. *On the onset of life's pulse, man.* You're switching gears, remember.

The hurried footsteps of clicking heels catch my attention, and I see an athletic-looking woman in her early forties wearing a stylish bun, a tight navy-blue skirt and ivory sweater, emerge from one of the corridors. I wonder if she's Docteur René Garneau, the director, the first-name *René* being gender neutral. But the woman screeches to a halt upon spying me, almost dropping her armful of files.

"Oh wow. Please, tell me you've got the government seal of approval, 'cause whatever you're selling, I'm buying," she says in a sultry voice, and the receptionist clears her throat a few times, trying to catch the woman's attention.

"Not quite yet," I answer in an even tone of voice, struggling to keep my face impassive, fighting a scowl. "I need to pass the last of my equivalencies first." I hope to hell she's not who I'm supposed to meet for this internship interview, the way she gives me the onceover. Great.

"Nathalie," the receptionist hisses under her breath, "he's *Docteur* di Fiori, not a sales representative."

Not Docteur Garneau then. Beyond relieved, the breath I didn't know I was holding swooshes out. The cougar wannabe swivels round and plops her files on the reception's counter.

"Ha! Good one." She shakes her head at the receptionist but is only met with her stony expression. "You're pulling my leg, Nicole, aren't you?" she asks her in a hushed, but surprised tone of voice, and I can't help but wonder.

What's with that? They both reacted with such disbelief. I check, making sure my buttons are all aligned. Jesus, I even dressed the part. Don't I look serious enough to pass for a doctor, or what?

Probably thinking I can't hear a thing they say from where I stand, the receptionist, Nicole, whispers furiously, "No, I'm not. He's Docteur di Fiori, Docteur Garneau's one o'clock interview."

The other one looks me up and down over her shoulder, shooting me an incredulous look before turning back to the receptionist. "You know as well as I do that we never get the young, gorgeous ones up in the north boonies. Montréal is their first choice, and they never look back. Québec messed up his assignment for sure." She shrugs, dismissing the matter, and pats down the files like they're her most prized possession. "At last, all signed and Québec approved for Félix. And in less than six weeks, how about that? He's on his way over to collect them," she instructs Nicole before turning on her heels to face me once more. "Well, too bad you're not selling anything, I'd buy in bulk," she says as she breezes by me, returning from where she came from, down the east corridor.

Six weeks to get it signed, she said, like it's an unheard of record time. I stare at the files, and swallow another bout of uneasiness, but for a completely different reason this time. Am I getting myself mired down in bureaucracy? Will I feel hemmed in, my hands tied? Or worse, will tedium follow me through yet another decision of mine?

I want this, I remind myself.

Nicole, the receptionist, gives me a sheepish look, bringing me back to the here and now. "That was Nathalie, in charge of purchasing if you're wondering. She's ... a colorful sort, never a dull moment when she's around. Docteur Garneau should be right down, Docteur di Fiori."

"No problem, I'm a little early," I tell her, and she gives me a little nod before returning her attention to her computer screen. I'm too keyed up to sit so I walk over to the large bay window at the back of the waiting room, and soon get absorbed in the view. I see the rooftop garden of the hospital, below, and a crew busy shovelling mounds of slushy wet snow, toppling it over the side, most likely to prevent a roof collapse from the accumulated weight. Boy, it looks like a full-time job from where I stand, gusts of wind rattling the windows, and snow coming down almost faster than they can shovel it off.

My gaze sweeps the surrounding hills, their tree-covered tops encased in a mantle of the pristine white stuff. Beauty everywhere I look. A small grin curls on my lips. I like what I see, and how I can breathe in this wide-open space, how it makes me feel grounded, for once in my life.

A discreet male cough sounds behind me. I turn into the waiting smile of a tall, grandfatherly figure of a man.

"Docteur di Fiori?" The man angles a brow, cocking his head to the side, and his brown eyes narrow by a fraction, his smile congealing.

"Yes. Are you Docteur Garneau?"

His eyes pop wider, bushy white eyebrows lifting. "Well, I'll be," he says under his breath, but one hand extends, and I accept the firm handshake.

"Pleased to meet you," I say, unruffled by his first reaction, by now, more or less expecting it. We exchange a few pleasantries while he motions for me to follow him down the west corridor.

"You don't mind if we take the stairs, do you?" He gestures to a dark oak, grand stairwell sweeping up all three floors, complete with curving balusters and a polished banister. "My office is on the top floor and I constantly argue that it's to keep me in shape, but really, the elevators are probably as old as I am," he says, eyes twinkling, as we start our ascend. "I don't trust them." He chuckles low.

"Duly noted, sir," I reply, my lips tugging up one side.

On our way up, I admire the ornate woodwork adorning the risers, and I like that the solid treads are worn down the middle, trampled by generations of men and women having used these very stairs before me. Upon reaching the top floor, we walk down an elegant corridor, our footsteps echoing on the hardwood floor, closed doors on either side of us letting out muffled conversations and background office noises as we walk by. The walls are painted a soft mellow yellow, brightening up what would otherwise be a gloomy space, and the patina of the original tin ceiling captures my attention.

"Pretty impressive, isn't it?" Docteur Garneau comments upon noticing my interest in the architectural details. And I don't have the heart to tell him that it's quaint rather than impressive, coming from my European background. I give him a tight nod. "This place used to be the end of the line for affluent Montrealers afflicted with tuberculosis by the end of the 19th Century. And now, its former grandeur is one of the perks of working in administration, you could say," he says, motioning me to a small, round conference table sitting four. The bland, government-issued pieces of furniture are in stark contrast to the intricate moldings carved with vines and birds, and ornate window casings. A clash of two worlds.

"Sit, sit." He absently gestures to me all the while patting his desk, looking for something under the mess of files and papers strewn across. "There they are!" he exclaims with a hint of triumph, locating a pair of reading glasses underneath what looks like a monthly report, before reaching for a cobalt-blue file, it's bright color sticking out among all the manila ones.

My name is written on the cover, I can't help but notice, alongside a long-ass named governmental sub-department of the Health Ministry.

Just as he settles in opposite me, someone knocks on the doorframe.

"Ah, Eugénie, ma douce, come in, come in. Glad you could make it," Docteur Garneau says to the newcomer, getting up to close the door as he introduces me to the head of the pediatric department under which the prenatal care division reports to directly.

Almost as tall as I am, her white hair shorn in a buzz cut shorter than mine, Docteur Eugénie Labonté's faded blue eyes give me a pointed look, all the while taking in my measure. We exchange a firm handshake, and get a few weather updates and other such noncommittal icebreakers out of the way as we all settle back around the conference table. I see an entire conversation silently taking place between the two, and judging by the slew of expressions crossing both their faces, they're either long-term acquaintances or an old married couple, and if so, I absently wonder how's that working for them...

Docteur Labonté clears her throat and I look her in the eye. "Seeing you, I admit to being curious," she says, tapping a finger on my file. I raise a brow, waiting. "Let me get this straight." She steeples her fingers, tilting her head to the side, and Docteur Garneau coughs once behind his fist. "You're coming from Cambridge University Medical School, can practice pretty much anywhere you'd like to, had a one-year stint with Doctors Without Borders, and you *specifically* requested to complete the last of your obstetrics examinations and internship, here?"

"Correct," I say, my brows dipping. "Is there a problem? I was assured my equivalencies were above standards, and my license is to be issued accordingly any day now."

Docteur Garneau slides the blue folder my way. "Québec accredited your practitioner's license; it's in the file we just received," he says, both of them eyeing me warily. "Québec also assigned you to a pilot program we were selected for in Sainte-Agathe to train midwives, as explained in your schedule binder."

"And ... the problem is?" I ask, baffled.

"Technically, none," Docteur Labonté replies, giving Docteur Garneau a quick, sidelong glance.

He sighs, brushing a hand down his face as though giving in to her non-verbal prompt. "Here's the thing. To be perfectly honest, we never retain the attention of young doctors out here in the regions, not for long anyway, once they're fully trained. So to be fair to everyone concerned, as a newly arrived foreigner, maybe you're unaware that Montréal counts three children's hospitals with top-notch obstetrics, and four pediatric research centers? Or, for that matter, that Saint-Jérôme is our chef-lieu in Les Laurentides with a much bigger hospital, or that we do have a rather small obstetrics' department here. We have generalists, but you'll be the only obstetrician, and we do cover a pretty large territory," Docteur Garneau says, leaning back into his chair.

"Frankly, with your credentials, you could bypass all of the waiting lists and get right into a more prestigious environment. Are you sure you're where you want to be?" Docteur Labonté asks, leaning over the table.

"I am." *I absolutely am.* "I specifically chose to be here. I have family here and I'm not interested in being anywhere else." Not by a long shot if it means I have a chance of a do-over with Magali.

"Say no more, that settles it." Docteur Labonté slaps both hands on the table in a decisive manner, and I'm hard pressed not to grin. "According to your schedule, you're to report to me for your first rotation at five tomorrow morning. Welcome aboard." Her angular face softens with a welcoming smile.

And just like that, I'm in.

Thirteen

ZAC

The next three months zip by me at the speed of light and see me settle into a routine of sorts in between clinical rotations, undergoing the last of my obstetrics examinations and equivalencies, monitoring the twins, and living at the old farmstead.

Yeah, if living in Leo's temperamental house can ever be called routine...

Christ above, I swear under my breath as the better part of the lower wood casing of my bedroom's window splinters in my hands, leaving me holding the brass handles.

"Leo," I yell over my shoulder, "get your ass in here."

Footsteps sound on the hardwood behind me.

"Aww fuck, man." Irritation clouds his features as he skids to a halt just inside the doorway. "I've been back less than twenty-four hours, and you're breaking shit already? Are you doing this on purpose?" He grumbles, but helps me secure the rest of the dry-rotted window frame with duct tape before the window itself topples down the side of the house.

"What'd you do? Yank them off?" he mutters as I drop into his hands the antiquated handles.

I grab from my bedside table the information binder I've yet to read on the midwives' pilot program, and start down the stairs. It's already July the eighth, and I'd better hop to it. That group's first round of three months' clinical rotation is scheduled to start this upcoming Monday, and I'm the appointed supervisor.

"For your info, they don't make windows like that anymore, and I don't think I'll be able to salvage it," Leo gripes from behind me. "You pulverized it."

"I may have done you a favor, then. Look outside, it's finally summer, man," I say, my voice oozing sarcasm as he follows me down to the kitchen. "I'm sure you'll find some other window frame more technologically advanced to replace it with, like one that opens once in a while."

Leo shoots me a look, clearly unimpressed, and I can't help but snicker. "Man, you do realize that in between Liam and me, the only thing holding your house up now is duct tape?" We now keep a roll of the "Duck" brand in every room, world-acclaimed, at least here at the farmstead, three of them just for the downstairs L-shaped floor plan.

"What have I done this time?" Liam says, sliding off his crusty work gloves on the kitchen table, his construction helmet and tool belt following.

His brown hair is matted to his skull, and his face shines, sleek with sweat. Streaks of dirt line his cheeks and forehead, and his shoulders droop with fatigue from his day working construction, helping where he can, alongside the contractor he hired to build the barn at the end of their road up to the meadow. Even so, the sparkle lighting up his eyes is blinding me. He's that happy.

I sigh, leaning back on the counter, a familiar envy burning a course through my veins.

I take my phone out and discreetly check the countdown on my agenda. One hundred forty-six days left before Mont-Saint-Sauveur officially reopens for the season on my twenty-sixth birthday. I take the coincidence as a good sign. Focus, man. You're getting there.

November 22. I'll come get you, Magali, wherever you are. *Just watch me.*

"*You* haven't done anything," Leo says to Liam, throwing up his arms. "But ZeeMan here killed a window upstairs with his bare hands." He shoves past me, grumbling on his way to the fridge.

"Let me guess, another dry rot casualty saved by the Duck?" Liam angles his brow at me, fighting a laugh.

"Just your typical day at the quack farm," I say to Liam, and we low five on it.

Leo lets out a snort but refrains to comment. Instead, he picks up a black sharpie, squeezing in another line on his never-ending Honey-Do list, now two pages long and tacked on the cupboard door right beside the fridge.

"Éolie's still napping?" Liam asks, checking on her from their downstairs bedroom doorway before quietly closing the door.

"Yep. For the last couple of hours, and doing great," I reassure him. He comes in every once in a while to take a break and check on her, see if she needs anything, even though Leo and I are on babysitting duty today.

"Yeah, she's doing great." Leo shakes his head, and a small grin forms on his lips as he pops the fridge open, selecting some seedless grapes. "Speaking of which, I owe her our last two Maillé's dark chocolate squares. She beat the shit out of me at Mille Bornes but she conked out before collecting on her winnings."

We all share an amused look. I found a 1964 edition of the French auto race card game at the back of my bedroom's cupboard when I first unpacked. Liam wasted no time in teaching Éolie the game we spent many a rainy Saturday afternoon playing in Berlinger's rec room. Life's funny that way sometimes.

"I'll Doppler the twins when she wakes," I say over my shoulder, retreating to the living room. "She wanted to wait for you."

"Hearing them both, man, it never gets old," Liam replies, pulling his sweat-soaked, long-sleeved tee over his head.

I plop my ass down on the old couch in front of the fireplace, unlit for once, on this fine Friday afternoon. Propping my feet up on the huge tree log we're using as a coffee table, I settle in more comfortably, cracking open the three-ring binder on my thighs, intending to read.

"You know, Leo, no rush on the plumbing now that summer is here. Cold showers are kind of growing on me," Liam wisecracks, wiping his face with his bunched tee before shedding the rest of his mud caked clothing, letting them drop to the kitchen floor.

A lethal grape flies by and hits him on the back of his head, but he only chuckles as he ambles off to take his Scottish shower.

"It's all Zac's doing, anyway," Leo calls after him.

"Me? It's your bloody rotten house's doing, you mean."

"Hey, no dissing my house, you might hurt her feelings." He leans back on the counter, crossing his arms. "Besides, cold showers are good for him. Didn't you put them on a strictly no-sex regime?"

"That's them, what about us?" I demand. Call me spoiled, but I like my creature comforts, like hot water.

"Relax. It's on my list, I'll get there." His gaze sweeps the place, narrowing on a few strips of tape gracing the wall behind me, very art nouveau. "What was there before, I can't remember?"

"A shelf, and it left holes the size of craters, and before you ask, no. The shelf didn't make it." I point to the fireplace. "Made great kindling, though."

"Bloody hell, man. My list is growing a third page. I need to get to it before you get to me," he mutters.

"Now you're talking. So, what's first if not plumbing?"

"Soil sample analysis," he deadpans, as though it's evident that new strains of soy beans he sees yielding results five years from now are more urgent to deal with. My eyes upturn.

"Ever heard of prioritizing?" I eye the muddy rubber boots he's pulling on. "Éolie will have a stroke as it is next time she goes to the bathroom; the kitchen's a mess. There's no need to add mud all over the place on top of it, man." You'd think none of us got a Swissy clean upbringing from the look of things in here.

"Down, boy. The mud room's door is fixed."

"You what, changed it while I was upstairs?" I let out a snort. Last winter, the door frosted over and the doorknob fell off when Liam pulled too hard. But now, it can't even be screwed back on. The wood panel flakes; it's like trying to put screws through sawdust.

"Nope. If you can't beat them, join them. I duct-taped it." Leo smirks.

"You, *taped* the doorknob on?" I shake my head in disbelief. "Let me guess, they don't make doors like that anymore?"

"You said it. I'll find a cabinet maker that's willing to change only the rotten parts and salvage it. Meanwhile, if no one yanks on it, it'll do."

"Yeah, good luck with that." I chuckle under my breath.

Should be interesting at the very least. P.O. and Yann are expected back today for their summer break, almost done now with their respective grad programs at MIT, and with only Theo missing out on the fun, it will be, once again, a full house over here.

I hear a clanking noise and some thumps. Leo curses a blue streak in the back room. I make a mental note to stock up on some more tape rolls; probabilities are we'll need it.

I settle back to read all about this midwives' program, soon absorbed.

Opinions among my colleagues vary on the subject, as midwives will be licensed to practice somewhere in between a nurse and a doctor, taking over some of our responsibilities. But I really don't get the fuss against the program some of them are making, as from what I read, they're to be paired with one of us for consults at all times. The way I see it, it's a good mix, both from a medical standpoint and the mothers' well-being to be accompanied in such a way.

I turn to the last few pages, quickly going over them. Sainte-Justine Children's Hospital in Montréal gets six candidates; the Eastern Townships, one; and the Laurentians, one. So, eight at a total to start with, and if it proves successful, in two years, it will be launched across the board.

I quickly flip through all the reports I'll have to file on my candidate for the next three months. "Great. I'll be stuck on paper duty for the most part," I grumble under my breath. *Probably why they appointed the newbie to it ... Never mind that you also happen to be the only obstetrician up here*, I argue with myself, *which is beside the point*, I grumble some more. They could have appointed her to a bigger center, like Saint-Jérôme.

I skip ahead to the Candidates tab and read through their list of requirements, and whistle low. Quite the laundry list they had to contend with, there. Why go through all of this for something in between, and not go for a full medical license, I wonder. But I don't get to dwell on it too long as Éolie's door opens, and she shuffles out, carefully balancing her steps. Her belly's big enough I suspect she can't see her feet anymore.

"Hey, there." I jump up to help her cross the room, and she smiles her thanks, but Liam comes out of the bathroom at the same time, knotting a towel at his waist, and beats me to it.

"I've got you, luv." Liam scoops her up in his arms, kissing the top of her head.

Her whole face lights up. "You're home early," Éolie says, clear delight echoing in her voice.

He murmurs something in her ear that has her snuggling deeper against his naked chest as he takes her to the bathroom, closing the door with his heel.

And man, it gets to me.

I want what they have.

Bad.

Fourteen

MAGALI

The first Monday morning of my clinical rotations finds me in a few hours early, lost in warm sensations as I croon nonsensical words of love in the low light of the hospital nursery. I can hardly believe that I made it here, at last. The past six months of non-stop studying are the most intense ones I've ever lived through before, and kind of a blur around the edges at the same time now that they're over with.

One of my hands gently rubs the naked back of my little bundle, kangarooed on my chest, skin to skin. I've been volunteering all of my spare time in the nursery for the past two days, now that the last of my theory exams are over with. The last time I volunteered up here I was seventeen. Even so, the personnel of the pediatric ward, where the neonatal care center is located, remembered me on sight when I checked in early on Saturday.

"It's one of the perks of living up north," I murmur to baby Camille, relishing the gentle fall and rise of her little chest. I could stay thus forever. My medical face mask sporting teddy bears with little hearts, matching my hat and scrubs top, prevents me from kissing the top of her tiny head like I'd like to, though. "Soon, Camille," I murmur. "You'll get to be kissed, over and over. The real deal, promise."

"Magali! You're still here?" the head nurse of the pediatric ward, Chantal, whispers, coming to an abrupt halt upon spying me in Le Coin Tranquille, the quiet corner, where all the rocking chairs are. My eyes grow wide. "I thought you had to report for your shift?"

"Oh no. What time it is?" I whisper back, alarmed, already on my way to Camille's isolette, and Camille instantly picks up on my distress, and whimpers. "Sssshh, it's okay, I'm here," I say, slowing down, my palm soothing her. But as I round the corner and face the clock on the wall, any which way I look at it, it still reads ten minutes after eight, which means I'm ten minutes late for my first clinical pre-rotation meeting, even though I've been at the hospital since five. Awesome.

"Here, I'll take her, you're already late to report." Chantal cringes in sympathy, but I shake my head, loathe to relinquish my little one. Five more minutes won't make any difference for me now, but for Camille, it will mean one less bump in her ride as I deposit her gently under the blue light, re-hooking her monitors.

"You're worth being late for," I murmur, stroking Camille's back one last time before turning on my heels, ready to make a run for it.

"You won't say that once you meet Dr. Handsome di Fiori. Nothing is worth being late if it's for him. He's to die for," Chantal gushes on as she follows me out of the ward.

It's all I've heard, all weekend, how absolutely to die for my internship supervisor is. And I'm thinking that if I hear that comment one more time, I'm likely to puke. But really, did no one read the guy's amazing credentials? We're so lucky to have him here after a stint of one year with Médecins sans Frontières, his short bio read. Not to mention, Cambridge Medical is renowned, and I can't wait to discuss the latest prenatal researches and technologies with him, regardless of what he looks like.

"To die for. How nice." I lose the fight, and roll my eyes.

Correctly reading the tone of my sarcastic disinterest, she adds, "Girl, don't knock it. You're two of the rare singles around here, and you haven't seen handsome until you see him." She keeps pace with me, our shoes squeaking down the hall. "We may be all married, but we're not dead!"

"Chantal, trust me. I've seen handsome before," *and what I saw can't be topped,* I silently add. The kind that gives you a bazillion butterflies, swoony grins, delicious shivers, intense burning looks, the whole works—even six months later. I cluck my tongue. Great, now I'm thinking about my insanely hot foreigner. This is not the place nor the time to fantasize.

"I'm glad it's not me that's paired off with him, though," Chantal prattles on, our brisk walk to the nurses' central station not in the least deterring her from the subject. "I get tongue-tied every time I see him, but working with him? God, I wouldn't remember my own name."

Really, the whole female population of this hospital needs to get out more. Yeah, myself included, I inwardly snort.

"Magali, you're late for your pre-rotation meeting," Adélaïde, one of the nurses manning the station this morning, points out the obvious, wildly gesturing in the general direction of my face. Something I don't have time to decrypt.

"I know, I know." *Please don't remind me.* I cringe as I rush by her, glad I had the foresight to leave my stethoscope and program binder on the conference table earlier on. Facing the staff meeting room closed door, my palms grow unaccountably sweaty on me. I rub them once on my scrubs, before taking a deep breath. "The rest of my life starts here," I say to myself with true conviction. I knock once, and enter, closing the door behind me.

My sincere apologies die a swift death on my lips. I'm rendered speechless at the sight of the man sitting at the conference table.

My eyes bug out, my stomach bottoms out, and I have to lean on the closed door to support my back, weak-kneed.

I close my eyes.

No way.

There's just no way. I've been awake too long, not enough coffee. I'm hallucinating.

"Vous êtes DESM 6093 2208, je présume," my hallucination's voice rumbles across the open space, deep and magnetizing in a French no longer so rusty, and goose bumps travel up my arms. By now, the familiar, delicious sort of heat he evokes floods my lower belly just at the sound.

My eyes pop open.

My bronze-skinned foreigner, it would seem, is truly sitting on the other side of the conference table. No hallucination. And he's wearing a lab coat and a hospital ID badge.

The hint of a frown is pulling down his kissable lips as he taps his pen on his clipboard after having read out loud my permanent code, the one every citizen gets at birth, identifying us into the system for health care as well as education, the former for life if you reside, the latter all the way through university.

At least, I think that's what he said. I can't be sure. My ears are ringing, my heart's in my throat, and my head is spinning.

"Vous êtes … Docteur Zac di Fiori?" is all I can squeak.

"Correct." He looks up, cocking his head, and my eyes widen. In the light of day, he's even more handsome than I remembered, if at all possible.

I stare at him a minute longer than awkward, rendered mute. I'm torn between elated and horrified. My unforgettable stranger, the one I accused of being nothing more than a self-centered, adrenaline junkie out for kicks, an entitled prick to boost, he's an obstetrician? In my hospital? My maître de stage?

In what alternate universe is this even possible?

One in which it doesn't seem like he remembers you, Magali.

Huh. There might be hope, yet. I straighten from the door.

He stills for a fraction of a second as our eyes lock together, and I swallow, wondering if he's starting to recognize me now. His copper-brown eyes narrow as he holds my stare in a searching gaze. I hold my breath, but he shakes himself off.

I almost slump in relief.

My eyes dart between the floor and the conference table as his magnetic voice rumbles on, "You won't need a surgical get-up this morning, unless you're contagious, in which case you shouldn't be here."

Wait, what? Surgical get-up? Contagious?

One of my hands comes up and brushes over my mask. A small groan escapes from my lips. No wonder he doesn't recognize me yet.

"I just came from a NICU visit and it's why I'm a bit late, sorry. It's just an added precaution I took," I manage to say, hardly recognizing the high-pitched tone of my voice. "I forgot I was wearing them," I add, stating the obvious, standing there, struck stupid, self-evidently. And now, to be honest, I'm afraid to take them off, my fingers unaccountably fidgeting with the hem of my top.

Adélaïde's gesturing makes total sense now, and I just had to zip by her without stopping, didn't I? And Chantal, probably much too busy swooning over him, didn't noticed me wearing them as she wears them herself pretty much all the time, anyway ... like I'd like to do now.

And what, pretend you're contagious for the next three months, or something? I argue with myself. Good one, M. Who knows, maybe you'll grow on him like a recurring virus, plaguing him anew for all eternity while at it. I can hear CD's snarky remark from here. I almost groan out loud.

"Do you have a name to go with that code of yours, or should I call you DESM?" he asks without looking at me, busy scribbling down notes in one of the files he picked from the top of a small pile of patients' manila-colored ones sitting next to him on the table.

I watch his spidery writing, and absently wonder if he had a hard time adjusting to being left-handed in a right-handed world as a child, like my brother Lucas did at times. Probably not. The effortless glide of his lean-fingered hand exudes self-confidence in a take-charge attitude. I can't help but admire the way it moves, nor can I help imagine its warm smoothness skimming down my skin...

His pen stops moving, and his left hand tightens in a white-knuckled hold on a mumbled expletive. I look up, startled out of my reverie.

He raises a brow, expectantly.

I stare, uncomprehending.

He clears his throat, tapping his pen, clearly waiting for something.

I frown in thought. Wasn't he busy writing notes? Focus. Oh, yeah, question. He asked if I had a name.

"Um..." I nod and shake my head, quite the feat really, almost giving me whiplash. But for the life of me, with coppery brown eyes I never thought I'd see again drilling me, I can't seem to articulate any coherent words.

"Is that a yes, or a no?" he asks, his voice vibrating somewhere in between irritated and fascinated.

Dieu du ciel, Magali, get a grip already, answer him. It's been what, six months? Right. He probably forgot all about you by now, anyway. Get over yourself.

I take a deep breath, and slide my teddy bear surgical hat off, stuffing it in my scrubs' front pocket. "It's both. Yes, I have a name and no, you can't call me DESM." I peel the mask off my face. "But you can call me Magali, Docteur di Fiori. Magali Deslauriers," I hold my hand out across the table to shake his.

"Magali?" he cries out, talking over me, his chair upending on two legs from his forceful shove as he stands. He almost topples over, blinking. "Christ," he swears under his breath, brushing one hand down his face.

I inwardly wince and slowly retract my hand. Well, I was wrong about that.

He remembers.

This is a disaster of epic proportion, or a wondrous, miraculous occurrence, depending on which viewpoint.

But it can't be both.

My heart thuds in my ears.

Our eyes fasten on one another.

My skin prickles. I fight a shiver and the urge to rub my arms.

A yearning echoing mine, surprisingly enough, etches onto his face, and my whole outlook shifts and locks into perspective.

I lick my lips, my mouth suddenly dry.

I made assumptions on that night, bad ones.

It's time for me to own up to them and be held accountable, like I've been taught to all my life.

Fifteen

ZAC

"Magali?" I almost topple over from the shock, sucker punched in the chest.

Magali.

How in the bloody everlasting hell did she end up here? In scrubs? My midwife *intern* of all things? Really, what are the odds? Fuck me sideways, but I can't seem to form a coherent thought beyond this. I blink a few times, but no. She's still there.

I throw my pen on the conference table.

"Christ." I brush one hand down my face, fighting the urge to pull at my hair.

She's even more exquisite than I remembered. Limpid silver eyes stare me down. A few wisps of glossy, mahogany hair tease her delicate cheekbones, escapees of a once neat braid that I'd like to muss up some more. And right now, she's too adorable for words in yellow teddy bears and pink hearts-printed, sage-green scrubs that fit just right. I can't help but notice all of the things I'm most likely not supposed to notice any longer as her immediate supervisor. Yeah, like that's going to happen, I curse some more.

"Fuck," I mutter, frustration bleeding into my tone.

Her spine grows rigid. "I'm so sorry for that night," she murmurs, her light-grey eyes entreating. My stomach drops, and I almost lose it, wanting nothing more than to kiss her six ways to Sunday as she stands there like a personal miracle waiting to happen.

"Look—" we both say, talking over each other.

"I don't usually do awkward quite so well," I mutter, motioning for her to sit.

She tilts her head to the side, sending her messy braid tumbling down her shoulder. I stare, unable to help myself.

"Me neither," she says on a wince, taking a seat opposite mine. She looks me in the eye, her bright gaze drawing me in. "I never meant to blacklist you, not really. What you did only deserved a warning, a stiff one, granted, but only a warning nonetheless. I know it's no excuse, but on that night, you threw me for a loop. My emotions were all over the place, and I couldn't deal with them and I'm truly sorry I took it out on you. I know better than that. It was wrong and impulsive. I overreacted, and judged you on circumstantial evidence alone without giving you the benefit of the doubt, and condemned you on the spot. It's not something I'm proud of, and you have every right to be livid. If it's any consolation, your eternal sentencing ended early the following morning when I rescinded the order, and resigned. So, technically speaking, you've never really been blacklisted anywhere."

I'm not actually blacklisted. The guys will be glad to hear it. But to hear, on top of it, that she quit after that night when I had every reasons to believe she'd be there next season... "Well ... thanks," I say, although I couldn't care less about the skiing. Which is just as well because she doesn't stop long enough to hear me anyway.

"And since I'm on a roll, confessing here, I never in a million years thought I'd ever see you again, and I've never felt as grateful to be wrong, ever. And if you can find it in you to forgive my ill-advised reaction, I'd like to start over and wipe the slate clean, and, you know, move on."

Her long-ass speech is delivered all in one breath and, thunderstruck by what she just apologized for, my mind drifts off, held in a sort of haze.

I look at her for a long moment. I couldn't keep my eyes from roaming even if I wanted to. Her cheeks blush rosy under my stare, her plump lips part, and her chest heaves. Her silver gaze drops to the table, and she bites on her lower lip, worrying it. *Jesus.* Give me a bloody break, but all I want is to soothe the little hurt away with my tongue.

But then again, as her immediate supervisor for the foreseeable future, I'm shit out of luck, aren't I? Not that a workplace romance is frowned upon here; the place is chock-full of loving couples working together on some level or other, after all. But as her *maître de stage*, they're just not quite at the same level of power imbalance we both stand at ... And she'll likely think the worst if I make a move on her. My jaw clenches as I hold in a scowl. The rebel in me roars, unused to being denied.

I tap my pen on the table, her speech replaying on a loop in my head, my mind latching onto the last of it, *and I've never felt as grateful to be wrong, ever.* Maybe she's not that indifferent after all. So why should you lie, man, and pretend this is strictly business, exactly?

"I don't think that's possible," I say after a beat.

"You don't think you can—"

"Forgive? Yes. Done. But forget it?" I shove away from the table, walking over to the window with a view of the mountains. "No. I don't want to move on." My hands bracing on the upper frame, I exhale a long breath.

"I ... huh ... All right, fair enough," she says, her tone decidedly contrite, "but can you do one thing for me before I'm reassigned somewhere else?" her voice pleads, and I whirl on her, frowning.

What? She wants to transfer out? Brow dipping, I open my mouth to ask her what she means, but she launches into a quick spiel, beating me to it. "Since I'll most probably be held up in the usual limbo in between red tape and enquiry committees for months, if not a year, as soon as you request my transfer, can you reconsider and give me a week to prove myself?"

"What's to reconsider, here?" I scoff, crossing my arms. "You have nothing left to prove."

Her face drains of all color. "I understand." Her shoulders sag, and she makes a move to gather her things.

I burst into action and push her stuff out of the way with the back of my hand, and her head snaps back up, her eyes shooting me a startled look.

"You understand nothing, then, if you think I'm letting you go. And I won't deny the truth," I say, unable to help the gruffness of my tone as my heart hammers painfully against my ribs. *Please don't let me fuck this up this time around.*

Confusion flickers over her face. My pulse is pounding in my veins as I consider how this needs to be done, but nothing comes to me other than the overwhelming urge to make her mine...

"What ... What do you mean by you won't deny the truth?" Her eyes drop to my mouth, and she swallows, licking her lips.

Bloody hell.

"Do you have any idea what you do to me?" I push back, needing the small distance, shoving both my hands in my hair. Taking a deep, calming breath through my nose, I give her my own truth. "I don't want to move on. I've thought about you every day since that night ... Your words sliced right through—"

"I'm so sorry!" Her hands press down on her chest. "I had no right to judge—"

"No, but you did." I cut her off, capturing her gaze solidly within mine. "And that's what I'm getting at. Don't apologize. I'm here, in this hospital, because those words kick-started a change in me. One that needed to happen to challenge me to step up and be a better version of myself. And I have you to thank for that."

"Oh." She blinks as my apology hangs between us, her expression drains of tension, and her eyes once again land on my mouth.

My voice is low, steady. "So here's the deal. I want to move *beyond* that night. I won't deny there's something electric between us. I want more and I won't let the fact that I'm your appointed maître de stage for the next three months stand in the way."

Attraction springs up between us once again, and I pause to let myself enjoy that I've thrown her off balance.

"You can't say things like that, and then expect me to behave," she cries out, her eyes darkening to pewter grey, full of unleashed desire, searching mine.

I start to advance on her, the predator in me lit up by the intoxicating commands swirling in my head. A low growl escapes from deep within my throat.

"Please don't. I can't go there." Christ above, my stomach bottoms out, her words effectively stopping me in my track. But the small, needy whimper that follows shoots straight down to my dick in such a swell move.

She holds up a trembling hand. My heart flips, wanting nothing more than to curl her over my chest, and soothe the trembling away. "Magali ... I would never force you to do anything you're not comfortable with, or abuse my—"

"No, *you* don't understand. It's not you that I don't trust. It's me. I don't know how to do half-measures. I always end up giving it my all. All in, or nothing. And I can't pretend otherwise. It's who I am. I'm wildly attracted to you, and those very feelings are scaring me right now. I can't fight both attractions, mine on top of yours. I'm not cut out for casual."

I put my hands on the table and bend down at eye level with her. "There's nothing casual about the way I feel." I gesture between us. "The pull is just too strong, and I've never felt the likes before. I need to see where this goes, Magali."

"So you say, but just where does it go from here? You tell me. You're my maître de stage. I never had to pretend one thing while living another. I can't do this to you, or me. I'm committed to this program," she says, her eyes clouding over, her voice impassioned.

My heart hammers out of my chest.

"And you think I'm not? That what? Just because we're getting to know each other on a personal level, I won't be impartial in my reports and kick your butt if you're slacking on the job? The hell I won't."

"That's the easy part! If I'm slacking on the job, you'll have to stand in line as I'll be kicking my own butt. Becoming a midwife means everything to me." Her eyes close, and she takes a deep inhale through her nose. She exhales on a long breath, "I can't go there; I'll get too attached and mess everything up. Don't you understand? We briefly met six months ago, and I'm halfway there already."

"Do you really think that we can't be colleagues, friends, lovers? Think again." I lean closer, my voice dropping to a low timbre, and she inhales a sharp breath.

"I'm pretty sure we can, au contraire, and that's the problem. I'm afraid you'll burn me to cinders and obliterate me when you leave."

"Just so we're clear, I'm not going anywhere. And unlike that night on the slopes, I'm not taking no for an answer." My brow arches, daring her to argue. "*I want it all.* Set the pace, Magali."

Tension crackles in the air as she searches my eyes for what feels like an eon or two. "Okay," she whispers into the stretching silence.

Something inside me unfurls. "Okay," I repeat, shoulders sagging in relief.

"Okay," she says again, this time more resolute.

I straighten, shifting the folders on her side and doing my best to swallow a victorious grin. "You have an hour to review those files for comments before we report to the prenatal clinic for our first appointments." My voice is oddly steady for a guy whose pulse pounds like mad in his ears.

Magali's gaze drops to them, and then back to me. There's quiet for a moment as we stare at one another. Her gaze, searching. Mine, steadfast.

A beat, or an eternity pass between us.

Her bright, silver eyes clear, filling with strength and resolve. "On it."

She gifts me with the most blinding smile, and suddenly, I'm on top of the world, freefalling on the best possible high.

Sixteen

ZAC

Apprehension

noun

3. a view, opinion, or idea on any subject.

L eaning on the corner credenza of the exam room, I take notes on my clipboard, letting Magali be in charge. Not even an hour into our first clinical appointments, and here I am, falling just a little harder, watching her interact with her first patient.

Magali's soft, graceful hands smooth down in gentle, circular motions the ultrasonic gel she took care to warm up beforehand, applying it on both Laurélie's twenty weeks' exposed baby bump and the Doppler's probe.

"I realized the very first time I heard his heartbeat that what they say is true. A baby fills a place in your heart you never knew was empty, and I just can't wait to cuddle him," Laurélie, one of the seven first-time moms enrolled under the program, says on a dreamy sigh, totally at ease with Magali, relaxed in a way she never was with me.

"I know what you mean; they're so precious. A sense of total peace washes over me every time I cuddle a baby close to me, heartbeat to heartbeat," Magali says warmly, and yeah. That, right there, does it for me.

"Éric says pregnancy gives me no other choice but to learn patience, at long last, but he's the one who went and bought baby skates and this tiny hockey jersey when we found out we were having a boy."

Magali shakes her head, chuckling low as she programs the monitor's script terminal.

"Boys," they say at the same time, fast friends, probably having forgotten that I'm standing there not three feet away in the corner of the exam room. A slow grin spreads on my lips, and I shake my head, writing the date and time on Laurélie's chart clipped to my board.

"All set. So, let's hear this little boy of yours." One of Magali's hands expertly handles the probe while the other adjusts levels on the monitor, up until the swooshing sound of the baby's heartbeats fill the room. Just like Liam said, that sound never gets old. Completely in her element, Magali shares a radiant smile with the mom, one full of joy, and I want that smile, I realize, aimed at me.

Laurélie chatters on, asking Magali a million questions, so it seems, discussing all sorts of small concerns she never addressed to me before. Magali reassures Laurélie on every little thing she comes up with, her voice soothing, never rushing her.

I let Magali do her thing, absently listening in, as I sit behind the desk in the cubicle adjacent to the exam room, jotting down some additional measurements on the chart and a few notes, to compare with hers later in our debriefing session.

From where I sit, I see her scribbling down notes, her slender back bent over the credenza, and I stare absently at the pattern on her scrubs. I'd give a lot to be one of the teddy bears hugging the hem of her top right now.

"How about rescheduling them on Fridays instead of Mondays, that way Éric can be here with you, non? Tell him I want to see that tiny jersey, and we'll take his future hockey player's measurements to see how much he's grown into it."

"Can you do that?" Laurélie squeals.

"Sure, let's see this agenda." Magali types away on the keyboard, logging onto the clinic's agenda from the exam room's computer. "I can put you down either on Friday, August the twelfth, same time in the morning, or on the nineteenth, at two in the afternoon. Tell me which time slot is more convenient, and I'll switch around all your other appointments accordingly." She looks up at

Laurélie, and Magali's expectant expression fills with warmth as she witnesses the other woman's happiness, and something snug unfurls in my chest.

"Oh Mon Dieu. I just fell in love with you for rescheduling them, you have no idea," Laurélie raves over Magali. "Éric was so bummed when he received his new work schedule keeping him in Toronto for three days instead of two, and from Monday instead of Tuesday, like before, and the clinic's secretary insisted that she couldn't switch any of my regular appointments. We'll both be here on the twelfth."

"It's a date," Magali says, pressing enter on the keyboard with a jaunty index finger. "Just stop by the reception desk and pick up your printed confirmations on your way out, and we're all set." Magali helps her get down from the exam bed, steadying her as they walk out of the cubicle.

"Docteur di Fiori, I seriously love her," Laurélie says upon noticing me tapping my pen on the clipboard, leaning in the chair, absorbed by my thoughts. "*Please* keep her."

I shoot Magali a look, before replying to Laurélie, "I intend to." And Magali looks down with a small grin, face glowing.

"Oh, wait, before I forget." Magali takes from a small wicker basket she brought with her a little care package she prepared with a few samples of homeopathic and herbal tea products she had me approve beforehand. She gives it to Laurélie, explaining what they are and how to use them. "If you have any other concerns, Laurélie, give me a call or write me an email, day or night. My cell number and email address are on the fridge magnet in there."

"That's so thoughtful," Laurélie says, her eyes flooding with tears. She takes out the handcrafted magnet made from a natural tree limb cut in a thin slice palm size in diameters, the wood grain sealed with a clear matte finish. "Sorry. Hormones," she sniffs, abashed, smiling her thanks as Magali passes along one of the essentials in here, a box of tissues. She picks one, dabbing at her eyes. "But really, it's so thoughtful, and cute!"

I crane my neck, trying to see what's on it, and I'm caught mid-motion by Laurélie, who hands it over to me while asking Magali where she got them.

It's cute all right. There's a stick figure family drawn on it with colored crayons, a dad, a mom, and a baby at the end of a rainbow, and Magali's name, cell phone number, and email address written in a painstaking, block handwriting. Hmmm. Will she notice one's missing if I pocket one of her little packages for myself, I wonder...

"Do you know La Maisonnée?" Magali asks Laurélie, her cheeks creasing into another lethal smile, and two dimples appear.

"No, is that a store in town I don't know of?" Laurélie's forehead scrunches up.

"La Maisonnée? That's down the road from here, isn't it?" I ask, curious myself, having seen it written on a wooden sign posted on the door of a large residential Victorian in passing before. "It doesn't look like a store, though."

"It's not, it's a halfway house for young adults with intellectual deficiencies, and my best friend volunteers over there, teaching. They find so many clever ways to integrate into the work force, and well, some of her protégés came up with this fridge magnet idea for my calling cards, and custom designed them." She points at the magnet Laurélie takes back from me, admiring it. "One of their counsellors joked good-naturedly about the pickles and ice cream squad, explaining to them where it came from. So, they figured they'd save my mommies-in-the-making from eating that awful mixture by having me watching over them that much more closely. And I just couldn't argue with that kind of logic, non?"

"They're too clever by half if you ask me. I won't be able to sneak into the fridge for unauthorized snacks with your name and cell number plastered on it. No more guilt trips. I like that," Laurélie proclaims, putting it away in her tote bag. "You'll probably start a Binge Alert Hotline with those."

"No worries. I'll stick by you if it comes to that," she tells Laurélie, her tone growing mischievous, her eyes twinkling as she accompanies her to the door.

"Not to mention, it's such a simple way for me to keep your number handy around the house if anyone needs to get a hold of you." Laurélie's hands brush down her round belly.

"That's the plan. And I like just as much that each one of these calling cards is unique, just like my babies." Magali's face softens on that last thought, and they share a quiet smile.

"I think I'll stop by on my way home and tell them what a great idea they had, and that Éric and I will treasure it forever."

"It will mean the world to them if you do," Magali exclaims. "But I should warn you, though, they go nuts over anything baby. They might keep you," she admits as she hugs her goodbye.

"Then I'll be in good company," Laurélie chuckles. "I won't abuse your *magnetic* privilege, promise. Thanks again, Magali, really."

And it's pretty much how my morning goes. Each patient warms instantly to Magali, and when she gives them her handmade magnet and makes them promise to call if they ever need her, they light up. From my corner vantage point, clutching at my clipboard, I light up too.

I fall a little harder for Magali, one patient at a time ... And much too soon to my liking, there are none left to see.

"That's the last one for you today, but want to grab some lunch in the cafeteria before I'm due back?" I ask, unbuttoning my white coat and sliding my stethoscope in one of the front pockets. Obstetricians over here follow up closely on their babies for a year of monthly checkups before a pediatrician takes over, unless otherwise advised. And it's another part of the job I truly enjoy. But those follow-ups are not on Magali's roster, and today, my afternoon is filled with them. Hers, according to the schedule I read in the binder earlier, is filled with online courses. But I'm not ready yet to see her leave for the day...

"It's already time for lunch?" Her brow scrunching up, she checks her watch. "What do you know, it is," she says, dismay blooming on her face.

"Didn't believe me?" I ask, raising a brow.

"It's not you." She shrugs, stepping out into the corridor. "Wearing a watch and checking it regularly is on my list of resolutions."

"You realize it's the second time this morning you're giving me an 'it's not you it's me' speech." I give her a sidelong glance. A small grin tugs at her lips as she falls into step with me.

"I'm behind schedule, then. You should be up to three by now," she sasses me. "Seriously though, you should be warned that I usually get so involved in what I'm doing that I easily lose track of time, well, pretty much all the time." She shakes her head. "That's what my resolution is about, to change. But obviously, I'm only halfway there." She motions to the watch strapped on her left wrist. "I'm wearing it, but not checking it."

"I'm all for getting so involved in an activity you lose track of time. I've a few that comes to mind." I wink, and her eyes grow wide.

"There you are, Magali Deslauriers! And to think I'm missing out on my lunch hour because of you," the clinic's manager hisses as we pass by the glass wall of her office, now emerging from the corridor into the reception area. *What the hell?* The clinic is officially closed from twelve to two in the afternoon, leaving staff with an hour's overlap as leeway. "I'm fixing your meddling with the system," the woman rants on, typing away on her computer. "You just can't do that, you know!"

Magali's brows dip. "What—?"

"That," the skinny, dark-haired woman I vaguely recall as an Annie or an Angie, snaps, pointing to her screen with a forceful finger, and Magali bends over her desk.

"The agenda? What's wrong?" Magali asks, concern etching on her face.

"You can't change appointments, ever. And the summer intern at the reception gave away the confirmations too. If it gets out, everyone will ask to switch this, and switch that, and it will be unmanageable in here! Not to mention, we have specific days and time when there are *no* exam cubicles available, *at all*, like on Fridays."

"Really, Annie, it's just one patient. And what do you mean no cubicles available? The agenda was wide open on the Fridays I rescheduled her regular appointments, and mine certainly isn't filled out yet," Magalie says, her tone bewildered.

"What seems to be the problem?" I ask.

Annie huffs, "See that red code up here?" She points to a small red dot on top of her screen. "It means not available. Closed down. Compressions. Government cutbacks. You can name it however you want, but not available means *not available*." She throws her arms up.

Magali's shoulders sag, and she rubs at her temples. "Okay, okay. I get it," she says, holding up her hands. "But just this once, can't we reschedule? There must be a place I can squeeze Laurélie Trépanier on Thursdays so that her husband, whose job takes him to Toronto three days a week now, can make the appointments, non?"

"No exception." Annie crosses her arms, and her mouth thins. "Her husband should take it out with his employer to free his Mondays; it's part of his congé parental. It's not our concern."

"It is *our* concern. He works in Ontario more than half the time so his company is not governed by the Régime Québecois d'assurance parentale! He won't get the three-month paternity leave so he's racking up his annual vacation weeks as it is. And isn't it the point of this whole pilot program I'm in to accommodate them a little bit more?" Magali asks, a thread of impatience lacing her tone.

"If you want my opinion, it's to cut back on expenses and still look good while at it," she gripes. "You cost half his salary." She vaguely waves one hand in my direction, and Magali mumbles under her breath that she didn't ask for her opinion.

"This whole thing is beyond absurd." I frown, bracing my hands on her desk. "Look, I'm sure one exception won't—"

"Docteur di Fiori, with all due respect, we have quotas to meet, statistics to measure up to, and monthly reports to justify, so yes. No exception," she interjects.

I swallow down an angry retort, unclenching my jaw just enough to say in what can pass for an even tone, "Show me the agenda."

Annie's lips pinch, her face taking a turn towards mulish and a lovely shade of puce. She opens her mouth to retort but is cut short by Magali.

"No, leave it." Magali's hand comes up to rub on her forehead, and she mutters, "I'll call Laurélie back and fix this."

Another one of those slivers of unease slithers down my spine as the rebel in me can't help but twitch. Am I really cut out to contend with reports and red tape a mile long, on top of systemic rigidity if you so much as deviate by a fraction from the guidelines, here?

"I'll catch up to you in the cafeteria." She shoves away from the desk and storms out of the reception Carrefour through the connecting door leading back to the hospital without looking back.

I tilt my head up, count to five in my head to keep from starting in on Annie, and follow Magali at a slower pace.

So far, the pros of this place still outweigh the cons, but what if it gets to be too much in the long run? My stomach coils in uncomfortable knots. What if I'm a misfit through and through and can't really fit in here as well?

Then what?

Remembering Grégoire's advice to Liam a few months back about not worrying when you can't solve it, I shelve that worry away for now, and concentrate instead on catching up to Magali as she rounds the corner.

"Don't lose sight of the broader picture, here, man," I mumble under my breath. "You want it all, remember?"

"Magali, wait up," I call out, making a few heads turn, but she swipes her card and disappears into the staff locker room at the other end of the corridor.

Seventeen

MAGALI

My pulse hammers and blood pounds in my ears as I storm into the staff locker room, using some Lamaze breathing techniques in an attempt to calm down.

"Hey, Magali. How was your first morning with Docteur Le Handsome?" One of the neonatal nurses, Johanne, looks up as I walk by her.

"Way too short," I say, thankful the room is quasi-deserted on this torrid July day. I don't have time to chitchat my way through half the staff. I keep moving and turn at the third row on the left toward my locker.

"I know what you mean," she replies from a few rows down.

"No, you don't," I mumble under my breath. After a few unsuccessful tries I finally get the combination right on my keyless padlock—and to think I was afraid to lose a key.

"What's it like to work *under* him?" Johanne's voice drifts over, all dreamy like.

Really? "I wouldn't know, we work together as partners," I mutter into my locker.

"What?"

"Can't talk now, or I'll be late," I call out over my shoulder. The idealist in me is on a mission. I pick my messenger bag up and cross it over my shoulder, jiggling my padlock back into place.

"And you don't want to be late for our lunch date, right?" Zac says, a shoulder leaning on a locker two lockers down from mine, hands in his pockets.

My hands come up to my chest. Warm copper eyes greet mine. A lopsided grin indents a dimple on his cheek, zapping me on sight with a flurry of butterflies, flooding me with heat.

"Sorry, did I startle you?" A playful smile tugs at his mouth and I feel my own mouth tilting up at the sight of him.

"Not at all. But you might startle the staff if someone catches you in here."

"I weighed that against the possibility of you slipping out the back door and leaving me hanging," he says.

"I had no intention of passing up a free lunch. If we hurry, I even think I'll make it on time for once," I reply, striving for a playful note, willing myself to switch gears. *Focus, lunch, mission. Check.* "Come on," I grab his arm. "Bye, Johanne," I call out. "Give baby Camille a hug for me."

"I ... will," she replies, turning thirteen shades of red upon spying Zac as we pass by her row, where she is thankfully already dressed again.

I shrug both shoulders and walk out.

"Bon après-midi," Zac wishes her a good afternoon, opening the door for me.

I step out, and he falls into step with me. My average five-feet-five height is on the short side standing next to him, the top of my head barely reaching his jaw line. We nod in passing to a few colleagues walking by.

"Are you all right?" he asks with a sidelong glance.

"Yes, why?" My head tilts.

"You lit out of the clinic, not that I blame you." His brow creases, and his mouth thins.

"I wish I could say it won't happen again, but my Zen hasn't reached unshakable level yet. Working on it, though." My gaze drops to the tiled floor freshly scrubbed. "You might as well know that I don't conform to inflexibility all that well," I confess. "And the system is full of rigid guidelines."

"No argument from me," Zac grumbles. "Add to your list that it's full of absurdities, like illogical schedules and intolerant clinic managers catering to them at the point of service, and I'm with you all the way."

"Done," I say, touched by his grumblings, as they tell me all I need to know about where he stands. "But still, it's no excuse. I knew signing into the program what I was getting into, not that it's always easy to curb my inner-idealist." I sigh heavily. "I don't blame Annie, you know; she's under a lot of pressure. I don't envy her at all, in fact."

"You're a lot more lenient than I am then," he mutters, irritation clouding his features.

"Come on, give her a break, just a wee one," I say, my thumb and index pinching close together, and he lets out a snort. "You heard what she has to contend with, and prenatal care is always the first one hit by budget cuts, and don't let me get started on small regional centers." I steer closer to him, bringing my messenger bag close to my chest to clear an empty stretcher by the wall.

His hand settles at the small of my back, guiding me down the corridor. I shoot him a look, narrowing my eyes, unsure what to do. Noticing it, he takes a step back, letting me go. I fight a shiver, tempted to put his hand back on me and, yet, afraid to. He seems unruffled, unlike me. My pulse is all over the place. I take a few deep breaths, calming my racing heart.

"I haven't been here long enough to form a definite opinion on this whole state-run public health regime as the only choice, but isn't it kind of surprising, investing in the future of the nation and all that jazz if I read the paperwork correctly?" His brow draws in, and his forehead wrinkles. And just like that, I'm back on familiar ground.

"In theory, yes. The truth? Not really. Pregnancy isn't a disease, for one, so government policies or not, it will follow its natural course. Compressions in prenatal care are done quietly, so it doesn't make as good a scandal as cutbacks in emergency rooms or intensive care units when severely understaffed," I explain. "It's a question of balance I suppose, and they never seem to strike it completely right."

"Yeah, I'm starting to get the picture," Zac scowls. "And I'm not too keen on it. The whole process and the red tape a mile long are absurd. It makes the rebel in me twitch when his hands are tied."

"That makes two of us," I say, dodging another stretcher as we continue to wind through the halls, but he makes no move on me this time, and if I'm being totally honest, I am disappointed and relieved in equal parts. No. More disappointed than relieved. I sigh, exasperated with myself. I'm not used to this scared, indecisive Magali, blowing hot and cold. "We should probably start an

Absurd List to help us keep our perspective, or our sanity, whichever."

"Not a bad idea."

"And what would be your Absurd Highlight of the Day?" I ask, intrigued.

"A schedule that gives me the past weekend off, you on a Monday, and the following two days allegedly off, but on call, then makes me work for the next eight ones straight through." He quirks a brow at me.

"I know, right?" My eyes upturn. "Your schedule is my schedule by the way, except that I'm not on call for the next two days, like you, of course. And now you know, our healthcare system is not only public across the board but far from perfect."

"Why do you think it's such a mess?"

"Irreconcilable differences, the attorney in my dad would say." I frown in thought. "The decision makers and the field workers basically have two different agendas. It makes for an interesting tango, anyway. But even so, I believe in the guiding principles behind it; they're good ones at their core."

We share a quick look of understanding before I continue on, "But I won't lie. In their application? They bring their own set of unresolved issues and challenges, big time, and it's sometimes hard to navigate through them all with equanimity. But then again, is there such a thing as a perfect system anywhere out there?"

"I've seen so much worse, you won't see me arguing." His eyes takes on a faraway look, and the tight pinch of his lips makes me wonder if he's thinking of his one-year stint with *Médecins Sans Frontières* in third-world countries.

"Hey, doesn't mean I'm giving up on perfecting what I can on my own," I say, bumping my shoulder into his, and he looks at me a question in his eyes. "Midwives used to monitor and deliver babies at home, after all, and my whole thesis treats that very subject. In fact, I'm thinking I might just experiment with that very idea purely for research purposes, of course. Care to give me your expert opinion on medical-grade portable Dopplers?" I uphold my messenger bag. "I've brought my laptop to scroll through the choices and buy one online."

"Are you thinking what I'm thinking?" He raises a brow.

"Depends ... If you're thinking I'll go monitor Laurélie's little one on a few free Fridays on top of her regular checkups, then yes, we absolutely think the same."

The glint in his eyes reflecting something in between complicity, wonder, and tenderness, he says, "What I think is that we'll make one hell of a team." He puts his hand up, his mouth stretching into a grin, and we high five on it. And I fall under his spell a little bit more.

"I like the way you think, Docteur di Fiori," I say, a new bounce in my steps. "So, want to look over Dopplers with me? I'd really like your opinion." I dangle my laptop bag in front of him like a prize.

"I'd be happy to," he says, half a grin still tugging on his lips, but as he checks his watch a slight frown forms on his brow. "But looks like I only have some forty-two minutes left to spare. Want to grab a sandwich instead, and eat on the rooftop garden?"

"We won't make it then," I say, motioning for him to follow me. I veer right for the stairwells leading to the front atrium, and the nearest exit. "Trust me on this, by the time we get to the sandwiches, we'll have to eat them as we walk back to the ward. Been there, done that, too many times to count as a teen. Care to share this, instead?" With years of multitasking on the go under my belt, I rummage through my messenger bag, taking out a plastic container. I give it to him to carry.

He holds it up, studying the contents. "Fine by me. What's in it, pasta salad?"

"Yep. The best kind, I'll have you know, homemade for once since I finally had the time. Basil pesto, roasted pine nuts, cheese cubes, and raw veggies, and I always bring way too much." I step in front of him just to see the automatic doors swish open on me, gesturing with a grand sweep of my arm for him to pass through. He shakes his head at me, the ghost of a grin playing on his lips. "I just can't resist their open sesame effect." I shrug and Zac chuckles low, the sound filling me with joy. I can't get over how different from the self-centered entitled prick I thought I'd left that night on the slope, he really is.

I remember his words earlier about seeing where it all leads. I can only hope he meant it because, already, I know I will not be able to walk away from him. Not easily. Maybe not at all. And we haven't so much as touched. Well, not much anyway. Not as much as I want to...

We step out into the muggy July air of the high noon hour, the humid heat more tropical than northern. I tip my head up, closing my eyes for a brief instant, enjoying the warmth of the sun on my face.

"And where do you see us eating this?" Zac's gaze sweeps the concrete circular driveway, and the parking lots, staggered down the hillside, where a hot humid haze clouds over cars baking under the sun.

A fine sheen of sweat glows on his face, and my scrubs cling to my back as I start down the walkway toward a thin patch of green between parking lots, just a few hundred meters from the entrance where an old maple tree provides shade. I jump up and perch on one of the thickest, low-hanging limbs, my feet dangling, taking out my laptop.

I pat the tree. "Meet an old friend of mine, Albert." One of the few remaining vestiges of the former sanatorium's gardens.

"Albert?" His brows lift in amusement, and he looks up the tree's canopy. "Of course, she names things like trees."

"And you don't?" I tilt my head to the side quizzically.

"Only people," he says, a slow grin tugging up one side.

"You're missing out, then."

"Am I, now?" he asks, voice low and amused. I watch as he goes to work folding back his white shirt's sleeves.

"Definitely." I will my eyes to move away from the sight of his well-defined, lean muscled forearms and long, slender fingers. Nondescript white shirts and khakis never looked so good before, I swear.

The warm wind whips a few strands loose from my braid and ruffles Zac's hair, much longer now than it was last winter, the tousled look lending him a boyish charm tugging at my heart strings. Zac's full lips tug on one side. And I fall under just a little bit more.

He sits beside me, and we share a lunch, a fork, a laptop, and an animated discussion over the acuity of cordless probes versus wired ones, pocket Dopplers versus table top ones, digital or script monitors, and the best megahertz ratios. Zac's informed opinion is invaluable, as suspected, but most precious of all? I enjoy our undeniable subtext. A shared passion. The one behind animating the search for the best Doppler ... its usage.

Monitoring life conceived.

Zac's eyes are lit with unspoken excitement for birthing life—just like my own. It's a breath of fresh air talking to someone else who feels like I do about it. A kindred spirit.

I breathe in the moment, wishing time would stand still.

Cicadas sing. Crickets chirp.

Albert's leaves sway and rustle in the warm summer breeze.

All too soon, our time is almost up. I set the empty container aside and brush my pants off, steeling myself against the disappointment of having to leave already. Today went by way too fast.

Zac brushes a strand of hair behind my ear, and we get lost in each other's eyes in the space of a moment, or an eternity, I can't tell anymore. "I'd like to keep you with me," he murmurs as to himself, the words barely audible.

My breath grows shallow.

I lean in by a fraction. He leans in by another.

Three distinctive air horn blasts ring in the air, splintering the moment. We both straighten at once, abruptly brought back to reality. The ambulance rushes by us on its way up from the cross-road down below in the valley.

Zac's jaw clenches as he checks his watch, cursing under his breath.

"Are you late?" I ask concerned, hopping to it, closing my laptop.

"No, it's not that. I'll make it on time."

"Then what is it?" I ask softly.

Briefly looking up at the sky, he shakes his head, letting out a self-annoyed grunt, before looking me over. "I never had to deal with this type of frustration before," he admits. "I'm not good at this denying thing."

"Too much want, and not enough time," I tentatively say. And the idea that he wants this just as much as I do sends tingles straight into my core.

He rubs the back of his neck on a rueful sigh. "Yeah, that."

"Good news is, we're in the same boat." I sigh in sympathy, and his face softens as we gather the rest of our things.

"And the bad news is?" he asks, the hint of a smile now playing in his voice. He unrolls his shirt sleeves, buttoning them back at the wrists, his movements deft and precise. I stare at the muscles bunching and rippling along his forearms before they disappear from view.

"That we're on that boat," I quip back ruefully.

He takes a step closer and casually lifts his arm, placing his hand on Albert's trunk, beside my head.

"The good news is," his arm bends at the elbow and he's suddenly a whole lot closer, "I'm glad we are." I watch his lips spread into a slow, sensual smile. From this close, I can see tiny gold flecks shimmer in the depth of his coppery brown eyes.

I swallow. "And ... the bad news is?"

He leans a fraction closer, and I stand frozen as his stubble cheek grazes mine.

"That it's a bloody slow boat to China right now," he murmurs into my ear, and my heart flutters out of my chest. He takes a step back, his fingers brushing down my cheek. "See you tomorrow?"

Tomorrow? When is tomorrow again? Don't I have somewhere to be tomorrow, can't remember for now ... I nod, a bit dazed. He takes another step back, then another, his dark soulful eyes drawing me in.

"Wait," I say in earnest, stopping him in his tracks. "Would you mind terribly if I stick around for your little ones' follow-ups?"

Even if outside my realm of responsibilities, I'd like nothing more than to soak up some more hands-on experience, if only to observe the interactions and learn.

His face grows perplexed. "Don't you have a bunch of courses scheduled in the afternoons?" he asks in a puzzled tone.

"I don't anymore, all done," I say, my arms extending by my side in quiet bliss over the notion that it's now behind me.

"Are you saying all of your theory's over with?" His eyebrows lift.

"Mmhmm," I hum happily. "The only thing I have left to do is complete these clinical rotations and hand over my final thesis by the end of November at the latest, and voilà, fully licensed midwife." I gesture to myself.

He shakes in head in wonder, hands coming up on his hips. "For real?"

"Study is pretty much all I've done for the past six months." I shrug to make light of it, keeping for myself that one of the main reasons why stares me in the face, miraculously enough. "No big deal."

"No big deal, she says. You forget I've seen the syllabus," he says with something akin to awe in his voice, just before a slow grin creases his cheeks. He cocks his head to the side. "Mademoiselle Deslauriers, soon-to-be midwife, want to hang around the clinic for my follow-ups this afternoon?"

"Really? I'd love to!" I cry out, giving him a quick hug, but he holds on to me for a moment longer. Closing my eyes, I relish the sensation, inhaling his warm, clean musk.

My pulse picks up, letting it seep deep within me.

How am I to resist him? And is this what I really want? Not knowing what's it like to give it my all with him, even at the risk of being hurt? If I had regrets for a missed opportunity in the past six months alone, what kind of awful regrets will I harbor for the rest of my life if I refuse to take a chance and see where this thing between us goes?

He releases me, and the warmth in his eyes makes my chest expands. My heart thuds faster. "You got that wrong. It's the other way around. *I'd* love to. Really." He motions with his head. "Come on, we'll be just on time if we cut through the atrium." Taking my messenger bag, he hooks it over his shoulder, and we make a run for it.

My heart trips over itself and I'm breathless but not from running. It's him. Zac. Something about him and the way my heart seems to already know him. After months of resisting my body and heart, I give in to it. With a happy smile, I revel in the intoxicating sensation.

Eighteen

MAGALI

Zac and I make it back to the ward with no time to spare, skidding to a halt at the clinic's door. We slow down to a more dignified pace under Annie's scowl. Her thin-lipped mouth purses in a sourpuss expression, her forefinger pointing to her watch meaningfully.

"Magali, you're *not* on the payroll this afternoon," she mentions as an afterthought as we pass by her office.

"No worries. I volunteered." I scavenge a square of dark chocolate from one of my scrub pockets and double back. The paper foil oozes a bit of melted chocolate at the corner pinched between my thumb and forefinger. I pop in just long enough to put it on her desk. "Swiss, a personal favorite, try it." Annie blinks at it as though it might bite her, or worse, leak on her report. "It would be best if you wait for it to harden back before unwrapping it; it's pretty muggy out. Enjoy."

When I reach Zac, he bends close to my ear. "Are you trying to soften her disposition?"

"Nope, only sweeten it." He chuckles low.

The receptionist unlocks the outer door and a few patients trickle into the waiting room.

Inside the exam room, I mute the overhead lights and switch around the equipment for him. When all is set, I watch, utterly mesmerized, as Zac interacts with his first little patient on the afternoon's agenda of eight regular follow-ups on healthy babies.

Mélanie, six-week-old Julien's young mom, sits across the desk from Zac. One knee bouncing, she chews on her thumbnail. Julien sleeps on peacefully in his carry-on propped on the desk, his cupid bow mouth hidden behind a pacifier. I smile softly.

"So you'd say, every two hours?" Zac quietly asks. His left hand fluidly consigns in Julien's carnet de santé, the answers Mélanie gives.

You can tell a lot about someone just by observing their hands. The way they're shaped, the way they move, the language they speak. Zac's hands are a thing of beauty, spelling strength, guidance, care, and compassion in one gesture.

"Here, let me," Zac says, taking over from Julien's mom's nervous fingers, unbuckling tiny Julien from his carry-on, scooping him up. Zac's strong, self-assured hands cradle the infant to his chest; the same hands that welcomed him into the world.

"Hey, little man, you're awake now?" he asks, and Julien blinks into his eyes as he gently deposits him on the exam couch lined with the soft flannel cocoon expressly used for newborns. "It's been a few weeks already since we last met, hasn't it? Looks like you're doing great," he tells him in a soothing voice, unsnapping his short-sleeved onesie, as Mélanie hovers near, worrying her bottom lip.

"He spits up like a dozen times a day in between feedings, sometimes in a geyser. Is that normal?" she asks, her fingers fidgeting the hem of her stained, sleeveless blouse. I send her a quick, reassuring smile, and she gives me a weak, tired one in reply. She's around my age, and clearly on the verge of being overwhelmed.

"There's no reason to think otherwise at this point, but we'll make sure," Zac says, palpating Julien's tummy, warming the end of his stethoscope for auscultation.

I take two bundles of twelve muslin cotton diapers out of one of the credenzas, draping one over Mélanie's left shoulder. "They'll help you keep both the change of clothes and laundry down." I squeeze her shoulders in a side hug, giving them to her. "And I can't explain why exactly, but somehow, they always smell like baby powder no matter how sour the baby spit. Magic."

"Thank you," she says, looking down and her shoulders slump. "I took all the required prenatal courses, and you'd think I'd have a better handle on things. But well, ever since my mother-in-law's stay, I'm always second guessing everything now..."

"You're doing great," I reassure her, and she gives me a doubtful look. "I see it in Julien's eyes," I simply say, and it's like watching early sunrise the way her features light up with renewed confidence.

Zac's right hand automatically splays over Julien's body, anchoring him down while he awkwardly twists his torso. His left hand reaches over the equipment gurney for the wireless thermometer. His eyes land on the switched sides, giving him an easier access now, and he looks up at me, startled.

"I prepped them for you," I say quietly, gesturing with my left hand. Zac gifts me with a quick, dimpled smile, shaking his head at me.

All through his exam, Julien latches on to Zac's face, wide-eyed, cupid bow lips open-mouthed. And my heart cracks wide open upon witnessing the gentle way with which Zac's compassionate hands convey to Julien that he is safe and that all is right in his world.

Zac's an honest-to-goodness Baby Whisperer, and my heart fills up that much more.

"There's nothing to worry about for now, Mélanie." Zac brushes one hand down Julien's tummy one last time, before snapping back on his onesie. "His skin tone's excellent, and even though he's in the lower percentile in his growth chart, his weight-to-height ratio is normal, and his eyes are alert. Just be on the lookout for listlessness to be on the safe side, but otherwise, you should see a marked decrease in his reflux episodes over the coming months as his stomach matures some more, and his upper cardia closes. Right, buddy?" he asks, cradling the tiny baby in his powerful arms, and Julien's whole face beams up at him. "Now, I want you to keep that mindset next month when I give you your first inoculation, got that," Zac adds, buckling Julien back into his carry-on.

Mélanie's face, no longer tight with worry, relaxes into a genuine smile, before she thanks us profusely on her way out.

And that's pretty much how my afternoon goes.

I fall a little harder for Zac, one baby at a time ... And much too soon to my liking, there are none left to see.

Nineteen

ZAC

Leaning in the doorway separating the exam room and the office cubicle, I watch Magali. She's so beautiful. Her exquisite features replayed in my mind over and over again ever since that night, but nothing I imagined in the past six months comes close to her present radiance. She glows from within.

"You'll probably get a scolding for cleaning the room in lieu of the orderly," I say while she sprays disinfectant on the bottom shelf of the metal gurney, and wipes it clean.

"No, you'll get the scolding. I'm not scheduled to be here this afternoon," Magali tosses back, smoothing down a fresh layer of paper on the exam table, the crinkling sound echoing in the room.

"You trying to get me in trouble?" I ask, amused as she squeezes by me to gather her things. I probably could have moved aside but I wanted her to touch me.

"Absolutely," she says, picking up her messenger bag and brushing past me into the hall.

"I should warn you. I like trouble." I cut the light behind me, falling into step beside her.

"I already figured that." She shoots me a dry look, and I chuckle.

I want to know everything there is to know about her and I'm impatient as all hell on the best of days to begin with. How am I supposed to let her go home now, let alone for the next two days until our next rotation together?

We emerge from the clinic's corridor to a locked front door and dimmed lights, everyone gone for the night already. "Guess Annie didn't stick around to lay it on us for the few minutes of budget overrun."

"I had it covered." She walks over to Annie's desk, leaving another chocolate square on the memo pad, drawing a smiley face underneath.

I shake my head, utterly charmed.

"Do you need to stop by the locker room?" I ask while holding the connecting door open for Magali, hoping to buy just a few more minutes in her company. The fingers of my hand flex, fighting the urge to place them on the small of her back as we head down the hall leading away from the pediatric ward. Earlier on, at lunch time, she was kind of skittish about it and I could tell she doubted me still. Made me realize that letting her set the pace might be more of a challenge than I've ever encountered before. I take a deep breath. I'm in for the long haul, I remind myself. So I guess it will have to wait until I can convince her of such. I give her a sidelong glance. She's worth the wait.

"Nope. No need. Benefits of lunch dates," she replies, patting her messenger bag, "and hot, sultry July days." She gestures to her short-sleeved scrubs. "For a limited time only, no sweaters, no coats, no boots." She grins up at me, sidestepping two empty gurneys, stationed by the wall.

I know I should give her some space, but I can't get enough of her. I shove my hands in my front pockets, lest I grab her and make a run for it.

"Want to—"

"Would you—"

We both grin. "You first." She tilts her head, waiting.

"Want to go for a bite to eat?" I strive for a nonchalant tone, but it comes out rushed instead. Great, now I sound like a thirteen-year-old with a crush on her. What next, man. A note asking her if she likes you?

"Um ... like a dinner date?" she hesitantly asks.

"Any damn thing you want to call it." *I don't care as long as you say yes.* "Guess, I'm not ready to let you go just yet, but if you have other plans, I—"

"Well, I sort of did..." she interjects, stepping in front me, and the front atrium's doors swish open and she twirls out, shuffling backward for a few, tilting her head up to sky, arms wide open.

My heart thuds in my ears. Jesus, she's so gorgeous haloed out against the glow of the golden hour, or *l'heure douce,* as it is called here. How am I supposed to let her go if only for the night, not to mention for the next two days, and not think I dreamed it all?

"But I guess my catching up on some long-overdue reading on anything other than textbooks can wait a bit. Can I go change first before this dinner date?" She gestures to her scrubs, wrinkling her nose.

Her answer hits me in the chest, and I stop breathing. She's not ready to let me go either...

"Sure," I manage to say, but just as quickly frown on a new thought. Going back home to change? Up here, it's a pretty wide-open proposition, one that could mean anything from half an hour to two hours ... Doctors are required to live within a thirty minutes' drive from the hospital, but I don't know yet if Magali's status as a midwife comes with the same restrictions.

"You don't need to change at all. You're perfect as is." *Perfect for me*, I silently add, and she worries her bottom lip as though weighing her options. So, I push a little bit more. "I really don't want to put you out, driving back and forth. I thought we could hit one of the bistros by the lake, nothing fancy."

Sainte-Agathe-des-Monts is a small town by Lac des Sables, and the main street runs parallel to the south shore alongside a park, a beach, a dock, and marina, and a medley of retail stores and casual restaurants offering outside dining. Around summer solstice, l'heure douce lasts well past nine thirty at night with spectacular sunsets that go on forever. Who needs fancy in those conditions?

"I have a flat that's a ten-minute walk from here." She points to the hill behind her. "I really need to stop by my apartment first, and pick up Picolo from my neighbor," she says, checking her watch, backing away. "She'll worry otherwise. It's her first time babysitting, and I promised before bedtime. You can come with me or, if you prefer, I can meet up with you in half an hour or so."

"I'll give you a lift; come on," I reply, swivelling her in the other direction. Like hell I'll miss this opportunity. "Picolo's your pet or something?" I ask on our way to the staff parking lot.

"Or something." She holds in a laugh, eyes twinkling, but she doesn't elaborate. I seem to be missing out on the joke, here. I raise a brow in inquiry, and she gives me an innocent little shrug.

"Guess I'll know soon enough," I say, palming my car keys.

"Guess you will," she says, her lips tugging up one side.

Grabbing hold of my arm, she stops us dead in our tracks when we reach the last row of cars, where my Jeep is parked. "Wait..."

Her widening eyes dart between my Jeep, a Dodge minivan, and a Mercedes Benz parked beside it on one side, and an Alfa Romeo, a Volvo, and two Subaru's on the other. "Which one is yours?" she asks, her face wearing an arrested look.

"At least, you didn't pick the minivan right off the bat," I say, shaking my head, thinking of the ribbing I'd get from the guys if I ever were to drive one.

She chokes on a little snort. "I'd pick the Alfa Romeo, but I promised myself just this morning that I wouldn't make any other assumptions based on circumstantial evidence alone," she retorts drily. I chuckle, appreciating her sharp wit and the way she completely owns up to that night with grace and humor. Now it's up to me to do the same.

"Good to know I won't have to live up to any of those then." I unlock the Jeep's passenger door, cocking my head, waiting for her reaction, curious.

"Of course." She lets out a peal of laughter, tilting her head up to the sky. "He drives the Jeep."

"Do I want to know?" I ask, basking in the afterglow of her dimpled smile as she plops down on the seat, facing me, both feet still planted on the tarmac. I brace my hands on the upper crash bars, hovering over her.

"You're an interesting man, Zac di Fiori," she says, looking up, "and you'll know soon enough." She chuckles under her breath.

"In that case." I lean so close, my lips are practically brushing over her cheek, and I revel in her sharp intake of breath. My fingers trail down a trace of goose bumps all the way to her left wrist, stopping there. "Let's keep it interesting, shall we, and lose the watch." I straighten, pocketing it, hard pressed not to laugh at the incredulous look washing over her face.

"My, my," I say, "speechless, mademoiselle Deslauriers?"

She soon recovers from her initial surprise, and we banter back and forth on the short drive over to her place. And man, I love this organic ease we have going on, here. I could talk with her for hours, and it still wouldn't be enough. I follow her directions up a meandering avenue lined with small bungalows tucked away from the road.

"Okay, it's the next one to your right," she says.

I turn up her drive and cut the engine.

"No way." I bark out a laugh. "Yours?" I stare at a carbon copy of my matte charcoal-grey Jeep, Willis Edition, parked by the side entrance.

"I know, right?" she says, shaking her head at me.

Before I can further comment on that, the door of the bungalow swings open and a little tornado runs down the drive, calling out her name. Magali comes out and meets her halfway.

"Hey, Cassandre." She hugs the brown-haired pigtailed little girl, at a guess, not much older than six years old, mindful of the neon-pink arm cast she wears on her right side. Not an easy feat, considering she carries a well-loved, woolly looking brown teddy bear, half as tall as she is.

Magali crouches in front of her. "Did Picolo give you any trouble today?" she asks, softly brushing back Cassandre's bangs, revealing a stapled cut along the hairline.

I get out, leaning back on the Jeep's door. Crossing my ankles, I tuck my hands in the front pockets of my khakis, unashamedly eavesdropping. So little Cassandre with a broken arm and healing cut is Magali's babysitter? Explains the before-bedtime curfew, but not exactly what kind of pet, *or something,* she needs a six-year-old babysitter for.

"He didn't climb any trees. He won't anymore, ever, ever, because of what happened to me," Cassandre says to Magali in one breath.

"I'm so glad to hear that. So, no trouble all day?"

"Well, just a little, at nap time," she admits in all seriousness.

"Let me guess." Magali sighs in a commiserating tone. "He didn't want to nap."

"No, and he was growly. Said he wanted to go to summer camp, not take naps. So I told him a story just like you told me to. I did, I did, and it worked! We both slept for hours, Mamie said, like I'm supposed to," she says in an excited voice, and upon spying me, she grows wide-eyed. "He's Picolo's papa?"

I blink. *What?*

Magali takes it in stride, though, confirming it to Cassandre, before shooting me an impish look over her shoulder. "Guess the eye color gave you away," she says, beaming, and I just shake my head at her.

I look down, thinking of San Alessio and the story of my mom's lover, the royal pilot, my biological father. Wouldn't be the first time my eye color gave me away...

"Cassandre," a grandmotherly woman wiping her hands on her apron beckons the little girl from the screened door. "Give Picolo back to Magali, and say goodnight so that she can put him to bed too. Bath time, ma cocotte."

"Coming, Mamie." The little girl drops a loud, smooching kiss on top of her teddy bear's head, squeezing him to death in a one-arm hug. "Pleasepleaseplease, can I babysit Picolo again? He really really liked it today." Her big brown eyes entreat Magali before her good arm relinquishes...

Picolos's the stuffed bear?

Magali, by now sitting on her heels, plops him on her lap, dipping her head down as she attentively listens to the teddy bear whispering in her ear. Her eyebrows lift and she tilts her head. "You do?" she asks him, making sure, and he nods. "Okay, I'll ask."

Christ, she's adorable. I swallow, utterly caught in all that she is, and something snug unfurls deeper in my chest.

"You know what, Cassandre? Picolo says you're the best babysitter he ever had, and he'd like to stay with you tomorrow instead of coming with me. The only thing is, I'll be away late, and well, Picolo usually hates sleeping away from me but he really really likes you, and he says he won't miss me as much tomorrow night if he's with you. Can you two have a sleepover, you think?"

My hand rubs down my jaw, pondering. So, she'll be away late tomorrow, then? Where? Doing what? With whom, some other guy? And what in the hell is that god-awful squeeze in my chest making me feel like I just swallowed a spoonful of molten lava?

I eye the old-fashioned teddy bear, all arms and legs cuddled up to her chest, his face split into a beatific grin ear to ear. Yeah, mate, I hear you. I'd wear one of those too right about now if we were to trade places, and I'd hate sleeping away from her too, given half the chance. Jesus, why does tomorrow feels like an eternity without her stretching in front of me...

"Yesyesyesyes," the little girl squeals, jumping up and down. "Mamie, Mamie, Picolo's coming back tomorrow, and we'll have a sleepover. It'll be just like summer camp."

She gives Magali a quick hug goodbye, sending me a small, shy wave. I wink, and she giggles, running back up the drive in a whirlwind. She gives us one last wave at the door and Magali blows her a kiss, and her grandmother mouths "thank you," over her head before shutting the door behind them.

Magali straightens and sighs in a blissful way. Her eyelids half-closing, her whole face a study in sensuality as she breathes in the warm, gentle summer breeze ruffling through the leaves. She turns to me, a new softness in her eyes. "I won't be long. Do you want to wait outside, or help me put your son to bed?" she asks without missing a beat.

Not waiting for an answer, she pushes her messenger bag up her shoulder, anchoring the bear up on her hip, kissing the top of his head as she heads toward the side entrance.

Jaw dropping, I watch her walk away. "Help you put my ... *son* to bed?" I cough out the last. Guess thinking it in jest and hearing it said aloud are two different things.

In that moment, I see it all in fast forward, and the images slam into me, leaving me reeling. The two of us coming back from a day of joint appointments, picking up the kids, sharing our days, sharing our nights, sharing our lives.

Love. Home. Family.

Magali.

And damn if the bear with whiskey-gold eyes the exact same shade of mine doesn't smirk at me from his perch on her hip as she marches up the drive.

The yearning washes over me in a tidal wave, and something snaps. One minute I'm leaning on my Jeep, and the next, I catch up to her as she unlocks her door. Stepping in, I slam it shut with my heel, backing her up against her front door.

The bear hits the floor with a dull thud.

"Zac..." Magali whispers. Her eyes drop to my lips, whetting hers, and every single part of me surges with awareness.

I tuck a stray hair behind her ear and tilt her chin up. "God, you're so lovely." My hands cup her face, my thumbs stroking her cheeks.

Magali shivers in response to my touch. Her eyes darken to pewter grey as she leans into my palm, and I can feel the rapid rise and fall of her chest, or is it mine?

My head dips, and my lips graze her jaw, the corner of her mouth.

She whimpers and stretches on her toes, burrowing her fingers in my hair, pressing her chest into mine.

With a hungry groan, my mouth descends on her, and in the next instant, our lips seal in a scorching kiss etching itself onto my soul.

I stand on the edge of a cliff, and I know in that exact moment there's no turning back; the only way forward is to jump.

I let myself freefall into our kiss. The taste, like ... coming home.

Twenty

ZAC

The entire universe has been reduced to the silkiness of Magali's skin under my palms, her lips under my lips, her mouth soft and supple as she gives it back stroke for stroke.

I cup her bottom, lifting her up against the door, and her legs lock around my waist as she arches into me, and she still isn't close enough. I want her against me, on top of me, under me, all over me.

The air crackles with electricity.

I increase the pressure against her lips, and a restrained moan builds in my throat as her tongue seeks mine. My erection rages hard as my hips grind into her, and she gives as good as she gets.

The kiss deepens, and I'm enveloped by her taste, her smell, her touch, her feel, fueling my overwhelming desire to make her mine, be as one with her.

Magali.

Everything inside me tightens.

I get so lost in the kiss that I find it harder and harder to breathe.

I don't want a quick lay up against the door though, and that's what we're headed for, in about thirty seconds from now if I don't slow us down. But I can't make myself stop, not just yet. I need this too much; it's been too long.

Without breaking the kiss, my hands fumble with the buttonholes fastening her scrubs' neckline. Giving up, I tear it open, the three buttons popping off and hitting the hardwood at our feet with a clink. My fingers skim over the silken-soft skin of her bare shoulders, down her chest. She gasps into my mouth as my hands cup her, pushing inside the lacy fabric of her bra. Nearly shaking with need, I palm her small, perfectly soft breasts, stroking my thumbs over and around her beaded nipples. Magali's head drops back on a low moan. Her eyes close as my lips and teeth nip their way down to the crook of her neck, her mewls getting me high, intoxicating me.

At some point, my brain registers a persistent buzzing sound at our feet that can no longer be ignored.

My muscles lock into place, and we both grow still. "Do you need to take the call?" I pant in her ear.

"Call...?" she asks, leaning on me, her eyes a little unfocused. Her spine grows rigid and her head snaps back up, thumping against the door. "Oh no, it's late and I totally forgot to call." She grabs hold of my forearms, unlocking her legs, and as she slides off me, I mourn the loss. "He'll worry needlessly now that I didn't pick it up. I need to call him back," she says, worry and loving concern lacing her voice.

"Who's *he*...?" I drop my forehead on hers, trying to control both my ragged breathing and the surge of hot-white coals of jealousy now burning a hole through my gut. *Jesus, man, cool it.* I breathe through my nose, and lean away.

"Mon Papa," she murmurs, and I exhale on a long swoosh. She searches my eyes, and I don't know what emotions are swimming in mine, but she adds, "They're away on a road trip through Charlevoix and La Basse Côte Nord and they'll be out of cell range by tomorrow. I promised I'd call by the end of this afternoon to let them know how my first day went. And even discounting me being me, it's late, and if I don't call back, they'll try again every fifteen minutes or so, worrying something happened to me. I swear checking in like this is not the usual with my parents..."

"I ... never really had any parents myself, so I wouldn't know all that much what's the usual anyway," I say, but even as I say it, I think of Vie and Grégoire, and our long chat by the bivouac last winter ... Vie telling me, "You're never too old for a mom thing." Maybe Magali's parental concern is normal for her, but it sure as hell isn't normal where the guys and I come from.

And as though reading my mind, Magali whispers, "You can borrow mine any time you feel like it, with or without me in the picture." She gently brushes a lock of hair from my forehead, and I drink in the caress. Her fingers run through my hair, eliciting an involuntary shiver, and my eyes close on a new kind of bliss, savoring. I don't remember anyone ever touching me with such care and affection.

My eyes reopen, and I swallow a surprising lump in my throat. A new sense of protectiveness surges forth, making me fiercely glad that she grew up with caring parents instead of the void like I did. Magali's clear gaze searches mine.

Unable to resist, my fingers map the contours of her cheeks, down to her jaw, brushing her messy braid over her shoulder. "Go on. Call them now so they won't worry."

She gives me a hug. A hug. Me. "Make yourself at home. It won't take long."

"No hurry, take your time," I murmur, held under a spell, craving her warmth, her softness, the emotional connection. I'm on a new high, and it's turning out to be addictive, big time.

"Thanks, but knowing my Papa it really won't take all that long, and the rest of the evening will be ours." She presses a quick kiss on my cheek, and I give her hand a light squeeze before taking a step back.

She bends over, picking up the bear and her messenger bag.

"Sounds good to me," I say, distracted by the sight of her plunging neckline. Courtesy of my earlier lack of finesse popping her three buttons, I'm being afforded an unobstructed view down a butter-yellow bra, and her perky breasts with dusty pink nipples peeking through the lacy thing. And that's all it takes for my fingers to flex, my mouth suddenly dry, my reactions on a hair trigger. *Jesus, get a grip.*

Remember she's in charge of the pace, here, man, it won't do to back her up against the door and dry hump her like you just did, caveman style. She really has no idea what she does to me, and I don't either ... I never had any problems controlling my reactions before. I discreetly readjust, following her farther inside. Turns out, her flat is an open-room loft. One tiny room with a futon bed stretched wall to wall at the bottom of the stairs. I swallow to wet my throat. Must. Slow. Down.

I lean a shoulder against the kitchen pantry while Magali places her call. It's either that, or plop my ass down to sit on the bed.

"Papa, guess what?" Her features brighten as she recaps her morning in a few words, and when she comes to her afternoon, wow. She beams up, her face glowing as she raves about the babies, and how exceptional her maître de stage is for letting her stay and observe. Pretty sure it's the other way around. She's the one who made my afternoon that much more exceptional. Makes me wonder why she didn't choose to specialize in neonatal care, though. But then I get distracted anew as she braces her elbows on the counter by the sink, looking out the kitchen window as she listens to her dad.

I busy myself filling up a glass of tap water.

My eyes stray to the curve of her hips on display, and the arch of her backside, perfectly angled for...

I rub the back of my neck, my skin dotting with beads of sweat that have little to do with tonight's muggy temperature. I wipe my forehead with the back of my hand, doing my best not to lose focus. I will my eyes to stay put on the kitchen cabinets, and not on the unmade bed, wrapped in citrusy scented sheets.

I take a long draught of water, giving me something else to do besides staring at her, or the bed. No jumping her bones, I remind myself, guzzling down a few more swallows. *Unless she decides she wants to sooner rather than later.*

The bear, propped on the floor next to the fridge, gives me a look. Hey, come on, bud. Give me a break, will you? I'm flying by the seat of my pants here. The bear looks on, not in the least impressed. "Don't give me that look. I know I don't have a very good track record but I want more than just sex, got that?" I tell him, crossing my arms.

Magali gives me a wide-eyed look. She claps a hand over her mouth to reign in a muffled snort of surprise, her eyes darting between me and the bear. *Did I just talk out loud to the goddamn bear?*

"Non, non ça va. A special friend at my place having it out with Picolo, but by the look of things they're about to conclude," she tells her father.

Guess I did. Awesome. I rub one hand down my face. Well, this should make for an interesting meet the parents...

Shooting a glare at the bear, I swig down the rest of the water.

"No worries. He's totally safe from me, Papa. I'm not networking." She leans back on the counter. "I swear I won't get him pregnant, unless he wants to," she deadpans, and I choke, water spewing out of my mouth. *Jesus.* I thump on my chest in a bid to recover as she chatters on, asking if they spotted any whales yet in Tadoussac.

I look around for something to wipe up my mess, and she hands over a tea towel left to dry by the kitchen sink without missing a beat.

I listen to the excitement in her voice. Whale watching in Tadoussac, must be pretty cool. That's near the St. Lawrence River estuary where it starts to meet the North Atlantic, if I recall some of the detailed flight maps I pored over. Maybe I'll take her there on our next day off...

"Love you too. See you at the end of the month, and kiss Maman for me." She ends the call on a soft smile, sliding her phone on the counter.

Coming up behind her, I brace my hands on either side, trapping her there. She stills. I slowly lean over one side to replace the towel by the sink and pick up her phone.

Her spine grows rigid.

"Just programming into it my confidential number ... Please, feel free to use it anytime." I slide it back on the counter, my torso pressing down on her. She inhales sharply, and fuck me if I don't relish her reaction to me.

My pulse leaps, inhaling the citrusy smell of her shampoo. I close my eyes for a brief second, fighting the urge to grab hold of her hips and grind into her.

"I wasn't completely off the mark on that night. A wee bit sure of yourself, aren't we?"

I frown, unsure. Am I? "Why? You'll *never* call me?"

She tips her head up, eyeing me over her shoulder with a catlike grin. "Saved by the 'please' you tacked in there and the fact I like you. A lot. Yes. I'll call. Eventually."

"I'll take it." My head dips close to her ear. "Speaking of calls, you won't get me pregnant unless I want to? We may have to review some basic biology in a private study session."

She chuckles low. She leans back on my chest, the back of her head coming to rest over my heart.

"Mon Papa, he was just teasing me." She shrugs, a smile lingering in her voice. "I may or may not have been carried away when I first received my acceptance letter into the program, seeing gorgeous babies in the making pretty much everywhere I looked. My Papa mentioned at the time that at the rate I was networking, I'd soon ran out of potential moms and I'd need to innovate ways for guys to get pregnant to supplement my supply and demand. It's sort of been a running gag ever since."

She looks up at me from over her shoulder with her big, guileless eyes framed by impossibly long, dark eyelashes. From this close, I see tiny specks of light green mixed into the pale grey of her irises, and I want to memorize every minute detail.

My arms tighten around her waist. "You got that wrong." My mouth lingers close to her ear, and I murmur, "It's the other way. You're not safe from me."

I turn her around so we're face to face, her palms coming to rest on my chest, over my heart. Their warmth seeps through the thin material of my shirt, sending tingles down my spine and my heart into overdrive. "That's what scares me," she whispers. "It's too late for safe."

I cup her face with my hands and brush my thumbs back and forth along her cheekbones. I can feel the rapid rise and fall of her chest against mine.

"I'm going to do whatever it takes for you to see I'm not going anywhere. Your call, your pace, remember?"

Her lips part, her eyes darkening to pewter, and it takes everything in me not to ravish her mouth on the spot, and the rest of her while at it. Releasing her from my hold, I take a reluctant step back. And another.

Pushing her past the point of no return up against the wall is not on the long-term focus list. It'd be easy to do so, I can read the signs, but I don't want any regrets, either. *She has to be the one initiating the first moves, clear-headed, cold sober, not punch drunk on kisses. Roger that?* I almost growl down at the uncooperative dick in my pants.

"You. Me. This. I've thought about you every day for the past six months," she says softly, her words washing over me like rain after a drought, flooding me with warmth, seeping deep into my soul. "The first couple of times I stood on top of the steepest freestyle ramp, I got so scared, I froze. When I finally pushed past the fear, I soared." She takes a step closer, her fingers brushing over my lips, trailing down my jaw. My breath grows shallow. "I want to embrace what you make me feel, falling fast and furious. Show me, Zac, what it feels like past the fear. Kiss me."

I drop my forehead to hers, panting a breath, close to undone.

"Magali, the way I feel right now? If we kiss, there will be no turning back. You sure?"

And before I know what hits me, her mouth crashes down on mine while both her hands fist on my shirt.

I'll take that as a yes.

Twenty-One

ZAC

how her? Man, she doesn't need to ask me twice. I'm more than willing to.

"Zac," she moans my name like a prayer as she mindlessly pulls at my shirt, and I grab it by the back of my collar, hardly breaking lip contact to whip it over my head, inside out, not bothering with unbuttoning it.

We both inhale a sharp breath as her smooth hands splay on my naked back, exploring, brushing up over my chest, down my abs. I almost flinch from the aching pleasure of her touch, twitching in my pants as heat arrows straight down my cock. Brushing her hands aside, I crush her to me while my tongue seeks hers and swoops in as she opens up for me.

I kiss her senseless, lips smashed, tongues diving as we paw at each other, shedding our clothes in a blur of hands and lips, until there is only skin standing between us. I may have lost all finesse, but Christ, I have never felt such an explosive mix of desires, sensations, emotions, and I can't seem to get enough. It's like we're possessed, lost in the feel of us.

She holds on as we kiss wildly for a minute longer, or an eternity, who knows, until we're both shaking with need, panting with want. I back away the two steps it takes for me to fall flat on my back on her bed, and she follows me down.

Heart pounding, I roll her beneath me, covering her body with mine, skin on skin. Heaven. Magali fits into me perfectly, like we've been molded for each other. I groan as my teeth nip the column of her throat on a downward path, the honey-flavored taste of her skin driving me wild. On a blissful moan, she clutches the back of my head as my tongue circles one nipple before my mouth latches on, and suckles on it.

"I've waited for a lifetime ... to feel this like this ... Please, more, now," she begs, devastating me.

I grit my teeth, fighting the urge to pound into her as she pushes her hips forward, moving rhythmically. My straining erection rubs flush against the plumpness of her mound, her whimpers driving me insane with lust. Half-delirious with need, I dip two of my fingers inside her body, feeling how silky wet she is, how ready she is for me. *So wet, so fucking wet.*

"Zac!" she cries out, chanting my name in a litany of want, her fingers flexing on my ass. I grab her hands and bring them up over her head, nowhere near ready for this to be over so quickly.

We still. Our shallow breaths are the only sound in the quiet of the room. Our explosive chemistry's an uncharted volatile combination, a first for me. My teeth clench as I try to control my raging hormones, so I'm not blowing in a nanosecond the minute I slide into her, when just at the thought of it, never mind doing it, droplets of pre-cum bead on my tip, leaking in pulsating waves.

Red light. Red light. Red light, my unplugged brain finally registers the warning signals blaring in the cockpit. And ... reality crashes down on me. "Fuck. Condom," I ground out, burying my face in the crook of her neck, panting like mad. I silently curse myself up and down. Not only didn't I think of putting on a condom, another bloody fucking first, but I don't have any condoms. Not one. A sobering fact, any way I look at it.

Magali whimpers, too far gone. She rocks into me, digging her heels, straining up. "Zac, I ... I ... now ... need..."

"I've got you, let go. I've got you." My thumb ghosting over her clit, I curl my fingers and push them to the hilt, giving it to her with slow, deep thrusts. The walls of her sex contract around them, her cry just about undoing me.

"Soon, Magali, so soon. I'll be buried deep inside you. So deep inside you, you won't know where I start and where you end, you understand?" My palm press down hard and my fingers pump twice. Her keening cry is music to my ears. "That's it, love, give yourself over. Let go for me. Now." I pump twice more, hard and fast, and that's all it takes to catapult her over the edge. She stiffens and cries out as her climax pulses around my stroking fingers, and I let her ride the crest to the other side, bringing her back gently. Christ, she's so gorgeous, inside out, she takes my breath away.

Her eyes slowly reopen with a look of wonder I've never seen on anyone's face. Not looking at me at any rate. My heart overflows, my emotions all over the place.

"It's ... an awesome feel ... Thank you," she whispers, awed. Totally given to the moment, unaware of her true beauty, she's a breath of fresh air, and my heart takes another hard tumble.

I roll her on top of me, kissing her temple. I don't know what to say for an answer, "My pleasure" much too tame for what I feel. I'm used to sophisticated women expecting me to perform at all times like some sort of sex god, and taking it as nothing less than their due. And here is Magali, filled with overwhelming pleasure and gratitude from such a quick, simple caress...

Her hands bracing on my pecs, she sighs in bliss as she sits back, straddling my hips. Her whole face is lit by a dreamy look and a sensual air of tousled I like seeing and intend to often. I lock eyes with her, bringing up to my nose the lucky fingers that got to be buried deep within the wet silk of her core a moment ago, inhaling her sweet musk before slowly, deliberately licking them off.

I'm fucking drunk on her.

I want my hands and lips all over her. I want her writhing underneath me. I want to drink in her cries of pleasure as I go down on her, over and over. I want ... I inhale a sharp breath as she sprinkles open-mouthed kisses down my pecs, down my abs, down ... My stomach clenches, as warm lips and fingers trail down, one of her hands cupping me.

I pull her up to my chest and roll her underneath me, but she protests. "Another time, promise. I'll let you touch me to your heart's content but I can't stand it just now; it's been too long."

"All the more reason—"

"No." I hold her narrowed gaze steady while my hands brush down her sides, anchoring her. "This is not about me." Her gaze trapped in mine, my mouth trails down her taut abdomen, my hands opening her to me. Magali shivers in response to my touch, and her eyes darken to pewter. Good.

My head slowly dips, ready to feast on her, but she gasps and pushes on my shoulders, locking her arms, halting me. "No, don't." She shakes her head, determined.

I still. "No, as in don't go there, too much too soon, or no, as in stop everything?" I ask, elbows bracing on the bed. I inwardly groan, willing myself to cool it down a notch or three.

"No, as in I won't let go this time unless you do. I want to feel all of this *with you*, not without you," she says, her eyes flashing with a glint of defiance.

"We will, but not tonight. As for you, you're not done yet, not even close." My hands curve underneath her ass and I lift her hips up. She pushes them down, squirming away. For such a small thing, she's surprisingly strong. "Magali, I want to be buried deep inside you when I let go with you the first time around."

"Then I'll wait too."

"Are you daring me not to make you come?" I raise a brow.

"Are you trying to force me to?" Her chin juts out.

Man, I don't know where's up and where's down. She completely throws me off my game in unexpected and charming yet frustrating ways, and ... I love every minute of it, exhilarated like never before from this strange, new sense of intimacy and ease I find quite compelling, truth be known. "Are we really arguing about who gets to come and under what conditions?" I ask, making sure, a wry smile blooming on my lips at the thought.

"No, we're not arguing," she says, shooting me a pointed look. "*Yet*."

Conceding to her will, I say drily, "We'll wait. Roger Willco." And at her blank look, add, "My friends and I used to pepper our gaming sessions with Royal Air Force lingo as teenagers and it rolled off my tongue, just now ... Message received, will cooperate."

I release my hold on her, and she rolls on her stomach to pull out a bin from underneath the futon bed. "Good, then. What we need is to find something to take the edge off *and* satisfy the both of us." I blink, confused. "There's got to be one in there that's not expired yet," she mumbles to herself.

"Do I want to know?" My brows lift.

"Pharmacies close at seven on Mondays, and you don't want to know how far you'd need to drive for the next dépanneur or how long their limited inventory's been sitting on their shelves," she says in self-evidence.

"Dépanneur? That's a convenience store, right?"

She nods distractedly. Clearly she's on a mission of her own as she takes out a picture box frame and drops it on the bed, rummaging some more into the bin full of knickknacks. She brings out three glass containers of different heights. Old-school cookie jars closed by a metal lid, and filled with some colorful wrappings that look, oddly enough, like condoms ... But I'm no longer paying any attention, head thrown back, laughing.

Christ, only her ... The frame contains four rows of four condom foils, in four different shades of blue with a caption, reading, *in case of emergency, break the glass!*

"No use breaking the glass, those are long expired by now, but you can start looking through these." She sits back on her heels, handing me a cookie jar in all seriousness, and I can't stop laughing.

"Oops. No use." Her nose wrinkles and she takes it back. "Spermicidal lubricated condom samples. They only last two years in optimal storage conditions; they're done for." She hands me another. "Stop laughing, start looking."

"Wait, wait." I bark out another laugh, as she takes the third jar and upends it, combing through little foil squares. Her eyes squint, reading the date before throwing them back in haphazardly. I grab hold of her hand, stopping her mid-motion. She looks up a question in her eyes. "No, wait. I need to hear this ... really. You keep cookie jars full of expired condoms? Are you trying to populate the world or it's just that you ran out of time to use them all?"

"Neither, and just so you know, had I met you during my university years, not one of them would be expired by now, and I wouldn't be finishing my masters a year ahead of time."

"Is that so?" I lean up on my elbow, looking at her, pleased to no end somehow ... and I just know a shit-eating grin is spreading, splitting my face from one ear to the other.

"You're such a guy." Her eyes upturn, but she shakes her head at me with some indulgence. "Anyway, what I'm messing with here is not my practically non-existent sex life heretofore, *c'est de l'art déco*," she says the last on an exaggerated snobbishly professor tone, which is funny as all hell in its own way, seeing she's sitting there, all prim and proper, but naked as you please...

"Art deco?"

"Inspiration du moment, if you prefer." She shrugs innocently. "A direct result of my faculty being the most popular one quite a few years back with sex workshops we held throughout campus, along free samples."

Leaning forward, I ask, curious, "*Sex* workshops? You mean Safe Sex Ed, no?"

"No, sex seminars for clinical research purposes." She spreads out the condoms on the bottom sheet and quickly discards them, one after the other, her forehead creasing in concentration.

"And by free samples, you mean...?" One of my brow angles, and I look at her pointedly.

She looks up. Growing wide-eyed, her jaw drops open and she backhands me on the thigh. "Not what you think! Free condom samples, and a questionnaire."

I grin, enjoying messing with her.

"The faculty was part of a data gathering group and it gave us extra credits. And you'd be surprised at the number of guys who don't even know how to use condoms properly." She shakes her head in disbelief. "I was floored not one in my beta group had admittedly ever read the instructions. Ripping it open with your teeth? Come on, and you're worried by the probabilities of needle's prick? Keeping one in your wallet, just in case? In your car? Hello, this is sensitive material. Don't even think of using it safely after a week. Not checking the expiry date on the gazillion boxes you got in a liquidation sale? You mean *it has* an expiry date? Yes, it does! And that's what we're checking for right now."

Still chuckling, I pick a handful of foils in the one I've been given, wondering what's behind the jars. "Why cookie jars?"

"That's all Amélie's doing. My leftovers used to drive her nuts, she'd find bunches all over our room," she says with fondness, diligently sifting through foils, totally unassuming, unconcerned by her state of disheveled, and nudity. Her cramped quarters are really starting to grow on me; seems like living on a wall-to-wall bed breeds spontaneity and implicit intimacy. I'll take it.

"Who's Amélie?" I ask.

"My BFFF, or best friend from forever," she says on a lilt, and the fierce concentration lines tightening her features soften. "Amélie's crazy creative. She's the mastermind behind my magnets if you're wondering. Same natural flair as my mom in home decor and arts and crafts, and they both can't stand living in a bland space, or chaos. We usually run in the other direction if they're both let loose in a room, but the results are off the charts when they're done. We were born on the same day, and we often joke that we were switched at birth, à l'évidence," she says in a self-deprecating tone as one hand gestures in a grand sweeping motion to her bare white-on-white walls and tiny loft, with its unmade bed and mess of papers and books strewn about.

"Except, I have my father's eyes as proof to the contrary."

Something else we have in common...

"Anyway, I digress, something I'm very good at." Her brow furrows anew, going back to her self-appointed task, finding the elusive, unexpired condom. "Do you know the French expression, *tremper son biscuit*?"

"*Dip your cookie?*" I let out a snort. "No. I've heard of a few others much more crude, but not this one." Something occurs to me, however, the picture not quite there. My eyes narrow in thought. "Not that what little Italian I still have in me is above smirching French lovers' reputation, but wouldn't softening a hard cookie by dipping it in milk defeat the whole purpose behind the euphemism?" I ask drily.

"I know, right?" She lets out an airy chuckle. "But the expression is from way back when sugar was at a premium, and a cookie was a rare treat. It was the ultimate sweet, and if dipped, made that much sweeter, and god knows why but it stuck through the ages, *ergo...*" Her head tilts to the side.

"The cookie jars." I shake mine, highly entertained.

"The cookie jars," she concurs on a small, infectious grin. "I'll need Amélie's help to redo the contents on the two we're messing with, though." She motions to the one left, untouched, still filled with condoms artistically displayed in color-coordinated layers in different shades of green tones, now that I take a closer look. She drops another handful of expired condoms back into her jar, half-filled already, and I haven't even started on mine yet. "She has a knack for transforming even the most mundane things into fun, quirky art, and our student apartment in Montréal was so cool because of it. A Dupré-Rousseau original. You saw her the night we met actually, flying off the ramp with me. Amélie's one hundred percent made of awesome, I'm pretty sure you'll like her."

"Pretty sure I will." *Just by the size of the smile you wear when you think of her.*

Enjoying this bubble out of time, and nowhere near ready to rejoin the rest of the world and go out in downtown Sainte-Agathe, I absently join in the search for the Condom of the Year on my side of the bed, just to make it last a little while longer. And wouldn't you know ... I hit pay dirt.

"Amélie and I, and some friends, are going to Montréal for the day tomorrow to see *Luzia*, the latest show from Le Cirque du Soleil," she says.

I look up from the handful of condoms I hold in my hand like the Holy Grail, my chest pinching in an odd squeeze at the reminder she'll be gone all day tomorrow...

"It's their last week performing that one under Le Grand Chapiteau in the Old Port before they go on their world tour. As usual, they're sold out, but a friend of a friend works there and we have a few extra tickets available. Want to come with?" she asks in earnest, her expression soft and hopeful.

And, man, am I ever torn having to decline. Not that being on call as an obstetrician up here gets a lot of traffic in the ER, but still. "I wish, but I can't. I have to stay in the area. I'm on call."

"Oh, that's right. I forgot," she says in a small, despondent voice, looking down. Her shoulders sag. "It's just one day, why does it feel like an eternity all of a sudden?" she asks, and my breath catches.

Heart rate at a rapid stutter, I tip her chin up, the back of my fingers trailing down her cheek. "It does, doesn't it?" I ask softly.

We stare at one another for a long moment.

"You, here, feeling this," she murmurs. "I never really thought I'd ever see you again. I'm afraid I dreamed while awake all day today, and that you'll disappear by tomorrow."

"Don't count on it. I met this girl last winter at Mont-Saint-Sauveur, you see, and she made a lasting impression on me. I came back to look for her."

"You ... did?" she asks, unsure, but with a touch of wonder in her voice, as though she doesn't trust what she just heard.

"I did." My lips tugging up one side, I send a silent thank you to whatever deity out there who was responsible for tossing us together again. "That girl, she grounds me somehow, and exhilarates me at the same time. I had this grand plan to march up to her at Mont-Saint-Sauveur come next November, blacklisted and all, and not take no for an answer." Drawing her hands to my mouth, I kiss her knuckles. "So thank you for dropping by that much sooner, much obliged."

"Seriously?" she repeats twice, a slew of expressions playing on her features in quick succession, from stunned to delighted, and all the colors in between, up until her expression stills, and she wears an arrested look. "But ... what if I'd been..." she stutters, blinking.

"What if you'd been, what? In a relationship?" I ask, and her nose wrinkles.

"I was thinking more along the lines of what if I'd no longer been at the resort. But yeah, now that you mention it, what if I'd been in a relationship?" She tilts her head, a pensive look crossing over her face.

"Magali, seriously, I don't think it would have made that much difference. Honestly, with that kind of spark, and pull? I would have pursued you regardless. But if it makes you feel better, I was willing to take my chances on a calculated risk. After you left that night, that other guy, Cédric, did let on that he had never seen you react this strongly before."

"CD?" She leans away, a question in her eyes. "What else did he mention?"

"Not much else. You left the both of us kind of slack-jawed up there."

"I'm truly sorry," she says, her voice growing contrite all over again.

"Hey, none of that, now." I tuck a stray hair behind her ear. "Some of what you said wasn't that far off the mark, and it made me take a hard look at my life and decide on a few changes, for the better." I run my fingers on her brow to smooth out the worry lines creasing her forehead.

"It did?" she asks, tentative.

"It did."

She lets out a pent-up breath. "I really felt bad the following morning, sort of two sizes too small in my own skin. But I can't help but think it's a wonder we met at all just now. Even if I hadn't resigned a few weeks ahead of time, it was still my last season as a patroller down at Mont-Saint-Sauveur, in any case. You wouldn't have found me there."

"Not finding you at the resort? I would have hunted down that Cédric guy on the slopes, day in, day out."

"You would have?"

"Damn straight."

Our eyes meet, and the soft, hazy look in hers makes my heart turn over.

"You don't know what it does to me to hear you say that?" She breathes in, briefly closing her eyes. "I usually listen to my gut feelings. They've never steered me wrong, and I trampled all over them that night. Ever since, I've had to live with regrets for a missed opportunity I was sure wouldn't come along twice."

I let my fingers trail down her jaw, cupping her cheek. "Well, considering the odds of you walking in on me, here, maybe," I bend low and murmur into her ear, "just maybe, it's quite simply that we were meant to be."

She leans into my touch. "Do you believe in love at first sight?" Her warm gaze searches mine.

"Do you?" I ask, her eyes silver pools of light I could so easily drown in.

She drops a tender, heartfelt kiss at the corner of my lips, and I stop breathing, absorbing her gentle touch.

"I do. I absolutely do," she says with quiet conviction, entrancing me.

Needing her warmth, needing her softness, needing to taste her again, I pull her up to my chest. My hands come up to her face, and my head leans forward.

"So do I."

"I believe I'm falling in love with you, Zac di Fiori," she whispers on my lips just before my mouth seeks hers.

I believe I'm falling in love with you too.

In the space of the next heartbeat, I'm gone. I've lost my heart, and found myself.

Twenty-Two

ZAC

I believe I'm falling in love with you, Zac di Fiori.

The powerful words play on a loop in my mind, inscribing on my soul, filling every raw, hollow part of me with warmth.

I lay her down on the bed, and my eyes close, savouring the sweetness of our kisses. Our earlier frenzy is nowhere in sight, replaced by an unhurried exploration of soft lips and hands on a slow burn, as though infinity now stretches in front us. Is that what forever tastes like?

I bring my fingers up, skimming them along the satiny skin of her chest, trailing them down her taut abdomen. She stretches out in a sensual move, eyes closed, humming in bliss.

"You're so beautiful." I gaze down at her, unable to recall a time when I'd been more aware of someone else.

She shakes her head, bringing my palm to cup her cheek. "It's this, us. It makes me feel beautiful."

My head dips and I nuzzle her neck; she sighs dreamily. "No you're beautiful all on your own," I tell her.

"Are we arguing again?" she whispers.

"With you? I wouldn't dare." My lips quirk up in a shameless grin. "Not if we can make out instead."

"You're dangerous," she groans, her fingers tracing my lips. "I know the mechanics of sex and reproduction in minute scientific details, but not this layer of emotions adding to it, and the feel is so crazy addictive. The more we kiss the less I care that we're lying down on top of a pile of useless condoms, which is saying something. We *have* to get dress and out of here, or I'm about to land us in big trouble." She scoots away, sitting up.

I take her hand and close her fingers over one of the foils I found still within its expiration date. "You decide where tonight goes, Magali."

She looks at the little square and, when realization dawns, her face brightens like the rise of the sun on a new day.

"All the way," she whispers, excitement thrumming in her voice. Her lips spread into a slow, voluptuous smile as she delicately tears the wrapping open, offering it to me. Her eyes are so intent on my full erection that I have to concentrate on rolling the condom into place, and not dive for her.

I tip her head up. "No turning back. I can wait, so please be sure," I say, my voice rough around the edges, my pulse pounding in my ears.

"I can't wait to feel this, *with you*." Her hands push back on my shoulders and, falling on top of me, she presses a string of open-mouthed kisses where my shoulder and neck meet. My hands curve on her ass, pinning her down against me. She whimpers. Moving her hips seductively, the wet softness of her core glides over my straining erection. The scent of her musk fills the air and a shiver of pure lust arches down my spine.

Growling deep in my throat, I roll on top. Her small breasts flattening against my chest send an ache of pleasure through me.

Her hips thrust forward while her teeth nip my bottom lip. My mouth swoops down, and in no time, we're lost in a world of sensations where deep moans, brought forth by every little touch against our skin, and our shallow breaths are the only sounds registering.

I set my palms on the mattress to brace myself.

"You with me?" I ask, barely pushing forward, the crown of my cock fitting just inside her silken wet entrance, waiting. My forehead dots with beads of sweat, and my arms tremble with the effort to hold still, while she squirms, arching into me, her breath coming out in short pants.

"Open your eyes, Magali," I enjoin, my voice urgent. She reopens them and I see all I need to know. She's totally, gloriously here with me. "Mine," I grit through my teeth, gliding to the hilt in one thrust, and we both suck in a breath.

"Yours," she breathes out on a long exhale and the look of pure ecstasy washing over her face almost makes me lose it.

I clutch her to me, lifting my hips to pump into her, so tight, so wet, so ... given to the moment.

I pull out of her slowly, coming to a halt just before I pull free, and then push back in, a little faster, a little harder. On a low moan, she wraps her legs around me, and I surge deeper within her, and it's still not enough. I grab her bottom to bind us together as tightly as possible, until we're as close to becoming one body as two people can get. I'm flying, the feel of her, in tune, the both of us given, heart, body and soul, so bloody amazing. My tongue tangling with hers, I thrust hard, I thrust slow, I thrust in long deeply arched moves and all the tempo in between, until she stiffens around me and her toes curl on the back of my legs.

"I've got you, let go with me. Come," I whisper, my teeth clenching, just about ready to come out of my skin from the exquisite squeeze she exerts. "Now," I ground out, my thumb pressing down hard on her clit.

"Zaaac," she screams my name, her sex flooding and pulsating around me. My cock tightens, and I feel my release bursting, pulsing in waves, emptying as we ride our orgasms together, my own guttural cry muffled in the pillow by her neck.

Holy freaking hell. I collapse on her, full weight, totally fucking spent for the first time in forever, my brains fried, and for some unfathomable reason, my hard-on is as stiff as ever.

"I ... I..." I have no words. She blew my world and all of my previous conceptions about sex out of the water.

Our racing hearts and panting breaths quieting, she squirms, shaking back some sense into me.

I start to roll off her, but she holds on tight, digging her heels on my ass.

"No, please. I love the feel of you just like this. Stay a little bit longer?" she whispers in a throaty voice, sexy as all hell. I grow from taut to tauter, and from ready again, to readier.

A shiver courses through me as the soles of Magali's feet brush down my legs to the back of my ankles in a lazy back-and-forth motion. My eyes drift shut, memorizing the feel. I hold her tighter, resting my cheek against the top of her head.

I could stay thus forever without complaint.

This girl owns me.

"I don't know how to tell you this..." she says after a minute, her tone indecipherable.

"Too heavy?" I brace on my elbows, and start to disengage.

"Not exactly," she says on a slight wince. My brow quirks up. "I thought climaxing would soothe the urge for a little while, but all I can seem to focus on now is you buried deep inside me, and soaring off with you ... I think you created a monster, just so you know. You're in so much trouble."

Grinning wolfishly, I turn my hands until they imprison her wrists and bring them up over her head. "My kind of trouble," I murmur in her ear. "Let me get rid of the condom and I'll be right with you."

"But only after I eat something, or I'm likely to pass out otherwise. Aren't you hungry?" she asks, dropping a kiss on my shoulder.

"That's the thing about trouble, no passing out from hunger allowed, only from pleasure. Get dressed, I'll feed you." I hop out of bed and draw her up.

"Um ... Would you mind terribly if we stayed in, instead? We could eat in bed and just relax, talk, you know, go with the flow." Her arms loop around my waist, and, snuggling close, her cheek comes to rest over my heart. I sigh in pleasure, my arms enfolding her.

My head bends, and I murmur close to her ear, "Put that way, pretty sure I'd mind terribly if we got dressed and went out now." And I feel her smile curling on my chest. "I like the way you think. Count me in." I kiss her forehead before taking a step back. "Bathroom?"

"Behind sliding door number one, to your left. Bath towels on the middle shelf. You can't miss them, but I can't guarantee you'll have enough room in there to unfold one properly. Fair warning, it's nouveau water closet," she says, her eyes glinting.

"If I'm not back in two minutes, send a search party."

She giggles, and I revel in the happy sound, feeling lighthearted in a way I've never been before. Is this what happy feels like?

We take turns showering in the cedar-plank stall, putting a new spin on what I've known in some parts of Europe as WC toilets, or water closets. Nouveau water closet indeed.

I grunt, banging my elbow for the third time in a row. I don't think the shower stalls at Berlinger's early-childhood dormitories were that much smaller. My six-foot-tall frame fills up the entire space. Halfway through, I step out of the shower in order to turn on the other side, and go back in to rinse off, which effectively crosses out any wet soapy sex session I may have entertained. We'd need to be Cirque du Soleil acrobats to get it on in here, and even then.

Knotting my towel at the waist, I rub my hands briskly through my hair, sending droplets all over the painted wood-plank floor.

Across the room, Magali, her skin still dewy and flushed from her shower, pulls my dress shirt up over her head, inside out as I left it on the floor. Closing her eyes there for a minute, she breathes in the lapel on a long inhale. I pause, witnessing the soft glow washing over her face.

"Sorry, Pico, but you're standing between us and food. You need to move over." She picks Picolo up off the floor by the fridge and props him on one of her pillows.

"If you're trying to make me jealous, it's working. You really sleep with the bear?"

"Yep. Guilty as charged. We've been cuddling partners since my diaper years, and now you owe me two."

The bear eyes me with what I swear is a smug-looking grin. "Two what?" I ask.

"Guilty secrets," she says, leaning into me. One finger traces down my jaw, and I catch it, holding it close to my chest.

"I have a few," I say despite myself, as I never really talk about it; there's even some parts buried in there, the guys know nothing about. "But they're not of the sweet variety like yours are. Not by a long shot." A familiar heaviness now sits in the pit of my stomach like a rock at the bottom of a pond.

Unbidden, thoughts of my official father flit through my mind. His home, San Alessio, is a Mediterranean island the size of a postage stamp, and could probably fit twice into Monaco with room to spare, but still, the weight of his estate and title—some sort of Italian crowned prince—now rest on my shoulders. A weight that I want no part of, I sigh heavily. Theo is looking into freeing me from it, I remind myself, and will report any day now.

Her head tilts up. "I'm a good listener." Her voice is soft, a verbal caress.

My throat suddenly dry, I swallow a couple of times, tempted by the offer and yet, afraid to taint the beauty of her world with some ugly parts of mine. I glance down to where her fingers splay on my chest then back up at her face. "Maybe someday, I'll take you up on that offer..." I trail off into silence.

Her eyes drop to the column of my throat, flashing with some unreadable emotion, and then flit back up. "Offer stands whenever, no expiry date." Her stare moves over my face, full of strength and understanding, and I fall in love just a little harder.

"I ... thanks—"

Her stomach growls in protest, and mine echoes twice as loudly. Her eyes widen, but the timely rumbles effectively trump my untimely introspections.

"Food," we both say at the same time and end up snickering.

The tightness in my chest loosens and a strange new sense of well-being rolls in.

I follow her to the fridge and wait while she peers inside. "I have an interesting selection of leftovers to tempt you with. Looks like pasta salad, pasta salad, and some pasta salad. Which will it be?" she deadpans.

"And to think all I wanted was pasta salad, this sucks. How the hell will I choose now?"

"Beats me." She thwacks me on the thigh with the tea towel, and I stumble to the side, laughing.

Taking two plates from the cupboard, she hands them over before rummaging inside the fridge, selecting a stainless steel serving bowl filled to the brim. Man, she really did cook enough of the stuff to feed a small army, but she can sign me up for an army of one if it means staying in bed with her. I wouldn't mind eating it for breakfast, either.

Dusk comes and goes as we eat in bed, laughing, talking about everything and nothing, getting to know each other just that much more over a bottle of French Alsace Pinot Gris. I make a mental note to introduce her to some Italian Pinot Grigio at the first opportunity, less fruity, more body.

We swap hilarious anecdotes, hers from the Junior Freestyle Ski Team, and mine from my GGS crew, and other funny moments the six of us had, growing up at boarding school.

"Awww, that's so cute." One of her hands presses down on her chest. "But just how old were you, anyway, when you hid crickets in your dorm to save them from the cold?" Her brow angles in question as she sips on her wine. The symphony of crickets chirping into the night outside our window is what brought back to my mind that particular one.

"Cute?" I ask drily, shaking my head at the memory. "Did you forget the part where they escaped inside the walls, reproduced like crazy, and drove everyone nuts for a year or so?" I refill half her glass, emptying the last of the wine. "But in my defense, I didn't know any better at four years of age."

Her shoulders stiffen. "Your parents sent you away at boarding school full time when you were that young?" Her mouth drops open.

I put my fingertips under her chin, and close it back gently. "In a way."

She frowns. "What do you mean, in a way?"

I sigh. "They died in a plane crash and I was sent to boarding school." Swimming in unshed tears, her expressive eyes, filled with sorrow, search mine. "Don't. I'm okay with it. I never really knew them," I say quietly.

"But still, at four years of age? They board preschoolers full time at BIA?"

"No." I rub one hand down my face, unsure where to draw the line on too much information and not enough. I don't want to muddy the waters of our budding relationship by needlessly shaking the thick layer of silt lying at the bottom of my pond. "I ... started primary school over there in the second grade."

She tilts her head back. "You're a child prodigy?"

"Not even close." A humorless snort escapes from deep within my throat. "I had several tutors by age two."

She blinks owlishly. "By age two—Never mind." Her lips pinch in a thin line. "You don't have any other family?" She looks down as she cups one of my hands, her thumb brushing gently over my palm in a soothing caress, giving me goose bumps. I drink in the sensation.

"Nope. None whatsoever." *Thank god for that.* "The guys are the only family I've ever known." I glance down to where her fingers touch mine then back up at her face. "By age seven, they got the six of us rooming together, as we were the only ones in our level more or less on a twelve-month basis over there."

"It's ... kind of sad." She squeezes my hand.

"Why? I've never seen it that way." *Being sent to boarding school is what saved me.* "If you only knew how much better we had it being forgotten there, free of family obligations," I say.

"Family *obligations*?" Her brow wrinkles in confusion.

"Expectations, obligations, it's all the same. Ancient ones I grew up uncaring about." *Thank the fuck.* I swirl the wine in my glass, tossing it back. "There were lots of boys from European dynastic families at BIA, so we had it way better than most over there. Anyway, BIA isn't exactly an Oliver Twist kind of place. Was it an idyllic childhood? No. We used to dream about what normal would be like, *but*, normal aside, we were more than well cared for and, all in all, we had a grand time over there." *A grand time, thanks to Liam's Tales from the Enchanted Forest of Laure that started it all.* My face softens on a quiet smile.

"It's evident from the way you talk about it, and I'm so glad you did." She drops a light kiss on my shoulder.

"So am I."

Having seen the bottom of the bottle, she takes my empty glass and puts it down beside the bed, next to hers.

The first quarter moon shines down on us, bathing the room in low light. A warm summer breeze skims down our skin from the wide-open window and ruffles our hair, cooling us as night settles. I lean back on the half-wall, propped on pillows, my arm inviting her in. I kiss the top of Magali's head, nestled into the crook of my neck as we lay, side by side, half sitting, half sprawled, my arm casually draped over her.

I tilt my head up to watch the northern night sky, satiny white with stars, something I never get tired of looking at. "Now I see why you shoved the futon underneath the window."

"During my years in exile in Montréal I used to long for this," she says dreamily. "A dark starry night on a wide-open window, letting in this pure clean breeze carrying the smell of the evergreens."

"You didn't like living in Montréal?"

"I liked it well enough as a temporary place to be, I suppose. Knowing it was only a means to an end made it easier," she says on a light shrug. "I can't complain, though. Montréal is a pretty cool city for a city, lots to do and see, considering. It's just that when I'm over there, I feel disconnected. That place isn't *home*, you know?"

"Huh ... no. No, I don't actually." I rub the back of my neck, and sigh.

She looks up, her expression growing sorrowful. "I'm ... so sorry ... You never really had a home, did you?"

I kiss her forehead. "It's my first time putting down roots anywhere," I reply quietly.

"There's a 'but' in there somewhere," she says softly, waiting.

She knows me well, already. I glance up at the sky, contemplating how to put it into words. "I don't have a very good track record of staying put." My jaw tightens. "The kicker is, all through medical school, I was so sure the non-conformist in me and the rest of my contradictions right along with it would find working for Doctors Without Borders my calling, *the ultimate me*." I let out a derisive snort. "I toughed it out for a little over a year, but it didn't take me more than two months to realize that it was nowhere near what I thought it would be, and that I wasn't cut out for it. I felt powerless just about every goddamn minute of every day, to the point I couldn't even see the little victories. It killed me." I thump my head on the wall and sigh heavily.

The back of her hand brushes down my cheek, coming to rest over my chest, her gesture comforting. I bring her palm back up on my cheek, cradling her hand, enjoying the feel of her warm fingers. Her, us, this intimacy we share, it grounds me, and I voice my biggest concern. "I've never felt that level of contentment before, like all my scattered pieces belong somehow in this wide-open space, and I love it. I've never felt at home anywhere, Magali. I hope it's here. But there's this inner rebel in me ... I won't lie. I hate having my hands tied up, and already at the clinic I've felt a few hard twitches toward the bureaucracy bogging it down."

"And it worries you," she states quietly, interlacing our fingers.

"It worries me."

"Isn't it a good kind of worry, though?" She squeezes my hand, encouragingly.

"Meaning?" I lean back, unsure what she means by a good kind of worry, or if there is such a thing.

Her fingers trail down my jaw. "Just maybe it means that all your scattered pieces made it home and your inner rebel is at peace, having found something worth fighting for."

Her eyes flit back up to mine, and I'm hit by a loving blaze of liquid silver. It's like a sucker-punch to the chest.

Her words etch on my soul, smoothing a few of its ragged edges, shifting my fear into a whole new perspective, a positive one. One I can work with.

"How did you get to be so wise?" I ask, my tone a little awed despite myself.

"I have two older brothers who'd beg to differ on that one," she says wryly. "But my Papa would be so pleased to hear you say that. If you only knew the number of times he sat me down for similar talks over the years. Yet, here you are, getting it the first go-around. You're one to talk." Her eyes are soft, filled with an inner glow.

"You'll have to tell me sometime how you got there. As for me, older, certainly not wiser, and a lot of catching up to do will make a guy hop to it."

I angle my head and kiss her; an all-possessive, heart-stopping kiss, until we're both shaking with need.

We let our bodies exult to whispered words of love, our joining excruciatingly slow and gloriously pleasurable.

"Can you stay until morning?" she asks softly in the dark, much later. Our erratic heartbeats slowing down, our sweat-slick bodies cooling off, her hands stroking my back lazily.

"You'll have to kick me out," I mumble into her hair, and I just love hearing the sound of her airy light chuckle, her breath tickling my neck.

"It's the other way around. You took my watch, remember?"

My lips quirk up one side.

"Come here, you." I pull her to me.

She curls in, her cheek coming to rest on my chest, her hand settling over my heart, organically fitting one into another.

"*Best* cuddling partner *ever*," she vows, her voice drowsy and full of contentment.

"Best ever," I agree quietly.

In the low light, the bear shoots me a glare from the foot of the bed. Hey, bud, no hard feelings, c'est la vie.

Soon, her breaths grow even and her hand goes slack, lying over my heart.

Careful not to jostle her away from my chest, I grab hold of the top sheet with my toes, inching it upward until my hand reaches the hem, and I pull it up to cover the both of us, tucking her in.

I close my eyes and drift off to sleep with my arms enfolding her.

And I just know that this, this is what happy feels like.

Twenty-Three

ZAC

A ray of morning sun wakes me and, to my surprise, not only did I sleep without waking once, but I'm still pretty much in the same position I fell asleep in, Magali spooned tightly on my side. I'm not exactly known as a peaceful sleeper and I usually hog the whole space, waking more often than not in strange, unexplainable positions.

I disentangle myself from Magali, reluctantly and carefully. She stirs slightly but settles again. My foot lands on the bear, forlorn looking, now sprawled on the floor.

My eyes upturn.

I sigh, picking him up, propping him next to her, and she instinctively cuddles him. I swear he smirks at me. I raise a brow. "Doesn't mean I'll share at night, got that?" I whisper.

The bathroom's rail door squeaks faintly as I start to slide it shut behind me. Stopping mid-motion, I pop my head back out, making sure it didn't wake her. Not a stir.

I debate going for a quick, hot shower, but change my mind, recalling I'll have to put yesterday's grubby clothes back on. Somehow, it doesn't appeal all that much and I blame my Swiss upbringing for that bit of fastidiousness. I'll probably need the cold shower awaiting me at the old farmstead, anyway.

I splash some cold water on my face. Tilting my head up, I hardly recognize the guy grinning like a loon staring back at me. I'll take it.

"Zac?" I hear Magali's tentative voice asking through the door. I slide it back open, and man, every cell in my body stirs, awakened, no caffeine required. Leaning up on one elbow, her half-lidded eyes blink sleep away. Her hair is sticking up all over the place, and gorgeous doesn't even come close.

I take a step closer and squat down beside the bed. "Sorry, did I wake you?" My fingers sliding into her hair, I comb through some of her tangles, brushing them away from her face.

"No ... Yes ... I don't know. I missed your cuddling. I thought you had left." The relief in her voice is palpable.

"No worries. I think you'll have to kick me out each and every time," I say, before dropping a kiss on her forehead. *Until you keep me for good...* "What time are your friends picking you up?"

"At nine, what time is it?" she asks, concerned, scrambling up.

"It's early still, not quite eight yet ... Want to go out for breakfast before I head out?" Her whole face beams up and my insides melt.

"I'd love to, give me ten minutes?"

"Take your time," I say, but the sight of her lithe body hopping to it and my new favorite dimples gracing her backside give me other ideas her shoebox of a shower can't accommodate.

The sound of the water running covers my groan. I mentally recite symptoms of the bubonic plague and every other virulent, infectious disease that can progress to septicemia in a flash just to fit comfortably in my boxer shorts. Popping my head in the bathroom's doorway, I call out, "I'll wait outside."

Letting Magali shower and dress, I step out of her flat into the early-morning haze, a sure sign of another scorching day ahead.

I check my messages to be sure I didn't miss one from Liam regarding my patient. I don't have any, which is good news.

Hearing the distant click of Magali's door closing at my back, I swivel around. My jaw drops. Her hair is held up in a messy bun with loose strands framing her cheekbones, light makeup enhancing her impossibly large eyes that much more. She wears a casual cotton dress of pale aqua flaring at the waistline, hitting her several inches above the knee, with flat heel sandals.

"Let me drop Picolo off and I'm all yours," she calls out and fuck me, but I grow weak-kneed at the words.

As though conjured up by Magali's thought alone, the upstairs screen door clacks and the little girl bounces down the stairs. "Chouette, Magali! Is Picolo ready?" Cassandre cries out the minute she spots her.

"Hey, Cassandre, just the girl I was hoping to see." Magali hugs the little whirlwind close to her. "I wanted to ask if you'd mind taking care of Picolo for the rest of your week at your Mamie's. Picolo gets bored during the day when I'm with friends or at work and he'd like to play summer camp if it's all right with you."

"For the rest of my week?" she squeals, jumping up and down. Never mind that when she sees the small overnight bag Magali hands over she screeches so loud that I watch for signs of swooning in case she injures her head. She gives Magali a killer one-arm hug before running back up the drive, holding the bear, screaming "Mamie" at the top of her lungs.

My heartstrings ping. Christ, my girl is too lovely by half. *My girl* saunters back to me, lacing her fingers through mine.

"What?" she asks, tilting her head, noticing my intent stare and unmoving feet.

"You're beautiful." I shake my head, a bit dazed.

"Then we're even. So are you." She stands on her tippy toes and deposits a gentle kiss on the corner of my lips.

"Not even close." I brush my lips over her temple and take a fortifying breath. I'll need it to let her go in an hour or so.

"Are we arguing again?"

"Not even close." My lips curling into a grin of their own volition, I tug on her hand. I never noticed before, but the only difference between sappy and happy is one little letter, and clearly, my mind is buzzing from one to the other this morning.

"And we don't even have time to make out instead, what a waste," she sighs dramatically. "What do you have in mind for breakfast?" she asks, swinging our arms, skipping down the road.

You.

"We could try one of the terraces by the lake?" I reply instead.

"Sounds good to me. Normally I'd walk there, but we won't have time to eat before I'm due back." She shuffles backward, pulling me along. "Mind if we take your Jeep? I'll even help take the top off, three minutes flat."

"Fully dropped in three minutes? Game on." Between the both of us, the soft shell top is off and folded in well under three minutes, a record.

Her eyes dart to the dash. "Just like me, you kept it bare bones, no electronics, not even a clock."

"Hey, it's a Willis. No frills for a reason. I'll find time eventually to go off road, doors off, the works," I say, hyped by the thought of off-roading deep into the woods. We share a look of understanding, adventures written all over us.

"Yesss! That would be so fun!"

I mentally fist pump, that's my girl. I put my hand up, and we high five on it.

She sighs happily, hopping into the passenger seat, buckling up. "Time for condoms, and breakfast."

Turning the engine, I cut her look. "Condoms and breakfast?"

"The local pharmacy is on the lakeshore road," she says. "Would you consider giving me a Depo-Provera injection on our next rotation?"

My right hand slips, and the fucking Jeep stalls on me. My heart as well. My left hand flexes, missing in on the action. Where's a bloody British car on the right side of things when I need one?

"That's why my Jeep's a five-speed automatic." She looks at me, all innocent like. "I'm abysmal at driving a manual transmission. I just can't seem to get the flow right."

"Magali, seriously, you want *me* to give you a contraceptive injection?"

"Well, I can't prescribe it on myself, and I'm the worst possible candidate for pill taking at regular intervals, so?" She shrugs.

"I can't give you a full exam and stay clinically detached," I mutter. No fucking way, not even close.

"Zac, that's not what I was thinking, nor asking!" she cries out aghast, thank the fuck. "Swipe my MédiCarte Soleil into the computer, and you'll see I've had a full medical less than six months ago in Montréal. The last time I've had something even remotely distressful health wise, I was ten years old with a capsulitis shoulder. I just need the prescription, and a professional arm longer than mine to inject my buttock."

Jesus. I breathe through my nose a couple of times, my fingers flexing on the steering wheel. I shift in my seat, blood pumping wildly in my ears, my dick probably harder than steel right now just at the thought of feeling all of her, skin on skin.

"I haven't requested a switch yet for a Saint-Jérôme's gynecologist. You know by now it will take weeks or months without an emergency, and I don't have the patience to wait that long for a prescription. I'd like to feel all of you with nothing but skin between us. What do you say?"

My raging boner running the show, my mind is running on fumes.

Bloody hell.

I shoot her a look. "This is going to be a fucking long day. Yes, I'll give you the injection," I grit through my teeth. Turning the engine back on, I slam it into first, then second, and third, peeling down the deserted road.

"Told you, you created a monster," she says knowingly, and a few sidelong glances confirm a vision. Arms rising above her head, hands sticking out, she tilts her head up to the sun. Eyes closed in bliss, the wind whips strands of her hair loose. It reminds me of the way she flew through the air on skis months ago. A flying ballerina. She's magnificent.

I shake my head. How did I get so lucky? I have no fucking clue, but I'll take it.

Parking on la rue Saint-Vincent, running parallel to the lakeshore, I cut the engine. "I'll take care of the interim condoms later. Come on, let's find breakfast. I'm starving." *But it's not for food*, I silently add. I better get this long day looming ahead of me on its way while I have yet a few brain cells still in working condition. In the horny state I'm in right now, I'm liable to take off with her and never look back.

"We can try La Brûlerie." She points to the restaurant I'm parked in front of. "They serve a light breakfast fare with coffee beans roasted on site. Their house blend is to die for according to hospital grapevine."

"Suits me fine."

Magali hops down, and a breeze sends her dress fluttering about her legs, flashing me a peek of baby-blue boy shorts, lace trimmed, leaving me lightheaded.

"Who's going with you to this show again?" I ask, distracted. As we move towards the café's entrance, I place a hand on the small of her back.

"For the day? Amélie, CD, and Benoît, which means yet another interesting foray into double dating, for sure," she says on a light chuckle, as I open the door to let her pass. My step falters. *What the what?* "We'll meet with a few others for the show tonight. I don't know yet who'll be there. CD arranged the whole thing," she adds over her shoulder. Her mostly naked shoulder, seeing she's wearing an off-the-shoulder dress capped with tiny sleeves.

My skin prickles. An instant, god-awful burn shreds my guts, spreading lava in my veins. My jaw clenches. Now it's a fucking long day in more ways than one and my mood fast dive at an alarming rate. Magali's limpid eyes smile up at me. I breathe through my nose, exhaling through my mouth, reminding myself this day out was planned some time ago and is not spur of the moment. Not even the fact she invited me along last night calms me down. I don't know what the fuck to do with my overwhelming darkening mood.

She sighs as we stand in La Brûlerie's foyer, waiting for the hostess. "CD owes me big time for agreeing to spend a full day over there. Montréal will be a muggy ten to fifteen degrees more than here, for sure." She frowns.

"Why go then?" I grunt in reply.

"CD hardly ever goes to Montréal," she explains on a shrug. "And Benoît, one of his new lifeguards at the resort, and fresh out of Le Témiscamingue region further north, has never been. I'm under strict orders to wow him into sticking around, showing him some of the sights. Le Vieux-Montréal, Le Vieux-Port, it's going to be torrid, I know. I worked over there one summer." Her eyes upturn, and mine narrows.

The hostess greets us, preventing me from commenting, which is a good thing as not only my teeth are clenched tight, fighting the urge to snarl, *I'll just bet the dude will be wowed by the sights*, but I only have to nod a few times in reply to her queries.

For two? Nod. Outside? Nod. Follow me? Nod. A cup of house blend to start with? Nod.

The waitress follows behind the hostess with the coffees and menus, unfurls the umbrella, and I ran out of nods well before she moves away. I take a look around, breathing a few times through my nose, calming the hell down, or trying to. My pulse is erratic.

The restaurant isn't lakeside. Instead, the round bistro tables are arranged on the sidewalk just like in Europe, and the crowd is mostly a business one on this early Tuesday morning, and fast thinning out.

"CD? That's the guy from the resort. Cédric, right?" I ask, feeling unaccountably edgy. Go figure.

Probably taking her cue from my splendid display of non-verbal answers earlier on, she nods quietly, selecting from a small red-enamel metal pail three low-fat milk cups. She rips their top off, pouring them into her cup one after the other.

I try not to cringe at the sight of cold milk being poured, and fail. A latte would have been less disturbing to watch.

Our waitress scurries back to us, enquiring if Magali would prefer steamed milk instead. "Non, non, I love cold milk, merci."

I suppress a small shudder at the thought of swallowing cold cow juice straight up.

"So, Cédric. You two hang out a lot?" I ask before I can stop myself.

Bloody hell. And here I thought I was done with any abandonment issues I may have had at one point in time. What with all of Dr. Englehart's endless therapies under the guise of what was called mandatory life orientation sessions we all to endure at BIA, tattooed on my brains. Guess joke's on me, there are a few hiccups remaining. Great. Just great.

"Cédric? Not as much as before, no. I hardly saw him, or anyone for that matter, in the past six months, which is the reason why he successfully guilt tripped me into going for a full day in Montréal today, why?" She tilts her head, her brow angling.

"No ... particular reason," I lie through my teeth, my chest constricting in a vise. "What about that Benoît guy?"

Fuck. Where the bloody hell did that come from? And I use to be so suave. Her eyes narrow.

I look down at the content of my black coffee cup as if it holds the answers I'm looking for. I shake my head in a self-deprecating way.

"Zac?" I look up. "I'm getting this weird vibe here, are you ... huh, jealous?" she asks, her facial expression clearly confounded.

I lean back, disgusted with myself, shoving my hands through my hair. "Double dating, Magali? After the night we just shared. I guess I am, yes."

She leans forward to rest her elbows on the table and pins me with a direct look.

My heart hammers with apprehension. What if she says all things considered, you're not worth the commitment? I curve both my hands around my coffee mug, willing myself not to squeeze it in a white-knuckled grip.

"I promise you, there's no need to be jealous. I love lots and lots of people, but I'm not *in love* with them, big difference," she says, without an ounce of hesitation, her limpid gaze stalwart, and I feel smaller than a two-inch dick. I made a conscious decision to leap, both feet, all in, I remind myself. I can't let old insecurities sabotage my jump.

Her palms open, the back of her hands coming down to rest on the table top, inviting me in. I swallow a lump, the gesture touching me, spreading a soothing balm inside my shredded guts. The vise grip wringing my chest eases somewhat, letting me draw a relieved breath.

Her fingers curl over my hands; her thumbs stroking back and forth. "CD has always been a friend. I didn't even think you might misinterpret my jest for something other. It was insensitive, and I'm sorry. The running gag is that whenever we go out with CD and one of his lovers, everybody thinks Amélie and I are a couple, and he plays it up every single time so that everybody thinks we're double dating."

I blink. She squeezes my hands once and leans back in her chair, taking hold of her coffee mug, tilting her head.

My breath swooshes on a silent sigh of relief.

"So, CD's gay?" I ask, striving for casual, taking a sip of coffee for countenance.

"One hundred twenty-eight percent gay. Oh, and he likes you by the way. He gave me hell for the longest time after I went off on you that night. I can't wait to see his face. He'll flip for sure when he hears about us," she says, grinning into her cup.

"No shit, now I like him too," I mumble under my breath, getting my feet back from under me. I love gay, gay is good. No blurry lines and I don't have to try and kill him now. My arms fold on the table, and I lean in. "So Benoît is *his* lover?" I ask pointedly, making sure I'm not inferring things, nonetheless.

"Totally." Her eyes are warm as she leans forward until our faces are but a few inches apart. "Next time something bugs you, raise your hand, tap my shoulder, whatever ... but just come out with it! Ask me. I can't guarantee you'll always like the answers, but I can guarantee you'll have answers, honest ones. I won't play you, ever, I promise."

I lean back in my chair and take a deep breath. "Look, I'm sorry. I'm not used to any of this stuff. I don't have any clear guidelines like you do, and I'll probably fuck up more than once getting the hang of it, so bear with me." I shake my head, looking down into the deep mocha brown of my coffee.

"You think I have clear guidelines?" she says, her tone incredulous. I glance up, surprised. "The only thing I know for sure is that I'll fuck up, as you put it, just as much, don't beat yourself up. Getting the hang of *us* is organic that way, but that's where I've seen the magic of love happen around me." She leans forward, cheeks flushed rosy. "Don't you see? We're uniquely us, Zac, and I've waited a lifetime for you. No one else before was ever us. No one else will ever be us. No one else gets to decide what works for us. And that's the beauty of us," she finishes, impassioned.

She falls quiet for a minute as we stare at one another.

I lift my coffee cup in toast and she clinks her mug against mine. "To us," I declare.

"To us," she echoes right back.

A slow, glorious smile lights up her features, mine right behind.

To one hell of an us, Magali.

Twenty-Four

ZAC

I swing an arm around her as we step out of La Brûlerie in plenty of time to get her back to her place before her friends are due to arrive.

"What about you, what will you today?" she asks.

I hold the passenger's door open for her, and she hops in. "Hang out with a special friend," I say tongue in cheek, waiting.

Right on cue, she raises an eyebrow, her gaze drilling me with silver laser beams, their tiny specks of peridot green flashing fire within. "Spill it."

I let out a snort. She's cute when she tries for intimidating.

I hold my hands up in surrender. "I'm making fun of me, really." My hands brace on the crash bar above her head. "I was sure you would ask, though, so don't give me that look. I'll be hanging out with my family."

Confusion flickers over her face. "Family? I thought you said you only had your GGS crew from your years in Switzerland?"

"I do only have them," I reply.

"And..." she prompts, gesturing with her hand, and I can almost hear her silent "out with it already."

"Oh, you mean you want the whole story? Cue my ass handed over by this girl on a ski holiday we all took last winter."

Her chin tips up. "You can skip the prologue, that part I know by now, thanks!"

I saunter over to the driver's side, enjoying this ease and well-being between us so much. "Two of my GGS pals bought property in the area. One is building a place on his empty lot, the other is, well…" I scratch my stubble. How to describe Leo's duct-taped house? "Renovating his house right now might be pushing it, but when he gets to it, I think it will be more along the lines of rebuilding from top to bottom. Anyway, most of us are crashing at his fixer-upper for the summer. It's a full house, or the funny farm, depending on who you ask." I shake my head, turning the engine.

"This is so cool." Magali cries out turning in her seat. "You didn't mention some of your lifelong friends were staying over permanently, too. I'm so happy for you! And I'm so happy for me," she says, cheeks flushed. Her smile flips my stomach.

It may have played in the beginning as it got me here, but it sure as hell wouldn't make any difference now … I'm head over heels, as Leo would say. Nothing would keep me away. I don't bother saying so. Instead, I just smile.

"Okay, which ones?" she asks, worrying her bottom lip in thought. I part my lips but she leans forward, her fingers coming up to press on them. "Non, non, don't tell me their names yet. I want to try and pin down all of their old BIA nicknames correctly when we first meet. Hmmm." She taps her index finger on her lips, eyes narrowing in thought. "Let's see. There's LawMan, MathMan, KnightMan, ByteMan, WeedMan, and…" She counts on her fingers. "Zut, I'm missing yours." She bats her eyelashes.

"Nice try." I check the rearview mirror and put on the blinker, waiting for a break in the traffic. I purposely omitted my own nickname last night, having too much fun letting her try wheedling it out of me. "And *zut*? What's with that word? Is it a curse word I don't know yet?" I ask, cocking my head to the side.

She lets out an airy laugh. "Not even close. Zut de flûte? It's more of a cute expression really, similar to … I don't know? Oops and darn, maybe? Anyway, you'll need to be ready to hand in your man card if you use it. Little kids use it too, just so you know." Her eyes twinkle.

"Duly noted. Zut is no longer on my list of swear words, thanks," I reply, shaking my head.

"So? Out with it."

"The two you're looking for are KnightMan and WeedMan," I reply, holding in a laugh.

"You know I'll find out yours eventually, right?" I give her a sidelong glance. She crosses her arms, pretending to pout. "Why not give in now?"

I snicker, clutching in first, then two. "You shouldn't have told me you'd soon be ready to beg on your knees."

"Ever heard of pleading? You're so taking it out of context!" she cries out.

My brows lift in amusement. "Am I, now?"

"Okay, what if I do beg on my knees, will you tell?" Her voice rings with clear challenge.

"You could try, and see what comes up."

She puffs out a laugh and man, do I love hearing the happy sound, makes me tingle all over. "Would you tell me if I guessed it right?" she asks.

"I would, but you won't," I say with confidence.

"Game on," she replies with just as much confidence. "StuntMan?"

Ha! "That would have been a good one, but no."

"BoobooMan?"

"No way," I say, having a harder time keeping a straight face. "I'm more of an ass man."

"I get why, emphasis on the jackass part," she says drily, and I chuckle under my breath. She says overly slow, making sure a toddler would get it, let alone the doctor in me, "Booboo, like kiss the booboo better."

"Aw, cute, but no." Thank the fuck. I don't think I would have lived that one down in a boys' school. I give her a sidelong glance as I drive. "That's all you've got?"

She taps her fingers on her mouth. "MedMan?"

"Come on, that's the best you can come up with?" I tease, egging her on.

"MadMan? MidMan? ModMan? MudMan?"

"Nope. But you get extra points for trying all those in a row like that. Your tongue is pretty nimble, impressive." I shake my head, chuckling, as I drive up her street.

"Funny man," she mumbles.

"Was that a guess, or are you stating a fact?"

"I will let you figure it out all by yourself," she says as I turn into her driveway and park. Seems like no one's here yet; even Cassandre's grandmother's car is gone, and I wonder if she expects me to just drop her off and go...

"Um. They should have been here by now, what time is it?" she asks twisting in her seat, looking up and down the road.

"It's only five past nine," I say, checking my watch, which reminds me. I fish her pilfered watch out of my front pocket and hand it over. "Here, you might need this."

"No, you can keep it. I won't need it at all until Thursday," she says on a slight frown, worrying her bottom lip. It makes me want to slip it back on her wrist now, and ask her to check the time regularly when in Montréal, and think of me.

Hair windblown and cheeks flushed, she's breathtaking, and my insides melt into a surreal pile of mush, thinking that she's mine ... And the feeling is unfamiliar, but not at all unpleasant.

"Something's up. They're freakishly early all the time; it's unnatural. It's the only reason why they're picking me up, instead," she says, her frown deepening. She adds, "I drive all of them bonkers by being a few minutes late, pretty much always."

"Have you checked your phone for—?"

"Merdouille, my phone," she gasps, unbuckling. "I totally forgot I left it sitting on the kitchen counter, what with getting Picolo ready and everything. You don't have to wait if you need to get going." She gives me a quick, but tender peck on the cheek, and I run my palm over her hair, keeping her close for a minute longer, resting my lips on her forehead.

"I'm not going anywhere. I'll wait outside while you fetch your phone." *I'm afraid I'll jump your bones if I follow you in.*

"That's probably best. I'm afraid I'll jump your bones if you come in with me." She hops out, and I thump the back of my head on the headrest.

I get out and lean back on the Jeep, crossing my arms, watching her bound up the drive.

She whirls round, shuffling backward for a few, her dress flitting about, showcasing her toned legs and the soft curves of her delectable thighs. "Thank you for this," she calls back. "CD will flip, and so will Amélie, if they see you. Otherwise they won't believe me. And really, who could blame them? You being here is like something straight out of a book." She opens her arms wide, twirling a few spins, dancing the rest of the way to her front door.

She lets the screen door clack close on her butt, and I get comfortable, slouching a bit, crossing my ankles.

I breathe in the quiet of the morning, bees buzzing in a small patch of wildflowers on the other side of the long driveway. The chirping of cicadas at intervals enhances the calm of the moment rather than break into it.

Up until the loud rumble of a faulty engine backfiring up the road catches my attention just before a beat-up Volkswagen Westfalia camper in a god-awful puke yellow eaten away by rust, turns up the drive in a puff of black smoke, sputtering to a stop right behind my Jeep.

I straighten from my slouch, frowning.

Three sets of eyes stare at me through the cracked windshield, jaws dropping.

"You've got to be kidding," I mutter under my breath, eyeing the driver. I'll lend him my Jeep if I have to, but there's no fucking way I'll let Magali go to Montréal in that guy's disaster waiting to happen.

"Cédric Daviault, are you nuts? You drove Hector in the shape he's in all the way up here?" Magali stomps past me, getting their full attention. She pats the flat-nose front, and says soothingly, "No offense, Hector, but you're lucky you weren't pulled over and on your way to the car pound right now." Having reassured the death mobile, she looks at her friends through the windshield and asks, "What happened?"

The girl, Amélie, I can only presume, slides the rail door open. The loud screeching of metal grinding against metal is not only jarring but wince inducing. I get the onceover, not so discreetly, from the young athletic-looking man in the middle seat getting out in Amélie's wake. *You're shit out of luck, bud. I don't swing your way. Or anyone else's now that I have Magali.*

From inside the camper, CD's head swivels back to me. I nod politely, and he nods back, eyes squinting at me. Well this is going to be interesting if the wary expression washing over his face is anything to go by.

"My car wouldn't start, not even with booster cables, and it had to be towed," Amélie explains. "We tried to get a hold of you early this morning so you'd come pick us up instead, but ... huh ... yeah ... Guess you were ... otherwise occupied. So, anyway, here we are. Finally." Her hushed tone wavers in between excited or incredulous, hard to tell, as she eyes my wrinkled clothes.

There's quiet for a moment as we stare at one another, the air heavy with unspoken questions from her friends—the loudest one being *what the hell did we miss between yesterday and today?*

Magali winks at me. The little minx, she's enjoying this, and taking my cue from her, I relax back against my Jeep, waiting.

CD leans over the front seat to talk to Magali standing with Amélie by the open door. "Holy freaking shit, M. I swear I'm having this weird déjà vu. Doesn't he look to you like? Huh ... just the eyes, maybe..." his voice trails off as Magali tilts her head, her eyes drilling into him. She raises a brow, daring him to say it. But he shakes his head. "Like that's possible, right? Of course not, I mean, what are the odds?" Cédric babbles his way to a stop. He gets his bulky frame out, using the passenger's door. He scrubs his hand a few times on the back of his buzz cut, as Magali saunters away from the wreck on wheels the guy drives, and walks over to me.

Taking both my hands in hers, she tugs me close, searching my eyes, a soft look in hers, and my heart skips a beat. "Actually, CD, I've been asking myself the same question over and over. What are the odds, and yet..." She squeezes my hands once before she turns to them. Running my arms around her waist, I nudge her against my chest, her back to my front. "Guys, meet Docteur Zac di Fiori, my maître de stage, and so much more ever since that night we met on the slopes. Zac, meet my friends, Amélie, CD, and Benoît."

"Pleased to meet you indeed, and under better circumstances," I say, a small grin tugging at my lips as I look over at CD.

Amélie squeals, "Get out!"

"Holy shit. Same accent, same voice," CD says, astounded. "He's really one and the same." He shakes his head, hands coming up his hips.

The other guy, Benoît, leans on the camper, picking at his nails.

"Hey, Benoît, looks like we're taking my Jeep. Mind taking the top off?" Magali throws him her keys and the guy's sullen feature brightens, catching them.

"No prob, on it."

"I'll need your help with the cookie jars. I made an awful mess of them," Magali says to Amélie. Her eyes grow wide, and her hands come up her mouth stifling a laugh. I wink at her over Magali's head and she laughs.

CD gawks at Magali, then me. "Wow. Guess you really were otherwise occupied." He crosses his arms. "Well, shit, M, thanks for nothing. Now I can't even rant at you for turning off your phone, can I? And I had my spiel so well-rehearsed too," he grumbles in a whiny voice.

"Very pleasantly occupied," I murmur into her ear and she nods, sighing contentedly. Her fingers interlace with mine over her abdomen, squeezing once, before stepping out of my arms. I take a step back, leaning once more on my Jeep.

She pokes CD on the chest. "Get it off your chest."

"Do you want the sarcastic version or the pissed-off one?" he asks.

"We heard both twice on our way here," Amélie says to us upturning her eyes. "Personally, I liked the sarcastic one better. It's way funnier. But I really don't need to hear it once more, CD. No one here does, so shut it and come with me. I need a glass of water." She drags him away by the arm.

"I don't," he complains, grumbling up the drive.

Coming up on the tip of her toes, Magali tangles her hands behind my head and takes my lips, plucking at my heartstrings like no one else ever has. I keep mine around her lower back as she kisses the stuffing clear out of me. I forget about everything else until she leans away, her fingers brushing on my lips. "This is scary, crazy, and awesome all rolled into one. I'm nowhere near the clingy sort, yet, I'll really miss you today," she murmurs.

"So will I." I brush a strand of windblown hair behind her ear.

CD clears his throat loudly from behind us. "We need to hit the road, M."

"See you tomorrow?" Her fingers curl on my forearms, leaning into my touch, and I let the loving warmth in her eyes infuse me inside out.

"You bet you will." I kiss her forehead.

She takes a few steps back and I have no other choice but to let her go. Her eyes taking me in, she says, "I just need to go lock up, and check on Benoît's progress, so we can all be on our way. I'll see you soon, then."

I nod once, sending her on her way, and Amélie, eyes twinkling, sends me a shy smile before falling into step with Magali, squeezing her shoulders tight, kissing her cheek. I see Magali nod at something she says, just before she disappears inside.

"Listen, man, no shit, I couldn't be happier for Magali, it's been a long time coming," CD says, watching them go, still shaking his head. He looks me in the eye. "But if you fuck with her heart, I'll hunt you down and feed you to her brothers."

I level a gaze on him. "If I fuck with her heart, I'll let you. And if you drive her anywhere in that death trap," I motion with my head, "I'll kill you myself."

"I knew I liked you for a reason." A slow smile creeps up his face, and we go for a fist bump. "Got any brothers?" he asks.

"You're shit out of luck, mate." I palm my keys and slide in the driver's seat.

"Yeah, figured as much."

Twenty-Five

ZAC

I enjoy taking sinuous back roads with breathtaking views on my drive back to the old farmstead, leaving Magali and her friends to their city adventures.

My heart brimming over, I'm running on an unparalleled high just at the thought of Magali and the short time we've spent together. She lives in me now, I realize.

Everywhere I look, colors are ten times more vibrant, and the warm wind ruffling my hair has never been this sensual, nor the sun's caress on my forearms ever felt so good. Every little sensation is magnified, and I revel in it.

Parking beside Liam's red station wagon by the woodshed in the back, I cut the engine and eye the deceptively innocent-looking mud room's door, debating. Nah.

Unwilling to chance it and be stuck on tape duty, I round the house and bound up the stairs of the covered porch. The old-fashioned carved wood door clacks, closing behind me, and I make a beeline for Liam and Éolie's downstairs bedroom. Popping in and out of the doorway, I report for babysitting duty with my best commercial airline voiceover. Éolie, propped on her sea of pillows, laughs when I give her a dramatic salute. Liam shoots me a knowing smirk as he takes in my rumpled clothes, and I hear him comment on my over-the-top mood.

"Hey, I had a pretty awesome day, yesterday," I say, popping back in. "I'm ready to take on the world!"

"Good to know," Liam chuckles under his breath, adding that it must have been quite the night too.

"You have no idea, bud," I say, on my way to a cold shower. Well, actually, I'm sure he does. I chuckle low.

Leo, sitting at the kitchen table, is poring over what looks like pie charts and graphs analyses on his laptop. I clap his shoulder in passing, and he spits coffee out, his mug upturning from the shove forward.

"You're lucky my laptop's weather resistant or you'd be dead by now," he grunts, mopping the worst of the spill on his keyboard with a few paper towels from a roll we keep on the table. Éolie's feminine touch in the downstairs rooms is sorely lacking by now. Only thirty-seven days left before the twins are due to make their appearances. I sigh in relief. We can all work with that.

"I survived worst," I tell Leo, unperturbed. "Who's turn in the shower?" I ask, checking the schedule.

"Mine," P.O. says on a yawn, shuffling in from behind me, rubbing his bleary eyes. His plaid pajama pants hang dangerously low on his lanky frame as he stretches from side to side, hands interlocked behind his head. P.O. with his pants dropping around his ankles is a sight I can do without this early.

"Want to swap?" I pop the fridge open, taking the orange juice carton out. Shaking it, I judge it's more than half-empty, so I chug it down straight up.

Eyeing my rumpled clothes, P.O. grunts, "Fuck, man, should be illegal to be this awake before ten in the morning after pulling a twenty-seven-hour shift," he says, disgruntled. Knowing him, he probably was working at his computer until he crashed. And it shows; he still has crease marks from, I'm guessing, his pillow case.

Who said anything about a double shift? I inwardly grin while guzzling the last of the juice. "So? Yes or no?" I ask, rinsing the carton, flattening it with my heel before putting it in the recycling bin.

P.O. stares at me.

"Go ahead, take my turn." He waves me off, overfilling a pot with water, shoving it on the stove. "I'll drink my weight in instant coffee meanwhile, and see what happens."

It's funny, as no one ever gets around to buying a kettle around here, or an espresso machine. Guess the authentic, rustic charm about the place is half the fun, and no one wants to mess with a good thing ... Or risk upsetting the delicate balance we finally reached between supply and demand from the antiquated electric plugs and wiring throughout the place.

"Thanks, I owe you one." I pull my shirt off by the back of the neck, once more foregoing unbuttoning it. The faint trace of Magali's citrusy scent wafts through my nose. I breathe it in, picturing her wearing my shirt inside out, and nothing else.

"More than one, but who's counting?" P.O. replies in an even tone. My tally is adding up. I may have switched rooms on Yann and P.O. before they arrived last weekend, leaving them stuck in one with no window to speak of, duct-taped and all. Leaning on the counter by the stove, ostensibly waiting for his water to boil, his eyes narrow, zeroing on the shit-eating grin I can't seem to shake.

"Leo?" he asks, eyeing me. "Is it me, or what?"

"What?" Leo frowns, studying his laptop screen as if by thought alone he can change the negative ratios the computer calculated from his current soil analysis.

P.O. flips down Leo's laptop screen on him, saying, "Pay attention. I need a second opinion. So, is it me?" Leo lets out a long-suffering sigh, but his gaze sharpens in on me.

"Holy..." Both eyebrows shoot up.

"What?" I ask them. I pull my shirt around my neck, towel style, hands on my hips.

"I've seen that look before," Leo says knowingly. "Hey, Liam?" he calls out as Liam stomps by in his steel-toe construction boots, on his way out the front, tool belt cinched around the waist, his hard hat tucked under one arm. You'd never know looking at him that not even five months ago the guy didn't know the difference between a wood screw and a metal screw. Not that I can talk; I still don't. "Come here a sec, will you."

"What?" Liam asks.

P.O. and Leo dart their heads between us two.

"Yep, that's the look," P.O. states.

Liam quirks a brow at me. I shrug.

"Man, you've got it bad. But for whom?" Leo asks me, baffled. "What the fuck happened between the time your grouchy ass left yesterday morning, and now? Talk slow, I'm taking notes."

I can't do anything else but laugh, feeling light-hearted, and for once in my life, it's a carefree sound, not of shared humor but of sheer joy spilling out of me spontaneously.

"I met my new intern, and she flipped my world, that's what happened," I'm finally able to say.

They all stare at me, shocked into silence.

Liam's the first to recover. His hand comes up and we high five, sharing a look of understanding. "She's *the one*, isn't she?"

I nod, feeling another loopy grin forming.

"Man, I need a shot of caffeine to keep up with you two," P.O. grumbles, rinsing a mug out of the pile of dirty ones left on the counter.

"I'm with you," Leo says to P.O., turning off the stove and pouring some boiling water into his own, adding two spoonfuls of powdered coffee to the mix.

"I didn't know you were in line to intern a new doctor so soon. They're branching you out from under pediatrics to head your own department of obstetrics, or what?" Liam asks, pulling up a chair and straddling it.

I lean on one hip and hold onto my shirt draped around my neck with both my fists. "No, I've been put in charge of a midwife trainee who work-shadows me for the next quarter rotation. A pilot program that Sainte-Agathe is a part of. And get this ... The girl from that night at Mont-Saint-Sauveur, the one I couldn't get out of my head? She walked in yesterday morning as said midwife intern."

"No way. *The* patroller?" Leo's mouth falls open.

"The one and the same," I reply, taking a glass from the cupboard and filling it with tap water, which is, here, sparkling spring water from an underground well. Cool drinking water, cold-as-fuck showers. One I need right now just thinking about her...

"Bloody hell, man. As soon as Yann wakes up, I'll have him do the math on the odds of that happening." P.O. shakes his head, leaning back against the counter.

"One in a million. Magali's completely—"

"Wait! *Magali* is the girl from that night? No shit, what a small world!" Liam exclaims, and I swivel, unsure I heard right, my glass forgotten in the sink. Liam knows Magali? When the fuck did that happen without my knowing? I just stare at him, uncomprehending.

"You know Magali, *my* Magali?" I ask Liam, incredulous.

Leo shuts the tap water still gurgling behind me and P.O. knocks back what looks like his second mug of coffee. I may need one or two myself.

"Well, know her is a bit stretching it, but yeah. I'm pretty sure she's the Magali we met on our first morning in Les Laurentides, at Le Vieux Clocher in Saint-Sauveur. I mean, the name is not that common and besides, how many Magalis could there be that fits? Patroller at Mont-Saint-Sauveur, check. Going into a two-year program to train as a midwife in Sainte-Agathe, check." Liam scratches his scruff. "Your Magali, would she happen to be grey-eyed, dark-haired, and scarily outgoing?"

And so much more... "Spot on, man," I say instead, all the while thinking, wow, this is cool. Magali will more than likely recognize Liam and Éolie, and be delighted by how small a world it is indeed when they meet again. She'll probably get a kick out of that, so I won't mention anything to her beforehand. "Nice. I'll surprise her with this."

"Oh, you will." A sly grin forms on Liam's lips as he tucks his chair back in. "Can't wait to see that." He flips his hard hat with a flick of the wrist and catches it, a smug look washing over his face. He snaps me a two-finger salute, backing away. "I'm off, boys, take care of my girl."

"Will do." I stare after him.

Why do I feel like I'm missing out on the joke here?

I shrug it off. I'll know soon enough.

Chucking my pants and balling them, I close the bathroom door with my heel.

Twenty-Six

ZAC

Not three hours later, I'm switching off the screen to the medical-grade, portable ultrasound I check the twins with weekly on top of Doppling them daily, Liam glued to Éolie's side.

"Okay, still no signs of premature labor and their vitals are comfortingly within normal range. Looks like all's good with our little dudes in there."

"I'm so so sorry ... I promise I won't get out of bed without assistance from now on. I swear to you," Éolie keeps saying.

"You won't, I'm not leaving your side from now on." Liam brushes his fingers in a back and forth, over the light-pink scar on the inside of her arm. She lost her balance earlier on in the bathroom, her arm sustaining a nasty cut on the antique glass cabinet when she braced against the fall. The three others left for a much-needed coffee break, down in the village, still a little green around the edges.

"Zac, please tell him he can go back to the barn site now," she entreats me.

"Nope. You shaved ten years off my life. It's as he says." I wipe the ultrasonic gel off the ultrasound probe and put it away alongside the Doppler.

"See? There's no getting rid of me, deal with it." Liam scoots on the bed, next to her.

"I'm not trying to get rid of you." She rubs her forehead. "You love being outside, helping with the construction of the barn, and I'm not going anywhere—"

"Éolie, let it rest, you're outnumbered," I say pointedly. "I'll Doppler them again tonight."

She holds her hands up in surrender. Liam catches one, kissing her fingers. She cups his cheek and he leans into her touch.

"I'll be upstairs, just holler if you need anything," I say over my shoulder.

I sprawl down on my bed under the eaves, and rub my hands a few times over my face. Next time, I'll be better prepared, I vow, and I won't freak as much witnessing Éolie go down, nor self-healing in a matter of minutes in a spectacular way. But still, the thought of having to perform an emergency C-section at home, if it comes to that, now that the hospital is definitely out of the question, is not exactly on my top ten favorites.

Theo's ring tone echoes in the eerily quiet of the house. I unsnap my phone from my belt holder and take a deep breath.

"Theo? What's up?" I ask, striving for a composed tone.

"Have a minute?"

"Why do have a feeling I won't like it?" My guts churn, intuitively knowing what's coming.

"Because you won't," he says in a monotone.

"Hit me." My arm coming over my eyes, I sigh heavily. Pretty sure it means I'm stuck with San Alessio's fucked-up legacy, then.

I know, deep down, before he even tells me. And yep, Theo confirms in the next instant.

Gut feelings, one. Foolish hopes, zero.

"You can't abdicate without exposing the dirty laundry, and it would be for nothing as they're prepared to sue your ass off through the next millennia to keep the title alive. They have a lot riding on this, so you better believe they will. You're already put on notice, Principe Raffaelo Alessandro Filippo Zacari San Alessio di Fiori."

"Don't call me that. I'm not even of the bloodline. A simple DNA test would show it," I huff. The courtesy title is not in the least figuring on *my* official papers, all superfluous names having been dropped.

"They don't give a fuck. On paper you are."

"Come on, it's been what, a few centuries? Pretty sure they're all fully Italian by now and no longer Alessian. What gives?"

"It's all pretty convoluted, but from what I've been led to understand, the special considerations and tax exemption the overseas territory benefits from hinge on that bloody medieval title. It dies, and poof. The ex-principauté is on a level playing field with the rest of Italy, and it's not something they like to advertise."

Fuck. Offshore banking is the bread and butter of the place nowadays, and has been since the end of World War II.

"Well, so much for my arguing that it's an outdated symbol they can do without." I rub the bridge of my nose, feeling a headache coming.

"Yeah, looks good on paper but doesn't cut it when you scratch beneath the surface, man."

Not long after the plane crash that took my mother's life, Principe Filippo, the original, died from a massive coronary under suspicious conditions. It was the last in a long string of unfortunate, incidental deaths that family had. Vendetta, greed, power plays, betrayals—the whole nine yards in a repeat cycle over the centuries. The old prince was nearing sixty, so it didn't make that big of a splash, and the investigation was quietly closed on the side. Not that he was greatly missed by anyone, but it's amazing what kind of dirt a little hacking from P.O. can unearth.

But why the fuck do they insist on my presence back on island now with nothing else to do over there but smile and look pretty? Yeah, like that's going to happen.

I've been left to my own devices my whole life by the board of five trustees appointed to "me," forgotten more like, both parties liking it just fine, considering. Especially coming from a previous era where heirs apparently eliminated one another, until the one left standing made it his life's mission to live off the fat of the land, and be obnoxious to the hilt, while at it. So yeah, they hit pay dirt inheriting me at five years of age, already parked at BIA at an unprecedented bargain price.

"Awesome. I can't get rid of them, so I'm stuck with the estate trust fund from hell as well?"

"That sums it up." Theo's voice is sympathetic.

He knows I'm not cut out to smile and look pretty at a bunch of cotillions, and that I'll likely poke my eyes out in under a week. *Is having control over my life too much to ask?*

I rub my temple, massaging some of the tension away before it blooms into a full-blown headache.

Well, too fucking bad for them. "I don't know if they're screwed, or I'm screwed, but here's the deal. They get me on paper only, or nothing," I snap. "I'm not going over there to be paraded like a puppet. I'm building a life here. My life."

It worked for the past twenty years, no reason they can't shuffle around whatever the hell their protocol is to make it work again for the next ... forever.

"That, I can work with, I think. Just give me a few more weeks," he says. "So, I take it you still like being a civil servant, your Highness?"

Not sure if I appreciate his dry wit to its full measure right this minute, but I know it's his way of saying he's confident he'll strike up a *status quo* deal. Otherwise, he wouldn't go near the "H" word, not even in jest. And like it or not, it works to dispel my darkening mood, and saves me from a self-pity trip, like he intended.

"You're a royal pain in my butt." I let out a snort. Growing up, he used to gripe I had it royally easy when his grandfather insisted he learn the Debrett's Peerage by heart, and his proper place. Theo's like two hundred thirty-sixth in line to the British throne. Although, he gives less than a single fuck.

"I'll take that as a yes," he says drily.

"On both counts, counsellor." I stretch, and settle more comfortably against the headboard.

"Get off, you ass," he scoffs good-naturedly. "Seriously, though, you still like it over there?" he asks incredulously. Not that surprising, given my previous track record. I've never stayed put anywhere before.

"Yeah, I do, believe it or not. The system gives me a few hard twitches, but I'm discovering brand-new perks to it that I wouldn't trade for the world," I reply, thinking of working alongside Magali. "I love it here, man." I admire the view from the wide open window, breathing in the pure, cleansing air. I take in the dips and curves of the hilly terrain, the mountains as far as the eye can see, and the sense of self and well-being the place brings. Flying my Piper, soaring high over clouds, is the closest I've ever been to feeling like this before. At peace. Like I belong.

"Yeah, I know. I'd love it too if I were there," Theo mutters under his breath.

"You won't be able to make it up here at all this summer?"

"No. Speaking of, have to go. I've got two lines blipping the fuck red."

The line goes dead. "Theo? You still there, man?" I'm met with static silence on the other end. I let my phone drop on the bed. Well, that was abrupt, even for Theo. Then again, ever since last winter, something has been brewing with him but he clams up whenever we bring it up. A Theo thing ... But I don't get to dwell on that for long before a text alert pings on my phone. My pulse picks up.

I swipe my thumb, and can't help the goofy grin.

Magali: Miss you. Having fun but still. Can't wait to see you. xx

My thumbs fly over the keys.

Me: Heads up, seeing you will not be enough.

I bend one arm behind my head and wait, my eyes fixed on the little dots hopping on my screen signaling a forthcoming reply, for what seems an eternity.

Magali: Heads up, we're staying in bed all day tomorrow.

I close my eyes briefly, savoring the concept, letting bliss seep in deep just at the thought of a day rolling in bed with her. Oh, yeah. Man, I love that girl.

I text back.

Me: Consider me warned and ready.

A floorboard creaks and I look up. Liam stands in the doorway, his hands shoved in his hair, a troubled look marring his features.

"Éolie?" I hop out of bed.

"No, all's good. She's sleeping peacefully," he quickly reassures.

My shoulders slump in relief and my breath swooshes out on a long exhale.

He rubs the back of his neck, staring at me. "Magali?" he asks quietly, motioning to my phone.

"Yeah, she's out with friends in Montréal for the day, and, man, she's texting that she's missing me. Me." I shake my head, awed.

"Yeah, I know the feeling, and it never gets old, man," Liam says.

I look at my phone, grinning as I read the texts that just came in, one after the other, in a quick succession.

Magali: Is this where I ask what you're wearing? :)

Magali: Oops. CD caught me texting. :(

Magali: Getting the evil eye.

Magali: Walking into SOS Labyrinthe, Old-Port Hangar Sixteen if I go missing.

Magali: Zut. Being dragged away. Signing off.

I make a note to look up the Old Port on my laptop, and SOS Labyrinthe.

"I'll come back later," Liam says, backing away.

"No need, she's off the grid for now. What's up?" I slide my phone on the nightstand and sit back down on the bed, forearms resting on my thighs, waiting.

He starts pacing the room, rubbing his hand over his mouth.

"Something worrying you about Éolie?" I straighten, growing concerned. When I left them downstairs, they were both calm and back to normal. I don't want him falling into another panic attack like the one he had last winter.

"Sort of." He plops his ass down on the bed next to mine, rubbing his palms over his thighs a couple of times. His forearms coming to rest over his legs, he interlocks his fingers, looking down at the paint-chipped wood plank floor, getting lost in thought. "Do you know one of the first things Magali asked Éolie and I on that morning?" He shakes his head, and the corner of his lips tugs in a ghost of a smile, mirroring mine, knowing what's coming. "Said we were lovely together, and that we'd make gorgeous babies."

Ah, Magali, love... "She'll be thrilled to see you applied yourself on the double," I say, relaxing back, the anecdote charming me.

"More than probably. Zac, man, your girl was over the moon, all lit up, and it was pretty clear to see that being a midwife means everything to her. She was celebrating making it into the program, so I guess if she was one of the chosen few, she's pretty damn good," Liam says, shoving his hands through his hair.

"Yeah, she's totally in her element, and so sharp and vibrant and passionate about..." My voice trails off into nothing as the dots connect. *Bloody hell.* I drop my head into my hands. If she meets them again before the twins are born, she'll be ecstatic for sure. But I don't have one good reason for her not to assist me in the monitoring like she does at the hospital, and the twins' metrics speak for themselves. And then what? I won't have any good explanation for monoamniotic, monochorionic twins born at home and doing extremely well, other than the truth ... A truth that I can't share. Won't share. Not if it might threaten Éolie's safety.

For a split second, I consider telling Magali. It's not like I doubt her. I know she's trustworthy. But just as quickly, I reject the idea. It's not about trust. Knowing something like that and seeing it ... It's a lot to take in.

I wince, as even knowing about Éolie's preternatural gifts, we all freaked anyway, witnessing it. I can well imagine the shock of being caught unaware.

Liam watches the byplay on my face, shooting me a tormented look. "After this morning ... Aww, man," he says, walking over to the window, bracing his hands on the upper frame. "You don't know how happy I am for you right now. But it's not my secret to tell, and I don't want Éolie to fret over it on the last few weeks left of her pregnancy."

"No, I get it. You're right. Éolie is special any way you look at it, and she needs to share by how much on her own terms, in her own time, and only if she wants to. I'll wait until the twins are born before bringing Magali over, no sweat."

In all probability, it's for less than the thirty-seven days left in any case, as twins are notorious for being early. I'll do my utmost to divert her attention away from the farmstead and meeting the guys for the time being. I think back to her text about staying in bed. Hmm. Going on a sex binge might do the trick. Harsh, I know.

"If I cut across the hills, using back roads, it's a fifteen-minute drive from her place to here, at a cruising speed of seventy kilometers per hour," I tell him. "We're good." Liam knows what signs to look for, and boy, does he look.

He sighs heavily, turning around.

"You'll need to keep it under wraps with Éolie as well, man. If she learns you're with Magali but that she can't meet with us for now ... she'll feel like a freak all over again, and it's the last thing I want."

"And the last thing I want is for either of you to worry. I'll do my part, and keep all this on the down low when I check on her." I walk over and fist bump his shoulder, looking him in the eye. "You're in charge of keeping it together. We'll need the both of you in top shape for what's to come. We're almost there and it's looking good. Let's keep it that way, mate."

"Thanks, man. I owe you." His hand comes up, and we fist bump on it.

"Don't mention it."

I'll keep her busy elsewhere.

Very busy.

Twenty-Seven

MAGALI

"And you think milk with cereal is disgusting but orange juice is okay?" I eye the orange goo warily from my place beside Zac on the steps of the minuscule deck that comes with my micro-loft.

"Absolutely," he replies, making a big production out of sipping his spoonful of soggy granola soup.

"You're not normal." I snort.

"I know, but don't I get points for trying? I'm a work in progress here," he says in a self-deprecating tone.

I inhale a sharp breath, my heart turning over just thinking of his early childhood. "That's not what I meant at all—"

"I'm just messing with you. I know what you meant." He winks, taking another spoonful, chewing the soggy lumps with exaggerated relish. "Mmm."

My eyes upturn before I check my watch. It's only seven twenty-six, ample time to report to the hospital by eight fifteen. With Zac's help, maybe I'll turn over a new leaf and begin showing up everywhere on time.

Leaving Zac to his weird taste in breakfast, I put my empty bowl down beside me, enjoying the early-morning sun on my face and arms. The warmth of the rays drying the dewy grass seeps through the thin material of my scrubs, and I stretch my legs over the two steps. It's already the last few days of July, the morning dew is heavier, the mornings, cooler, and August will bring summer to a close.

I marvel at how time flew the past two weeks, ever since walking in on a certain Docteur di Fiori. I tilt my head, looking at him, so handsome, so prim and proper in his pressed grey dress shirt and slacks. Very doctorly. I secretly grin, as not two hours ago we were anything but prim and proper, having wild hot monkey sex in my bed. My birth control injection makes for lots of spontaneous sex. It'd be hard to tell looking at him now, but it's like we've been on a sex binge for the last couple of weeks. I'm on the fast track to be all caught up from my previous years' dry spell.

"Wanna taste?" he asks playfully, bringing a spoonful up to my mouth, and I lean away, grimacing.

"Are you positive you're not pregnant?" I ask for the bazillion time.

"Want to get me pregnant?" He smirks.

"Yeah, then maybe you'd go for milk," I say, nudging his shoulder.

"Hey, I'm all for trying, but don't get your hopes up on the milk. The only way you can make me drink it is by eating it on a dipped cookie." He waggles his eyebrows. "Wanna go for it?"

"Oh, no. Nonono. What have I done?" I cry out gamely, one hand coming over my chest in an overly dramatic fashion. "I created a cookie monster of my own. What if I get sued for copyright infringements, then what?"

He laughs, putting down his bowl. "Come here, you. I'm your cookie monster, no one else's." One arm comes round my hips and he slides me up his side. "No time to make out, but I need a good hug to last me the day."

I kiss his temple and snuggle close. My head neatly tucked in the crook of his shoulder, I sigh, happy. For the next few minutes, we listen to bees buzzing in the nearby Echinacea flower beds in bloom. The plant's pink petals and burnt orange center cones are festive against the bright-green backdrop of the grass. They're probably my favorite flowers. I love their medicinal virtues and their sweet honey-scented perfume. In fact, all medicinal plants, and any forms of alternative medicine, ancient or new, fascinate me, really. Something else I'd like to integrate into my midwifery over time.

Zac takes my wrist and checks the time on my watch. Kissing the top of my head, before resting his chin on my shoulder, his arms enfold me. "We have five more minutes before we need to leave for the hospital."

"Speaking of which," I start, smoothing one hand over his thigh. "We have this Friday off, plus the weekend, and I checked. You're not on call. Want to go off-roading? Kayaking? Mountain biking? Meet and greet your friends? Hiking?" I ask, wondering if he'll deflect, like he did the last two days we had off, saying he was on call when he wasn't. He'd argued for staying in, claiming my bed was nearer the hospital than his, just in case. Not that I'd complained. My bed makes for a wild adventure all by itself when Zac shares it. But still, it's a Lilliputian island into itself, and I've been cooped up for half a year studying in there. I miss the great outdoors.

"Sounds ... fun. But you know what? It's only Wednesday, still early for plans, no? Let's play it by ear." His lips trail down my temple to my jaw, his tongue flicking on the corner of my mouth.

"See, that's the problem. Playing it by ear leads to your addictive lips and tongue, and the last two times we had days off, we never made it out of bed." I get up, brushing my scrubs off before picking up our dirty dishes.

"You don't see me complaining." His phone rings and his wolfish expression drops to dead serious in a flash as he answers it.

"I'm on my way," he says after listening in for only a second or two. Taking off at run, he palms his car keys, and I follow. He turns to me. "Family emergency. Tell them I'll be a few hours late, but I'll come in later on. I'll call when I can. If there's any concern you detect from this morning's appointments, ask them to wait for me to come back, okay? Otherwise, I'll sign your reports as you see fit."

"Yes, of course. Anything else I can do?" I ask, worried, my pulse in my throat.

"Nothing for now, love, thanks. I've got this," he calls out. "P.O., you with me?" he says into the phone he's still holding to his ear. "ETA ten minutes. Give me the stats."

He slides into his Jeep and shuts the door hard putting it in reverse.

I watch his taillights disappearing down the road as he peels off.

I take a few deep breaths, shaking out of my trance.

Zac needs me to handle things at the hospital on my own until he makes it back, and I won't disappoint.

Nodding once to myself, I lock up behind me and hoof it to the clinic.

"I've got this," I murmur.

Twenty-Eight

ZAC

I complete the last of the APGAR test on Nicolas, noting his score on his medical chart, satisfied with the results. The test, performed twice after birth, is designed to quickly evaluate a newborn's physical condition and to see if there's an immediate need for extra medical or emergency care. Appearance (skin color), Pulse (heart rate), Grimace response (reflexes), Activity (muscle tone), Respiration (breathing rate and effort). Each factor scores on a scale of zero to two, with two being the best score.

"And?" Liam asks, hovering over my shoulder as I go through the last of these standard newborn tests on Nicolas using the kitchen table as an exam bed, his anxious tone cutting through his euphoric moment.

I snap the tiny diaper back into place and adjust his miniature blue-and-yellow-striped beanie, before cuddling the tiny infant close to my chest, crooning sweet nothings into his ear. Man, the pull these little twins exert on me is off the chart. My heart pings in my chest, overcome by joy. "Ten on ten," I reassure Liam, taking pity on him. I can feel his swoosh of breath releasing on the back of my neck. Mine is not far behind, beyond relieved they made it here safe and sound despite the odds stacked against them from the very beginning.

Man, I swear Liam's floating two feet off the ground, and his elation is infectious I'm walking on air myself.

"You can go back to the hospital." Liam holds his hands out to take Nicolas from me, and I shoot him a look that says *not happening*.

"Get in line, man; we're good here. Aren't we, Nicolas?"

Liam shakes his head at me, chuckling low. "I can take over from here. Thanks, Zee."

"Your Papa is eager to get rid of me now that you're safely here, isn't he?" I ask Nicolas soothingly, one of my hands cradling his little head close to my chest. My heart expands as he starts rubbing his face on my shirt, wanting to burrow deeper into me. "Come." I kiss the top of his head. "Let's go check on your Maman and Sébastien one last time before I leave." I ignore Liam's outstretched arms and he grumbles behind me.

"Between you and the guys, I didn't foresee I'd need to take a number to hold my baby boys in my arms."

"Just goes to show your Papa knows jack about your powerful magic," I murmur to Nicolas, bringing him close to my nose, nuzzling his sweet baby cheek and inhaling his sweet baby scent as I make my way over to their bedroom.

"I'll see if I get better luck prying Sébastien away from P.O.'s arms." Liam overtakes us while I take my time, busy conversing with Nicolas.

"You know, you two brought me here in the first place, right? In turn, infusing me with the unparalleled thrill of welcoming new life into the world, giving me purpose," I confess softly, staring into his eyes. "But want to know what's your best gift of all?" Nicolas blinks at me, his face attentive, his cupid bow mouth hanging open, charming the socks out of me. "Well, since you want to know, I'll spill." I smile softly, thinking of Magali. "All of this gifted me with the best possible reason in the world to stick around and I'll eternally be grateful for it. You'll know why, soon." We stare at one another, and I get lost the space of an instant into bluer than baby blue eyes, all seeing, all knowing. "That's right. I'm bringing her over to meet you two later on today," I say quietly, my heart overflowing with happiness.

I'm not as clinically detached here, but I really enjoy being less technical in my approach to the twins; a rare threat for me. It gives me a firsthand taste of fatherhood. One I like. And suddenly, I can't wait to get back to the hospital and Magali.

As though reading my mind, Liam pops back out. "Are you bringing Magali over today, or tomorrow?"

"Today, just as soon as this afternoon's clinic appointments are over with," I reply enthused before stepping into the bedroom.

"Cool," Liam replies a twinkle in his eyes, fighting a grin. "Can't wait," he adds somewhat cryptically, but I don't get to ponder his last comment too much.

Everyone gathered round the bed looks up from Sébastien, cuddled in P.O.'s arms, Yann's index finger firmly held in his tiny grip. Yann's usual stern features are softened by a warm grin. The same grin we're all wearing and can't seem to shake.

"So, did he score as high as Sébastien did?" Leo asks, walking over to take a peek at Nicolas, who blinks owlishly back at him. "See, he recognizes me already." Leo smiles down on him, brushing the back of his fingers on a velvety soft cheek. The little dude in my arms sighs in what could pass for bliss ... or gas. Leo puffs up his chest and takes him from me before Liam can.

Liam crosses his arms, shooting me a look that says, *see what I mean?*

"Well, hello there," Leo coos at Nicolas, solemnly swearing to him, "I promise I won't poke and probe like Uncle Zac does. Stick with me."

My eyes upturn.

Nicolas yawns, his eyelids drooping. I smirk at Leo. "He recognizes you all right, you're as fun as a stick in the mud."

"Hey, I resent that!" Leo mock glares over Nicolas's head before saying to him, "Playing in the mud is my specialty, we'll have loads of fun, you'll see."

Éolie, her back resting against her sea of pillows, shakes her head at us with a glowing smile. "Just by the look on Liam's face, I know Nicolas passed his APGAR with flying colors. Ten on ten?" she asks me and I concur, the guys and I sharing in their joy for the next few minutes. She beams, holding her arms out, and Leo deposits his little bundle into her waiting hands. Liam scoots on the bed, close to them.

"They both got my seal of approval. Good work you did there." I brush one hand over Nicolas's head who looks on his Maman with fascination, no longer so sleepy.

"No, you got that wrong, Zee. They did it all; they're extraordinary. I'm in awe of them," Éolie says lost in Nicolas's stare, her voice warm and soft. She nuzzles her nose on his cheek, love outpouring from her. It warms my heart, witnessing it.

"You need to take credit where it's due just as well, you know," I say to her, propping one shoulder on the wall by the bed, hands in my pockets. "If only all of my patients had your ability to heal that quickly or deliver as painlessly—"

"Painlessly, man?" Yann shakes his head, fighting a laugh. "I'm scarred for life. You missed Liam in all his glory experiencing shared contractions with Éolie just before you got here. We thought he was dying the way he hollered his way through them."

"Éolie was doing great at the time. Liam, not so much." P.O. smirks, relinquishing Sébastien into his Papa's waiting arms.

I chuckle low, shaking my head. These two give new meaning to shared pain, or pleasure, as connected as they are. Must have been a sight.

"Yeah, if we recall, Liam, here, swore up and down he'd gladly eschew sex for the rest of his life if it meant the god-awful pain would stop," Leo snickers, and the others follow suit. "Abstinence, he screamed once or twice at the top of his lungs."

"That was then," Liam says, unfazed, totally absorbed in his twin adoration. "Try and stop me now that Zee gave us the green light!" Éolie shares a warm look with him before turning to me.

"I can get up and about, right?"

"Yeah, you can. Just take it easy, though," I warn her. "I know you've been looking forward to this moment for the past six months, but don't overdo it. Got that?"

"Got it," she replies enthusiastically, and I get the distinct impression that we don't ascribe to the same definition of overdoing it at this stage.

I give her a stern look. "I mean it."

"I know. I promise." She crosses a finger over her heart. "Besides, how can I possibly overdo anything with four mother hens hovering by?"

"We'll all see to it," Liam replies and the three others chorus.

I straighten away from the wall, giving the twins one last caress on their little beanie covered heads. "I'll be back by the end of the afternoon." *With a surprise of my own.* "But call me if you need anything meanwhile," I instruct Éolie.

"You're not staying overnight at the hospital today?" Éolie asks slyly.

The guys all give me knowing looks.

I can't help the loopy grin I feel spreading on my face at the thought of bringing Magali over to meet them all.

"Nope. Today's special. I'm bringing over the love of my life to meet all of you." I saunter out, hearing Éolie's pleased outburst in the background. "I knew it! What did I tell you? Zac's in love. Isn't it some kind of wonderful?"

I pop my head back in. "I know, right?" I repeat one of Magali's favorite saying and Éolie beams up at me. "Later." I wink at her, pleased to no end by the joy permeating this place.

Twenty-Nine

MAGALI

Zac made it back to the clinic just before lunch time. He's different than earlier. Lighter somehow. And when I asked what happened he answered, "Magic. The best kind there is," but refused to say more, insisting on a surprise waiting for me after this afternoon's clinic appointments ... Time hasn't crawled in such an awful way since Madame Fréchette's French grammar classes in Secondaire IV, but finally, we're off.

"So, I'm really going over to your place to meet your GGS crew—and that's not the surprise?" I buckle up.

Zac's lips curl up in my favorite lopsided smile, the one showing a dimple. He gives me a sidelong glance, reaching for his sunglasses in the cup holder. The late-afternoon sun gilds his dark-brown hair with auburn highlights. His animated features are so boyish-looking right now that I can't resist ruffling his shaggy mane.

"Looks like it." He winks at me, a contagious smile etching on his face.

He turns the ignition and shifts into first, then second, driving down the avenue, away from the hospital. He's been wearing that smile pretty much all day, and since I like him wearing it so much better than the shuttered look he wore this morning—and for the past two weeks before it—I'm more excited than he knows.

"Where are we headed?" I ask, curious. His friend's house sits in the middle of the great unknown. The few times the subject came up, Zac always gave me vague answers like "not far from here," or, "in the area," before giving me a scorching kiss the likes of which made me forget my own name.

He shoots me his patented lopsided grin, before replying slyly, "You'll see. No questions allowed, remember."

"It better be good," I say jokingly. "I'm still wearing scrubs for this meet and greet, I'll have you know." I smooth down my stork-printed scrub top, one of my favorites. The drawings of baby deliveries I find hilariously quirky on a blue sky and white cloud back drop. There's even a stork wearing a smirk and sunglasses that bears a faint resemblance to Zac at his most cocky.

"I like you in scrubs," he says, downshifting. "But my favorite look, by far, is you wearing skin and nothing else. Preferably wrapped around me."

"AAAaah, don't you give me that look," I cry out, putting my hands up to the side of my face to block the view of his smoldering grin. He slows to a stop at the Carrefour, and signals a left turn, towards Val-David, same direction as my hometown.

"What look?" He shrugs innocently, giving me *the* sinful drool-worthy look, complete with hot burning copper-eyed gaze over his sunglasses.

"You're doing it again, aren't you?"

"Doing what?" The light turns green, and he turns onto La Montée du Rang Deux.

"Distracting me. Seducing me away from knowledge? You all what, live in a bat cave, secretly wear tights, and have super powers no one knows about?"

Zac startles, and the clutch slips.

Oops? Have I offended him with the wearing tights in a bat cave comment?

"It'd be cool if you did, just to let you know, and my lips would be sealed." I zip my lips closed, even though he can't really see since he's focused on driving.

Rather than an answering quip and our usual banter, though, he asks, instead, his tone of voice curious, "If you had the choice of one, what super power would you choose?"

"Healing, hands down," I readily say, as it's one of the things that fascinate me with alternative medicine, the power to unlock untapped abilities within our bodies. "You?"

"Flying, hands down, but healing is a good one," he answers, pondering. "And to think I've always been the wizard healer type in games."

"That's okay, you can fly me over, WizardMan, and I'll heal them. We're a team, non?" A pleased look washes over his face.

"We are that," he replies. "And nope, that's not my nickname, by the way."

I tuck back into my messy bun strands of flyaway hair that keep whipping in my face. "You still play computer games?" I ask, wondering when he has time for that. He didn't show any signs of withdrawals symptoms in the past two weeks holed up with me, anyway.

"No, but two of my buds still do, from time to time."

"Um. Let me guess..." The wind whips out from my bun the same short strands, and the ends of my hair sting my cheeks like tiny needle pricks against my skin.

I search through my top's pockets for some hairpins or a clip before I go bananas. All of my everyday clothes have deep, zipped, or velcroed pockets that double as a purse on any given day. I rummage and come up with three hairpins. *Victoire.* I secure the flyaway strands, saved from madness.

I tap my fingers on my lips. "I'll go for ByteMan and MathMan?" I guess.

"Spot on," he chuckles low, shaking his head. "They'll never know what hit them," he adds to himself.

Hair combat and conversation no longer the sole recipient of my focus, I let my gaze sweep the vicinity, orienting, and my brows lift upward.

"No questions allowed?" I ask, making sure. Not that it's weird or anything, but we're turning onto the road, leading to my road, and there's not that much over there but my parents' place and Old Léon's place, in between patches of wilderness.

"None allowed. You'll see soon enough," Zac says, an enigmatic grin now playing on his lips.

All the way up the bumpy road, Zac stays quiet. Although, from the excited vibe he exudes, he's probably biting his tongue not to spill any incriminating clues that would spoil the surprise alluded to all afternoon.

My thoughts spin in a circle.

I didn't tell my parents about Zac *per se* over the phone, preferring to let them meet in person when the right time comes. Anyway, they aren't due back for another few days, beginning of next week to my knowledge. So, even if they guessed by my tone that I'm head over heels in love with Zac, aka Docteur di Fiori, from the quick conversation we had last week, and they contacted him and prepared some sort of surprise greeting, huh ... Nope. Not really their style, for one, and they're in Québec City, which puts some three hundred kilometers between us and them.

But nothing else makes sense. We never really talked in details about my roots, what with patients to discuss and sex binging in between. Oh, and sleep, a necessary evil what with all the physical exertion we've been engaging in.

But no two ways about it, either we're en route to my parents' place or a drive down to the village from the other side.

We're driving past the familiar bend in the road. Past Oscar, the centennial maple tree missing two of his four central limbs. Past the fallow fields and the abandoned barn with its roof caved in since the winter of 2013, and we're about to drive by Old Léon's farmstead, up on the hill.

My eyes grow wide as Zac turns into the winding driveway I know so well, parking by the woodshed in the back.

He cuts the engine, his matte-charcoal Jeep sticking out in a sea of Volvos, three Cross-Country station wagons, to be exact, one a bright red. Amélie would swoon at the sight; she's a Volvo for life kind of girl.

I just sit there, staring.

"You know Liam and Éolie, the new owners?" I finally squeak as he rounds the front of the Jeep and opens my door.

"Yeah, I live with them, and a few others of my GGS crew," Zac says, tucking behind my ear one of the strands that stubbornly keeps flying away from my bun, no matter how many hairpins I shove in it.

"Get out," is all I can manage to say.

His eyes twinkle, his lips fighting a pleased, "mission accomplished" kind of grin as he takes in my floored look. He bends over me to unbuckle my seatbelt, and tugs me out by my useless hands. Wow, looks like someone up there made sure we would eventually trip all over each other, over and over and over again, until we got the memo. I send a quick thank you to the Man Upstairs, filled with gratitude.

Zac swings an arm around my shoulders, steering me towards the front veranda, instead of the back door. I don't think I've ever walked through the front door of this place.

"Come on, there's a few people I'd like you to meet besides Liam and Éolie—" His hand stills on the doorknob. His brow furrows in thought. "Wait. Now that I think of it. Didn't you meet once at a bed and breakfast in Saint-Sauveur? How did you know Liam and Éolie live here?"

The door swings open and I miss the last of Zac's question, no longer listening.

"I thought I saw your Jeep driving up, Lili. Guess I was right. Are you coming in or staying out?"

"Papa?" I cry out joyously. Not bothering to correct him on the Jeep's ownership—they look like carbon copies from afar—I fall into his arms for a hug and two kisses. "I thought you were staying over in Québec City for the weekend on your way back from Charlevoix?"

I feel Zac hovering behind me, standing straight as a flag pole on the covered porch. My Papa arches a brow, giving Zac a funny look over my shoulder and a nod in greeting that Zac returns.

I shoot him a reassuring smile, but he's slack-jawed, struck speechless, staring at my dad who, I must admit, makes for an imposing figure standing in the entryway. Not that he's tall at five seven, but his broad shoulders fill up the doorway, and his stern features and light-blond hair, whitening at the temples, speak of his Viking ancestry.

"Turns out some sort of convention got in full swing in the city, and it got too overcrowded for our taste. Even before receiving Liam's call with his news this morning, we had decided to cut the last of our trip short."

"Liam's news? What news? And is Maman here with you?" I ask excitedly, taking hold of Zac's hand, hanging as limp as a used dishrag by his side. I squeeze it once, comfortingly. This is so neat. If my Maman is here as well, I'll introduce him to both my parents while he's in the midst of his own family.

"Grégoire is *your* dad," he murmurs for my ears only.

"You two already know each other?" I ask them, only to hit the palm of my hand on my forehead. "Duh. You live at Old Léon's." Not only are they my parents' closest neighbors, but my dad worked with Liam on clearing his road to the meadow all through Spring, so guess there were plenty of occasions for them to meet.

My Papa's stern features softens, silver-grey eyes crinkling at the corners, darting between Zac and me. "Yes, we've met before, and your Maman's in the back with Éolie, as everyone else is for now. You'll see why soon enough." My Papa shares a knowing look with Zac over my head. Zac's lips tug up one side.

UmUm. My eyes narrow on them. If Zac hadn't been so surprised about my dad, nor me for finding him here when I thought he'd be in Québec City, I would have thought they'd planned this all along.

My Papa leans a shoulder in the doorway. "Now the question is—"

"I'll see what?" I try to look past my dad.

"Always in such a headlong rush." My Papa shakes his head at me, hugging my shoulder to him, preventing me from crossing over the threshold. "Not so fast, young lady. Give your old man a minute here, to look at you." He leans back, searching my face. "It's good to see you all aglow. I'd say these past couple of weeks working under your Maître de Stage have been *exceptionally* good to you." He cocks a brow at Zac.

Zac chokes. I give him a look. Are the tips of his ears reddening?

"Yes—"

"Oui—"

We speak over each other.

"So, tell me, Zac," My dad interjects. He cocks his head to the side, rubbing his jaw, assessing, but his eyes twinkle. "You wouldn't happen to be my daughter's exceptional Maître de Stage now, would you?"

Zac only has eyes for me as he replies, "Her Maître de Stage? Yes. Exceptional? No. She's the exceptional one. That's all on her, Grégoire, not me." Zac brings my hand up to his lips and kisses my knuckles. His eyes are warm, making my stomach flip. "Your daughter's remarkable in every way."

"That she is."

"I know. Believe me, I know." When Zac drops an airy kiss on my forehead, my heart turns over. "You mean the world to me," he murmurs.

"Good. Let's keep it that way, shall we?" My Papa catches Zac's gaze, trapping it. I watch as a silent conversation passes between them. My dad ends the staring contest, patting Zac on the shoulder a couple of times. "I'm glad it's you, Zac."

"So am I," Zac says, eyes getting lost in mine.

"So am I," I whisper with quiet conviction, drowning in the warm softness of Zac's tender gaze.

"Well, guess that's my cue to go check on Vie and let you have your moment. Don't take too long, you two, or the horde inside will descend on you." The door clicks shut behind us.

Zac tucks a strand of hair behind my ear. "So, Grégoire and Vie ... Small world."

"I know, right? You're living where I grew up, my parents live over there." I point over the hill. "I played all over this place..." I gesture around. I still do, whenever I can. Some of my favorite spots on earth are here, in this forest ... It's where I come to think and dream.

"I know now. I didn't know then, or we would have met again months ago, I promise you." The back of his fingers trail down my cheek and I lean into his touch. "I met your parents last winter. The six of us had such a blast with them on the eve of our fateful meet at Mont-Saint-Sauveur, prepping the meadow for a surprise to Éolie." I watch a soft smile play on his lips. "Upon folding camp, a few days after we met, they ... sat me down for a talk. I didn't talk about you *per se*, to my everlasting regret now. But they helped me clear some of my muddled thoughts. And ... here I am."

My fingertips trail down his jaw. Warmth fills me, feeling gratefulness to be here, in this moment. "Makes me so, so glad, you borrowed them to un-muddle your thoughts." I brush strands of his overgrown shaggy hair back from his forehead and he closes his eyes briefly, sighing.

"So am I." He lowers his head and captures my mouth in a quick kiss. "If you ever doubted that we were meant to be, doubt no more. And now that I got the memo and stopped kicking my own ass for not talking about you sooner, you better believe I won't lose any more time than I already did, just so we're clear."

"I'm not going anywhere. Bring it on," I say, floating on a hazy cloud of happy.

He leans one shoulder on the door. "You bet I will." My cheeks flush with heat, and he grins like a kid. He straightens, dropping a kiss on the tip of my nose. "I'm curious though, they never talked about it? My meeting them, the guys?"

"Never in a million years would they talk about other peoples' business, unless specifically required. They'd consider even light gossip as a breach of confidentiality."

"That's ... refreshing." His eyes take on a faraway look.

"Refreshing? That's a new one, but then, I wouldn't really know any different." I frown in thought. "My mom is my dad's paralegal, and they worked together for some thirty-five years now. So I don't know how much of it is ingrained by their profession or how much of it is simply their personalities." I shrug. "Guess by now it's both." My brows clear on a new thought. "They're a team just like us." The smile that blooms on Zac's cheeks mirrors mine, I'm sure, and it's like watching the rise of a new dawn. I kiss the tip of my index finger before pressing it on his lips. "Anyway, the point is, you can continue to borrow them all you want. All of your secrets are safe with them."

"Duly noted." His strong arms squeeze me in a hug, and he drops a kiss on the top of my head. "Ready now for your surprise?" he asks tenderly. His infectious grin is impossible to resist, and I let myself fall into his smile.

"I've been ready for the past four hours; pretty sure your nickname's CruelMan, and if not, it should be," I tease, grabbing the doorknob.

He chuckles low, his hand pressing down on the door. "Before we go in, you should know I wanted you all to myself the last couple of weeks. So please don't hold it against me that I waited so long, because after today, you might not notice me again for a while."

"Duly warned, and ready," I quote him back.

Guess I wasn't near as ready as I thought.

In the best possible way...

Thirty

ZAC

Apprehension

noun

4. the faculty or act of apprehending or understanding; perception on a direct and immediate level.

Early evening finds me watching Magali from Liam's bedroom doorway. I rub my chest, feeling it expand some more at the nurturing vision unfolding before me.

Magali bends and kisses Sébastien's forehead, her liquid silver gaze showering love down on the tiny infant as she smoothes down his light-blue cotton beanie over his head. Éolie unswaddles him, careful not to snag the umbilical stump with its plastic clamp sealing it shut as she changes his diaper. They coo and reassure the little guy with soft words and hands.

Liam, half sitting, half sprawled, propped against the sea of pillows behind his back, cradles Nicolas in the crook of his arm, watching him sleep with something akin to adoration.

They're identical, and yet, so different, that we can already distinguish them by personalities alone when they're awake without a visual prop to know at a glance who's who. But for now, a little blue-and-yellow-striped beanie covered head pokes out from a light cotton flannel blanket swaddling him. A dead give-away for Nicolas.

Leo comes from behind, looking over my shoulder. "Guess you didn't factor in the twins' super powers when you brought your girl over to meet the lot of us. It's been what, five hours now she's been with them? She barely noticed her own parents leaving. You may have lost her, man."

"Yeah, but look at her, isn't it worth it?" I murmur back, her face washed by a Madonna glow that's holding me spellbound. I don't really get to see that side of motherhood in great detail, my part in it being more technical.

But Magali? Magali embraces it right alongside the moms and goes all out. Aside from Éolie, she's the most nurturing soul I've ever met. And she's falling for me. The thought alone is enough to bring me to my knees.

"I'll tell you when I get there." Leo claps my shoulder. "Meanwhile, I'm getting another bottle of Chablis, want some?"

"Might as well," I say as Leo continues on to the kitchen. "Magali wants to stay overnight." She's likely to abscond with the twins otherwise. I shake my head.

"You won't see me complaining. I haven't seen Liam this relaxed in … forever," Leo says, over his shoulder. "Your Magali sure knows her baby stuff, man, and she has a soothing effect."

"Yeah, that she does," I agree, leaning a shoulder in the doorway.

With my hands shoved in my pockets, I unashamedly eavesdrop, watching the girls interact with the tiny baby, one of the full-sized cribs in the corner, on the opposite side of the room, serving duty as a changing table for now. Until they start rolling over by themselves, the other one will be used for both the twins. Eventually, anyway, as they have yet to sleep anywhere other than in somebody's arms…

"I know, right?" Magali replies to something Éolie said. "Yesterday, you went through your day unknowing you'd wake up to a July twenty-seven that would mean so much. And, suddenly, what's always been just another date on the calendar will hold a powerful magic all of its own forever."

"Magic's the word. Even prepared for it, it's still a bit surreal," Éolie sighs dreamily. "I can't really believe they're here."

"I can well imagine." Magali folds the top half of a fresh baby blanket in a triangle and Éolie gently deposits Sébastien on top. "It's truly amazing how well you're doing so soon after giving birth, but still. Remember to take it easy for the next little while, even as tempting as it is to get it all done now that you're up and about." Magali enjoins Éolie as she stacks piles of onesies and blankets into the crib from a laundry basket by her feet.

"I'll see to it," Liam vows, his face set, daring Éolie to argue the point, as she was caught folding laundry in the mud room a couple of hours ago.

"I'll do my best, promise." Éolie crosses her finger over her heart, enveloping Liam in a warm, tender look, and yeah, my bud is done for. His set features soften as he shakes his head at her. Man, do I know the feeling now. The moon? No problem, yours.

"I really should insist you go lie down for this," Magali says, rubbing Éolie's back in circular strokes, comfortingly. "Getting to do it on your lap, comfortably sprawled in bed, is but one of the hundreds of side benefits to infant massages, just so you know."

"I know, but all I've done the past six months is rest and take it easy. Now, I've this overflow of euphoric energy coursing through me, and I really don't feel like lying down, *at all*." Éolie's index finger strokes Sébastien's palm and, in perfect grasp reflex, he grips it in a stronghold. "I'm pretty sure my oxytocin levels are through the roof, and I'm probably drunk on them. I feel so well."

"All right, p'tite maman, you win this one. We'll do it standing up." Magali squeezes Éolie's shoulders before giving her full attention back to tiny Sébastien. "Aww, chouchou. Aren't your little toes to die for? Yes, they are," Magali coos, and they both gush over Sébastien for the next few minutes. I crack a smile. Man, they're probably both high on oxytocin, commonly called the bonding hormone.

Éolie, smiling down on Sébastien, her eyes lost in his, coos to him, "Nicolas swooned in bliss. You'll get to know why, now."

"Okay, your turn." Magali hands over to Éolie a small bottle of organic infant massage lotion with chamomile extracts she showed me earlier on, the sample made locally from l'herboristerie La Clé des Champs. I shake my head, for really, what she keeps in her pockets is a universe in itself.

"Oh, non, non," Éolie shakes her head. "It'd be unfair to Sébastien," she says, kissing the sole of his feet. "After all, Nicolas got you to do it and I wouldn't know how to begin, so I'd rather watch and learn."

"No worries. I'll start and then I'll guide you." Magali squirts a few droplets of the lotion in one of her hands and starts rubbing her palms together, warming it beforehand. I watch, enthralled, held under the spell of her graceful movements and gentle ways.

The girls are so absorbed in what they're doing that my presence goes unnoticed, as busy as they are cooing all over Sébastien, who laps it up, all eyes, a sure sign of his great taste in women.

Liam shoots me a knowing look, and motions me over.

"Get comfortable, they're on a roll."

"You think?" I ask drily, crossing over to him. "I'd say Sébastien's got it made."

"Just as Nicolas never a stood a chance, rendered KO by massage," Liam concurs. Stretching his legs out on the bed, he settles the infant on his chest, his palms cradling him preciously. I rub a palm soothingly over Nicolas's head, and the little dude sighs in his sleep, tugging at my heartstrings.

"Yeah, he's a goner," I say warmly. *We both are.* Ever since Magali and I arrived here at the end of the afternoon, Nicolas stayed awake, wide-eyed, pretty much the whole time, but little Sébastien had to be woken for a feeding just now.

I lean back on the wall beside the bed. I'm in no hurry to return outside where the guys are celebrating their new status as uncles. I enjoy the sight unfolding before my eyes much more.

Éolie follows attentively as Magali cradles both Sébastien's tiny feet in her hands. She massages the lotion onto his skin, pressing on his soles gently with her thumbs, careful not to startle him nor trigger his Moro reflex— an instinctive response in newborns to a sudden loss of support, where his arms would spread stiff with a heart-wrenching cry. It is believed to be the only unlearned fear in human newborns, and swaddling goes a long way into comforting them in their first few days of life.

"We start at the soles, pressing gently down the center, and we work our way up, slowly, kneading the lotion in, one limb at a time," Magali explains to Éolie, but directs her words toward Sébastien in a soothing tone of voice, mesmerizing him, as well as me. I never get tired of watching her interact with moms and babies alike. "Now, you try it."

"Like this?" Éolie asks, unsure. Her hands curving over hers, Magali confirms, making sure the light pressure's just right, all the while talking her through, keeping Sébastien entranced. Under Magali's tutelage, Éolie's previous nervousness soon dissolves into newfound assurance. Her strokes are smooth and confident, and in no time, the lines of concentration disappear from her brow and her features clear, both baby and mother enjoying the bonding time.

"Hey, little one, your Maman's a natural." Magali kisses the top of Sébastien's head.

"It's all on you. It's so much more reassuring to have someone here to show me how to do it right from the first. I can't thank you enough, you really made our day." Éolie's movements are not only gentle but self-assured, now, as she swaddles Sébastien back in his light blanket, pulling him up to her chest, kissing him.

"Hey, seeing you both like this, well adjusting and all relaxed, makes *my* day, and it's worth everything," Magali sighs happily. "So really, no thanks necessary."

"No, really, it's worth saying, Magali. I studied nursery caregiving for years and years, and knowledge by itself gives you zero practice, zero experience. It's unnerving when faced with the real deal, and you made all the difference," Éolie insists.

"You'll have a gazillion more hands-on experiences than me in no time," Magali says, squeezing Éolie's shoulders in a hug, kissing her cheek. "But still, I know what you mean. Textbook learning is one thing but the real deal is trial by fire, and it's a bit terrifying when they're so small and vulnerable." Magali, her eyes warm and tender, trails the back of her fingers down Sébastien's cheek, and the little guy yawns wide, his face scrunching comically.

It's catching. I yawn and so does Liam.

With the massage over, I straighten from my slouch by the wall on the other side of the room, kept partially hidden from view by the blue wardrobe. "What's a guy to do to get a kiss around here?" I ask teasingly, walking over to Magali and pulling her to me.

"Um. Well, if he's taller than fifty centimeters and doesn't wear a diaper, he can always ask and see what happens." Magali, balancing on my forearms, gets up on the tip of her toes to drop a sweet kiss on my temple.

"And you wondered why I wanted to keep you a little while longer all to myself?"

"Good point, but in my defense, I thought you were out on the veranda with the other uncles. Have you been here long?" she asks, perplexed.

"There's no way to answer that without adding voyeurism to his long list of sins." Liam snickers, and I let out a snort.

"Sooo that's what it's called," Éolie explains to Sébastien, rubbing noses.

"Not when I do the watching," Liam deadpans. "Come here, you." With Nicolas sleeping on his chest, Liam holds out his hands, and Éolie transfers Sébastien into his papa's waiting arms while she climbs into bed. Sébastien's eyelids flutter close on another huge yawn taking over half his face, and he's out for the count. "And we have another one KO by massage."

"I would too, if you massaged me the same," I murmur close to Magali's ear.

"No can do. Your feet are too big, or my hands are too small, whichever." She bumps her shoulder with mine. "But really, you've been here that long, and I didn't even notice, like at all?" Magali asks me softly, clearly baffled, and I almost laugh out loud at her wide-eyed surprise, they were both so engrossed.

"You've no idea," I tsk tsk. "My ego crashed and burned."

"Good, then. Now that your ego's flat as a waffle, you'll still fit in the doorway when I finish telling you that you're my hero, and the twins are so very lucky to have you in their lives," Magali says the last in earnest, hugging me tight. Her words echoes the ones her mom, Vie, said to me last winter.

I don't really know what to say to that. I kiss the top of her head, touched, despite myself, but I can't help but think that it's the other way around. I'm the one who's lucky to have them in my life ... her included.

"Agreed," Liam concurs, and I give him a cut it out look over Magali's head. "You made all the difference, man. Own it," he says.

"See what I mean?" Magali insists. "Every family should have a *you*."

"And a *you*." Éolie beams up at Magali, and that I can wholeheartedly agree on. "I'm so happy you two hit it off; you're so lovely together," she says, her eyes dancing with joy as they dart between us. Her words fill me with warmth.

"And where have I heard that one before?" Liam asks Magali, amused.

"And was I right, or was I right?" Magali, eyes twinkling, says to him, enthused, daring him to say otherwise. "You two make gorgeous babies, *own it*."

"Yeah, you predicted right, indeed." Liam tugs Éolie close to him, and they exchange a warm, loving look, before they both get lost in the twins, Liam as high on them as she is. And I know I'll need to remind Éolie to pace herself.

"Yeah, she did. You do make gorgeous babies, and speaking of. Doctor's orders, they sleep, you rest, stat," I say pointedly to Éolie, and she looks up from her twins in contemplation.

"What he says." Liam motions with his head.

"I know, I know." Éolie pouts, and Magali helps them secure the twins side by side in the crib with one last kiss on each tiny baby.

"No worries. I'm sure rest will be over with quickly. They'll be up in no time for night feeding," Magali says, resolutely turning her toward the bed.

"Up in no time, all the time," I remind Éolie.

"I know. Resting now."

"I'll make sure she does." Liam's arms enfold her as he murmurs in her ear, and she cuddles next to him.

I close the door behind us.

I place a hand on the small of Magali's back as we make our way to the front porch, and the three others assembled there.

"Can I ask you something?" Magali's brows furrow in question.

"Shoot."

"Why did you wait until the twins were born to bring me here? I would have helped you with pleasure if I had known."

"I know you would have, you're a brilliant midwife." I close my hand around her delicate wrist, and pull her to a stop. I look her in the eye. "First and foremost, I selfishly wanted you to myself for a little while longer and that's the god honest truth. I crave this intimacy we have going on, something I've never had before. And, well ... beyond the fact I wanted to surprise you just as much?" I sigh. It's really not my secret to tell, but at least some of the truth can be shared easily.

"Éolie had an unusual upbringing. She lived her whole life on a scientific sailboat in remote corners of the world up until, well, less than a year ago. She's still getting used to living on land where lots of human specimens roam. The twins are bringing her out of her shell and I'm glad you two hit it off so well. But as she was on the very last legs of her pregnancy, Liam got worried it would be too much for her adding this late in the game another caregiver and that she would stress it out. I wanted both not to fret on the small stuff, you know..."

"Thanks for sharing the info, I understand better now. Like I said, they're lucky to have you." She kisses my cheek warmly, and I'm touched beyond words. "Want to have hundreds and hundreds of gorgeous babies with me?" She tilts her head sideways, her face a study in angelical innocence, discounting the impish glint in her eyes.

I give her cute stork-printed scrubs the onceover. Good to know where she's coming from with this proposition, otherwise a guy could just keel over from the shock. "Hundreds and hundreds, hey?"

She takes both my hands, interlacing our fingers, leaning into me, stars in her eyes.

"Yeah, I mean, look at those two back there. Gorgeous all the way. And Éolie blows my mind. She's living proof that I'm on the right track with my dissertation. She's the embodiment of all those stats on births taking place in a cozier environment doing wonders for both mother and baby that I pulled out from clinics in Finland and Norway to beef up my proposal," she says all in one breath. Shuffling backward, she pulls me along towards the front door. "I really hope we can build a regular program over here, similar to theirs. One that's less clinical in its choices, with a homey feel thrown in there, just like the twins had, thanks to you."

"Thanks to me? Nope. Pretty sure Éolie did all the work here—"

"*And* she had you."

With her back now pressed to the wood-carved door, I brace my hands on either side of her.

"Are we arguing the point?"

"Not if we can make out instead." Magali sighs, clinging to my shoulders as I nuzzle her neck, inhaling the sweet baby smell clinging to her skin.

"Good answer."

However, no sooner said, the momentum of the door swinging open sends the both of us stumbling into Yann. He staggers back a step under impact but prevents us all from toppling over.

"Oops. Busted," Magali says, wide-eyed, holding in a laugh.

"You two need a crash course on the laws of probability or gravity?" Yann deadpans, sending Magali into spurts of airy laughter as I extricate us.

"Throw in a refresher on the laws of physics as well." P.O. smirks, slouched into one of the Adirondacks, hands laced behind his head.

My eyes upturn and Leo snickers, saluting me with his wineglass. "Weird déjà-vu, here. Liam, Éolie, *The* makeout of winter 2016, well, discounting the almost face plant."

"Discounting the door as a prop, you mean. Man, you almost gave me a heart attack." Yann plops his ass on a section of banister that still has its balusters intact.

"About that, for chrissakes, Leo. I swear, yours is the only bloody house whose bloody front door opens from the inside, out," I grumble, sending Magali into another fit of giggles.

"That's because it's not the front door, it's the outer door," she says as I pull her down on my lap on the improvised porch bench, one of the many twin beds from upstairs we brought out so Éolie could rest outside a few hours a day. The bed squeaks, and the mattress dips as she twists sideways, curling into me in a tight little ball. I settle back against the banister, testing my weight, making sure we're good, a necessary reflex to develop around here.

"You mean to say his bloody house doesn't even have a bloody front door?" I grunt, one of my arms enfolding her. But I must admit, it's a pretty neat way to spend a warm summer evening: outside, my girl comfortably snuggled up to me. No matter the lumpy mattress and the wood ramp digging into my shoulder blades. Maybe some horizontal tango if we lose the guys ... I make a quick estimation of the odds of that happening on a full house. Not happening.

And I ditch the plan, for a new one. A house of our own. No, not just a house, *a home*. We could have met again six months ago upon my return here if I'd opened up about her sooner, now knowing her parents are our neighbors. I could kick my own ass for that, but I'm still ahead of schedule of the original plan to go after Magali this upcoming November by four months. And didn't I just vow earlier this afternoon not to lose any more time?

I drop a kiss on Magali's head, envisioning a quiet evening at home with her, after our day at the clinic. I'm unused to all of this, but one thing's for sure. In this newfound intimacy we share, Magali completes me in many ways, and we're better practitioners for it. And I love it.

My heart thuds in my chest.

I want all of her days, all of her nights, more than ever.

Now to make it official...

"I'm supposed to have *two* front doors?" Leo asks, getting up to inspect said door, pulling me out of my thoughts.

"Not with newer doors you wouldn't, but as old as this place is, yes," Magali answers, straightening from her slouch, and I mourn the loss of her kittenish curl on my lap. "That's the winter storm one. It opens from the outside so that the two combine in an SAS effect, and it's supposed to be switched to a screen door for the summertime. I don't know where the original front door went, but with only this one, you must be freezing in winter with the draft."

"So I have a missing door?" Leo asks, nonplussed as he pours me a glass of Chablis and Magali declines, stating she'll take a few sips from mine.

"You're missing two, man, if you ask me," I tell him, and Magali brows crinkle. "Back door is uselessly duct-taped to death, don't ask."

"And a few upstairs windows," P.O. mutters, and I hold in a snort.

"Depends on what you think constitutes a few," Yann adds.

"Stop complaining, boys, it's on my list." Leo rubs his jaw, his gold eyes turning speculative as he eyes Magali under the low glow of the veranda's light fixtures. "Means you know the place pretty well, then?"

"Not so much the house, but the land? Like the back of my hand." She sighs again, her eyes wide and luminous. "My eldest brother, Renaud, worked for Monsieur Léon on the farm on its last two operating years, and Lucas, my other brother, and I, used to spend our summers running wild around here. And what a time we had, at turn fairies, wizards, and knights on quests in the nature preserve at the back. I love everything about this place. It's a magical kingdom," she says, enthused. "You'll see."

The guys and I share an arrested look.

"Can you run that by me again?" I request.

Thirty-One

ZAC

We all straighten to the edge of our seats, now four pairs of eyes fastening on Magali.

Under the low lights of the porch, her head darts between us, unsure. "Which part?"

"Tell us all about you running wild and free in this magical forest kingdom," I say, fascinated.

I feel the thick, old-fashioned spring mattress shift and dip as she sits on her heels. Propping her elbows on the banister, Magali rests her chin on her hands. Her gaze lost into the forest beyond, she tells of magical quests she embarked on all through childhood, building fairy castles and sorceress towers in what the guys and I have known as the Enchanted Forest of Laure.

"You don't say..." I blink.

"Man, that's some Kool-Aid," Leo says under his breath.

"But seriously cool." P.O.'s eyes dart from us to the woods beyond, the line of trees silhouetted against the twilight sky. "Hey, Yann, three out of six. What are the odds for the rest of us?"

"This I'd like to know." Yann whistles low.

"Uh ... guys. What am I missing out on, here?" she asks in a tone of voice that lets me know she clearly thinks we're lunatics now.

The back of my fingers gently trails down her cheek. "Your childhood memories in that forest are something straight out of Liam's *Tales from the Enchanted Forest of Laure*. It's uncanny."

What if Liam's *Tales*, inspired by three-year-old Éolie's visions, had the right of it, and the six of us are all destined to find Home within these very woods in the Normal Kingdom, closest neighbors in actual fact? Would I recognize my place if I saw it, like Liam and Éolie, then Leo?

Her head tilts, and her luminous gaze searches mine. "I like the name; it's a story book?"

"No," I say gently, memories flooding me. "Liam's bedtime stories we all grew up on. They were full of knights on quests for freedom, looking for Home in the Normal Kingdom in the midst of an enchanted forest, just like this one, here."

We all stare in the direction of the woods. *This very one, really, and odds are, that happily ever after is meant for all of us, here, it would seem.*

"You must have missed home a lot while at boarding school." Her full lips are warm and soft as she deposits on my temple one of the most adoring kisses ever. My stomach flips.

"We didn't miss what we've never known," I say quietly. We dreamed about what it would be like at night, imagining. Love. Roots. Family. And what I feel for Magali is nowhere near anything I ever imagined. It's so much more.

"Guess what we missed was the concept of home," Yann ponders. "You lived in one growing up; your parents are the coolest." He cocks his head at Magali. "We'll pick your brain once in a while."

"Anytime." Magali smiles softly.

"Well, at least, Liam's *Tales from the Enchanted Forest of Laure* swept us along when he joined us at BIA at seven, giving us something to dream about, focus on," I say, my arm snuggling her up closer.

"I'll drink to that," Yann adds, raising his glass in salute before taking a sip.

"I'm with you. Thanks to those tales, we'd miss boarding school away from it whenever we visited what passed for home for some of us." Leo's gaze darts over the fields, to the abandoned barn. "Thank god those visits got fewer and fewer over the years."

The guys and I share a look. At first, only Liam and I were there full time;

the four others joined our full-timers rank over the following years.

"Yeah," P.O. agrees, looking down at his wine. "At least over there, the only expectations were academic ones and the intellectual challenges agreed with us, less pressure."

"Well, let's not forget Zac, who could never pass up a dare ... Remember when what's his name dared him to bungee jump in the middle of the night? Talk about undue pressure." Yann waggles his eyebrows.

Aw, man. I cut him a look.

Leo snorts and P.O. cracks a full smile.

"What?" Magali jerks her head back. "In the dark?"

"Yeah, a bunch of jocks poked the beast, here, saying Zac didn't have the balls to do it, so he did. Bare-ass naked," Yann says.

They all smirk, knowing the outcome. Literal blue balls that hurt like a bitch for weeks on end, caught in one of the harnesses I had tied too loosely in the dark.

I groan. Christ, if they start, she'll run for the hills. Last I remember she wasn't too keen on the reckless thing.

"Ooooh, DaringMan?" Magali asks, bumping my shoulder, and they all bark out a laugh.

"Good one, but no," I whisper close to her ear.

"You did a bungee jump in the dark, naked? No way." She shakes her head in disbelief. "You're making this up, WildMan?"

"Okay, okay, enough said." I cut them another look. "And no, it's not WildMan."

"Hey, we just got warmed up." Leo puts his hands behind his head and crosses his ankles at the feet, getting a tad too comfortable...

"Yeah, we have lots more where that came from," Yann says, and P.O. low fives him.

And so it begins.

A few stupid but harmless dares retelling later, like wearing the same socks for a month before the offensive odor became too much, even for me, and already Magali finagles out of P.O. that Microsoft Flight Simulator was my all-time obsessive-compulsive computer game by age nine. At this rate, they'll soon drop my nickname on her. I shake my head. She has them eating out of the palm of her hand.

Then Yann mentions my Piper and Leo my helicopter flying for DWB. The guys regale her with stories on how much time I spent flying once I earned my private pilot license in my early teens.

"Wow. You've been flying your own plane since age *fourteen*," Magali says, wide-eyed.

"Yeah..." I rub the back of my neck. It's not like I go around dropping in conversations that I own a plane or used to fly a helicopter. Coming from where I hail from, I'd feel like an ostentatious prick doing so—just like she accused me of being that night on the slopes—and I just can't go there. Not even a little. But really, in the past couple of weeks, it's just that the subject never came up with Magali before, and I'm glad she understands I wasn't deliberately cutting her out of an important part of who I am. Being on call twenty-four seven for Éolie notwithstanding, surprisingly enough, I didn't miss my usual Me Time. Not even a little.

"And you fly helicopters too?" She sounds awed by it.

"Not anymore. But don't make it sound more than it is, it's only a thirty-hour session to get your rotor blades certification if you're already certified on fixed wings with a grade three medical." I shrug it off. "It's not like I flew sophisticated Coast Guard Helo. No big deal."

"Modest too." She nudges her shoulder into mine. "But you did mention on our way over that flying is your choice of superpowers. I should have guessed you'd take matters into your own hands, and take control."

She knows me better than I know myself.

"Well, now that the twins are here, I'll take you up with me this weekend if the weather holds." I kiss the tip of her nose.

"I'd love to, and I'll show you all of my favorite spots on our next day off, if you'd like. You'll see for yourself the magic within the Enchanted Forest of Laure of both our youths."

One by one, the guys get up and file back inside, leaving us alone. I send them a silent thanks and vow to buy them all a stiff drink at some point for giving us some privacy. My heart pounds in my ears.

"I'd like that more than you think." My forehead drops to hers, our fingers interlacing. "It's really uncanny all that we have in common."

"I know, right?" she says softly. "But this place is chock-full of magic if you know where to look." Her gaze returns to the darkened horizon, and I look. And I see hundreds of fireflies lighting up the woods like fairy dust, and, back through the eyes of a seven-year-old, the Normal Kingdom.

"Magic in the making," I murmur.

"Like us."

"Just like us." I pull her to my chest, and her cheek comes to rest over my heart, her palm over my breast.

We lay quietly on the improvised porch bed. Listening to crickets, watching fireflies dance in the dark of the night under a canopy of stars, while my fingers stroke the satiny softness of her upper arm in a lazy back and forth.

Soon her breath grows even. She's fast asleep.

I kiss her forehead.

I'm no longer falling for you, Magali. "I love you," I whisper in the night.

A shooting star crosses in a flash the midnight sky, and for the first time in forever, I get the feeling all of my wishes are about to come true.

And that I've finally made it home, in more ways than one.

Thirty-Two

ZAC

Enjoying the view from behind, I follow Magali at a more sedate pace as she bounces down the stairs the morning of our second night at the old farmstead, on our Friday off, energized by our spring-water shower. Her words, not mine ... And the promise of three days off the grid, as none of my moms-to-be are due to deliver in the near future.

I grin in passing at the double-face little blackboard sign Magali tied with a bow to Liam and Éolie's doorknob. For now, reading **Twin Feeding in Progress, do not disturb**; finding the flip side she wrote last night, adorable, **Twin Fix Inside. Come and get it.**

"Seriously?" Magali abruptly stops in the kitchen doorway, and I almost plow into her back. "You all smother your cereal with orange juice?" she questions the room at large, aghast, and three pair of eyes swing her way. The guys and I exchange a look, and I hide a grin.

"What? We're fighting the odds of contracting scurvy by a daily intake of vitamin C." Leo feigns shock.

"Studies show that too much vitamin C and not enough calcium will addle anyone's brains out, and impair vision," she says.

"Touché." Yann chokes on a laugh, saluting her with his coffee mug.

"Don't we get extra points for creativity?" P.O. asks around a spoonful of liquefied lumps.

Her nose wrinkles in distaste. "You get extra points for eating it. That stuff looks vile. The only thing it has going for it is the orange smell. It looks like puke." She shudders, crossing over to the fridge. "Guys, really? I get that you all caught the same cow juice aversion Zac has, but what's wrong with plant-based milk, like sesame, almond, or soy? The fridge is full." She pops the fridge open in a grand *ta-da* gesture.

"Why ruin perfectly good cereal?" I ask, and her eyes upturn. I rummage through for the makings of our picnic lunch, taking some camembert cheese out and what looks like leftover grilled chicken breasts for baguette sandwiches.

"No comment." She cuts the crusted bread in halves. "Mayo or Dijon?"

"Both." I blink. "Hey, boys, what's the game of Mille Bornes doing in the fridge?" I take the distinctive green cardboard box out, hidden behind the mammoth-sized square glass jars of mayonnaise and Dijon mustard kept on the half-shelf.

Both Magali and Yann exclaims over each other.

"So that's where I left it on Éolie's labor day? Christ, we looked everywhere!"

"Is that Monsieur Léon's Mille Bornes?"

"You know the game?" My brows shoot up.

"Oh boy, do I ever." She takes it, quickly shuffling through the cards, growing misty-eyed. "I learned to count to five thousand and infinity and beyond with it. My brothers and I spent so many rainy afternoons playing, inflicting on each other strategic speed limits and every road hazards we could come up with to slow us down, on this very table." She closes the lid on a sigh, brushing her hand over it.

"Cool. I'll pump you for some more deets about the place when you guys get back from your hike, and we'll play a game of Mille if you want," Leo suggests.

I wonder if I can come up with a new version of one-on-one strip Mille Bornes in the upstairs bedroom. *Hmmm.* The bed squeaks like crazy, but with the mattress on the floor...

"Sweet, and if I win you get to tell me his nickname?" she asks Leo, batting her eyelashes, bringing me out of my lurid thoughts.

"Hey, that's not guessing, that's cheating," I huff, crossing my arms over my chest.

Leo props his arm up on the side of the chair. "I'm not touching this one."

Magali beseeches Yann with her eyes.

"What he said." Yann's thumb points to Leo, and she turns to P.O.

"Don't look at me. You got me revealing that Flight Simulator was his fetish computer game, but that's it. You're on your own for this one, ZeeGirl." P.O., using the name they dubbed her with upon meeting, hides a smirk behind his laptop screen, the little shit.

For now, Magali thinks it's just a cute, dorky play on words derived from my name and no one disabused her of the notion as it is, in part, just that. But the guys are having too much fun with this, dropping clues in plain sight, watching me inwardly squirm. I'm in a pickle of my own doing, as I'm the one who hyped up the whole affair in the first place. What I hadn't really factored in before is that once she gets it, she'll ask how I came by the nickname. And they all know I don't particularly look forward, not as much as they do, in any case, to the retelling of *all* the stupid dare stories that got me the nickname. The one they dropped on her the other night not only got me a WildMan guess, but didn't even make the cut. Magali thought it was an entertaining tall tale, and it's a mild one...

My nickname, after all, stems from a play on words from my name at my most reckless self, and the guys don't even know the half of it. If they knew what dangerous recovery maneuver I practiced over and over again flying the Comanche in my teenage years...

"Tell me already," Magali groans, fisting my tee, and I stumble back a step, her grip surprisingly strong for one so slender.

I let out a snort, holding my hands up. "Not a chance; that ship has sailed. By now your expectations of it are so high up, you'll feel let down once you know. It's the last thing I want," I say, only half-kidding. She wasn't particularly enthused, nor impressed by my bit of recklessness on that night, now was she? "Unless you guess it right, I won't tell you."

Her face scrunches up. "Ever? Not possible."

"He's the man for the impossible," Liam deadpans, crossing over on his way to the kitchen sink. I cut him a glare over Magali's head, but he raises a brow, daring me to comment.

"Hey, there's a good one. ZeeMan for the Impossible." Magali chuckles under her breath, rinsing Éolie's water bottle for him, filling it up.

I mutter an explicative, tipping my head back, while the guys bark out a laugh.

I sigh. It was bound to happen, might as well get it over with. I lean back against the counter, crossing my arms.

"Remember I know where you sleep, man," I tell Liam without much heat.

"Oh mon dieu! That's it, isn't it? ZeeMan for the Impossible?" Magali, wide-eyed, looks around. "You were feeding me clues all along?"

P.O. low fives my girl with an indulgent smile as the two others get their hands up for a high five. "You said it, ZeeGirl."

"With a little help from my friends," I mutter under my breath with a sidelong glance. Liam stacks two yogurt containers in one hand and slips two spoons in his sweat's pocket alongside two granola bars, unfazed.

He leans beside me against the counter, and we watch the three others exchanging with Magali back and forth on the clues they dropped over since last Wednesday as they retreat to the living room. She exclaims, "No way. The naked bungee jump's a true story?"

"Hey, don't hold it against me. It was too good to pass up, man, in more ways than one," Liam says the last cryptically.

I cock my head to the side, giving him a sidelong glance. "And that would be?"

"Now that it's out there, you'll quit worrying it will blow up in your face. You don't fully realize yet Magali loves you for who you are—past, present, future. I know the signs. And I'm telling you, there's nothing anyone of us can say to her about you or about this reckless streak you think you have, that will change the fact." He fist bumps my shoulder. "Own it."

I stare at him.

"And on that note, I'm off to feed my world. Later." Balancing the yogurts and water bottle in one hand, he grabs a green apple from the fruit basket kept in the middle of the table, buffing the fruit on his tee on his way back to Éolie feeding his little twins.

I finish wrapping the sandwiches and grab a few granola bars myself. Adding a large bag of sweet potato chips and trail mix, along with two full-sized water bottles, I stash the whole lot into a backpack.

"Your family is not only great, they have great taste in nicknames," Magali says with authority, giving me an enveloping hug from behind before releasing me from her hold.

"Is that so?" I turn around, a brow angling.

Her fingers curl around my shoulders and I pull her toward me.

"Totally. My expectations of it have been exceeded, just so you know. In my humble opinion, yours is the only one still open to interpretation. So many possibilities, it boggles the mind." She nods gravely.

"Why do I get the feeling I'll never hear the end of it?" My brow lifts in amusement, my hands interlacing on the small of her back.

"Could be because you've got this interesting reputation to uphold now, and in view of the recent sex binge we've been on, it adds a certain je ne sais quoi to the whole thing." She angelically shrugs, her hands curving on my forearms.

"You daring me to top four orgasms in a row?" I grin wickedly.

"Maybe?" Her eyes drop to my lips. "Éolie says to tell you there's a sleeping bag in one of the mud room's backpacks—"

"And, we're out of here." I swing her over my shoulder, and she squeals in laughter, the sound inscribing itself on my soul.

Thirty-Three

ZAC

"It's your first, ever?" Magali murmurs, crouching low behind the high grass.

"Great Blue Heron, yes," I murmur back, standing still so as not to startle the graceful bird, not ten meters away from us. He's a majestic sight, with his subtle blue-grey plumage, wading belly deep into the marsh, with long deliberate steps before striking like lightning, snapping up a frog. The Great Blue takes flight with slow, deep wing beats, his long legs trailing out behind, and my gaze follows his ascent until he's nothing more than a dot on the horizon.

"When was the last time you flew your plane?" Magali asks, and my gaze darts back to her. Warm eyes quietly observe me in that special way she has when she contemplates, soft with tenderness, compassion, and understanding.

"A little over a month," I reply, sitting down beside her, hidden within our own cocoon of shamrock-green high grass growing wild on the banks of the marsh. Their long blades, rendered translucent by the mid-afternoon sun slanting to the west, sway around her pensive face, their tendril shadows gently kissing her cheeks.

"Is that the longest you've gone without?" she asks, subdued.

I search her eyes. "Aside from a few stretches here and there in medical school, yes."

"Is it because of me?" Her chin drops to her raised knees, and her fingers fidget with a blade of grass at her feet.

I put my fingertips under her chin, tipping her face up. "Never think that. I love every minute we spend together, and I'd take you up with me, any time. I was on call pretty much around the clock these last few weeks with Éolie, and that's the only reason why I couldn't take off for a flight."

I'm so grateful Éolie and the twins are doing great, I'd go without flying for months on end, no sweat, for the same results.

Silver eyes, flecked with peridot green, search mine. "You never talked about it at all, and I gathered from what the guys told last night that it's your utmost Me Time. I wondered and worried a bit that you might have missed it since we've started spending so much time together."

"Nope, didn't miss it once ... You, the feel of us, you make me soar, Magali."

Her hand curls on my cheek and she smiles softly in understanding.

I take hold of her hand and we lay flat on our backs, cushioned by a thick layer of humus and soft grass, watching Cumulus and Stratocumulus clouds drift by against their powder-blue backdrop for the next little while.

I never brought a girl up for a flight before, never had any desire to. Magali's right, solo flights are my sacred Me Time, or used to be, prior to her. "I can't wait to take you up as soon as the weather holds, truth be known."

A column of Cumulonimbus is forming on the far horizon, as warned by the Aviation Weather Center alerts programmed to pop on my laptop. It will bring unpredictable wind patterns and rain by this evening and all day tomorrow. I checked before breakfast this morning, and if the predictions hold, and the weather completely clears by Sunday, I'll take her up. I'll wait if I have to, unwilling to take one iota of chance as far as she's concerned, not even for a two-hour trip in the air.

"Well, now that you guys got me all hyped up about it, I can't wait either. Must be something else, soaring high above the clouds in a plane small enough to feel like an extension of yourself," she says, wonder lacing her tone of voice.

I get up and tug her up beside me, enthused as always, by the subject. "It's something else all right!" I grab the backpack, and she brushes the bottom of her sage-green cargoes before taking the hand I hold out for her. "It's one of the things I love the most flying my Comanche. It connects me directly to the feel of soaring, as one with the machine." My chest expands, stoked that she'll soon share into the experience.

Her eyes are bright with excitement. "Sounds like when I break free from gravity for a split second, flying off the ski ramp. Only longer, of course," she says, full of enthusiasm.

"I've never flipped as high as you on skis, but you'll see just what I mean with your hands on the controls."

"No way. I'll get my thrill just being a spectator, thanks. Put me behind a wheel and I'll get by, but it's nothing to write home about." She wrinkles her nose. "I swear I can't get the feel of motors, *at all*." She shrugs as though it's one of life's great mysteries to her.

Our hiking boots hiss through the long blades of high grass; the only sound to be heard now, from the marsh, as we retrace our steps back through the fresh trail of crushed wild grass. A few birds sing in the distance, but otherwise, all is quiet, not even a breeze rustling in the leaves.

The foot trail leading away from the marsh is narrow, and we walk in single file. Entering the undergrowth, Magali unfolds her raspberry-pink Henley tee's sleeves, hiked up to her elbows, briskly rubbing her arms.

"Need your light jacket?" I ask from behind.

"Thanks, but no need," she says over her shoulder. "The hike will warm me in no time."

It's definitely cooler in here, with little to no sun filtering through the dense canopy to the undergrowth, even on the best of days, and I'm thankful we had the foresight to wear long sleeves. When we get back to the hospital clinic on Monday, it will be the first day of August, signaling the end of the summer up here, according to Magali, and leaves will turn color by the beginning of September. Not hard to believe as last night, already, we had to wear sweatshirts to stay warm, even sitting around the bivouac.

She hops onto a fallen tree log, smoothed out to a dull shine by a few years of recurring snow and ice accumulations, and pirouettes.

She grows still, her eyes entirely focused before launching into a front flip. I reattach my galloping heart, reminding myself that she knows what she's doing, not to sweat it. Her feet land firmly on the log five feet ahead and I exhale.

"Do I have years of ballet lessons to thank for your perfect balance?"

"Years of gymnastics as a little girl." She walks the rest of the log's length with poise and balance. "Sad to say but, alas, the pace of learning ballet was too slow for me, putting an end to my aspiring prima donna career at the tender age of three. My brothers would say that's because I only have one speed, fast forward. But gymnastics was where I met Amélie, so all was not lost. And, of course, it's a great plus for acroski." She pirouettes, hopping down.

"What made you quit freestyle competitions at the junior level?" I ask, curious now. She's so in touch with her body, and her ability to focus and visualize ten steps ahead is off the charts. Something I lack ... or I wouldn't have gotten that impossible nickname.

"Um ... The competition, I'd say. Acroski is something I fell into with my friends for the pure pleasure of it, and even at the junior level it was more of an intense hobby, really. I was offered to go pro but I declined," Magali answers, her voice growing thoughtful, as we resume our hike onto the sinuous trail. "High-level competition isn't for everyone. The stakes are such that there's a lot riding on the outcome, and my very short stint at it sure didn't agree with my personality. I lost it, the passion as well as the joy behind it. I stopped having fun and stressed all the time." She tilts her head in my direction, her features softening. "It was one of those times my Papa sat me down for a talk. He made sure I knew that it's okay to quit on your own a dream of a lifetime that's not yours, and go on to find the ones that are. So I did."

I take her hand and tug her to a halt, grateful she never had to meet impossible expectations growing up but was instead cherished for who she is.

"It takes a lot of determination and maturity for one so young to get there and back," I say, impressed as all hell that she knows herself so well, and acts on it.

"You're one to talk!" she exclaims in awe, her cheeks flushing a rose color. "You blow my mind, acing your theory and getting your private pilot's degree by the age of eleven. Three full years ahead of reaching legal age to actually clock the solo flights required for your license? It takes a lot of determination and maturity," she quotes me back.

I let out a snort. "Obsessed, more like."

We soon resume our hike into the nature preserve, walking side by side as the trail widens for a stretch into the dip of a valley, and talk some more about what it took to make it all the way to the pros' knocking on your door, and decide upon changing course on your own steam.

"Where the hell are you going?" I mean, there's off the beaten track and off the track altogether.

"On an adventure, just like when I was little, come on. Those firs are the gatekeepers to the secret garden and the only way to make it past them is to follow the secret trail. No cheating allowed."

She climbs like a mountain goat along a faint path carved by a spring torrent, long dry by now, effortlessly balancing, hopping from one boulder to the next.

Me, not so much.

Soon lagging behind, I simply find it easier to haul myself up the slope, using the low-hanging limbs of the evergreen trees like a chimpanzee on crack.

Cheating, granted, but much more effective.

Taking a sniff, my eyes instantly water, and I blink moisture away, the pungent smell that potent. Looking at my hands, I yell up, "Can you run by me what happens if I cheat?"

"Then you're in a sticky position," I hear from above.

I stare down at my hands.

"You cheated, didn't you?" she calls out.

Uh...

"And if I did?"

Jesus. My fingers are fucking glued together, full of a fragrant-thick resin, sticky as all hell.

Magali takes one look at my hands and diagnoses, "The good news is, you smell amazing, plus your respiratory tracks are getting a deep cleansing with instant aromatherapy."

"What the hell?"

She shrugs, face impish. "This oleoresin is full of medicinal virtues a page long."

"Awesome," I grit through my teeth. "And the bad news is?"

She holds in a laugh, patting me consolingly on the chest. "The bad news is ... you'll literally stick everywhere."

I eyeball the sticky mess coating my palms and pretty much all of my fingers. "Well, that's not so bad. Want to hold my hand?" I ask slyly, lunging.

She sidesteps, holding her hands up to ward me off. "Oh no. I'll stick by you of my own accord, thanks. Besides, you need my hands to be your hands right now."

"We have a bottle of saline in the first aid kit..." My voice trails off into silence as she shakes her head, a laugh building behind her twinkling eyes.

"Won't do anything."

"What about the baby wipes you packed?"

"No go. Not even the bottle of expired hand sanitizer lying at the bottom of the backpack will help you with that," she says, leaning on one hip. Arms crossing over her chest, her brow slightly raises, upping the ante on her knowing look that asks, "Aren't you glad you cheated now?"

I stare, incredulous.

"What in God's name is that bloody fir from Hell," I mutter, and she chuckles. I take a closer look at the bulbous, yellow-tinged resin oozing from the bark of the mature evergreens surrounding me, seeping onto the limbs like some kind of liquid plague waiting to happen on the next unsuspecting victim.

"That's the greatest fir of all." She teasingly bumps her shoulder into mine, and aren't we just full of puns. "Also known as the balsam fir, a widespread Québec native all the way to the Ungava. And that wonderful resin can greatly increase your chances of survival in the wild, just so you know." A smile lingers in her voice.

"Really? Could have fooled me," I grumble as she slides the backpack off my shoulder.

"Seriously, just, you know, not on your fingers."

I shoot her look. "No shit," I say drily. "Now what?"

"Hold on, your plight has a few home remedies ... but you probably don't want to know some of them—tried out of desperation, no doubt." She barely holds in a laugh, rummaging through the backpack side pockets, where we shoved the remnants of our lunch.

"Define desperation?" I ask suspiciously. My eyes narrow, wondering what kind of whacked-up thing I'll have to do to get rid of my mess.

"For now, the only one at our disposal is butter, or the likes," she says, taking out our empty sandwich wrappers.

"What exactly am I supposed to do with that, cellophane wrap my fingers until we can buy two matching tubs of butter?" I ask, remembering, a scant millimeter away from disaster, not to put my hands on my hips and spread the mess around.

"You're supposed to rub it in until it scrapes off. Might take a while, but nothing too drastic. Fear not, or should I say *fir* not?" She ponders, drumming her fingers on her mouth, her serious tone belied by eyes glinting with merriment, her full, kissable lips fighting a smile.

"I'll never live this down, right?" I ask, resigned.

"Probably not, and it's half the fun. Here, let's see if we can rub some mayo and Dijon on your hands, and have it listed as an alternative."

"By all means, let's rub it in," I quip, a tad sardonic, but wipe my hands dutifully, nevertheless, on the leftover scraps from Magali's baguette sandwich to collect the grease, never as thankful for extra mayo. Guess desperation will do that. It's not a miracle but it will do for now.

Wondering if olive oil will do the trick just as well as butter is supposed to, as we don't have any at the farmstead, either, I wash my hands with the saline solution, topping it off with a squirt of hand sanitizer Magali hands over.

Catching her palm in passing, I bring it flush with mine, pressing on it back and forth a few times, test-driving the sticky factor.

I still have tar on my fingers but at least it's no longer as sticky. On a scale of one to ten, I'd say a five, not so bad considering that thirteen is what I started with.

I eye the trees with new respect.

"Where to?" I ask, hoisting the backpack over my shoulder.

"We go beyond the gatekeepers, through the Cathedral." She drops a quick peck on my cheek, adding mischievously, "Just stick with me."

"Have no *fir*, you bet I'll stick by you," I retort wryly.

"You're such a dork, I love it."

I wink. "I'm your dork, though. Lead the way."

The line of trees is thinning out, thank the fuck, so this time I have no problem keeping up with her. We climb the rest of the way up in companionable silence, and I inhale with relish the woodsy aromas of ferns and moss, underlying the strong hint of eau de Christmas tree I can't seem to shake. Not that I'm complaining now that I got full use of my hands back. Magali's right, I smell amazing.

She frequently stops, her face deep in introspection as she lets her soft gaze sweep the mossy undergrowth, and I let her have her moments.

Her eyes shine, lit from within as she takes in the vista.

She's so fucking gorgeous, I want to bottle her up. This moment. Her expression. An eternity preserved inside a container I can hold close and protect.

"We're entering my favorite spot in all of your Enchanted Forest of Laure." She lets out a happy sigh, breathing in her surroundings. "A magical kingdom, worthy of fairies and long-ago knights." Her face tilts up to the sky, arms wide open, her eyes closing in total bliss.

The hairs on my body stand on end, and my skin prickles in some sort of unforeseen anticipation. My heart pounds, pulse racing as a strange, new awareness takes hold, like a portent of things to come. The last time I even got close to that visceral reaction, I was dangling back and fro, stuck on a jammed chairlift, watching Magali ski away, my gut screaming at me not to let her out of my sight...

Unbidden, an image of a little girl with glossy dark-brown hair, and bright, silver eyes, running wild and free in this very place comes to me. The image is haunting but so real it punches me right in the solar plexus, so hard that I almost double over. When the vision fades, I'm breathing hard, but Magali is still caught up in her moment and hasn't noticed.

Tamping down on my growing exhilaration, I retrace our steps in my mind and orient. I estimate that we're about twenty degrees northeast of the old farmstead, having followed a trail circling the perimeter of Liam's meadow from the back since leaving the marsh, up until we veered off at an eighty-degree angle, here. At my guess, we're no longer in the protected area of the nature preserve, but in the woods surrounding the old farmstead, and if so ... it'd be possible to obtain a building permit for a residential. That much I know from Liam's own odyssey into the local bureaucracy.

My heart thuds in my ears. I don't know how it will play out exactly, if I do recognize a place like Liam and Leo did.

I close the distance between us, joining her on the summit. The view from the top is spectacular. It's the highest peak in the vicinity, and green mountains unfold as far as my eyes can see, swelling gently like rolling waves on a peaceful ocean. And to our right, tucked into the picturesque valley, the abandoned barn appears in all its decaying glory, surrounded by its fallow fields, taken over by wild flowers in bloom.

Running my hands around Magali's waist, my arms enfold her from behind, and her hands curl over my forearms. My chin comes to rest on top of her head as we contemplate the horizon, absorbed.

"Pretty awesome view. I get why you'd fiercely guard this Cathedral of yours." I sigh in her hair.

"Oh, we're not there yet, this is only the Belvedere pit stop. The Cathedral is down that way." She points behind.

"Oh?"

"We came in from the back and I usually go there direct from the farmstead, crossing over the fields." She kisses my still mildly tar-stained fingers before taking hold on my hand. "Makes me happy we took the long way, though. I haven't entered the Cathedral from this side in years, and it's the best way to experience it, especially the first time," she says, letting out a long, breathy sigh.

"Why?"

"The view's different for one side to the other, and from this one, you don't see it coming," she whispers reverently.

"Why are we whispering?" I whisper back.

"You'll see. Now shush."

She makes a shushing motion with her index finger, pecking it before pressing the kissed finger down softly upon my lips, and I shake my head at her.

Lead on, I mouth.

We walk unhurriedly down the slope on the other side, the slant a gentle two-degree gradient, keeping quiet. Not hard to do as I stare, slack-jawed, as the terrain changes suddenly.

We just entered a wood sprite palace. Dozens of ancient maple trees, probably centennials, border the meandering trail we're following, their far-reaching limbs forming an arch over our heads. The majestic trees grow tall and proud, protected from the fierce winds and severe cold by the lee of the mountain. Their intermingled canopies reflect a myriad of translucent green tones through the sunlight in a stained-glass, church window effect, some rays penetrating in arrows of light, illuminating phosphorescent ferns and mossy trunks.

It's breathtaking and awe-inspiring.

Magali shoots me a smile, and my lips curve, echoing hers.

"On a breezy summer day, you would have found me here, in the chancel between sanctuary and nave, listening to the choir of leaves singing."

Eyes turned skyward, I make a slow turn, marveling. "It's quite a feel."

"If those trees could talk..." she says feelingly, and my brow angles.

"What would they say?" I ask, cocking my head.

She interlaces her hands with mine, her chest leaning onto my chest.

"Lots of things only a little girl would understand." She drops a sweet kiss on my cheek.

I bend close to her ear. "Try me," I whisper enticingly.

"Not on your life, no boys allowed." She looks down to hide a smile. "But I'll share my little girl's secret home away from home, and we'll have a tea party if you'd like."

At her words, a tingly sensation fires up every nerve ending in my body. "I'd like."

"Tea party it is," she decides, eyes twinkling. "Just remember you volunteered."

The glint in her eyes makes one briefly wonder what kind of stew she brews in there, or what kind of pretend stuff she'll make me do ... Could go either way, but then again, can't be that much worse than glued fingers.

"Bring it on." I tweak the end of her braid. "How far is it to the finger food?"

"Not far at all." Her eyes are wide and luminous. "As a matter of fact, the Cathedral sits in the middle of my make-believe backyard."

"Great taste in real estate," I say offhandedly.

"À l'évidence, and no mowing the grass, either," she deadpans.

"Sold," I quip.

"Figured it'd be a selling point." She flicks a tiny pine cone onto my dark-blue tee. "Come on, you're invited to a tea party just across the Secret Garden of Dreams," she says with a secretive smile. She tugs on my hand as she cuts directly across the patch of giant maple trees, veering off trail.

Wading ankle deep, our hiking boots trudge to the crinkling sound of crunched, dried leaves following in our wake.

Coming out of the Cathedral's thick carpet of dried leaves, my eyes dart around the mature forest's undergrowth of saplings, bright-green ferns, and moss-covered ground we found ourselves in. The gentle slope, the dips and swells of the hilly terrain, the mossy boulders, the crisp freshness of the woodsy aromas are so special, the overall uplifting vibe of the place makes for a lighthearted feel. You can't help but be at peace.

"So? You have a Secret Garden of Dreams, huh." She really must have had a grand time in here as a little girl. "Is this another one of your No Boys Allowed type of thing?" I ask, readjusting the backpack straps over my shoulders.

"No worries, boys allowed," she says warmly as we step into an unexpected pool of light. "All dreams sowed in my Garden of Dreams are gender neutral. See for yourself."

I look around the tiny clearing flooded with sunlight. Only one younger spire-shaped tree grows, strangely enough, contrary to the cool umbrageous woodlands of the mature forest found everywhere else around. Wild blueberries, their pale-green fruits not yet ripe for the picking, surround the lone tree in a mantle of coarse ground cover, their stubby shrubs running rampant.

"What am I supposed to see?" I ask, giving her a sidelong glance.

"A dream come true, what else?" She tilts her head in my direction, assessing if I do get it or not.

"No pressure, here." I say under my breath, and she gives me an indulgent look. "Remember I'm a guy. We need spelling out. What do *you* see?" I ask, my voice low and amused.

"A universal wish, love."

I blink, really confused now.

"Zac di Fiori, Knight of the Laure, meet my wish trees, *Moi-et-Toi*." Her lips spread in a slow, sensual smile as she eyes the tree.

Of course, she named it. I chuckle under my breath, charmed. Me-and-You, only her. But then something else occurs to me. "Trees? Plural?"

"Very much so, look closely."

My eyes narrow, taking a closer look, and that's when I see it.

Unlike what I saw at first glance, there are two trees, not just one, about seven meters tall, one a little smaller than the other, their slim grayish trunks growing separate by a few centimeters, but their limbs lovingly interlaced one into another. You can't really tell where one begins and the other ends, yet, they're both distinct. They're wicked awesome, and magnificent taken as a whole entity. Understanding dawns. "Me and You," I murmur. Together, they form an *Us*.

"You're something else, you know that?" I shake my head in wonder, enchanted by all that she is, and her little girl's imagination.

Her wish trees look like evergreens, but only softer, not at all prickly, more like vaporous puffs of light blue-green.

"What are they?" I brush my hands tentatively over their needles, silken soft under my touch, proving me right.

"They're the only deciduous conifers and my favorite. They turn a glorious gold in November, and it's spectacular against the white backdrop of early snow," she says warmly, running her palm over one, then the other. "They're Larix Laricina, commonly known as larch. Lucas and I came upon them as tiny seedlings, and these two have been fascinating me ever since."

"How old were you?" I take a few steps back to better gauge, but at a glance, these trees are about four times as tall as I am by now, shooting up to the sky. Which is a bit surprising if she found them as seedlings, growth rate slower up north, that much I know.

"I remember being bummed Lucas was going back to school and I had to wait another eternity, or a whole year, to follow in his footsteps, so ... end of the summer when I was four," she says, peeking over at me with a soft knowing look. I was seven.

She waves around, pointing to the sizeable, charcoal-grey trunks of mature evergreens, straight as new pencils, circling this little spot of sunlight. "Larches are pretty common on lowlands, especially around bogs and marshes, but in mature forests, not so much. They need a lot of sun exposure for growth, and for some unknown reason this forest never encroaches on their little clearing. So, here they are, and twice as tall. What are the odds?" she says, awed.

"I'd say pretty good ones, considering they're *Moi-et-Toi*." I glance at her sideways. My lips tug up one side as clear delight washes over her face, brightening her eyes. "Told you we were meant to be," I add cockily.

"You may have said that once or twice, now." She gives me a quick joyful hug before stepping out of the clearing.

"Damn straight. Now where's that tea you promised?" I ask, following from behind.

"Le thé des bois? You're walking all over it," she says over her shoulder with a twinkle in her eye.

Shit, she's being literal.

My gaze drops to the ground, covered in thickets of shiny forest-green leaves, with a leathery surface not even close to appetizing. Thé des bois, she said. I make a mental note to ask Éolie at first opportunity to put me up to speed on indigenous plants so I'll keep up with Magali on a more level playing field.

"And what are we supposed to do with it?" I ask warily.

"Gather some fresh ones and have a tea party on my make-believe veranda while chewing on the leaves," she informs me, crouching to gather a handful of the leaves in her hands.

Who the hell was the first human hungry enough to think that stuff was edible, I wonder...

"And chewing on these magical leaves will what—get us high?" I quip, admiring the sway of her hips, and the swish of her thick braid above the small of her back.

"Le thé des bois has many medicinal virtues, Docteur di Fiori; none are hallucinogenic," she assures me, doing her best lecturer intonation. She drops the sour puss professor's façade, enticing me with a sassy look. "We'll just have great kissing breath. They taste minty terrific. So, could be ... if we get high, it will be on love."

"Works for me." I move around to gather leaves by the handfuls.

"Careful, you're stomping all over my kitchen."

"What? Where?" I ask, turning in a circle.

"Look at my view of the Cathedral from over the kitchen sink." She turns me around. "Right. There."

The view.

A splendid déjà-vu hits me in the chest, jolting me.

A warm sensation of familiarity floods my insides.

I stare, and stare some more, letting those long-ago delightful images wash over me.

I'm staring at the picture-perfect view I once saw in my mind's eyes, an indelible memory of this place I called Home in the Normal Kingdom.

Liam, Leo, and now, me. Three out of six.

I made it home.

Thirty-Four

MAGALI

I look up from my leaves gathering upon hearing Zac's sharp inhale. He drops his handful of thé des bois leaves, at a standstill.

"What is it?" I whisper, wondering what seized him.

In the nearby trees, a couple of blue jays call to one another, but otherwise all is peaceful.

My gaze tracks his, locked onto my Moi-et-Toi duo of trees up ahead. My hand curves on his forearm. "Are you all right?"

Zac's stare flickers back to me and I'm hit by a blaze of melted copper, his eyes burning brighter than I've ever seen, lit from within.

"Magali." His gaze darts up toward the sky before flashing back to meet mine, and I see stark vulnerability lurking in their depths. My heart turns over. "I'm not good at finding the right words ... I'm not used to this."

I open my mouth to ask what he means, but he grasps my face with warm hands and kisses me slow, long and sweet. I lean against him, clutching his back and opening for him when he seeks entrance into my mouth with his tongue, sending an ache of pleasure through me.

He brushes his thumbs back and forth along my cheekbones. Full lips, firm yet tender, trail down my jaw in a gradual retreat, ending the kiss on a quiet note. His forehead drops to mine, and I can feel the rapid rise and fall of his chest against mine. He swallows.

I sense he is gathering his thoughts, so I wait.

My fingers begin to trace soothing circles against the small of his back, and he sighs into my touch.

"Magali, I know this place. I've been here before in my mind, dreamed about it at night. The only thing I didn't see coming in my youth was you. No amount of imagination could ever come close to all that you are to me, all that you've come to mean for me. I'm past falling for you. I love you." He puts one hand on my cheek, cupping it. My hand comes up to cover it, feeling like my knees are about to give out.

"I waited for you my whole life, right here. You're my wish for love come true. I love you. Heart, body and soul, love you, Zac. You're the *you* to my *me*."

He kisses me. Hard. Passionately. I drink in the sensations of completeness washing over me, floating on a cloud, my heart soaring.

The sun disappears behind a wall of clouds. The breeze picks up, and the muted symphony of leaves by the thousands rustling in the wind travels down to us from the Cathedral in rolling waves of sounds.

Zac runs his hands over the curve of my shoulders, his earnest gaze searching my eyes. "I want to make this place real, grow with it." His voice gets husky, "I want to live here with all of this, Magali. With you."

My breath hitches, hoping he means what I think he means.

"And by *this,* you mean...?" I stare, wide-eyed, my thoughts running a mile a minute.

He takes a step back, shoving his hands through his hair, muttering about making a muck of things.

Pulse pounding in my veins, I meet his eyes.

"If I were to ask you to come live with me, right here, what would you say?"

"Yes, a thousand times yes!" I cry out, flinging myself into his arms, and he laughs a relieved laugh, whirling me around in a circle before setting me down.

Living here, with Zac? Already my eyes are looking at the place differently, knowing it will no longer just live in my mind, through my little girl's dreams, but in my heart, living them.

Magic in the making.

"Awesome." He beams up at me. "Let's do this."

My face splits into a grin while I nod, my chest bursting, full of uncontainable joy.

"Oh." I swallow, unsure if we rejoiced too soon as I take another look around us. I wince, looking back at Zac.

"What?" His smile drops by a notch or two. "Oh God. Magali, if you're not sure—"

"No, no. It's just that I'm not sure where the property lines run between the farmstead and the nature preserve. I mean, can we build here?" I ask, concerned.

His features softening, he brushes away from my face strands of flyaway hair, this morning's neat braid long turned into a messy one. "It's the first thing I estimated when you said we were entering your favorite place of all." His usual self-confidence is de retour in his tone of voice, I'm happy to note. "We're firmly standing on one of the farmstead subdivisions, of that I'm sure, if just from the many nights Liam and Leo pored over the land survey map, discussing it in details. And knowing Liam, he will have no problem selling me this parcel of land, no worries," he says, elation inscribing all over his face, and my cheeks hurt from smiling so hard.

I send a heartfelt prayer of gratitude up to my Secret Garden of Dreams for another dream come true as we both contemplate the site. I will turn Zac's dream place into a loving home, filled with cherished memories, I vow.

"So, what does your Home look like?" I rest my head against his strong chest, bringing his arms to cross over my abdomen.

"Beats me, I have zero knowledge of that stuff. What did yours look like?" Zac's chin drops to my shoulder, and he rocks us gently from side to side.

"We're two peas in a pod, then. Aside from make-believing this patch of moss is a bed and this rock's an oven, beats me too," I readily admit. "Oh, and Adirondacks spread throughout the forest in the backyard in little nooks and crannies, like my parents'. It'd be a super awesome thing to sit comfortably inside the Cathedral."

"Done on the Adirondacks," he says. "Jury's still out on the bed and the oven, though."

"Great, we're going to have to eat the resin to survive." I dodge left, then right, trying to flee, but he's quicker, holding me prisoner.

A gust whisks through the canopies, the leaves invert, belly-up, and settle down again. Everything quiets, birds no longer singing, leaves no longer rustling. Our laughter fades as we both finally notice the storm clouds closing in above us.

Zac's gaze darts up to the sky, assessing.

"We have twenty minutes max before the downpour. Which way back is the quickest?" He hoists the backpack over his shoulder and holds out his hand.

Thunder rumbles faintly in the distance.

I grab his hand and we make a run for it, emerging from the woods keeping pace with each other through the fields. We make it back just as the first raindrops spatter on the ground.

Taking the steps two at a time, Zac swings the outer door open.

"Guys, the Normal Kingdom's really out there in the back," Zac calls out breathlessly as we stumble inside the old farmhouse. "I've made it home; she said yes!" he shouts, pulling me into his embrace. "Ma douce," he whispers in my ear, and I bury my nose in his shirt. My heart brims over, overcome by love for this man.

The place erupts into cheers, welcoming us, warming my heart that much more.

Thirty-Five

MAGALI

This early on a Sunday, there are not many people in the guests' waiting room area of the one-room chalet housing the local pilots' center at the Mont-Tremblant International Airport compound. In fact, I'm the only guest.

Across the room from me, two long tables sit empty, regional maps spread all over. A coffee machine and a board full of notices occupy the other side of the room. Kitty corner, a skinny man, mid-fortyish, wearing a light-blue polo with the AéroClub La Macaza logo, checks a computer screen from behind the counter. Over the counter, Zac scribbles down numbers and a bunch of other stuff in his flight log. The guy, Étienne de la Durantaye, the back of his shirt reads in bold letters, confirms he'll have unlimited ceiling for the next three hours.

Zac pretty much said the same thing on our way over, which is the reason why we're this early in the first place. After which, he explained that it basically just means clear skies.

It's a toss-up as to who's the more excited by my small plane baptism this morning, but for now, as I sit on my hands, waiting for Zac to fill in his flight log, I win.

I look down at my red canvas sneakers, a splash of color swimming in an ocean of brown, absently noting that my feet drum against the rich walnut-tile floor. *Oops.* I make a conscious effort not to.

I squirm in my seat, and the thick espresso leather of the armchair crinkles.

Bush pilot magazines litter the dark stained-wood coffee table and I pick one randomly, fanning the pages.

My gaze darts up and I find myself studying Zac instead of the magazine.

Truly, Zac's slim-fit, washed-out jeans are a thing of beauty as he leans against the counter. His long-sleeved heather-grey tee fitted to his lean-muscled shoulders is not bad to look at either.

His head turns. We exchange a warm glance and he winks at me, before returning his attention to his flight log book.

My stomach flutters. *Oh, le sigh.*

His profile set in concentration lines, with his aviator sunglasses tucked into the collar of his shirt, windblown hair and scruffy jaw, Zac is the epitome of handsome. And he's all mine.

A glowing warmth spreads inside my chest and I sigh, touched once again by his willingness to include me in his ultimate Me Time.

A mid-sized chrome cistern truck, labeled Aviation Fuel in bright orange letters, rumbles by the bay window and parks beside the chalet. Behind the counter, a side door creaks open, and in wafts the acrid smell of diesel fumes. My nose wrinkles, and I hastily sniff the hem of my cobalt-blue shirt sleeve so the comforting smell of citrusy soap fills my nostrils instead.

A twenty-something guy pops in, dressed in dark-blue coveralls. "The Piper's all fueled, and ready to roll," he says to the guy manning the counter before popping back out.

Finally, Zac saunters towards me.

I bounce off the chair.

"Ready?" He shoots me a killer dimpled grin and swings an arm over my shoulders as we set out for the half-kilometer walk onto the graveled lane running parallel to the single runway. A dozen or so small airplanes sit in the distance, parked side by side, past the luxurious log cabin main terminal. There are no hangar facilities on this minuscule international airport. Mont-Tremblant is a port of entry into Canada from the United States via flights offered by Porter Airlines in the wintertime, mainly, flying skiers over to Tremblant's posh resorts, and really, it's the only reason why the label "international" is tacked on it. It is that small. Also the reason why it's my first time here. I've only ever flown in a large commercial aircraft, a far cry from the fifteen passengers regional planes or private jets the place accommodates otherwise.

"So, ready to fire up at me all those questions you promised?" he says with boyish charm, and my fingers entwine with his over my shoulder.

"You really don't know what you're asking for," I say, only half-kidding.

"Hit me."

I point to the black hardcover log book with its gold letterings reading Private Pilot Flight Log, he carries with him. "What were you calculating back there?"

"The single engine climb gradient on our takeoff based on the current weather conditions, meaning, temperature, pressure altitude and winds, among other things."

"Okay, why just one engine? Your plane has two, non?" My brows dip in confusion.

"Assuming one engine quits on takeoff, I've already computed climb feet per nautical mile, available and required."

Quits on takeoff? "Available and required ... meaning?" I ask, torn between reassured and unnerved by the information.

"Available means given our weight in fuel, passengers, and bags, what's our aircraft capable of achieving on only one engine. And required means based on the terrain ahead, what's the minimum single engine climb for our aircraft to clear all obstacles by a minimum of thirty-five feet."

"And there's a specific way to know all that with all the variables?"

"Absolutely, there's a specific number I derive from performance charts." He gives me a reassuring peck on the temple. "No worries, it's something I compute before each takeoff."

Before each takeoff? I shake my head, impressed. "So you really had to figure out *my* weight in there, today?"

I know about the importance of payload on planes, of course, but honestly, I never thought he would need to. His plane sits six, total, and we don't have any luggage. I mean, it's not something you factor in when you go for a drive. You just go. It makes sense now, though, to know beforehand at all times as we're going up in the air.

I bring our joined hands up to my mouth and drop a light kiss on his knuckles in thanks for being so well-prepared. And I send a quick thank you, while at it, to car engineers everywhere who factored it in for me in advance so that I can take it for granted, and just drive.

"Sure did," he replies.

"And you came up with?" My eyes narrow, curious as to what he'll say.

"That all things considered, you make all the difference in the world," he says, smooth as Swiss chocolate truffles.

"Aww, so many layers to that statement."

He shoots me a knowing look saying you really thought I'd willingly go there didn't you, give you a specific number of kilos at the risk of being way off. "Aren't we smooth?" I elbow him, and he playfully stumbles to the side.

"I know." He waggles his eyebrows. I roll my eyes. "Come on," he says, chuckling under his breath. "Time for our pre-flight checklist." He leads me to the end of the strip by the runway where his plane is parked.

"Wow!" I blink a few times. "If you hadn't told me your Comanche is a '72 model, I would never have guessed that plane's forty-four years old." I shake my head in wonder. "It looks brand new and contemporary."

The elegant low-wing plane with its pointy nose and sleek fuselage sits among single-engine, high-wing Cessna planes like a race horse among plow horses.

"It's been overhauled more than once since, but that's how it looked coming out of the factory in its last year of production in 1972," Zac says, pride in his voice, while inspecting the tires, the retractable landing gear, the baggage door, moving on to the propellers, the windshield, the wings, his movements methodical and self-assured. "In the sixties, the design was pretty avant-garde, and it fast became a mythic plane."

"That's what made you choose the twin-engine Comanche?" I ask, following him around like an overeager puppy, fascinated.

He hesitates for a beat before replying, "It's the other way around. It chose me."

I tilt my head in question.

A brief shadow clouds his eyes, gone in a flash. "It was my mother's plane. I inherited her."

My breath hitches, and my hand presses down on my chest. *No wonder then.*

My heart goes out to him. "Your mom's—"

"Don't sweat it," he interjects, lips thinning. "It's been mine for twenty-two years now, much longer than it was hers."

"But still—"

"Fuel check." He dips a gauge stick, reading the measurement, effectively closing the subject. I frown at his back, a bit upset by the brush off, but I let it drop. Now is not the time to insist, Magali. Patience, I remind myself. He's not ready to share details yet about his family of origin, and I need to respect that. But sometimes, it's hard to do ... I'd like to know all there is to know about him.

"Why another fuel check if that guy refueled it a moment ago?" I ask instead.

"It's the pilot's responsibility to read the level by the stick. Instruments fail and we'll be up there, that guy won't," he explains matter-of-factly, checking that the landing gear doors are secured.

"Oh." I blink. I'd need to reprogram my trusting nature on this one.

He stows the tow bar, securing the hatch, and motions with his head. "Time to hop in," he says, eyes aglow, and I bounce on my toes, my pulse picking up.

He pops the cabin door open on the left side and his head bows. My steps falter. "Is this show and tell before takeoff?" I ask, unsure. I climb in, and he secures the three seat belts on me with quick, efficient hands.

"Nope. The real deal." He tweaks my nose. I stare, aghast.

"I'm not sitting in the pilot's seat, no way," I cry out, remembering what he said, *you'll know exactly what I mean with your hands on the control.*

"Relax, I pilot from the right side; left-handed, remember?" He rolls his eyes at me on a head shake that says *seriously?* And I don't even care, I welcome it.

"You just gave me heart failure." I exhale loudly, looking at the instrument panel now that I can relax back. "Is this why there are two of those?" I eye the two-handled U-shaped type of thing on a column. Calling them driving wheels sounds weird; flying wheels, even weirder.

"Control yokes? In part, but mainly so you can take over at any given moment if something happens." He stows his log book in a side compartment, bending over me.

"I'll pretend I didn't hear that," I say in an even tone despite my pounding heart.

"It's true nonetheless, just ask my first instructor," he says wryly. "Okay, your feet need to stay," he pulls them up on a middle platform low to the floor, "right there on the footrest at all times. Those two on either side are the rudders and brake pedals, and we're linked. There's only one input to command the control surfaces. Got that?"

"Got it. Can I sit in the back now?" I ask, only half-kidding.

I pull my knees tight together. No feet bouncing allowed, I sternly enjoin myself.

He kisses my cheek sweetly. "You got this, ma douce, no worries." He seals my cabin door closed tight and rounds the plane.

"We have another ten-minute check list to go through before taxiing." He hands me over a pair of sophisticated headsets with a microphone attached, hooking them on the console. "Okay, ready for your last set of instructions before I get this show up in the air?" He cocks his head at me, his handsome features relaxed, filled with boyish enthusiasm.

I nod eagerly.

He pulls his shades on, and I follow suit.

He points to the headsets. "We'll have to put these on for now on, not only for noise reduction in the cockpit, but to allow conversations between us. There are no Air Traffic Control towers, or ATC, in the Laurentians. We fly on visual flight rules, or VFR, so every aircrafts transmit their intentions and position on a specific waveband, Universal Communication, or UniCom, we're tuned in. There's not much air traffic up here, it's heavenly, but even so, don't be surprised if you're cut mid-sentence. Same goes for the transmissions I'll make via a push-to-talk switch."

"Roger." I nod once, putting it on. "Can you hear me now?" I facetiously ask, unable to help myself.

"Good." I hear loud and clear in my headset. "Master switch on."

And for the next few minutes, I listen with rapt attention as he loudly calls out one after the other his series of checks. "Starters engage." His left index finger flips two switches on the bottom half of the instrument panel.

The engines fire up, my seat vibrates, Zac's plane roaring to life.

I fist my shoulder harnesses if just to make sure I won't accidently touch anything I shouldn't in the small cockpit.

"UniCom Mont-Tremblant, this is twin-engine Piper, Bravo Kilo Tango, taxiing to runway twenty-one."

"Why twenty-one? There's just one runway," I say.

"Taken from a three-hundred-sixty-degree circle, Mont-Tremblant's runway cuts a line across two points on the axis, at two hundred ten degrees southwest and thirty degrees northeast. We drop the zeros when calling it," Zac explains while he taxies into position.

"So, it means if we'd taxied to the other end you'd have transmitted we were taxiing to runway three?"

My heart beats in my throat at the sight of the long cement runway stretching before me. The view afforded us from the windshield, panoramic. Nothing obstructs my vision, not the low console, not even the nose of the plane with its downward slant.

"Exactly. Now, it tells others I'll takeoff in the southwest direction, better lift conditions into the dominant wind—"

"UniCom Mont-Tremblant, this is amphibian Cessna Lima Zulu Echo on final approach to Lac Inattendu. Bravo Kilo Tango, I have a visual on airport with a five-minute clearance, twenty-six degrees southwest."

"UniCom Mont-Tremblant, Bravo Kilo Tango, go ahead Lima Zulu Echo, I have a visual."

"You do?" I squint.

"Eleven o'clock." Zac points to a slight left and I see a little dot plane circling low on the horizon, disappearing below the line of trees. "We'll wait for his signal, in case he needs to abort his landing, and retry."

"UniCom Mont-Tremblant, Lima Zulu Echo, landed on water, signing off."

My head hits the headrest, my spine gluing to the bucket seat as Zac's Comanche accelerates down the runway.

My stomach bottoms out and my breath swooshes out as the plane lifts off in a graceful arch.

No amount of nose pressing on airplane windows on commercial flights, or pictures I may have seen before of the land from above, come even close.

No longer earth bound, my arms extend by my side of their own volition and I let myself fly.

I'm soaring, the feeling indescribable, and in that moment, the plane truly is an extension of myself.

Thirty-Six

MAGALI

I t's early evening, and according to my agenda, I should be more than halfway done by now, revising Docteur Labonté's notes scribbled in the margins on my draft dissertation, but somehow, my mind keeps going back to this morning's glorious plane ride.

Flying low over the wilderness beyond Mont-Tremblant, in touch all at once with the wide-open space of an endless sky and the lush greens and pristine blues of mountains and lakes, from above, seemingly untainted by mankind, is burned on my soul. Zac gifted me with this out-of-body experience and my re-entry suffered hiccups. Something straight out of my favorite scene in *Out of Africa*, one of my mom's favorite movies. We must have watched it a few hundred times, give or take a few.

He gave me a glimpse of the world through God's eye, Meryl Streep said, and I get it.

My bed dips as Zac's long frame shifts beside me, hunched over his laptop balanced on his jeans-clad thighs. A sidelong glance confirms lines of concentration furrowing his brow, as he scrolls down house plans online.

I sigh, trying to refocus on the blinking cursor at the top of a blank page my own laptop screen displays, mocking me. I'm usually fast absorbed in my dissertation, but the past magical three days off the grid with Zac fairly ruined me. Might as well admit my concentration is shot, and so is my personal agenda. I flip the lid of my laptop closed and put it aside.

"You're done?" His head cocks to the side.

"Not even close," I grumble, uncrossing my legs. "You ruined me with that plane ride."

"Good, now you can help with these. How about this one?"

"Nope." My fingers smooth the furrows on his brow.

"Might help if you look," he says drily.

"Don't need to, your face wasn't into it. Next." I snuggle up to him, and for the next half hour or so he scrolls through more house designs and floor plans per minute than I've ever thought possible.

"At this rate, we'll still be here next winter," he mutters under his breath. "I never thought there'd be so many designs to choose from, and none so far that appealing to the senses. I've been at it for hours and hardly made a dent in the pile left to see." Zac sighs, a forlorn-sounding sigh to my ears, reminding me that he waited some eighteen years to come Home and that, like me, *all in means right now.*

I search underneath my pile of textbooks still littering the glass table and locate an unused notebook. Now for a pen...

I plop back down next to him. "I think you're on the right track with your search online. But we just need to narrow the field a bit or our eyeballs will shrivel up to the size of raisins if we look through the thirty-eight thousand plans your search request hit."

"Yeah, well, what if we settle for the narrowed-down search, and miss something we don't even know exists out there?" he asks, unsure.

"Not possible, as we won't settle for anything less than being struck by le coup de foudre absolu, and then, it's no longer called settling, it's called loving it," I say with utter conviction, busy doodling on top of the sheet of paper I separated in two columns.

"How do you propose—What are you drawing?"

"A Home Wish List to whittle down the search a bit, see?" I show him the stick figure couple beaming in front of a blank stick house I drew, intending for his dimples to reappear, only his eyes narrow to slits.

"I'm cool with it, but there's something missing in this picture." His tongue clucks, and he grabs my notebook and pen, his left hand flying over the paper, drawing with a flourish. "Ah, much better, see?" My favorite dimpled smile of his blooms full tilt.

I love this man. He filled the entire house space with stick babies, and drew the sun shining over it. "You realize for that many babies, we'll need fifteen bedrooms?" *I'm so framing this.*

"So? Put it on the list."

"And what else?" I ask, scooting back on the bed, propping my head with a few pillows.

"I'd love to sleep under the stars a bit more than what you have going in here, and I like the eaves at the old farmstead," he says right away. "How about an attic bedroom under the eaves with skylights?"

"Love it column." I write it down. "How about a converted veranda with windows on three sides overlooking the Cathedral as a family room?"

"Love it column," Zac says, his face animated, eyes glowing.

"I don't really care for the log cabin's chunky look, but I like the rustic feel of them, and vertical wood sidings. How about mountain chalet meets country cottage vibes?" I ask, and I begin to see it, writing the description in the Maybe Column.

Zac types the key words, *mountain chalet country cottage*, into the search engine, and we browse through a manageable selection for the next hour. He clicks on a few maybes, studying the floor layouts, but just as quickly, it fizzles out, and we move on.

"This one!" we both cry out at the same time.

The house is modern rustic, nouveau farmstead. An inspired A-frame, with a rugged exterior look, sturdy, exposed beams, lots of windows, vertical wood sidings on the bottom half, and cedar shingles on the upper half. The floor plan needs a slight remodel to fit our attic specs, but the rest of it, layout and all, is love at first sight, we both agree and gush all over it. Well, I do. Zac is more measured in his verbal flights of enthusiasm.

"Only, in a deep Wedgewood blue to pop against the Cathedral backdrop, not brown on brown like shown here. Deal?" I hold my hand up.

"Deal." Zac, beaming, high fives me.

My small printer whirrs. I flip through the pages spewed by it, and I must admit, despite the black-and-white el cheapo printout we have for now, the draft plan still turns out pretty neat. "You know, if we let both my Maman and Amélie loose in there for the home deco, they'll have a blast helping us, and we'll have a Home."

"Works for me." His eyes glint with suppressed excitement as he puts aside his laptop. "Now that that's settled, what are the odds it can all be done in four months?"

Before the snow settles in? "Slim to none, ZeeMan for the Impossible." I nod gravely into his velvety copper-brown eyes, and what I see in them makes my breath catch.

He smiles—a lazy, confident grin—and his voice is soft, a verbal caress, when he speaks. "Are you daring me?"

His eyes lit from within with a predatory glow that spells trouble, the best kind of trouble, I poke the beast some more. "Oh, I am." I bat my eyelashes coyly.

"Are you now?"

"I absolutely am. What are you going to do about it?"

He pulls the sheaf of papers right out of my hands, letting them drop to the floor. "Just watch me."

His mouth stretches in a wolfish grin as he tugs me down to straddle his lap, a man on a mission.

I cup his face in my palms, relishing the feel of his firm body shifting suggestively beneath me, and I respond in kind, rocking into him. Intimately pressed against him, just a few layers of fabric standing between us, every twitch and swell of his lengthening erection shoot arrows of pleasure tingling through my core.

Our eyes stay locked on one another until his full lips touch mine.

Our kiss starts slow and tender, and our breaths mingle as we touch in feather-light brushes, teasingly. His warm tongue licks a path along the sensitive edge just below my jaw, raining down shivers as I hold on to his shoulders, my head falling back on a small whimper. Burning lips trail up and his tongue sweeps into my mouth, his hands curling on my ass, pushing my pelvis down harder, flush against him. He swallows a groan of satisfaction when I whimper louder, his hips flexing, grinding into me.

I tangle my fingers in his hair, pulling, and his mouth crashes down onto mine, wrapping his arms around my body, tight.

I run my hands underneath his shirt, over his satiny, sleek-muscled chest, tugging the material up while I greedily return his kiss. I groan in pleasure as his tongue flicks over the pulse point below my ear, before he bites down gently. Moaning low, my head falls back once more, as he stops just long enough to shrug his shirt off, letting it drop to the side, and peels mine off.

"I'll never get enough of you," he whispers right before he captures my mouth in another scorching kiss. His smooth hands slide up over my body, his thumbs tracing my nipples, fingers plucking them. Hot palms cup my breasts, teasing them, firing up every single one of my cells, alive with need.

He flips me over my stomach, tugging down my sweat pants and boy shorts in one fell swoop. I whimper his name. He moves his hands over my ass, squeezing in appreciation, his lips leaving trails of liquid fire behind. Pulling my hair to the side, he runs his lips over my neck and up to my ear. "Spread for me." His teeth tug at my lobe as he pulls me higher up by the hips, arching my back. Deft fingers reach around, massaging my engorged, aching clit, swollen and tender.

I moan deep in my throat, weak with wanting, spreading my legs as wide as I can, my hips humping into his hand as two fingers slide in and out of my slick folds, his thumb pressing down on my nub.

"So pretty, so pink, so wet, so mine."

"More. Now. Please," I beg, seeking release from this delicious friction, wanting him embedded deep inside of me, filling me up with a glorious tension.

His body brackets me and I welcome its weight as he presses the heat of his erection into me. He pushes himself to the hilt and a low cry of ecstasy escapes me.

From this angle, he fills me completely, until I can feel the weight of his testicles drawn tight against my folds, and soon my hips are rocking mindlessly with him as his thrusts speed up. "Zac," I groan his name loudly, "sogoodsogoodsogood."

His thrusts come faster and faster as he slams into me, until words are impossible, replaced by the sounds of desire, the slap of flesh against flesh, deep moans, and keening mews. Sensations heighten as our orgasms build to its peak. His silken touch, the musk of his scent mingled with the smell of sex and arousal, the drugging rhythm of his powerful hips rocking my world, soon obliterate me.

"Zac!" I scream his name as I fall over the white edge of bliss into orgasmic oblivion, milking him, my shaky legs weak at the knees. Zac growls my name on one final push, emptying inside of me in deep pulsating throbs. His face buries against my shoulder on a silent scream, his hot breath tickling the hairs at the nape of my neck.

"Pretty sure I'm the one who'll never get enough of you." I arch underneath him as soon as we regain breath, my inner muscles clenching his stiff length lodged deep inside, making it twitch.

"By all means." He rolls me over, burning eyes gleaming, and challenges, "Prove it." His buttocks flex, sliding out, thrusting in.

Plunging my hands in his hair, I pull his face down, murmuring on his lips, "I will. Just watch me."

And well into the night, we let our bodies love. Intimately speaking of want, need, desire, perfectly met and matched, setting out to prove it, over and over one more time, before, lovingly spooned, limbs entangled, we drift off into slumber.

"I love you," Zac murmurs drowsily. "I always will."

Me too, is my last coherent thought before sleep claims me.

Thirty-Seven

ZAC

Magali closes the door to the exam room, leaning on it. I look up from my laptop. "That was our last patient of the day, Docteur. I'm off, have fun reporting on me." She grabs her light wool peacoat from the back of my chair and brushes a hand down my arm in a light caress.

On the first of the month, I have a slew of progress reports to fill out on Magali before meeting with Docteur Labonté, the head of pediatrics, to hand them over.

It's already the first day of September. September ... Liam's right. Time does fly when you're drunk on love. And happy doesn't begin to describe how I feel, home planning with Magali in between hospital rotations.

"Whoa, whoa. Not so fast, Mademoiselle Deslauriers." I pull her on my lap so she can see my laptop screen. "Check this out." I just received an email from the Municipality confirming that the construction permits are approved.

She scrolls down, reading it. "You did it, ZeeMan for the Impossible!" She tangles her hands behind my head and takes my lips in a quick, joyful kiss.

"With a little help from your dad submitting them over at La Mairie, I now believe anything's possible, and so does Liam," I say, shaking my head. She lets out an airy chuckle for an answer, reading the rest of the email confirmation.

As Old Léon's attorney and estate executor, Grégoire, knowing all the ins and outs on the epic paper trail the old farmstead comes with, cut to the chase with the Municipality, and all permits were approved today. In less than a month, a record.

Magali's spine straightens, her head jerking back. "Huh ... Zac? This just popped in your inbox and it's addressed as ... Your Royal Highness?" she asks, her voice uncertain. "Are you—?"

I mutter a bunch of explicative, flipping my laptop's cover down. "No, I'm not." Fuck. Not again with the emails. I make a mental note to call Theo.

"Then who are they looking for?"

The charge in the air thrums between us.

"Someone who doesn't even exist," I reply quietly before dropping a kiss on the top of her head. She gets up, searching my eyes.

"It's addressed to you, Zac. Are you some kind of royalty?" She frowns, unsure.

"No," I insist, adamant. "Don't be upset. It's not worth it, he's no one. Please leave it at that." My eyes plead with hers.

"Do you have to go back to Europe?" she asks in a small voice. She swallows hard, cutting me in half.

"I'm here to stay, that I promise," I solemnly swear.

She nods a couple times, her face softening. "All right, when you're ready to share, just say the word."

I pull her to me, sighing into her hair, thankful. If I have to fight the trustees, I will. "Come on. I'll walk you to the atrium and collect on a goodbye kiss."

We talk some more about the permits and construction schedule on our way over to the atrium and, once there, I dial the contractor to let him know.

Magali's head tilts to the side, waiting for the outcome of my call before leaving to meet with Amélie, who just came back last night from a month's visit with her family at les Iles-de-la-Madeleine, on the Atlantic side of the Gaspesia region. To say she's enthusiastic about our home deco project is putting it mildly. My ears are still ringing from the resounding OUI! she shouted over the line.

The hospital's automatic doors swish open, letting in a middle-aged couple and the nip in the air.

"Green light on the permits. I'll email them later tonight. Are we still on track to finish the exterior before winter settles in for good this year?" I ask Réjean Monette, the general contractor Grégoire recommended we use.

"The driveway access and preliminaries will take a week to complete, and your house plan's a pretty simple one, so we'll get it done within the next two months, no sweat," he confirms anew and, seeing it all taking shape, gets me high.

"You made my day," I say, giving Magali thumbs up and she mouths, *awesome.*

"You made my winter," Réjean quips back, good-natured, and we end the call.

"Pinterest will never recover from Amélie, now. Or maybe it's me who won't after tonight," she half-teases, eyes shining. "Later." Magali gets up on the tip of her toes, and I bend at the neck, meeting her halfway as her lips kiss mine in a sweet goodbye.

"Have fun with Amélie." I fuss with her peacoat's collar, tugging it up. "Button up, it's getting cold out," I say. "No sniffles allowed in here, got that." I kiss her forehead.

"Oui, docteur," she replies, taking a step back. She dutifully buttons up her collar for her short walk back to the micro-loft we stay at a few nights a week, in between her twin fix. And if I'm being perfectly honest, mine as well. Someday soon, we'll be filling up the four-bedroom home I'm building right now with lots of little cousins for Sébastien and Nicolas to play with, if I have my say.

"All bundled up. Now go fill them up, or you'll be late, and then, you'll be late getting back tonight, and that won't do. Amélie can only stay two hours. After that, you and I have plans," she calls over her shoulder, the sexy glint in her eyes a very promising one.

I raise a brow, giving her the onceover for an answer. She blows on her hand one last sweet kiss before stepping out into the late afternoon blustery wind, her lithe silhouette fast disappearing from my sight.

Gotta love End of the Month Report Day. I sigh at the thought of the endless forms, not exactly what I'd like to fill up right now.

"Bonne fin de journée," a couple of older nurses, Chantal and Adélaïde, from the pediatric ward, singsong on their way out. Chantal, the head nurse, tacks at the end, "Docteur di Handsome," under her breath as if I cannot hear. *Really?*

Resisting the urge to roll my eyes, I say, instead, "Bonne soirée."

My phone vibrates with an incoming text message, and my brow dips as I read, the annoying nickname bandied about the hospital already forgotten.

Theo: Call me.

I walk out, speed dialing. I pace on the sidewalk bordering the atrium, the cool mountain air cutting through my light wool sweater now that the sun is low on the horizon.

"You heard back from them?" I ask the minute Theo answers.

"And to think I wanted to make you sweat."

I exhale a slow breath, knowing by his jaunty tone that he has good news, or at least, what I would consider good news. "Sorry to disappoint. What can I say, you caught me at a good time. So?"

"You'll never guess. Are you sitting down?"

"Now you're making me sweat. Spill it, man."

"Get this. Your ugly mug is to blame. In a sum up, they wanted you to play Prince Charming to hike up their fledging tourism as offshore banking is nose diving."

Say the fuck what! "Are you shitting me?"

"Not even a little. They finally admitted that one of the five trustees came up with the idea at the end of last year after finally going through the fifteen yearbooks BIA used to send over there with Swiss precision. Congrats, man. You're the first handsome prince they ever had, apparently. Helps you're not of the bloodline, of course, but hey, details. They wanted me to ask you to reconsider." I can see his smirk from here.

"Christ, I'll disappear into the wilds of Québec before I agree to that."

I'm not even mildly interested. Not even a little. Not only do I loathe the lifestyle, but even if I didn't, I would die of sheer boredom within a week. And just the thought of an army of paparazzi tracking down my every move, like Liam had to shake not so long ago, makes me shudder. No thank you, freedom is my currency of choice.

"Relax. I suggested they build a casino instead, much better odds. Told them I had a clear mandate. They're not happy campers, but status quo is reinstated. Voted four to one, under duress, I might add, but they took you seriously. They'll leave you the fuck alone if you don't rock the boat. I assured them you won't by document signed, sealed, and delivered. Their confirmation email is on the way."

I'll take it.

My head tips back and I close my eyes, taking a moment. War has been averted.

Seventy pounds of pressure I didn't even know I carried lifts off my chest. Magali won't be inconvenienced by any of this useless shit, now, either. Under the circumstances, the only other thing that could make any of this a bit more perfect would be to find a neat way to unlock the Swiss trust fund, and dispose of the obscene amount of money sitting there, doing nothing. Swiss bankers don't mess with instructions sealed tighter than their vaults, even obsolete ones a few centuries past their prime.

"Job well done, counsellor. I owe you a solid."

"Glad I could do it, Your Royal Highness, but don't think I won't collect."

"Ass."

After the call, I saunter back inside, ready to take on the world, give or take a few reports I still have to write.

"I agree with your overall assessment. Magali is ready," Docteur Labonté finally concludes after grilling me more than usual with questions on this month's progress report.

Avoiding my gaze, she studiously cleans her half-moon reading glasses with the hem of her white lab coat before readjusting them on the tip of her nose.

The scratching sound of her pen resonates into the quiet as she co-signs Magali's eight-part report in triplicate copies. After six thirty, the administration pavilion is pretty much a ghost town, and without the usual office background noise acting as a filler, every little sound eerily echoes in the high-ceiling room.

"Have you read Magali's final draft?" I ask as she shuffles the documents back into Magali's folder.

Her unadorned hand stills. "Yes, I did." She clears her throat, fussing with the papers. "It's ... interesting."

Interesting? She worked her ass off. I frown. "I find her suggested improvements insightful, well-documented, and all in all, quite resourceful, don't you?" My eyes challenge her shifting glance.

Her chair squeaks loudly as she leans back, eyeing me. "From the way you talk about her, I gather you two are quite close," she says, her tone indecipherable but her meaning clear, which I find kind of ironic, coming from her, married as she is to the head of departments, Docteur Garneau.

"It's no secret. We are," I answer honestly. "And as with her progress reports evaluating her strengths and weaknesses, it has no bearing on my assessment of her thesis. It's objectively what it is, a promising way forward increasing the parturient well-being, most of which is feasible at a low cost."

Subdued lighting. Baby Mozart music. Inasmuch as possible birthing in the quiet of the moms' private rooms, painted in deep meditative colors instead of sterile white, as well as increasing privacy by better sound proofing in said rooms. A wide screen displaying soothing images of the mom's choosing to help her stay focused beyond intense contractions, to name but a few easily implementable things Magali's dissertation outlines.

"Agreed."

Her index fingers start a slow drum on her armrests, the noise grating on my nerves, somehow.

"Is there a specific problem you'd like to address?" My fingers steeple in front of my mouth, and I cock my head to the side.

"Docteur di Fiori, all department heads received this today," she replies instead.

A withered hand takes from the top of the pile a slim, cobalt-blue folder with the embossed fleur-de-lys logo. She slides it towards me.

"This government notice will go up in all departments come next Monday."

My brow angles, unused to being in the know before anyone else, but I pick it up nevertheless.

I briefly wonder if it's a revised staff policy having to do with interpersonal relationships, given my enquiry.

My eyes scan the official bulletin quickly. "They're closing down orthopedic surgery?" I look up, surprised. There are more broken bones than there are pregnancies up here in ski country.

"All operating suites on floor B, due to budget compressions. Incoming ER patients with broken bones that cannot be set in a simple cast will be shipped to Saint-Jérôme, starting this December."

"And the reason why I know this before anyone else?" I ask warily.

Budget compressions or not, implementation of a candidate's suggestions is not a requirement for approval, feasibility is, and Magali's thesis meets the criteria.

"It's so you'll understand what I'm about to say next." Long tapered fingers with blunt, square nails fold primly on her desk.

I raise a brow. "Okay..."

An uncomfortable knot forms in the pit of my stomach.

Are we transferred to Saint-Jérôme? Is that what she's warning me about?

It'd be tight but doable by stretching it to forty minutes, no weekend traffic, I quickly calculate.

"I'd hate to see you two get too attached," she continues in a monotone.

My spine grows rigid, and I still. "Excuse me?"

Her extended index fingers on a slow tap dance above her joined hands, she clears her throat. "In the midst of those budget compressions, Magali is being reassigned to Victoriaville as of December, and it won't be as a midwife. The pilot program will end in November."

My stomach bottoms out and I slump back in my chair, floored. "What?"

"It's out of my hands."

My nostrils flare. *Compressions in prenatal care are done quietly*, Magali had said once. *We should probably start an Absurd List on the side to help us keep our perspective, or our sanity, whichever*, she'd also said. But holy fucking hell, this one takes the cake. The program is still brand new—the powers that be would let me train Magali only to cut her out before she ever really begins?

"This is absurd!" I lean forward, gripping the edge of the desk, sorely tempted to send all of its blue files flying with the back of my hand. My voice is low, restrained. "You know as well as I that she's ready, right now, and a whole year ahead of schedule? They're getting a gem at half the price they'd normally pay for a two-year training. Isn't that cost effective enough to make an exception in her case?"

"I've already put in my recommendations to the same effect," she says, her lips pinching in a tight line. I hold my breath, hoping she'll say she's still waiting for the decision. The powerless feel that comes with it galls me, taking charge and seeing results, much more my speed. "I just received confirmation Magali will be granted her license at the end of November since she completed the program ahead of time, but that's it. She won't practice. She'll be affected to pediatrics as a regular nurse."

"Then why in God's name Victoriaville and not here?" I shove away from the desk. *Where the fuck is Victoriaville anyway?*

"Do you see an opening I'm unaware of?"

My hand rubs over my mouth. My mind is spinning a thousand miles a minute as I pace behind the chairs.

"Look, I understand," she says, her tone placating.

No you fucking don't.

I know she has nothing to do with this, but Christ, it takes everything in me not to snarl. Magali is a born midwife, a natural, in her total element. This is such a waste of funds and potential I can't even wrap my head around the concept. And I don't get a fucking say in any of this.

Christ, is a little control over my life too much to ask!?

Hands on my hips, I concentrate on the gold patina of the ancient hardwood floor at my feet, and take a few calming breaths.

"What you need to understand," her voice carries across the room, irritatingly composed, "is that Magali doesn't have much say this early in her career." *What career, you're taking it away,* I inwardly sneer. "She's really at the bottom of the pile as far as preferences and choices are concerned, but they try to accommodate. Montréal is her last choice on the list; small regional centers, her first. She's officially listed as single, she has no dependents—"

My head snaps back up. "Would it make a difference if we marry?"

Docteur Labonté's white eyebrows shoot up. My gaze is unwavering, drilling.

"Even if you're willing to marry her on the spot, it won't do anything now. She'll be put on a waiting list, at best," she says.

"And at worst?"

"If she refuses, she'll be laid off. It's a cutback, a courtesy reassignment."

Courtesy, my ass. "Do you realize how absurd it is for everyone concerned to qualify then discard highly trained personnel?" I grit through my teeth. "Why not cut first into wasteful expenses?" Like filling out convoluted eight-part reports in triplicate.

"You're preaching to the choir." She yanks open her middle drawer, filled to the brim with a hundred red pens that no one fucking uses around here. Washed-out blue eyes give me a world-weary look. "It's the way it is."

Jaw tight, I nod in understanding. I know resigned when I see it. But I'm nowhere near that yet.

"It's privileged information until she's officially notified by letter."

"I'm not keeping this from her. She deserves to be told in person after working so hard." I fight the urge to shove the armchair back against the wall as I walk away.

"You really make a difference in the region, I hope you know that."

I don't look back.

"*We* made a difference," I snarl aloud to the empty hall. "A big difference."

I think of Magali and my heart breaks into a million pieces.

Thirty-Eight

ZAC

My Jeep's headlights illuminate Magali's, parked in front of me in her narrow driveway.

My phone screen glows in the darkening interior, the twilight sky with its extended ribbons of pink and mauve hues, for once not worth a second glance. I stare at the results of my internet search and swallow, my throat tight.

Victoriaville is more than four hours away from here, impossible for Magali to commute on a daily basis on such a distance. *I'd hate to see you get too attached...*

My head thumps against the headrest.

Guess I'll get intimately acquainted with the regional airport over there. But that's not to say we'll even be able to coordinate our days off.

I run my hand down my face.

"What a goddamn fucking waste."

I pinch the bridge of my nose and take a few deep, calming breaths, but to no avail. The lump in my throat sits like an anvil just at the thought of breaking the news to Magali. Never mind what it does to me and a few lingering abandonment issues still clinging to my heart.

My hands slam on the steering wheel. I'm not that good at finding the right words, but Christ. It has to be better than finding out by letter. I cut the engine, and drag my ass up the drive.

I clear the landing, my steps slowing to a halt.

From Magali's open laptop on the kitchen counter, mellow jazz music croons straight out of Yann's latest playlist she pilfered the other night, to his delight. Her micro-loft is bathed in the soft golden glow of dozens of tea candles set in outdoor lanterns on the glass table, cleared of all textbooks and papers for the first time in the known history of this place. Home deco magazines are spread open all over the rumpled futon bed, on Magali's thick, white duvet. A stack of colorful sticky note pads and colored markers momentarily abandoned.

I'm loathe to ruin the mood in here by telling her right now, but I don't think I'll be able to fake it, either...

My feet are still rooted to the last step as the bathroom door slides open, squeaking lightly on its rail. "You're here." Magali walks straight into my arms, before I even clear the staircase, tightly holding onto me. My arms enfold her. And I know I can't ask her to stay. Not for me. Not if it means giving up what's left of her dream.

"Yeah ... I'm here." I swallow a few times, but nothing more articulate comes out of my mouth.

My eyes close, and I take a deep inhale of her freshly shampooed hair not yet dry, the zesty smell of citrus mixing with the sweet vanilla scent permeating the place from the lit candles. And I remember those very flavors being discussed in the ski resort cafeteria when I first saw her.

Magali.

Magali, who'll be living more than four hours away three months from now.

I blow my cheeks on a slow breath. *Don't go there, man. One nuclear fallout at a time.*

I drop a kiss on her head, the sting of tears behind my eyes.

Bloody hell.

I feel the rapid rise and fall of her chest. Or is it mine?

"Amélie says hi," she says to my chest in a subdued whisper, probably taking her cue from my off vibe. "You just missed her."

"Looks like you two had fun," I say, injecting enthusiasm into my tone, but it sounds forced, even to my ears.

Her stuffed bear, Picolo, catches my eye. He's propped on the floor at the foot of the bed, facing me with his long arms crossed over his chest, giving me the stink-eye, clearly in a snit at being left out of bed. Magali props him in different poses, different places, and normally I'd find it amusing, but not tonight. I'll even miss seeing the damned bear on a daily basis when she's gone. My heart is weighted down, too heavy for my chest right now.

"Her ideas are wonderful. You'll see. She not only left us with these cute outdoor lanterns she found on her way over, but some homework and some eggplant lasagna we couldn't resist tasting." She brushes her hands on my soft wool sweater, smoothing it over my chest, the ghost of a smile playing on her lips. "I'm not very hungry, but want me to reheat you some?" she asks quietly.

"Don't bother, I'm not that hungry, either, thanks."

My stomach roils just at the idea of food. Already our conversation feels stilted, and I don't even know how to broach the subject matter yet ... Ease her into it, or just come out and say it bluntly?

She takes a step back. "So ... then..." She visibly swallows, and I still. Something is decidedly off besides me; her cheeks are too pale, and her eyes are red-rimmed. Is she coming down with a cold? "I had a letter from the Health Ministry waiting for me here—"

"Christ." I run my palm over her head and pull her close, holding her tight, and she melts into me. "I'm so sorry you received it already," I murmur into her hair.

"So you know," she says in a small voice.

I stare over her head at the tea candles' tiny prick of flames, their shadows dancing on the white walls.

"Yeah, I know ... Docteur Labonté told me at the end of the meeting," I say, my voice gruff around the edges. "I would have told you myself, and spare you the communiqué."

My jaw clenches tight.

I would gladly tell off whatever technocrat at the Health Ministry who sends out marching orders by way of a laconic letter from high above his ivory tower, indifferent as to whether it's good news or bad news. And I can't help but inwardly curse Docteur Labonté, who knew last month and could have told me so that I could break it to her gently beforehand. It's not like she's unaware Magali takes being a midwife to heart. Even if she could claim she never observed it on the field, which she can't, it's written all over their goddamn reports.

We both sit in the stairway overlooking the softly lit micro-loft. My hands link in between my knees, my elbows resting on my thighs as I look down at my feet.

"I didn't know how to tell you myself just now. We work so well as a team and I know how much you love it," she says quietly. "And so do I. So I can well imagine it didn't make your top ten list of topics either." She drops a soft kiss on the curve of my shoulder. "It's very kind of you to volunteer to tell me in person, Sir Zac of the Laure, noble knight in shining armor." Her attempt at lightening this falls flat. Neither of us smile.

I shove my hands through my hair, and drop my head into my hands. "I feel so far removed from a noble knight right now ... It's fucking killing me. You're this absolute amazing midwife, and I'd fight for you if I could, but I feel so goddamn powerless in there."

Not to mention they're taking you away from me. And there's not one damn thing I can do about it.

I stare at the dark stain of a pine knot in the wood plank floor. A soft hand rubs down my back, its warmth seeping through my sweater, but the tightness in my chest doesn't let up.

She sits on her heels on the floor in front of me, taking both my hands in hers.

"Don't say that. You're not powerless. You're this amazing doctor I've had the utmost privilege to work with, and learn from. I'm grateful for all of it," she says earnestly, her reddened eyes welling up, truly, fucking killing me. She presses her palms against my much larger ones, and my fingers curl over her fingers, delicate, yet their inner strength and warmth so comforting to both moms and babies ... and me. Her face softens, and a subtle glow washes over her features as she drops her gaze to my hands, her thumbs stroking them. "On that first day at the clinic, I fell in love with these very hands, strong, yet gentle and compassionate while reassuring tiny baby Julien that all was right in his world. If mine can't welcome into the world hundreds and hundreds of babies, I'm glad these will for me."

My forehead drops on her shoulder. "You're killing me." I swallow hard.

She tips my head back up, cupping my cheeks, her eyes bright with unshed tears. "I don't mean to; knowing it brings me comfort." She nods reassuringly before warm, supple lips kiss the corner of my mouth, the gesture consoling. I should be consoling her, I know, but her heart is bigger than mine. I just can't right now. I'm likely to roar instead for having my hands tied. "Give me a couple more hours, and my inner-idealist will recover from the shock, and I'll go on."

"I don't think I'll recover," I say under my breath.

"Yes, you will. Don't say that." Her fingers come up over my mouth, then trail down my cheek gently. "In the grander scheme of things, I'd rather they cut into my program than cut into the one-year paid parental leave, or child allocations each family receives, you know."

"You're way too nice about this. I'm not feeling particularly lenient towards the Health Ministry right now."

"If I'm ahead it's not by much. Amélie got the worst of my self-pity party." She shakes her head on a forlorn sigh. "Not pretty. You've been spared."

My right hand fists and slams sideways into the wall. "Not with you more than four hours away in Victoriaville for who knows how many years," I utter despite myself. *Fuck. Way to go, man, that should make her feel really good, so mature.* My shoulders sag. "I didn't mean it quite that—"

"Zac!" she cries out, aghast. "I'm not leaving."

Say what? My heart takes flight, and crashes down to earth just as quickly.

"What do you mean you're not leaving?" I demand. "Of course you are, otherwise you'll be laid off; Docteur Labonté confirmed as such. I have a plane, remember. Hell, I'd commute every day if not for being on call, but I'll come see you every chance I get. We'll figure it out—"

"Whoa. Simple as that. You decided for me?" She jerks her head back, effectively silencing me.

"Huh?" I manage to say, sifting through her black-and-white options. "Do you have a choice in there I haven't seen?"

Leaning into me, her hands come to rest over my thighs, her exquisite face softening with a look of love. My heart stutters.

"There's always a choice. What if I decided that *we* are more important? If I told you I choose you, Zac, what would you say?" Her eyes, wide and luminous, search mine.

My heart skips a beat, then another, and another. "That no one has ever chosen me before," I murmur before I can stop myself.

"It's long overdue then." She drops a tender kiss on my cheek, her lips lingering for a beat or two.

I pull her up to sit on my lap. "Christ, Magali. You don't know what it does to me to hear you say that." I tuck a long strand of hair behind her ear. Have her stay? Bloody hell, it's so tempting, it's tearing me in half. I close my eyes briefly, and take a deep inhale. "I'd love to keep you right here. I'm selfish that way. But in good conscience, I can't let you. You don't see how lit up you are in there at the hospital with the moms and babies. You'll miss it, and where will that leave us?"

"It will leave us a little bit more in love each and every day, because I'll be where I choose to be, with you. That's where," she emphatically says, and something warm and bright unfurls in my chest, lifting some of the heaviness lodged in my heart. Magali fixes me with a thoughtful gaze. "Zac, being a midwife is not who I am, but an expression of who I am. What I'll miss, I'll miss here much less than in Victoriaville, trust me."

I don't want you to miss out on anything. I want all of you, fulfilled, not just some parts of you.

"Have you ever thought of getting your full medical license? With your equivalencies you'd be more than halfway through already. I'll be there every step of the way if you'd like to go back to l'université—"

She presses her fingers onto my lips, shaking her head. "I know you would, but there's no need. I already went through all these considerations, choosing my path a few years back." Getting up, she tugs on my hands, shuffling backwards. "So you can feel a hundred and ten percent reassured about my decision to stay. Even without us in the picture, I'd refuse the reassignment."

"Why?" I lean a shoulder on the upper cabinet as she divides the last of a bottle of Côtes-du-Rhône red wine into two glasses, offering me one.

"I wouldn't last a month as a nurse in pediatrics, and even less as a doctor. I like the learning, but I'm not cut out for those responsibilities." She stares off into the claret robe of the wine in her glass. "My overflowing emotions would always get in the way, clouding my judgement." She tilts her head, eyeing me. "I'd need to curb them all the time, and I don't want to, and generally speaking, I hate hospitals."

"You what?" I choke in disbelief, putting back down my untouched wine.

The tiniest of grin plays on the corner of her lips as she leans back against the counter. "Okay, well hate is a bit excessive." Her face turns reflective, and her eyes glint, a faraway look in them when she speaks. "What I'm really hooked on in there is the joy and wonder permeating the maternity wards. It's energizing, a parallel universe within the hospital, and it brings forth a part of my personality I want to keep on nurturing. The one that accompanies, fusses over, cuddles, marvelling right alongside the moms over their babies, looking out for them ... That's what agrees with me." She nods a few times, then sighs, putting down her own, untouched wine. "And as a midwife teamed up with you as a doctor, I had the best of both worlds. I could really let loose, and be myself."

I shake my head. *Such a waste ...* "We really made one hell of a team, I'm so sorry."

"So am I."

I hold her stare in a searching gaze. "What do you want to do now?" I ask quietly.

"In the long run, I don't know, yet. The curse of living in a place where a public health regime is the only viable option with no access to private insurance, I suppose. But it will come to me," she reflects upon, her voice infused with quiet confidence injecting a shot of serene into the disquiet of the news, smoothing some of my ragged edges. Her arms wind around my neck, and my fingers curve around the small of her back. Wondrous eyes lock on mine, full of strength and determination. "For the next three months, though, I'm teamed up with this wonderful doctor I immensely admire, and I intend to make the most of it, and be grateful. You in?"

Roger willco.

"All in." I kiss her forehead, rocking us gently from side to side.

"Good." She drops a light kiss on my shoulder. "He's the love of my life, by the way, and it so happens I'm building a home with him, his first ever."

My adoring gaze tracks the loving warmth shining through on her face, drinking her up.

"Is that so? Lucky guy." I smile softly.

"No." She shakes her head, eyes aglow. "Lucky us."

I bend my neck, my lips trailing down her jaw.

Home. Forever. Happily ever after. The words swirl in my mind, seep into my soul as I cover her mouth with mine, recapturing in that instant something precious in my life. Something I thought we'd only have once in a while for the next forever, and not of our own choosing.

She meets my lips with hers, and I capture them hard, a melting exploration of lips and tongue making my heart beat fast and strong. I groan and angle my head to penetrate deeper. Her hand grips my hair, holding me closer.

I back her up to the bed, and she brings me down with her.

"Love me, Zac."

"I do. I absolutely do."

And I set out to show her just how much I do love her, well into the night, one caress at a time.

I brush the back of my fingers on her silken cheek as she puffs out a sigh in her sleep.

Head on the pillow next to hers, unable to find sleep yet, I watch the shadows dance on the wall until the last candle flickers out.

Thirty-Nine

ZAC

Sunday afternoon finds Magali and me sitting around painted wood bistro tables on the quaint terrace of C'est La Vie Café down in the village, saying goodbye to Yann and P.O. over one last coffee, at P.O.'s insistence, before Leo drives them to the airport for their flight back to Boston.

The sight would be comical anywhere else but not in Les Laurentides. Everyone's outside, even with the cold front that's moved in with a brisk wind blowing down on us from the hills into the valley. Patrons, bundled up into wool beanies, bulky coats, gloves, and scarves huddled around faïence coffee bowls, lazily sip café au lait, hold the milk for some of us. The whole ambiance, complete with some olden French songs playing in the background, is reminiscent of a Paris sidewalk café in the spring time. A subarctic version of it anyway; one I'm getting used to, which proves that with thermal underwear, anything's possible.

P.O., sitting across from me, furtively darts glances around my shoulder every once in a while. I watch his not-so-subtle maneuvers.

"See anything of interest?" I ask drily. Trust him to find a girl to his liking half an hour before he's out of here. Literally. A classic.

"Nope. I just thought someone looked familiar, that's all." He busies himself with his phone, texting, his cheeks now sporting red splotches. Interesting. On both counts. The denial and the flush of color.

Leo and I share a look, clearly thinking the same thing. Something more than good coffee served in exquisite faïence brought him down regularly to C'est La Vie the past couple of weeks. All is not as he claims.

"Wow. You normally would have flown them back to Boston if you weren't on call today?" Magali asks me, wanting to confirm whatever Yann said to her just now. Her impossibly large eyes appear even more so underscored by her burgundy beanie pulled low over her brow.

"*We* would have flown them back." One arm draped casually over the top of her mustard yellow bistro chair, I cross my ankles. "And that's a big maybe. I want to be there for ground breaking at the home site early tomorrow. Nice try, man." I smirk at Yann over my cup, taking a sip of my black coffee.

The guys are still marvelling over the fact I'm settling in one place, and they like to witness the phenomena by testing it. Not so long ago, I'd have flown them back to Boston, detouring by Miami in the blink of an eye. They really thought I'd be the last one to settle down. Truth be known, so did I. But not for lack of wanting. My fingers brush Magali's arm in a lazy back and forth.

"Harsh, man," Yann grumbles good-naturedly. "You're pulling the plug now that we're used to being chauffeured around."

"Porter Airlines has a direct flight from Tremblant to Boston. I'm sure you'll recover well enough." I roll my eyes at him.

"Hell, I'll drink to Porter, saves me a trip to Montréal on the weekend rush hour." Leo and Magali clink their white and blue earthenware coffee mugs in complete accord. Apparently, road conditions in and around the city are pretty atrocious, so much so as to be the stuff of legends among the locals. I'll take their word for it; being stuck in traffic and dodging potholes the size of craters is not really my idea of a good time. I'm in no hurry to visit.

"It's really a neat city but you need to go there without a specific timetable, otherwise you'll curse up and down," Magali concurs with Leo. "But, Yann, you really should come earlier next summer; the Montreal Jazz Fest starts at the end of June. You'd love it—"

P.O. slaps his hand on the table, barking out a laugh loud enough that it's a conversation stopper. All eyes swivel his way. He looks up from his phone.

"Huh ... Email. Don't ask. Inside joke," he mumbles, not so subtly craning his neck for a furtive look over my shoulder. His fingers, all thumbs, fumble to put his phone away. Magali catches it just before it hits the floor deck.

"Good catch, thanks." P.O. pockets it with a sheepish look.

"You *like* her like her, don't you?" Magali asks him.

"Who?" he asks warily.

She cups her hands over her mouth and stage whispers, "The girl behind me you keep peeking at."

"No! Yes. Never mind." P.O. rubs the back of his neck.

I check behind my shoulder for the most likely suspect, or prospect. Bingo. There's a lone girl with her back to us, two tables down, with straight strawberry-blonde hair sticking out of a black woolen hat.

"Go and say hi," Magali encourages him.

"No way." He sends her a quick, panicked look.

"Hey, maybe I know her. Do you want me to pass a note?" Magali says half-teasingly.

P.O.'s fair complexion turns red as a boiled lobster, starting with the tip of his ears, which he promptly covers by pulling down his black beanie so low it now hides half his face.

"Nice." Yann chuckles low.

"Shit," P.O. mutters, lowering himself in his chair. "Magali, do you really know her?" he whispers anxiously.

"No, I don't. Relax." She pushes P.O.'s beanie up his brow.

"You're panicking over nothing. She's not even looking this way, dude." Leo upturns his eyes.

He's right. The girl's so absorbed by her laptop she doesn't react in the slightest to her surroundings, almost unnaturally still, wrapped in a bubble of her own making.

"Please tell me it's the girl and not the laptop you're drooling over." If looks could kill, I'd be dead by now.

"You know, women don't bite unless you ask for it," Magali deadpans, and Yann nearly spits coffee, thumping on his chest.

"A little warning next time, Magali," he coughs up, flustered.

"I don't recall asking this morning," I murmur into her ear.

"It was implied." She elbows me. I chuckle low, brushing my lips on her temple.

P.O. straightens in his chair, his intent gaze following the girl as she leaves, walking by the terrace.

"No, really, guys. Are women that terrifying as a species?"

"Duh," we all reply as one, fist bumping, and she shakes her head at us, complete with eye rolling.

Gender-oriented quips fly high and low around our table for the next little while, up until Coldplay's *Up & Up* chorus plays out of Magali's coat pocket, interrupting the flow.

"That's Amélie." Her brows dip as she fishes her phone out. "She'd text normally. I need to take this; sorry, guys." She walks down to the edge of the Linear Park the terrace overlooks, a frown etching on her face as she takes the call.

"Amélie, that's her friend from her freestyle competition days who jumped off the ski ramp with her last winter, right? The one on the pictures she showed us?" Leo asks, rubbing his chin.

"Yep, what about her?" I ask distractedly, keeping an eye on Magali, relaxing back when I see her face break into a soft smile.

"Heard Magali mention to Éolie last night that she's helping with your home decor, and she seemed pretty enthused. Think Amélie can do something to tone down the duct tape at the farmstead?" Leo asks in all seriousness, staring at the bottom of his cup as if it holds the answers to his impossible request.

Both Yann and P.O. snicker, mumbling under their breath it'd take a miracle to tone that down. I have to agree.

"Leo, come on, there's not much she can do on repairs. She deals with the finishing touches as a hobby of hers. Gut the place down or own the duct tape, man."

Leo cuts me a look. "Well, since I'm not gutting it down until our little twins move into their new house next summer, I just thought Amélie could, I don't know, enliven it meanwhile." I raise a brow. He shoves his dark-green beanie down his brow. "Long winters, I've been warned enough," he grumbles, slouching into his chair.

"Riiight. That's what you call it now? Enlivening long winters," P.O. says knowingly.

"You're one to talk," Leo mutters.

"I like Magali's suggestion of playing tic-tac-toe on the walls." Yann drains the last of his coffee.

"Actually, that's Amélie's suggestion, not mine." Magali drops a kiss on the top of my head, before plopping back down on her chair.

"Really?" Leo visibly perks up.

Magali gives me a sidelong glance.

"Don't look at me. I'm not touching this one." I hold my hands up.

Last month, Leo was less than enamored by the idea when we ran out of paper one night and started writing Mille Bornes scores on rolls of tape, sticking them every which way on the walls. The witty commentaries on life at the farmstead written alongside them might be to blame for it. Leo's sense of humor didn't extend quite that far.

"Told you the idea would grow on you," she says to him. "But I'm sure Amélie can come up with other ones, if you're interested. I can ask her to drop by the farmstead and take a look. She hasn't been there in ages."

"Oh. Cool. Yeah. Sure. Anytime," Leo says, all the while nodding casually, as though pondering the matter at great length. He leans forward on his elbows, and asks "Is tomorrow all right?"

Magali and I share a look.

Well, well, well. This should be interesting. I grin into my cup.

"Huh ... She's going for a few days to Kuujjuaq, but since I'm going with her for the day, I'll put her up to speed and ask her to call you when she's back. How's that?"

"Great—"

My head jerks back, uncertain I heard right. "Whoa. Back up. Did you just say you're going to Kuujjuaq for the day?" I ask, my brows pulling in as she nods. "Who's flying you? What's going on?"

Later, she mouths, a shadow passing over her expression.

I frown, unclipping my phone. I haven't pored over flight maps recently like I used to, but if memory serves me right, Kuujjuaq's in Nunavik, the part of Nunavut that spans Québec's Ungava region at the edge of the Arctic Circle. Why the hell would Magali go there?

"And on that note," Yann motions with his head to the other two, "don't we have a plane to catch ourselves in less than ninety-six minutes?"

Leo jumps to his feet, humming the *Thunderbirds Are Go* theme song, an iconic sci-fi puppet show we frequently watched as kids at BIA. He ruins the dramatic effect by knocking his car keys right off the table. But Magali catches them in one swift move, and hands them over with a quick smile.

"That's some reflexes." He whistles low. "Man, next time we play Frisbee, you're on my team," Leo says to her, a little awed, palming them. "Suck it up, Zee."

Preoccupied by my search online, I refrain from commenting that we don't even play Frisbee. It's as I thought, Kuujjuaq is in Nunavik... A rough flight. And there's no way in hell I'm letting anyone else fly her up there.

At Leo's car, Magali says her goodbyes to P.O. and Yann, kissing both their cheeks, hugging them with well wishes for a safe flight back and a bang-up dissertation to finalize their last year at MIT.

"Ditto, for yours," they wish her, and she nods in quiet thanks. Her mouth pinches in a tight-lipped smile. She's putting on a brave front, making my chest compress in a vise. She'll be a fully licensed midwife, but without any means to practice.

Hands shoved in my coat pockets, I don't say anything. She wouldn't want me to. Aside from Amélie and her parents, Magali's decided to keep quiet about the news for now.

Leo drives by, and on a last wave goodbye, Magali buckles up in my Jeep.

"So, what's the story behind this sudden day trip to Kuujjuaq?" I ask with a sidelong glance, shifting in first.

Her booted heels coming to rest on the seat, she curls on herself, her arms enfolding her bended legs. "Amélie spent four months over there on her last student-teacher assignment last winter, and she stayed with a host family. Three women. A grandmother who only speaks Inuit, a daughter who speaks a bit of French, and a granddaughter, about our age, who doesn't speak at all." I shoot her a look sideways. "She's developmentally disabled. Amélie suspects she's somewhere on the deep side of the autism spectrum." She rubs her forehead, her beanie shoved up in the process.

"She's not diagnosed?" I ask with some surprise. My temperament might not be the best fit to work within the system, but it's not to say that I'm not impressed by the extensive health care coverage citizens get.

"No, and she probably never will from our standpoint, Amélie says." She looks out her window. "Inuits have their own language, their own beliefs and views on life, and with the rise in eco-tourism over the past decade, the younger ones now stand on the threshold of two worlds."

"Must be difficult for them, not fully belonging anywhere," I say in sympathy, knowing exactly how that felt, and how that still feels, in part, now that Magali will no longer work with me in the foreseeable future.

"It's ... difficult, assuredly. Long story short, from what Amélie understood, the granddaughter will probably require some medical attention outside of their traditional remedies. The grandmother is still convinced you only go to the clinic to die, and the mom is, herself, more than half-convinced of the same. Even so, she contacted Amélie, for her daughter's sake, as she responded well to her," she says, her tone of voice subdued. "Amélie will accompany her if need be, but she wants me to confirm if she's pregnant. The mom can't tell, the symptoms are mixed."

Christ. My left hand squeezes the driving wheel in a white-knuckled grip. We both know there's only one way that could happen, given her condition. My fingers clench on the shifter. "I'm coming with you." I say grimly.

So much mental sickness and emotional distress that goes unaddressed, such a vicious cycle. I scowl darkly.

Magali lightly strokes my forearm, and it gets my attention back from its dark place. "I need to rule out pregnancy, but for now, by symptoms alone, it's more likely uterine fibroids."

And it will show on the portable ultrasound. Uterine fibroids are very common, benign growths that develop within the uterus muscular wall, their sizes far ranging, from tiny as a pea to a sizeable honeydew melon, and there are non-surgical ways to remove them now.

"Doesn't change the fact I'm coming with you." I firmly say. "In fact, I'm flying you both."

"No, you're not." Her booted feet thump back down on the Jeep's floor and she crosses her arms over her chest, jutting her chin.

My teeth grind, and I make a concerted effort to unclench my jaw. "Give me one good reason not to."

From the corner of my eye, I see her shift in her seat towards me, and count on her gloved fingers. "One, she negatively reacts to the presence of men, and the whole point of my going is to avoid unnecessary stress for her," she says pointedly. "Two, AirBoréal's Cessna planes are equipped with AirGlide skis, yours isn't. Three, you're supervising ground breaking at our home site, something you've been looking forward to for the past eighteen years. Need a *fourth* reason?"

I swerve by the shoulder of the road, gravel crunching, and the Jeep skids to a halt.

Holding on to the crash bar, she cries out, "What are you doing?"

"Clearing up a few things before we reach the farmstead, and risk upsetting the twins if it turns into a shouting match." I jam it into park, my eyes drilling into hers. "One, I'll stay outside the house if I have to, and wait for you, but I'm coming with you. Two, nonnegotiable, if I'm not satisfied with what I see at AirBoréal, no one gets up there until I equip the Piper with skis, and that's final." I grab my phone and dial quickly.

"You don't need to—"

"Allo, Grégoire? Zac, here. Listen, something came up, and I can't make it tomorrow morning. You know the tighter corner around the last bend we marked? I'd appreciate if you can make sure the mossy boulder Magali loves is protected by tarps so that it stays untouched." He assures me he will, and I end the call.

"Any other reasons?" I ask tightly, and she shakes her head, wide-eyed.

"Good." I shift into gears.

A cold fist of dread twists my guts for absolutely no good reason. I don't know why exactly, but I have one hell of a bad feeling about this round trip.

I'd die a thousand times if something happens to her.

But it sure as hell won't be on my watch.

Forty

ZAC

Apprehension

noun

5. the act of arresting; seizure.

A light sprinkle of snow dusts Kuujjuaq and the surrounding tundra like powdered sugar on a confiserie. The Koksoak River sparkles in the distance under the early-afternoon sun.

The pilot, a taciturn old timer, grunts, as I recheck the cargo weight distribution myself, yesterday's unease letting up, somewhat, now that we're preparing for the return trip.

Not pregnant. The ultrasound revealed uterine fibroids the size of an overblown cantaloupe to my and the girls' relief. As for the two older women's acceptance of the diagnosis, it is best described as stoic. I clip into place the medical-grade, portable machine, originally bought to monitor the twins, into the Cessna 208 Grand Caravan's wide cargo bay.

Magali and I are the only passengers flying back south on this utility plane version of the 208, Amélie staying behind for a few more days. The Grand Caravan, in its mainstream version, is a ten-passenger short-haul regional airliner mostly seen with an add-on, underbelly cargo pod stretching its entire length in between the fixed tripod landing gear. This one, though, a four-seater, has an interesting configuration I've only seen once before on the internet. It has the usual bucket seats in the open cockpit, but a bench on the left side of the cabin, and on the right, a folded stretcher, clipped sideways to the floor when unused for medical transport, leaving a narrow aisle in between the cockpit and the backseat.

I have zero contention with AirBoréal. The plane is recent and in top condition, and their pilots stay overnight and only fly once a day, on a rotation, even though the flight's only three hours. I'll take it.

This morning's pilot was much more talkative, though, and I thoroughly enjoyed reacquainting myself with the Cessna's specs sitting in the cockpit, leaving the girls quietly chatting in the backseat.

This one mumbles about know-it-all private pilots with fancy-ass clothes, and the plague of last-minute passengers he's not ready to cater to on a cargo flight. His thick, French Canadian accent is as dense as deep-freeze peas and hard to follow. I trail behind his trudging gait to the company trailer, sitting high up on stilts, rolling my eyes behind his back to Magali.

With the dip below normal in seasonal temperatures, we're wearing our high-tech ski jackets, turtlenecks, and soft-shell pants, to the amusement of locals, I'm sure, most of whom are only wearing light jackets over flannel shirts. We get negative forty-five in the winter months from wind chill factor, but they get negative forty-five before wind chill factor. At negative four, with a light accumulation of snow from last night on the ground, it's probably still considered a balmy autumn day up here in Inuit country, so we might as well wear a sign that says *thin-blooded tourists.*

I nearly plow into the stocky man as he unexpectedly stops to take a breather on top of the stairs. One hand gripping the handrail, he clears his throat of phlegm, spitting out a load of chewing tobacco coated in yellowish snot. I almost laugh out loud at Magali's incredulous stare from the window as she eyes the wad, adding to an already impressive collection frozen solid on the landing.

We resume our climb to the top. I wait while the pilot works the latch. Its hinges protesting the use, the door squeaks open. The plane below is in pristine condition, the barrack, not so much. Before I even step over the threshold, my nostrils quiver, assailed by the smell of stale coffee and cigarettes permeating the stained carpet. Empty fast food containers litter the folding card table and the two metal chairs, overflowing into a wastepaper basket, near the counter. Since there are no fast food franchises in any of the small Inuit communities this far up North, quite the feat.

Magali sidles up to my side, whispering, "I think there's a black market on fast food going on here." She points to a cleaning service schedule pinned to the billboard.

If this place really gets cleaned once a week, what I'm looking at is clogged arteries happening live, and if not, a Petri dish of bacterial colonies. Probably both.

"Boarding," the disgruntled grizzly bear grumbles without looking in our direction. His yellow-tinted fingers reach behind the counter and produce a grease-stained paper bag harboring a well-known golden arch. Who the hell knows how long it sat there, at the very least, since we landed mid-morning today. On the other hand, the place is cold enough to be an open air fridge.

"Are you going to eat that cold?" Magali asks, holding in a wince.

"What's it to you?" He gives her a baleful glare, and she raises a brow. He lowers his gaze, his feet shuffling towards the door, muttering under his breath that he hates fish, which is apparently supposed to serve as an explanation. "Step on it. Poker night," he rasps in my general direction.

"By all means," I say drily, following behind Magali, adding under my breath, "Poker night in Mont-Laurier, who wants to miss that?"

AirBoréal is based in Mont-Laurier, a small logging town an hour-and-a-half northwest of Mont-Tremblant by car. Not that I have anything against logging towns, but I guess I'm still smarting over the fact Magali and Amélie had to translate for me at a local diner over early breakfast at five this morning. The two waitresses' and the few scattered clients' dense accent and quick run-on sentences didn't even sound like French to my ears. And here I thought I was bilingual, with a smattering of Swiss German thrown in the mix. Goes to show.

"You know a lot about Cessna planes for a Piper guy," Magali says, following me as I follow the grizzled pilot around his pre-flight checklist like a tick snacking on a caribou, making sure he manually checks the fuel cells, uncaring of the loaded glares he shoots my way. Fucking too bad, mate, if you don't like it. Deal with it.

"I clocked a few hundred hours on a 172 model," I explain to her, doing a visual on the landing tripod and tire pressure, AirGlide skis an add-on affixed to the wheels. "You can't get certified on a multi-engine unless you're certified on a single engine."

"Oh. I never really thought about that." She nods in acknowledgement. "Makes sense, though, now that you mention it."

"Yep, it does. A pilot adds on certifications, one at a time." I tweak her nose. "Ready to go home?"

"Home with you, I like the sound of that." Her eyes glint with inner joy as she hugs me, and I hug her back. *So do I.*

The Ungava region is hauntingly beautiful in itself, with its spectacular cliffs, ice turquoise waters and drifting icebergs. Its long stretches of tundra exposing grey granite polished to a dull shine by recurring glaciations, adorned with crusty patches of lichen and clumps of stumped-growth balsam firs. I eye them, remembering my sticky encounter with them in my own forest at home. However, the Ungava's stark grandeur doesn't resonate in me quite in the same way the Laurentians' lush green hills do.

I help Magali buckle in and, in no time, we're airborne.

Twenty-some minutes into the flight, we're cruising at one hundred forty knots at twenty thousand feet. I have to hand it to the guy, antisocial and sourly he may be, but he's an experienced bush pilot, no contest.

I relent on my watching him like a hawk and relax for the first time on this trip. I lean back, my arm inviting Magali in. We settle back more comfortably on the bench, her head propped in the crook of my shoulder.

Magali's hand resting on my thigh, I cover it with my own, stroking my thumb over it.

We stay quiet, lulled by the hum of the engine. The day catching up to her, no doubt, Magali stifles a couple of yawns discreetly behind her hand.

I kiss the top of her head. "Nap. I'll wake you in a couple of hours when we're about ready to land."

"I'm good," she replies drowsily, her eyelids fluttering close.

"I know you are," I murmur suggestively into her ear, and her chest rumbles on a faint chuckle, ending on a huge yawn she can't contain.

I let my cheek fall back on her head, an answering yawn stretching over my mouth.

My eyes drift close. *Just a few minutes*, I tell myself.

A jerking motion to the left, followed by an overcompensating swing to the right, makes my eyes pop wide open and land on the pilot.

Magali startles up.

The pilot's hands quake and his head bobs lightly, sweat pearling on the back of his neck.

Fuck.

I unlatch my two seatbelts and cross over to the cockpit.

Beads of sweat dampen his coarse hair at the temple as one shaky hand unbuckles his shoulder harnesses. Trembling fingers undo his flannel shirt buttons, ready to pop at the seams, his grey tee underneath already sporting a darker charcoal color around the collar, wetted through. "Get back there," he sputters over his shoulder when he spots me coming through.

I ignore his command, sliding into the right-end seat, buckling up into the three-point harnesses.

Lips thinning, the guy nostrils flare, two red splotches appearing on his cheeks in stark contrast to his tanned complexion turned sallow. Not a good color combo on him.

I pull the headset over my head, plugging it in. "Get some rest, I'll take over for the next hour." *Or two.*

"It will pass in a minute, just heartburn," he wheezes before popping the last three antacid tablets from a roll into his mouth, chewing.

Heartburn, imagine that, I inwardly vent, eyeing the half-eaten hamburger laying on the grease-stained paper bag left on the console, pissed at the guy. If you can't stomach it, don't fucking eat it while piloting. "Buckle up. Until it passes, *I'm* taking over," I say, my jaw tight, my hands steadying on the yoke. *Don't make me wrestle for control of the yoke, you arse, 'cause I will if I have to.*

"Not ... in ... insured—" I'm jerked forward as his forehead hits the top of the instrument panel with a hard thump, slumped unconscious.

The plane nose dives, dropping altitude in a straight line at eight hundred feet a second, his unrestrained torso leaning on the yoke in a dead weight, locking it into place.

"Zac!" Magali screams from behind me.

With the increased air intake, in a matter of milliseconds the turbo prop accelerates, one sixty knots, one eighty knots, past the unsafe zone of the plane's engine specs of one eighty-six knots. Horns blare in the cockpit, red light alarms firing up all over the panel.

I pull the thrust lever aft, shutting down the gas intake, but we still make it past two hundred ten knots, well into the red zone. *Come on come on come on,* I incant, willing it to reduce speed now that I stalled the engine. The yoke shakes under my hands, pressured by the opposite directions of push and pull stressed upon it. Two hundred knots, one ninety-six, one ninety-two, one ninety...

My feet brace in the space between the pedals and the instrument panel as I bend over the yoke on my side as far as the harnesses let me to steady my weight behind the pull I'll need to exert slowly; otherwise, an abrupt swing upward would pulverize the wings from the undue stress put on them.

The vibrations abruptly quit, my body instantly locking into place as the yoke miraculously lightens from its dead weight, giving me back full control.

Magali.

I look over and find Magali holding the pilot by the shoulders, yanking him off the controls and back against the seat.

I let myself exhale, vowing to kiss the fuck out of her later for that, and focus on what I'm about to do next. I practiced this recovery maneuver ninety-four fucking times in my teenage years, and a thousand more on Flight Simulator, I remind myself; granted, not once running in the literal red, but still.

Go.

An eerie calm washes over me, my hands holding steady, as I pull the yoke towards me gently, and we angle out of the dive in a wide arc.

Under one hundred eighty-six knots, horns stop blaring in the cockpit, and a few red light alarms turn off.

The plane stabilizes at an altitude of eight thousand feet, cruising at one hundred thirty-eight knots. I breathe out. These have got to be both the shortest and longest seven seconds of my life.

My left hand pulls the thrust lever fore, reengaging, and I start a descent to five thousand feet, decreasing speed in increments to get to one hundred fifteen knots, which will alleviate some of the stress the engine went through.

I switch to the emergency frequency.

"PAN PAN, PAN PAN, PAN PAN, this is AirBoréal Cessna 208 Whiskey

Sierra Lima on Unicom Ungava, to any aircraft in my vicinity. My position is two hundred seventy-two miles south east of Kuujjuaq, seven thousand feet, one hundred twenty knots, main pilot unconscious, engine over torque conditions, requesting direction to nearest landing strip and medical assistance."

"Magali," I call out to her, but with the headset on, I can't hear her. I turn and lock eyes with her. Magali's whole body is shaking from the effort of holding the guy upright, but she responds to me like the trooper she is, her eyes full of determination.

Her mouth firms with resolve. "I've got him," I read on her lips.

God, I love her.

"Magali, listen," I enunciate calmly. "I need you to re-clip his shoulder harnesses without letting go of him, and I need you to buckle up on the aisle side. Can you do that for me?"

She nods. Trembling fingers digging deeply into the guy's fleshy upper arms, it takes her a few tries before she manages to unfreeze them from their death grip. Her palm holding him upright by the forehead, she rounds the seat to brace her torso against him. Shaky hands buckle up the two-point harnesses into the lap buckle, securing him back.

Over Magali's leaning form, the pilot's waxen complexion and lifeless eyes stare through the windshield.

"Christ," I say under my breath.

Magali starts CPR but to no avail, the stench of death now permeating the cabin. "No pulse."

We share a look. In all likelihood, he's been struck by a sudden cardiac arrest. And even though I'm pissed he endangered us all needlessly, it's probably a blessing for the poor guy who'd have suffered tremendously through a milder myocardial infarction, otherwise, given the circumstances.

My eyes flit back to hers and then drop to her mouth. I read on Magali's lips, "I know."

I tap my headset and motion to the pilot's. She swallows, wiping his headset on her pants, unwinding the cord as far as it goes in order to sit back on the bench, buckling up, before she pulls it on.

"You okay?"

"Oui—"

282 • SYLVIE PARIZEAU

"Unicom Ungava, this is Fifty-Five Degrees North Outfitters' outpost on the Koksoak River calling to AirBoréal Cessna 208 Whiskey Sierra Lima, are you amphibian?" a baritone voice crackles into my headset.

"Unicom Ungava, this is AirBoréal Cessna 208 Whiskey Sierra Lima, negative Fifty-Five Degrees, AirGlide skis equipped, please confirm nearest landing strip."

There's none, I'm too far inland, according to the outfitter, only thousands of lakes to choose from if we'd only been amphibian.

I need to follow a road of some kind as an emergency backup plan. There's no road to Nunavik, so our only option is onward, flying home, following the remote James Bay Road we're looking for right now. If we don't and the abused engine fails over this vast wilderness area of some six hundred kilometers of taiga, a moist subarctic forest dominated by conifers that begins where the tundra ends, it will mean crashing to a certain death. A risk I'm not willing to take. My jaw clenches.

I alternate glances between the controls and the snow-dusted taiga below, scanning for the road.

"There it is, to my left. I see a white ribbon in a straight line cutting through the trees," Magali says and I veer left, exhaling.

Sunset and fuel will be tighter than what I'm comfortable with, but the risk of engine failure from the over torque it endured is greater than the risk of running out of fuel or flying blind, with no landing lights anywhere.

Less than forty minutes later, as though conjured by thought alone, the oil pressure buzzer blares to life, the red alarm light blinking in sync, confirming the right call on this.

But, bloody hell, do I hate being right sometimes.

"MAYDAY, MAYDAY, MAYDAY, this is AirBoréal Cessna 208 Whiskey Sierra Lima on Unicom James Bay, to any aircraft or control points in my vicinity, main pilot presumed dead, engine down, no oil pressure, requesting Coast Guard assistance when crash landing is completed on James Bay Road."

Fuck me, this is going to suck. I'd probably kill the guy if he weren't already dead.

"UniCom James Bay," the radio crackles. "This is James Bay Caniapiscau hydroelectric outpost, Whiskey Sierra Lima, mayday relayed, we're standing by for a safe landing confirmation, over and out."

Adrenaline and fear shoot through me as I think of Magali strapped in with a simple shoulder harness. If anything happens to her...

I stop the thought before it can finish. Nothing will happen to her. Not while I have breath. I force myself to concentrate on sticking this to landing. Nothing else matters.

"Magali, brace for impact."

Forty-One

ZAC

On final approach, the plane wavers, caught in the crosswind.

I listen to the soothing rhythm of Magali's deep, calming breaths, the sound of her filling my headset, her focus and calm keeping me on top of my game.

"Magali, hold on, ma douce. Just hold on," I murmur. "I'll get you there safely, I swear I will."

This is it, man, no retake on this one.

Reduce flaps, check. Steady, steady. Swaying from side to side, keeping the nose aligned with the center line, the white ribbon of snow-covered road stretching ad infinitum before me, I steer with both the ailerons and the rudders.

We're coming down onto the deserted road a little too fast, at an angle that's not perfect, a bit too low for one more turn, but I've got this. I just know I do.

Coming down, down, down.

Contact in three. Two. One.

The nose wheel hits first, hard, and I prepare for a face plant if it can't withhold the shock, but the landing tripod makes contact and I know the worst is over.

Still, I bump and toss in my seat, only held in place by my harness. I want to look back, check on Magali, but I can't spare a glance now. Almost there...

Steering with the rudders, I let the plane lose speed on its own, gracefully gliding to a halt by the side of the endless stretch of road bisecting the dense wilderness in a straight line.

Finally, after an eternity, the plane comes to a stop.

"Unicom James Bay, AirBoréal Cessna 208 Whiskey Sierra Lima, emergency landing completed, aircraft secured, James Bay Road, Kilometer Four Hundred Twelve, waiting on rescue."

I finish the message and fumble with my harness, twisting in my chair to check on Magali. She's breathing hard but her eyes slowly reopen, lit from within with a soft glow. "I love you."

I push back from my seat, meeting her halfway and pulling her tightly against me. "I love you," I whisper over and over again between breaths.

The radio crackles to life.

The pilot's death confirmed, no longer requiring medical assistance, and us in no immediate danger, waiting on rescue in the middle of nowhere at sunset translates into at first light of dawn tomorrow morning. The exchange with the Coast Guard mission control confirms it. We check the plane survival kit, and it's more than well equipped to see us through the night, geared for a week in the wilds.

Now that everyone concerned will be contacted by AirBoréal administration or Magali's parents, who'll relay the news at the farmstead, I don't really mind spending the night out here, Magali by my side, under a night sky white with stars.

"Come on," I say, pulling a headlight on and then fastening Magali's. "Our first order of business is building a fire. Then we'll get comfortable."

Magali's head lamp helps light my workspace and I go to work. Wielding the axe, the pungent fragrance of the evergreens releasing into the crisp night air, I hack down the conifer's limbs encrusted by slushy snow turned icy, adding to the growing pile.

We need to stay awake and keep alert through the night with unseasonal cold temperatures now hovering below negative five Celsius.

"Not sure we'll get the fire going, these are soaked through," I mutter.

Magali's LED headlight bobs in between trees at the edge of the road.

"No worries. It's the only known tree whose sap doesn't freeze in the wintertime. It gets gelatinous instead, and if spread on logs it will burn for hours. No matter how wet the wood is," she says, collecting blobs of sap in a decapitated, empty water bottle, incising the barks with a fishing knife taken from the emergency kit.

"If this works, you'll have officially reconciled me with the balsam fir." My gloves are toast, covered with the sticky sap, and that's just from picking up the soaked logs I chopped down. Then again, better those than my fingers.

Great grip on the axe handle, though.

"I'll do you one better. Here." She gathers a wad of the stuff on a tongue depressor and offers it to me. "Insta-energy. It will help us stay awake."

I eye it warily. Doesn't look that appetizing. "I outgrew eating snot by age five, thanks."

"Come on, it tastes way better than it looks, just put it on the middle of your tongue, and swallow." Sticking her tongue out, she demonstrates with one scoop of her own.

I raise a brow, all sorts of innuendos on the tip of my tongue, but refrain to comment. I'm not in a position to deliver on the goods, what with the shriveling cold temperatures reaching every part of me just now.

"Just don't put it anywhere near your teeth and you'll be golden." She pats my shoulder.

It actually tastes good, in a tangy, refreshing way, but I can't help but think it must have been a pretty harsh winter for the very first human who tried it.

I strike a couple of waterproof matches to our improvised bivouac by the side of the road, without much success. Plumes of smoke puff out in a hissing sound. Magali dribbles some of the goo on my attempts, and flames instantly lick the drenched wood.

"We. Have. Fire." She thumps once on her chest.

"Sweet."

We click our headlights off, conserving battery life, and settle for the long wait until dawn, sharing a seat on the inflatable sled, part of the survival kit found in the plane. "You know a lot about this stuff."

Her arms fold around her bended legs, her chin coming to rest on top of her knees. "My brother, Lucas, survived a few times on it, on extreme camping trips. He likes to push the envelope," she says quietly, watching the fire crackle to life. "Guess you pushed the envelope once or twice too. You knew exactly what to do up there, and did it with calm and practiced ease, and I never once doubted that we would make it." She tilts her head my way. "But if it weren't for you insisting on coming along, I'd be dead by now."

I don't know if it's my adrenaline rush fizzling out, now that we're no longer actively busy, but her words hit me right in the chest.

I look up at the sky, searching for the North Star, Polaris, in the constellation Ursa Minor. I stare at the bright star, feeling grateful for the whole story behind my years of reckless behavior, for the first time ever.

My heart thuds painfully against my ribs.

"I used to accept every stupid dare, taking unnecessary risks. It's how I got the nickname in the first place." I shake my head, throwing into the fire a few twigs at my feet, remembering a few instances of pure idiocy that any level-headed guy would have walked away from. "You called it right on that night, an adrenaline junkie, a jaded thrill seeker, that's what ZeeMan for the Impossible is really all about."

"Hey, don't beat yourself up." She puts her hand on my arm, and my glance darts her way. "I'm interested in every little thing that makes you, you. But it's not who you were that's defining *who you are*."

Who I am ... is in love with you. It's my biggest thrill.

"I have this reckless streak in me, Magali," I murmur, finally making peace with it.

The fire crackles, flaring up, licks of flames consuming in a flash the fresh needles of the branches I just threw in, turning them a phosphorescent red for an instant before they turn to ash.

"Why do you say that?" she asks softly. One of her gloved hands picks my left one up with something akin to reverence. Bringing it up to her lips, she kisses my palm tenderly over my sap-encrusted glove, dewy from melting snow, uncaring of it. Her fingers curve mine in a fist, safekeeping her kiss. "When it comes to people you love, you're the most conscientious guy I know."

"Maybe I am, and I never knew..."

She tilts her head in question.

"Getting certified, you learn all the basic recovery maneuvers on dual flights with instructors. Always practicing with a safety net. Nothing too drastic." I crouch by the fire, putting some more wood on, and stare at yellow, orange-tipped flames crackling into the quiet. A rush of glowing sparks swirl high up in the dark. I've never shared what I'm about to with anyone, but somehow, tonight, alive, underneath the stars of this northern sky, it feels right, the words needing to come out. "Flying solo in my teenage years, I provoked spirals and nose-dive recoveries, pushing the envelope as you call it, over and over again, hooked on the thrill of it. If for no other reason it made me feel victoriously alive, relishing the power behind seizing control back. Needing the proof I could do it and go beyond my own mother's meaningless death, and senseless life." I nod up at Polaris, and the star twinkles back at me, my earlier epiphany ringing clear in my heart, in my soul. "I've been reckless, for a long, long, time, but it was time well spent. I know that now. If for no other reason, every single one of those times got me ready for today."

"You did save the girl, Sir Zac of the Laure."

I swivel round to face her, touched beyond reason by her reference to the *Tales from the Enchanted Forest of Laure*. Tales that saved us all as children, blessing us with hopes and dreams of a better time, a better place, empowering the six of us to be who we were meant to be, come what may. On the softest of smile, she wipes an overflow of tears with her sleeve. "And she's eternally grateful you did so."

I crouch in front of her, taking my glove off to brush the back of my fingers on her damp cheek.

"And I'm eternally grateful the girl saved *us*, so that the story could begin," I say tenderly. "It was quite the catch up there."

She leans into my hand. "Just like you for me," she says.

Magali, my Normal Kingdom waiting to happen.

My friend, my lover, my soul mate, my forever.

"What happened to your mom?" she asks quietly, and I nudge her towards me so that she's sitting between my outstretched legs, leaning back into my chest.

I stare into the flames. "She married a prince, and ended up paying too high a price for it."

As we sit under a canopy of stars, I tell Magali the sordid tale I pieced together from snippets of diary entries my mother hid in her private pilot log book. The story feels so far removed from me now, that it might as well been someone else's in another lifetime.

How this young woman readily sold herself in marriage to a man thirty years her senior, agreeing to any and all stringent conditions in exchange for a lifestyle that brought her to the next level. How she had to breed one heir, and only one, a male to please his royal highness. How she agreed to have this one child only, as per dynastic tradition, so there would be no diluting the line's centuries' old personal wealth, dividing it equally, as called upon the *legittima* under Italian succession laws.

"It's you, isn't it, you're the heir?"

"I am on paper."

I tell Magali how the old prince made sure she abided by the contract, and had her abort four healthy eighteen-week female fetuses in a discreet clinic, officially claiming unfortunate miscarriages. How she grew bitter and resentful of the obligation. How the prince's pilot became her flight instructor, as well as her lover; ergo, how I had a fifty/fifty chance of being conceived by either men. And by then, how she thought it'd be a fitting, subtle insubordination if I wasn't really of the true bloodline. How the old prince took one look at me, at four years of age, and knew I wasn't his. How the "royal" jet's engines conveniently stalled over the Mediterranean Sea, out of fuel, less than a couple of days later. A faulty panel to blame, the investigation would reveal, and how the old prince died, himself, shortly thereafter of a massive coronary.

I stare at the star-dotted sky. Magali's hands soothingly stroke my forearms, loosely crossed over her abdomen.

The waxing crescent of the moon is more than halfway through its journey by now, Polaris tagging along on the western horizon.

"You would have had sisters ... It's so sad for all of you," she says, her gentle tone full of compassion. "Do you have at least one good memory of your parents?"

Do I?

"The old principe was rarely on island, and never bothered with me. So up until I was deemed worthy of his attention at age four, he'd been this portrait on the wall and a complete stranger to me. With the both of them living the high life in between Naples, Monaco, and Ibiza, so was my mother for that matter.

As for my biological father, even if my mother hadn't confirmed his paternity in one of her entries, in one of P.O.'s teenage hacking forays into archives, I saw a picture once, taken around my age today. Spitting image."

"What was it like for you before BIA?" She curls her hands over my forearms, holding me to her tighter. My chin drops to her shoulder. I stare at the flames.

"I lived on island, confined to a nursery on a strict schedule with tutors, locked into a daily regimen dictated by a protocol outdated by some two hundred years. There are less than a handful of stolen moments with my mother that I remember. More like impressions really, where she would hug me, promising to return soon as she left for another trip."

She looks over her shoulder, frowning. "That's pretty messed up. I never thought I'd say that, but I'm so happy you were sent to boarding school full time."

"Yeah, so am I." I kiss her temple. "I was born into a pretty fucked-up lifestyle." *One I want nothing to do with.*

"It's of no matter, you know," she stoutly says. "You carved your own lifestyle, on your own terms. One I admire even more, now."

I grow still. "What did you call it?"

"Your own lifestyle on your own terms?" she asks unsure.

Holy hell.

Sustain the *lifestyle*. I shake my head, my chest rumbling on a dry, self-deprecating laugh.

Could it be that simple?

I've been locked into this one-dimensional perception, blinded by something ingrained from birth, I realize.

But now, seeing it from outside the box through Magali's eyes putting a new spin on it, it makes me wonder...

What if I can do something worthwhile with the Swiss funds, on my terms?

Forty-Two

ZAC

Magali sends sparks flying, stirring the red coals with the narrow tip of the aluminium folding shovel, another useful yield from the survival tool kit. I put the last of the chopped logs and branches into the fire, flames blooming back to life. My thoughts still churn.

"If you had all the money in the world, what would you do with it?" I ask Magali, curious as to her answer.

Her head tilts in my direction. Her delicate features haloed by the warm glow of the revived flames, her wholesome, natural beauty strikes me anew.

"Um. Depends on your definition of all the money, and the zeros attached to it. Are we talking global world peace or purely selfish desires?"

"Purely selfish. Lots of zeros. First thought that comes to mind."

"I'd build a huge fifteen-suite sprawling estate somewhere near the village," she replies without missing a beat, her gorgeous face lit by a dreamy look.

My brows shoot up. "You would?" I ask, floored.

I don't know what I expected, but yeah. That is the last thing I would have thought she'd say. Right up there with "I'd buy ten times my weight in diamonds and wallow in it."

"In a heartbeat. It's an impossible dream of mine my inner idealist is fond of." She shrugs, plopping back down on the sled. "What about you?"

I shift my weight on one leg as I stand before her, hands on my hips.

"Uh-uh, you can't leave me hanging. Why is it an impossible dream you're fond of?"

"Because I'm a pragmatic idealist." She hands me a protein bar, part of the ration packs, and I absently decline the offering, my stomach still gurgling from my latest sap ingestion.

"We still have a few hours left to wait. Humor me."

"It's my version of a prenatal CAM clinic," she simply says.

I plop down beside her, surprised anew. "CAM as in Complementary Alternative Medicine?" I ask, more than intrigued by the idea.

She nods repeatedly, eyes aglow.

"Go on."

She scoots sideways, sitting on her heels, facing me, her features lit by what she sees inward. "See, my dream clinic is this hybrid concept," she animatedly says. "A place where prenatal medicine meets holistic medicine head on, in a multitude of complementary choices underneath one roof, in a spa resort ambiance set amidst a garden forest. Besides the usual clinical follow-ups, my moms-to-be would have access to any and all healthy alternatives out there, like homeopathy, aromatherapy, meditation, yoga, aqua gym, massage therapy, acupuncture, a variety of seminars, nutritionists, name it, we'll have it. The whole, culminating into a birth week of in-house pampering with beauticians on hand, cuisine fusion fares, the list is endless." Her hands flutter about while she talks, their graceful motion unconsciously used to underscore each of her points.

"It wouldn't feel at all like a hospital. There'd be private suites all done in Zen decors with airy living rooms for visitors, and double beds with dual control that can accommodate new fathers as well, cuddling close. En suite with air bathtubs for relaxation and water births. There'd be tall windows everywhere with a view on nature. A dining room with a bistro feel instead of a cafeteria. A cozy library. Common rooms with fireplaces and deep sofas. A cool nursery and daycare playrooms for the little ones with a story-time corner for volunteer Mamie's and Papie's. And this lush atrium with a saltwater swimming pool for baby swimmers and aqua aerobics sessions. An art gallery for a gift corner, exposing local artworks, from knitwear to wood toys to framed poetry and photographs, exposing as well all of La Maisonnée's protégés creative ideas. And speaking of, there are so many simple tasks they could be hired for besides selling their unique wares." She's absolutely fucking gorgeous. Luminescent, so full of passion, she hardly ever takes a pause, the words flowing out of her mouth. "It'd be this gathering place for new parents, bonding over shared concerns and wonders, welcoming new life and each other."

Her vision lights me up. I want this for her, for me, for us. I want to wake up every morning, seizing this joy and lightheartedness building inside me, capturing it, mirroring hers.

"And, of course, it would offer a gamut of birthing choices, from water births to friendly surgical suites with music in surround sound, and—"

"How do you see the inner workings of this concept within a public health regime?" I interject, almost tasting it as I picture this place, the both of us working side by side, on the onset of life, protecting it, nurturing it.

"That's where the zeros come in, and the fantasy starts, so there goes my reality check," she sighs on a little puff of breath. "It would be run as a free, private clinic, no Absurd List anywhere in sight."

My pulse picks up. I see it all, even the spin I'll put on the trust fund to seize control of it. "Magali, you're an absolute genius!"

"Oui, a dream genius." She nods on a half-hearted shrug.

I grab her shoulders, flashing a toothy grin. "No, we can do this." Her brow scrunches and she gives me a look.

I jump up and start pacing, an uncontainable chuckle bursting forth. Plans ignite, firing up my nerve endings, a familiar wave of adrenaline flooding me. My beanie flies up my brow, my hands all over the place, and I catch it before it lands on snow, shoving it back on.

"A fifteen-suite estate, it's fucking perfect actually." My lifestyle, on my terms. "It would require a slew of full-time staff, of course, from butler to gourmet chef, from concierge to housekeeper, maids, nannies, beauticians, gardeners, you name it, even an art curator thrown in there." I chuckle low, Magali's openly gaping at me. "And we'll need a plethora of health caregivers and CAM therapists on staff—"

"What? Zac, I know you're independently wealthy, but this goes beyond it." Her nose crinkles adorably, her face torn between "you're nuts," and hopeful longing.

I pull her up, laughing, swinging her in a circle before putting her down. "You don't understand. This is the key to unlocking centuries of accumulated wealth gathering dust in the old prince's personal trust fund, part of his twisted heritage I'm stuck with."

Poetic justice, I can't help but think. I'll spend his money on a prenatal clinic nurturing to life hundreds of babies with Magali by my side.

"You lost me, there. I assumed you were disowned from not being of the bloodline when he sent you in exile at BIA," she says.

"Not exactly." I explain the fine print, and the assurances I'll be left alone, thanks to Theo's intervention.

"So, it means they require an heir to carry on this empty title of theirs?" she asks, eyes narrowing in thought.

I still.

I haven't even thought that far ahead, yet, since Theo's call.

Not the children part; I'm really looking forward to it. In fact, I can't wait to see Magali's beauty in full bloom, round with our child. *My family*. The thought alone brings me to my knees, leaving in its wake this indescribable warmth glowing inside. They'll even grow up close to us at the estate manor clinic ... and if that's not perfect in my book, what is?

No, it's the other part, the carry on the title part I haven't really thought about until now. But, in my defense, I've lived so long on my terms, all but forgotten, that were it not for the trustees suddenly making demands on me last year, all of this San Alessio's business would have remained a distant memory of no consequence.

Things happen for a reason, Leo would undoubtedly pick from his vast collection of proverbs. And indeed, how else would I be able to breathe life into Magali's dream just now. In a much more suitable position as for myself as well, making all of my wishes come true, if it weren't for them irking me to no end, out of the blue, in the first place?

Will Magali see it that way or will this be too much? My pulse beats in my throat, my age-old insecurity resurging.

"Well, seen that way, now that you mention it, pretty much, yeah," I confirm, ruthlessly stomping on my panic. I take her hands and bring them up to my chest, cradling them with mine, close to my heart, the very one about ready to drop to my stomach. I lock eyes with her, vowing, "It's just that, though, an empty title. I'll make sure it does not affect in any way any child of ours, other than the name of our firstborn scribbled on a piece of paper buried on the other side of the pond, I swear to you."

"Well, I swear to you," she fiercely vows. "They'll never know what hit them, 'cause we'll flood them with many, many daughters, and a dozen or so cherished children, all of them loved to pieces. Just watch me."

"Come here, you," I say. Hugging her close, I breathe her in, closing my eyes. "God, I love you."

For the next little while, ideas, summaries, plans, and lists are whipped into shape, our combined energy, passion, and enthusiasm bringing Magali's clinic concept to the next level already. No longer an impossible dream but one ready to be turned into reality in the coming years, grounding me, exhilarating me.

"Oh, look!" she exclaims, awed, her head tilting back as she gazes at the night sky. "I've never seen one," she whispers, wide-eyed.

Pinpricks of fluorescent green light flash dance in the sky like the play of sunlight on a clear surface of water. The particle shower increases in intensity, until the shimmering veils of iridescent colors light up the entire sky, the spectacle of an aurora borealis frolicking above absolutely breathtaking, taking over the darkest hour of the night just before dawn.

"Neither have I," I murmur, just as awed, my glance darting around.

"It's otherworldly beautiful," she sighs breathily as the swirls of eerie greens and turquoise slowly fade, melting into the lightening sky. "One of the Inuit legends, Amélie told me, refers to the aurora as the spirits of unborn children coming down to play on Earth for a short while. I can see why," she says softly, reverently.

I bend low, murmuring close to her ear. "I'll bet a few hundred of them just checked you out, ecstatic you'll catch them on their way over with these very hands." I kiss both her palms.

"I will, I really will, won't I, right alongside you?" she says, wonder lacing her voice, her eyes so warm and full of love, so alive ... A look I intend to see often for the next forever if I have my say.

My chest fills with love and well-being to overflowing.

"You bet." My lips brush over hers, sealing it with a kiss that not even the distant whir of the rescue helo can interrupt.

Lost in our kiss, I'm home.

Seven months later...

ZAC

Yesterday's spring blizzard is nothing more than a memory, the warmth of the sun melting the last of the snow into puddles of slush under the brilliance of a cloudless blue sky. I park my Jeep on la rue de l'Église down in the village, hurrying to Le Vieux Presbystère where *Cutting Edge Custom Jewelry by Anaïs* is located, hoping to make it before closing time.

The doors are locked but I can see Anaïs through the side window, sketching a design at her counter. I knock on the window pane, joining my hands in a pleading gesture, and her face blooms with laughter as she unlocks the door.

"I was waiting for you to show up, no pleading required," the lovely young woman, who we all suspect captured Theo's attention last winter, says, eyes twinkling as I step inside.

"Sorry, my last appointment took longer than expected, but I couldn't wait one more day when I read your text confirming that it was ready," I reply. I feel this lightness in my chest at the thought of surprising Magali in the next hour with the ring I commissioned for her. She's not that into jewelry, but she's always been quite taken with Anaïs's custom pieces, particularly the rings she designed for Éolie and Liam from small pebbles found in their meadow. I wanted to give her something just as meaningful.

"And that's what I like to hear," Anaïs says, her face filled with quiet joy. "So, tonight's the night?" She slides a little box over the counter, opening it.

"Tonight's the night—" I pick it up and stare in awe, turning it this way and that. "Wow, just wow, Anaïs. It's more perfect than perfect..."

Magali's ring is exquisite in its rendition of an aurora borealis, made from two different granite pebbles. One I found at our home site, the other found on the twenty-acre lot where our CAM clinic will be built in the upcoming summer months on the outskirts of the village. It was surprisingly easy to unlock the old prince personal trust funds to build a luxurious fifteen-suite mansion. Magali's vision was the perfect foil to meet the two requirements for that to happen to the satisfaction of the Swiss bankers in charge of the monies, just like we first anticipated on that unforgettable night we shared underneath an aurora borealis, waiting on rescue. Yes, it's for my personal use, gentlemen. Yes, of course, it's maintaining *the* lifestyle of the old principe's bloodline in the lap of luxury, and will continue to do so in the years to come. The many, many years to come. A new legacy, starting now. *Ours.*

Buoyed by that last thought, I state to Anaïs, admiring the ring from every angle, "I can't wait for Magali to wear it."

Anaïs designed intricate swirls of light-silver platinum fitted with the irregular pebbles, sliced sideways and buffed to a pearly shine, showcasing their iridescent blue-green hues. A never-ending circle of love ... Anaïs's motto, she readily admits comes from Éolie saying just so when she commissioned her for Liam's ring.

"Can't wait for her to wear it either," Anaïs says mischievously. "All of you guys are turning up to be the best free advertisement I can hope for. Keep on spreading the love."

"Will do." My grin matches hers as I bounce out of there.

Fifteen minutes later, I cut the engine by the side of our rustic Wedgewood blue home, our very own magical Normal Kingdom within the Enchanted Forest of Laure, parked in the shade of mature spruce trees. I'm not even out the Jeep when I see Magali running towards the side door through the large kitchen bay windows overlooking the Cathedral at the back of the house.

I take a moment to savor the happy the place exudes, my heart brimming over with love and peacefulness. Here, is where I belong.

The door is yanked open and Magali slides on her socks, halting her flight by bracing her arms over the doorway, stopping short of the slushy deck.

Her whole face is lit up. "You're back!"

And, man. Being welcomed home with such joy ... It never gets old.

"Come here, you." I gather her in my arms, kissing the top of her head, inhaling her fresh citrusy scent for an instant before shrugging out of my coat, hooking it on a wooden peg.

"You had a good day at the hospital?" She takes my hands, pulling me into our country kitchen, and I'm met with the warm aromas of oregano, garlic, and basil, a pot of homemade spaghetti sauce simmering on the stove top.

"Not as good as when we'll be back to working together at our clinic, but good enough, considering." I nuzzle her neck, brushing her hair over her shoulder.

"Can you believe it's the clinic's ground breaking tomorrow?" she sighs dreamily.

"Can you believe you still didn't come up with a name for the place?" I tease her.

"Hey, no pressure allowed, I still have a few months to come up with a good one, ZeeMan for the Impossible," she teases right back, her woolen sock-clad feet stepping on mine. Her arms looping around my waist, she holds on as I walk us over to the stove top and turn it off.

"Impossible is no longer applicable. With you by my side, I believe anything's possible," I say in earnest. "Even finding home."

"And you say you're not good with words?" she replies, her nose rubbing on my chest in a kittenish way. "The sauce isn't ready yet."

"Food can wait, this cannot." My hands slide down her ribcage and hips, cupping her bottom. I lift her up on the counter. She leans in for a kiss but I lean back, brushing my thumbs in a gentle back and forth along her cheekbones, my eyes adoring her.

"What?" she asks, leaning into my touch, her eyes soft with that special glow she has when she looks at me, full of loving warmth.

"On the night we met, I said to you, tonight, I'm yours. I could just as easily have said, from tonight on, I'm yours, and it would have been the truth, even then." Her eyes swim in emotional tears as she tenderly brushes back a lock of hair from my forehead.

"My heart knew, my soul knew," she whispers, "but my mind refused to believe on that night that I was yours too. But I've been yours ever since, Zac, and I'm so grateful you came back for me."

I take her left hand in mine, sliding the ring on her heart finger, kissing it. "You're my new beginning, my aurora that brightens the night, my journey, my anchor, my roots, my companion, my soul mate, my perfect match. I love you. I always will come what may, as I can't imagine a world without you in it. This summer in the Cathedral, we'll make it official for the rest of the world out there I know, but this, you wearing this pledge of mine, cannot wait ... I want it all, Magali, right now."

"You do. You absolutely do," she says on a blinding smile that I capture with my lips, jumping together deeper into forever. No fear of the future, no apprehension. Just us.

Incandescently
(Liam's story)

By Design
(Theo's story)

Indigenous
(Leo's story)

Exposure
(P.O.'s story)

Apprehension
(Zac's story)

Gravity
(Yann's story)

Journey Into the Incandescent World
of Sylvie Pariseau...

The Forest of Laure

Exposure

Incandescent Series

Book 3

Prologue

Olivier,

I'm so sorry.

I knew this would come. My fault entirely. I ignored it too long, liking it too much.

I can't talk to you...

I can't write to you again.

I can't meet with you.

I'm not who you think I am.

I wish.

Lost in a world quilted by silence is who I am.

A world in which I remember the sounds of life, echoes of the distant past.

A world in which I was whole, perfect for a short while.

A world passing me by, soundlessly.

I've fallen in love with you.

Forgive me. I didn't mean to.

—unsent email.

One

P.O.

Val-David (Québec), seven months earlier...

A rivulet of hot water streams down my neck, trickling down my chest. Of course, the bar of soap I've been chasing slips away from my fingers for the zillionth time. Goddammit!

Wait.

This can't be right.

There's no hot water at Leo's old farmstead, just cold-as-fuck showers.

I crack my eyes open, my glance hitting the slanted ceiling with its peeling paint in an ugly-ass shade of... Whatever the heck that puke color's called.

It's as I thought, too good to be true.

Fucking hell, I curse, waking up more fully. I'm drenched, sweating like a pig roasting on a pit.

I flip onto my back, rubbing at my eyes.

It's only midmorning, my wristwatch confirms, but the couple of hours of sleep I managed to catch will have to do for now. There's just no way in hell I'll be able to snag any more zzzzs in this oven.

I roll out of bed, eyeing balefully the useless window duct taped to death.

If this unusual heat wave hitting Québec's Hautes-Laurentides this late in August goes on much longer, I'll probably do something drastic. Like switch bedrooms behind Zac's back the minute he stays over at Magali's place for the night. A window in working condition letting in the cool night breeze is at a premium around here, and I have no compunction in doing so, either. After all, Zac switched bedrooms on us first, the little shit, just before Yann and I flew in from Boston a month ago for our summer break.

Coming out of the sweltering bedroom tucked under the eaves, I wipe my forehead with the back of my hand, missing MIT's air-conditioned computer labs for a minute. Who knows, though, this might be just what I need to grow a brand-new fondness for icy cold showers.

Eyes shrivelled to the size of raisins, I shuffle down the stairs in dire need of a few shots of caffeine after pulling another all-nighter debugging new lines of code on the firewall program I'm developing. Probably the reason why my body considers coffee a food group by now.

Absently swiping beads of sweat dotting my chest with the tee I picked up off my bedroom floor, I yawn on my way to the kitchen in my boxer shorts.

Hitting the last step, I sigh with relief at the summer breeze coming in from all the opened windows downstairs. It instantly washes over me and cools my skin. Makes me briefly wonder if it would be worth waking up with yet another sharpie-drawn goatee, or worse—like it's been known to happen before—to hitch a hammock in between the staircase newel posts, tonight.

I stop by Liam and Éolie's closed door, noticing that the whimsical blackboard tied to their bedroom doorknob reads: **Twin Feeding in Progress. Do not disturb**.

That explains why the house is so quiet at the moment.

My chest expands, filling with warmth as I think of the twin babies that belong to Liam and Éolie. Those two little guys pull at my heart strings like nothing else.

Even with my lack of experience with kids, I'm not surprised I took to being an uncle so quickly. And I'm not the only one. We all have.

Fascinating phenomena.

It's not like the six of us guys growing up at a Swiss boarding school had a lot of hands-on experience with family life... "And tiny infants at that?" I scoff underneath my breath. "Might as well have been talking foreign species from another planet altogether."

I flick the sign with my index finger in passing, chuckling low. Before that little blackboard came into being, we all had a hard time letting our twin baby boys have a little peace and quiet, always bickering about whose turn it was to hold them. Now, we're more disciplined, waiting for the flip side to appear. **Twin Fix Inside. Come and get it.**

Guess for now coffee it is. I keep moving, shaking my head at Magali—the mastermind behind it—and her creative thoughtfulness. The love of Zac's life is a midwife through and through.

I stop short in the kitchen's doorway, inwardly groaning. *Aw, man.*

The other reason the house is quiet. Zac and Magali are making out like oversexed teenagers, hogging the counter space and blocking access to the stove. Not that shit tasting instant coffee made from a pot of boiling water is worth all that much, but still. Caffeine is caffeine and beggars can't be choosers, as Leo would say.

With two couples madly in love living here for now, Leo's place no longer qualifies as a quack farm as much as a remake of *The Love Boat*. Theo's the only one missing in on the fun, stuck at his uppity law firm in Boston for the summer and grumbling weekly about it. But sometimes, like now, I'm not so sure Theo isn't the one better off. Leo, Yann, and I literally trip on one, or both couples, either cuddling, gazing into each other's eyes endlessly to the oblivion of everything else, or making out ad nauseam pretty much everywhere we turn.

Not that I'm envious or anything.

"Hey, you two," I say to Zac and Magali, eliciting zero reaction and no refraining on the action.

"Mind if I step in for a minute?" I ask drily. "You're standing between me and coffee and that might be hazardous to your health," I say, only half-jesting.

Their lips on lock down, their hands all over, they don't even acknowledge me, lost to the world around them. Surprise. Surprise.

"Okay, well, guess that's my cue to go hunt coffee elsewhere."

Still nothing.

I double back to the stifling bedroom upstairs and pull on the first pair of passable cargo shorts I can find on the floor, not bothering to shower first nor hunt down a clean shirt.

I. Need. Caffeine. Try, yesterday.

It's as urgent as my dampened, wrinkled tee implies with the text. **COFFEE. EXE not found: (A)bort, (R)etry, (F)all asleep.**

I shove my other half, Lucie, into my computer bag and make a beeline for the front door.

"Later!" I shout, grabbing from the peg a set of car keys from our Volvo Cross Country station wagon fleet of cars on my way out.

No answer. Go figure.

As I stumble over the threshold, I spot Yann comfortably sprawled in one of the Adirondacks spread out on the front porch. He's reading some sort of quantum physics textbook like, say, a normal person would a novel. When he sees me, his brows shoot up above his classic tortoise-shell glasses.

"Let me guess? You've been cut out from your usual caffeine supply by the ongoing kissing fest?" he asks.

I stop in my tracks. "They've been at it that long?" I shake my head, wondering what that would be like. To kiss someone for that long. To want to.

"Longer."

I grunt in reply, "Christ, maybe we need to check if they're turning blue from lack of oxygen." Yeah, and maybe I need a bit more breathlessness in my own life. I feel a tad depressed by my lack of a love life all of a sudden.

"Been there. Done that," Yann says, making a big production of swiping clean his eyeglasses with the hem of his dark-green polo shirt before shoving them back on his nose. "Do so at your own peril, man. Some images cannot be unseen once they're burned on your retinas."

"Did they fog up your lenses with the applied physics, Math Man?" I rib him, and right on cue he turns red, the flush spreading like wild fire from his neck up to the roots of his mahogany-brown hair.

"Something like that," he mumbles under his breath, and I take pity on him. The guys and I aren't even sure he ever kissed a girl. Hard to tell with him, but out of our band of intellectual misfits he's the geekiest, so, not improbable. And considering I've known him since I was a kid and we tell each other everything, the fact he's never divulged anything remotely physical with a woman speaks volume.

Not that I can talk. I can count on the fingers of one hand the number of brief encounters of the girl kind I've had. A few weeks at the most is my record. But it never bothered me before tripping all over Liam's and Zac's brand-new kind of happiness.

"I'm going down to the village for a shot of espresso. Want to come with?" I ask him, hobbling down the front porch stairs into the hazy morning sun.

"I'm good nerding it over here but feel free to bring one up."

"Will do."

On my way to the woodshed in the back where our herd of station wagons is corralled, I spot the sixth member of our little guy-tribe taking measurements by his ruin of a barn with its roof caved in.

I hail him. "Hey Leo, want to go down to the village for coffee?"

His shoulder-length, ash-brown hair is half undone from its usual leather tie, blowing in the wind and lending him an air of mad scientist. Not entirely a lie.

"Thanks, but no," Leo shouts back, hyped by whatever he sees in this pile of barn crap. "I need to get back to my architect with some more ideas I came up with during the night for my greenhouse."

I eye the mess and snort, shaking my head at him. Guess experimental farm means just that, experimental. With the ink still wet on his PhD in agronomy research, he wants to integrate into his projected, state-of-the-art laboratory greenhouse the remains of the old barn, salvaging it. But the rotten thing is so far gone that even his architect is scratching his head over that piece of the puzzle.

"Looks good to me," I snicker before cupping my hands on either side of my mouth to yell, "Maybe you'll breed a new species of magical mushrooms out of it."

"You wish!" he yells back. "Get out of here, you arse, and bring back coffee while at it."

"Looks like it's you and me, Lucie." I unlock Volvo Cross Country number three, the silver-colored one we all chipped in to buy, dropping Lucie's bag onto the passenger seat.

Sliding in, I adjust the driver's seat forward by rote. When you're surrounded by guys over six feet tall it kind of goes with the territory when you're barely topping five feet six.

I cut the engine in front of C'est la Vie Café alongside the linear park, Le P'tit Train du Nord—a two-hundred-kilometers-long ancient railway reclaimed as a cycling and cross-country skiing venue bisecting the village, hopping from one to the next. The village boasting dozens of bistros and cafés, but I haven't tried this one yet. My eyes cut to the display easel standing at the foot of the stairs, advertising an in-house blend blacker than black. And just like that, I'm sold on the place.

"Come on, Lucie, let's hit the terrace and get some work done," I mumble into the empty car, my sleep-deprived brain salivating over the vision of a double shot of espresso.

Stepping out, I'm greeted by an old '40s French song, *La Mer*. A popular classic the guys and I heard many a time on weekends in Paris in our A-level years, the lyrics of which are a poem in itself. The music spilling onto the terrace from the open door of the café transports me in the space of an instant to La Place du Tertre sur la butte Montmartre and its quaint sidewalk cafés. Well, minus the sidewalks, the sheer masses of gawking tourists and the blasé attitude we used to wear around us like a scarf. I chuckle low, remembering. Yeah, when we hit eighteen we thought we were the shit for a little while. Thank the fuck it passed quickly.

I follow the coffee aromas inside, my mouth watering at the smell of roasted beans permeating the place.

On my way over to the counter at the back, I shake my head at the barista who dries some cups as he sings along in a pleasant, baritone voice.

To be heard, I practically have to shout over the loud music. "Nice voice you got there, but I never thought I'd hear a Charles Trenet's soft ballad blasting the speakers at a nightclub's volume level," I joke.

Chuckling, the tall, skinny guy, not much older than me, dabs a few beads of sweat from his temples with the corner of his black apron with the bright-white C'est la Vie logo written across his lean chest. "Yeah, sorry about that. We're not allowed speakers on the terrace but at *la belle saison* everyone's outside and it's kind of our trademark, coffee and French oldies. What can I get you?" he asks over the sink, washing his hands.

I place my order, my French no longer so choppy now that I get to practice it daily. *"Un double espresso allongé, s'il-vous-plaît."*

You'd think that with my Swiss Romande origins I'd be organically more fluent in French, but I grew up with the guys in English at Berlinger Academy, a Cambridge International boarding school—a Swiss boarding school as ironic as it is, given the size of a country that rivals the size of the city of Montréal. But what's left of my family wasn't into the whole commuting daily thing. Nor communicating for that matter, I inwardly snort. So my French is pretty much as fluent as what I learned in school, and not much else.

The dark-haired barista nods once. *"Installez-vous où vous voulez et je vous l'apporte à l'instant,"* he says with a knowing look at my half-awake, rumpled appearance as he enjoins me to sit where I want, my espresso coming right up.

Magic words if I ever heard them.

I step out into a blast of humid air that makes my tee stick to my back.

"Great," I grumble, faced with either having my eardrums splintered by sitting inside or have my brain cells liquefied by sitting outside.

Thankfully, it's too late for the breakfast crowd and too early for the lunch crowd. So, apart from a few tourists pouring over activity pamphlets, I have the deck overlooking the linear park pretty much to myself. And the only table on the side shaded by a bouquet of mature apple trees grown wild, their gnarly branches reaching to the sky some forty feet up.

You won't hear me complaining.

I swipe the sweat pearling on my forehead with the back of my hand, waiting for Lucie to boot up.

"*Merci beaucoup*," I thank the barista when he arrives with a full tray and begins setting items in front of me. First, the steaming coffee he places just so. A water glass and a small bowl with lemon wedges and what looks like fresh mint leaves by smell alone, follow. I fight the urge to roll my eyes and hurry him along. As he fills my water glass, I slurp my coffee and scald my tongue in the process.

He makes a face before turning on his heels like I just made the worst faux pas ever by not taking the time to savour the heavenly concoction.

I don't give a damn by now; I'll savour the next one. I let the shot of caffeine spread through my veins, sighing in quiet bliss even though my tongue stings like crazy. All that matters is that I may survive the day with eyes wide open after all.

On my fourth cup, pleased by the yield results of my latest lines of code, I look up from my screen and stretch my arms over my head, ready for a break. At this rate, I'll be able to present on schedule the final version of my firewall app in a marketable form by the end of this upcoming year at MIT, my last before I earn my double Master degrees in software engineering and computer science. The beta version is already attracting interest from the big five but, for now, I'm happy to go solo and do my own thing.

The air is still thick with heat and kind of soggy. Sunlight filters through the branches of the apple trees covered in shiny leaves and ripening fruits, which reminds me I haven't eaten anything since last night. Right on cue, my stomach growls loudly. I should probably order some kind of croissant sandwich to go with my liquid diet or fold and grab something at the farmstead. Undecided,

I stretch my neck to the side to work out the kinks in it. That's when I see her.

I still mid-motion, eyes locked on the woman on the lawn below me.

My heart starts to beat in a weird staccato rhythm.

I could blame one too many hits of caffeine on an empty stomach, but that's not it. A pair of toned legs stretched out on the grassy area bordering the park overlooking the deck is to blame. The legs are attached to the most beautiful girl I've ever seen. The breeze has kicked up from earlier, and the wind is playing peek-a-boo with her pale yellow sundress, showcasing her perfect backside and white lacy boy shorts underneath. If she notices, she doesn't care enough to stop it.

But I care.

I definitely care.

Unable to help myself, I stare.

She bends low and then sprawls flat across the grass, facing me now. Wonder brightens up her exquisite face as her bent legs swing charmingly to and fro, and she talks to. . .a dragonfly cupped in her hands?

Not that I can judge since I regularly have long chats with Lucie, my trusty laptop. Still. A beautiful girl like that deserves better company than a bug. And coming from someone who used to hack into computers to plant them, it's quite the admission.

For the first time in my life, I'm seriously contemplating debugging a flesh-and-blood female. Slowly, and oh, so pleasurably...

Exposure

Lots of love from P.O. & Aurèle coming your way!

Acknowledgements

Curious about the pretty amazing people who contribute to my story-telling journey behind the scenes? Take a look :

http://www.sylvieparizeau.com/behind-the-scenes/
Book cover design provided *By Hang Le* ❤
Copy editing provided by *Red Road Editing* ❤

Heather, I have no words to describe your amazingness. See? I had to make up my own, and even then... My stories would never be the same without you (and I hope they'll never be without, hint hint on Exposure coming up). But just so you know, my characters love you quite simply, and so do I! Hugs. xo

Grégoire, you know why... it starts with a 'K', and I'll always remember it. Je t'aime pour les prochains mille ans. xx

Philippe-Olivier, for all those (very) early mornings spent at Mont-Tremblant Airport in your (very) early teen years, waiting for your solo flights to take-off and land safely. Time well spent if just to watch you soar through life (and well, the firsthand knowledge I acquired along the way did come in handy here ... Who knew?) Stay passionate in your pursuits. Love, Maman. xx

If I did pique your curiosity and you'd like to know just a little bit more about me? Feel free to peek inside my head by exploring this website: www.sylvieparizeau.com

Curious about the real village my characters live in? Feel free to explore right here:
http://www.sylvieparizeau.com/sylvies-chronicles/

STAY IN TOUCH. Spread the love. ❤

Sign in and get both, the Forest of Laure Map as a gift screensaver and your first email-tribe-only bonus scene, featuring Liam and darling little Sébastien.

Warning: May contain traces of Zac and become addictive.

Gift map, excerpts, teasers, bonus scenes, village news, upcoming releases, hugs.

Don't miss out!

My e-mail tribe gets it all. So can you.

http://www.sylvieparizeau.com/link-to-newsletter/

About the Author:

A paralegal by day and incurable romantic by night, Sylvie is a cross-genre, and she takes Happily Ever After very seriously. The End just isn't in her vocabulary.

An incorrigible daydreamer, she now feeds her obsession with epilogues by concocting stories in which heroes deal with the happy from the get-go. Ready, or not. And she confesses under oath to loving every minute of it.

Sylvie lives her own Happily Ever After in the beautiful mountains of Les Laurentides in Northern Quebec, alongside her whole set of characters.

In between treks in their backyard wilderness, you can find them hanging out at www.sylvieparizeau.com

https://twitter.com/SylvieParizeau
https://www.facebook.com/Sylvie-Parizeau-romance-novelist-526307707511745/
Come and say hello, they'd love to hear from you!

www.ingramcontent.com/pod-product-compliance
Lightning Source LLC
Chambersburg PA
CBHW070649180626
46817CB00006B/2296